If only she could see his face better.

Her gaze drifted over to the telescope. Why not? She rushed over, pointed it in the man's direction, and peered through the eyepiece.

Oh, yeah, he did not disappoint. His eyes looked sharp and intelligent. Pale, though she couldn't tell the color. He had a straight, strong nose, a wide mouth, and a strong jaw with a sexy hint of dark whiskers. There was a grim expression on his face, but it didn't make him unattractive. Quite the opposite. It added to his aura of masculine power.

She lowered the scope to his body. His chest expanded with each deep breath, and she found herself matching her breaths to his. Even lower, she noted his muscular thighs and calves. His white running shoes pounded on the sand, leaving a steady trail.

He continued down the beach toward the rock known as Petra, giving her a glorious view of his backside.

"Opa."

By Kerrelyn Sparks

The Vampire
and the Virgin

KERRELYN
SPARKS

AVON

An Imprint of HarperCollinsPublishers

AVON BOOKS
An Imprint of HarperCollins*Publishers*
10 East 53rd Street
New York, New York 10022-5299

With all my love to my hero at home,
My husband and best friend,
Don

Acknowledgments

Even though this is the eighth book in the Love at Stake series, the journey from beginning to end was just as tough and arduous as the first book. For those dear friends and critique partners who made the journey with me—MJ, Sandy, and Vicky—you have my love and gratitude. My thanks to my editor, Erika Tsang, for her wisdom and patience. My thanks to everyone at HarperCollins for the best publicity, marketing, and artwork in the business. My thanks to my agent, Michelle Grajkowski of Three Seas, not only for her expertise, but for always being there with a smile and word of encouragement. My thanks to all my readers. You guys are the best! And finally, my love and thanks to my husband and children. Whether we're celebrating good news or enduring the rigors of deadline hell, they are always there for me.

The Vampire and the Virgin

Chapter One

Robby MacKay had murder on his mind as he approached the rendezvous site in Central Park. The peaceful scene did little to dissuade his violent thoughts. Moonlight sparkled on the still lake and gleamed off the aluminum hulls of overturned rowboats along the shore. The boathouse sat nearby, empty and quiet. Robby only took notice because he was checking for signs of an ambush.

He and his companions halted in front of a series of steps that descended into a dark gully. At the bottom was a tunnel with a Malcontent waiting inside. Waiting for his death, if Robby had his way.

He started down the stairs with Zoltan and Phineas. Angus MacKay and his wife Emma charged over the hill with vampire speed so they could investigate the far side of the tunnel.

"I told you . . . come alone," a Russian-accented voice whispered from the black interior of the tunnel.

Phineas stopped on a landing halfway down the stairs, his hand curling around the hilt of his sword. "You've been trying to kill me for months, Stan. Of course I brought some mean and nasty dudes with me. One wrong move and they're gonna make you look like beef Stroganoff."

After surviving entirely on blood for almost three hundred years, Robby wasn't sure what beef Stroganoff looked like, but he took grim pleasure in being called a mean and nasty dude.

Unfortunately right now, he was more of a clumsy weakling. Each step felt like he was sinking into wet shifting sand. The casts and bandages had been removed last night from his feet and hands, so tonight he'd claimed he was ready for action. It was a bluff he could pull off only if he didn't fall down the stairs.

Meanwhile, the other mean and nasty dude, Zoltan Czakvar, zipped down the stairs at vampire speed and positioned himself against the brick wall to the right of the tunnel entrance.

The Russian had insisted earlier on the phone that he would come alone to meet Phineas. Robby and his fellow Vamps suspected a trap, but the question was, where? No doubt the Malcontents realized a group of Vamps would accompany Phineas to Central Park. Did the Malcontents plan to attack in the park, or were they hoping the Vamps would leave their base at Romatech Industries understaffed and vulnerable? Either way, the Vamps knew they had no choice but to divide and protect both Phineas and Romatech.

Robby had asked to go with the group to Central Park, figuring it afforded him the best chance at killing a Malcontent. One wouldn't be enough, but it was a good start. He made it to the bottom of the stairs and stationed himself to the left of the entrance.

"Yo, Stan," Phineas called to the Russian. "You paying rent for that tunnel or what?" He drew his sword and affected a gangster voice. "Come out and say hello to my little friend."

The Russian vampire, dressed in black cargo pants and a black sweatshirt jacket, eased slowly from the tunnel. The hood was pulled over his head, casting his face in shadow, although the icy blue of his eyes glittered as his gaze darted nervously about. He flinched when Zoltan whipped his sword out, the blade gleaming in the moonlight mere inches from the Russian's shoulder.

Robby followed suit, reaching overhead to draw the claymore from the sheath on his back. When his grip faltered, he grasped the hilt with both hands to keep from dropping the weapon and making a dent in his thick skull. Bugger. He should have brought a lighter weight sword. He lowered the sword and rested the tip on the ground.

The Russian lifted his hands in surrender. "I did not come to fight. I have no weapon."

"And he's alone." Emma emerged from the tunnel and sprinted up the stairs to stop on the landing next to Phineas. "The tunnel's clear."

Angus exited the tunnel, returning his claymore to the sheath on his back. He patted the Russian down from behind, then moved in front of him to pat him down again. He jerked the hood off the Russian's head, then stepped back to glower at him. "Stanislav Serpukhov. What are ye up to?"

Robby stiffened at the sight of the Russian's spiky white-blond hair. He'd seen that hair before. His newly healed fingers flexed jerkily around the hilt of his sword. "Ye were there. In the cave."

Stanislav whirled around toward him and his eyes widened. "You?" He moved back, stumbling onto the first stair step. "You're alive?"

Memories shot through Robby's mind. Images of the torturers with their twisted, gleeful faces. The stench of his burning flesh. The snap of his breaking bones. *"Ye bloody bastard. Ye were there."* He used both hands to raise his sword.

"Robby, stop!" Angus ordered.

"He was there!" Robby lurched toward the Russian, who scurried up the steps to the landing.

"I said *stop*." Angus planted one hand against Robby's chest and his other hand on Robby's arm, forcing the sword down.

Robby glared at his great-great-grandfather, who only looked a few years older than himself. "I require revenge. Ye canna stop me."

Angus glared back. "I expect you to follow orders."

Robby pulled away from Angus's grip and focused on the Russian. "I know who ye are now and where to find you."

"I do not want trouble." Stanislav sidled closer to Phineas.

The young black Vamp gave him an incredulous look. "What the hell are you doing, man? You think *I'll* protect you? You've been trying to kill me."

"I did not want to," Stan grumbled. "Jedrek said I must kill you . . . or he will kill me. But he is dead now. Everyone who heard the order is dead. So I do not feel that I must kill you now."

Phineas scoffed. "That's real sporting of you."

Stan glanced warily at Robby. "I did not like what Casimir did to you—"

"But ye stood there and watched," Robby growled. "Ye helped tie me to the chair with silver chains. Did ye enjoy the smell of my burning flesh?"

Stan's jaw shifted. "*Nyet*. But I tell you this. If they catch me here, talking to the enemy, they will do things to me that make your torture look like . . . walk in the park. Instead of thirty pieces of silver, they will take thirty pieces of flesh from me, and the first piece will be my tongue."

"Then let me kill you now and save you the misery!" Robby lunged toward the stairs, but ran into Angus's outstretched arm.

"Enough, lad," Angus hissed softly. He turned toward the Russian. "Are ye thinking of betraying yer master?"

"If you mean Casimir, I never met him till he came here to America and said he was our leader. I am not killer. I never was. I was . . . farmer. I stayed with Russian vampires because I am Russian, and they helped me learn how to live here."

"And ye learned how to kill mortals," Robby grumbled.

"I never killed," Stan insisted. "I feed from mortals, that is true. But I never kill mortals."

Zoltan snorted. "He expects us to believe that?"

Stan stiffened. "You are one to talk. You killed my best friend at the Battle at DVN. I lost another friend in South Dakota. You Vamps act like you are . . . better morally, but when it comes to war, you do the most killing."

Phineas cocked his head with a grimace. "He has a point there. We've been whipping their ass."

Angus shrugged. "They're bloody fiends. They deserve to die."

"Then I can kill him now?" Robby muttered.

Angus ignored him. "Ye have two minutes, Stan. Talk."

"And then I can kill him?" Robby asked a bit louder.

Angus shot him an annoyed look.

"I came to America seven years ago," Stanislav began. "Me and three vampire friends from Moscow. We wanted . . . new life with no tyranny and no terror. We went to coven in Brooklyn so we could learn English. We hoped to get jobs someday and our own place—"

"The American dream." Phineas pretended to wipe away a tear. "I'm getting choked up."

Stan scowled at him. "But all we found was more tyranny. Ivan Petrovsky liked to capture mortal women for food and sex. If we did not follow orders, he would kill them. He killed so many, and he abused the vampire women. I was glad when Katya and Galina murdered him."

"So you just fell in with the wrong crowd." Phineas rolled his eyes. "Where have I heard that one before?"

"My friends and I, we hated following orders from the ones you call Malcontents, but we knew if we try to escape, they would kill us. I lost two friends in battle. And last night—" Stan glanced away, his eyes watering. "My last friend died. Nadia killed him because he was blond."

Phineas winced. "Tough break."

"Isn't she the one who stabbed Toni?" Emma asked Zoltan, and he nodded.

"Nadia is crazy bitch," Stan growled. "And Casimir put her in charge of the coven."

"Bummer. So what do you want from us?" Phineas motioned to Stan's white-blond hair. "Some L'Oréal hair color? I'm not sure you're worth it."

"I want asylum. If you can hide me from Malcontents, I will tell you everything I know."

The Vamps grew silent as the Russian's request sank in.

"Doona trust him," Robby whispered. "He did nothing while they tortured me."

"Robby has a point," Angus said, regarding the Russian sternly. "Ye've never given us reason to trust you."

Stan glanced nervously about. "You checked the area? It is clear?"

"Yes," Emma answered. "What can you tell us? Do you know where Casimir is hiding?"

Stan licked his lips. "You scared him very much. He thought Apollo's place was secret, but you knew about it. And he thought his camp in South Dakota was safe, but you attacked with no warning. I do not understand how you knew about his camp."

Robby snorted. "He's fishing. He's still working for them. Let me kill him now."

"No!" Stan raised his hands. "Please. I can see how it is going. Ivan, Katya, Galina, Jedrek—they are all dead. You killed over sixty Malcontents in South Dakota. Casimir will lose. He must lose. He is evil."

"Nice speech," Zoltan said. "Where is Casimir?"

"He was afraid you would find him if he stayed in America, so he went back to Russia. He is very angry, and he cries for revenge. He will come back."

"When?" Angus asked.

Stan shook his head. "I do not know. He lost too many men in South Dakota. And then he killed more himself, because he thinks one of his men betrayed him and told you our location. He is . . . paranoid now. He trusts no one, and many followers have run away to hide. He is in very bad shape till he can find way to rebuild army."

Robby leaned close to Angus. "We should go after him, finish him off while he's weak."

Angus nodded, then addressed the Russian. "We appreciate the information. We'll have to verify it first, of course—"

"Then you will take me?" Stan asked.

"Eventually, perhaps." Angus crossed his arms. "For now, I want ye to go back to the coven in Brooklyn and continue to bring us information."

Stan grew pale. "You want me to spy for you." He ran a hand through his white-blond hair. "You know how dangerous that is? If they find out—"

"We're no' asking you to die," Angus interrupted.

"Speak for yerself," Robby muttered.

"If ye have the slightest inkling of danger," Angus continued, "ye must teleport away immediately. Then call us, and we'll take you somewhere safe. Phineas will give you his cell phone number. Memorize it. What do ye say?"

Stan took a deep breath. "All right. I will do it."

"Good." Angus turned to Phineas. "He'll be reporting to you. Take him away and make yer plans."

"Yes, sir." Phineas took hold of Stan's arm. "Let's go." He teleported away, taking the Russian with him.

Robby shook his head. "I should have killed him."

"Nay," Angus said. "He's much more valuable as a spy."

"We canna trust him," Robby argued. "Casimir could have sent him as a double agent. I should have killed him."

"Robby." Emma descended the stairs, frowning. "All this talk about killing—it's not like you. I know they did terrible things to you, and it breaks my heart, but—"

"I doona want yer pity," Robby growled. "And I'm no' sorry for what happened. It bloody well opened my eyes. We should have killed all the Malcontents years ago. I say we teleport to Moscow immediately and hunt Casimir down."

"We will." Angus motioned to Zoltan. "Call Mikhail in Moscow. Find out if there's any news about Casimir."

"Got it." Zoltan headed up the stairs, slipping a cell phone from the pocket of his black leather jacket.

"If it's still dark in Moscow, we'll teleport there right away," Angus told his wife. "If no', we'll go as far as our castle in Scotland."

Emma nodded. "I hope Stanislav was telling the truth."

"'Twill be bloody well impossible to find Casimir in Russia," Robby grumbled. "The place is huge, and he knows it much better than us. I think we should divide up—"

"Robby," Angus interrupted. "Lad, ye're no' going."

He stiffened. "Of course I'm going. My hands and feet are healed—"

"Nay," Angus said softly. "I can tell that ye're struggling, lad. Ye're slow and weak."

A flash of anger sizzled through him. "Dammit, Angus. I'll heal quickly, ye know that. By the time we locate Casimir, I'll be ready—"

"I said ye're no' going."

Robby squeezed the hilt of his sword so hard, his newly healed fingers ached. "Ye canna do this to me. I have the right to avenge myself."

"That's all ye're thinking about, lad. Ye're obsessed."

"And much too angry," Emma added.

"Of course I'm angry!" Robby shouted. "The bloody bastards tortured me for two nights."

"You need to get past your anger," Emma said gently.

Robby scoffed. "Believe me, my anger will be miraculously cured once I've killed the bastards."

Angus sighed. "Lad, ye're a loose cannon. I'm ordering you to take some time off."

Robby glowered at his great-great-grandfather. As the CEO of MacKay Security & Investigation, Angus was his boss. And his sire. Angus had transformed him as he lay dying on the battlefield at Culloden, so Robby felt an extremely close bond. His fierce sense of loyalty had kept him strong during captivity and torture. He'd managed to endure the pain without betraying his family and friends.

But he also had plenty of money set aside. He didn't need to work for MacKay S&I. He could look for Casimir on his own.

"I can guess what ye're thinking, lad," Angus said softly. "Doona consider it. Ye're too full of rage to take off on yer own. And ye're too weak. That makes a lethal combination. Ye'll get yerself killed."

"Yer confidence in me is touching."

"Robby." Emma touched his arm. "We do believe in you. You just need some time to recover. That's all we ask."

He groaned inwardly. He hated to admit it, but they had a point. Maybe a week off wouldn't be too bad. He could lift weights, get his strength back, then go after Casimir and kill him. "All right. I'll . . . think about it."

"Excellent." Emma smiled. "I know the perfect place for you. The West Coast Coven Master invited you to stay at their vacation spot in Palm Springs. It's a luxury resort and spa just for Vamps."

Robby blinked. "A . . . spa?"

"Yes. They have all the latest, state-of-the-art equipment. Jacuzzis that will be wonderful for your hands and feet. Fully trained physical therapists. An Olympic-sized heated swimming pool. A huge exercise room—"

"They do fencing and martial arts?" Robby asked. He could use some practice with his sword.

"Well, actually, they're more into Pilates and yoga." When Robby snorted, she raised a hand to stop his objection. "Now listen. Those are excellent exercises for gaining flexibility and balance. You need that right now."

"And do ye expect me to kill Casimir by holding a yoga pose for thirty seconds?"

Emma frowned. "There you go again with the killing.

This obsession is not healthy, Robby. You're lucky to be alive. You need to learn how to smell the roses again. Yoga will help you relax and find your center."

"I doona think I ever lost it." He touched his flat stomach.

"If you don't want to do yoga, fine," Emma snapped. "I was looking at their brochure, and they have lots of ways to help you achieve inner peace. There's the hydrothermic massage in the Tropical Tranquility Grotto or the rejuvenating body wrap with aromatic oils. When's the last time you exfoliated?"

Robby looked at Angus. "Is she still speaking English?"

Angus snorted. "Show respect to yer elders, lad."

"Are ye joking? I'm a few centuries older than her."

"True." Emma's mouth twitched. "But when I married Angus, I became your great-great grandmother."

"Stepgrandmother," Robby corrected her, then arched a brow. "Make that *evil* stepgrandmother."

She laughed. "That may be, since I expect you to stay at the spa for at least three months."

"What?" Robby gave her and Angus an incredulous look. "Ye canna be serious. If I doona practice with my sword for three months, I willna be fit for duty."

"They also have an excellent Vamp psychologist—"

"Nay!" Robby interrupted her. Now he knew why they were pushing this damned spa on him. "I'm no' going to a psychologist."

"Lad," Angus began. "Ye're suffering from post-traumatic—"

"I know damned well what I suffered. I doona need to whine about it to a therapist. 'Tis a complete waste of time." There was no way he was going to talk about what had happened to him. Why on earth would he describe every painful, humiliating detail? It would be torture all over again. No, it was much better to simply put the whole nasty ordeal behind him. And kill the bastards.

Emma took a deep breath. "If we made it an order—"

"Then I would quit," Robby interrupted again. He could hunt down Casimir on his own.

Angus gave his wife a sympathetic look. "I knew he wouldna agree to yer fancy spa, but ye gave it a good try." He glanced at Robby. "We doona want you to quit, lad. We just want you to get better, both in body and mind."

"I'm no' crazy," Robby growled.

"Nay, but ye're angry as hell, and it makes you too unstable for work. No' only would ye be risking yer own life, but the lives of anyone working with you."

Bugger. Robby ground the tip of his sword against the brick pathway. Angus knew exactly how to get to him. He could never put the lives of his friends at risk. "I might agree to a short vacation. That's all."

"Good." Angus nodded. "Ye can use our castle in Scotland, or Jean-Luc has offered his home in Paris."

"Been there, done that," Robby mumbled. He'd been head of security for Jean-Luc in Paris for ten years.

"Jack said ye could use his palazzo in Venice," Angus continued.

"Does everyone want rid of me?" Robby grumbled.

"We all want you to get better," Emma insisted. "Roman offered his villa in Tuscany or his new one on Patmos."

"Patmos?" He'd never been there before.

"'Tis a Greek isle," Angus explained. "Verra lovely, I hear."

"It's where Saint John envisioned *Revelations* and the end of the world," Emma added.

"Well, that's comforting." Robby shrugged one shoulder. "Fine. Whatever. I'll go for a week or two."

"Four months," Angus said.

Robby gaped. "*What?* The spa was only three months."

"The spa had a therapist," Angus reminded him. "We figure if ye're on yer own, ye'll need more time. Of course, ye could change yer mind about therapy—"

"No. Hell, no."

"Then four months it is," Angus said. "All expenses paid. Plus yer usual salary. Ye canna beat that, lad."

Emma smiled. "We'll see you at Christmas, and you'll be so much better."

Better, his arse. This wasn't a vacation. It was a bloody exile. Imprisoned on an island like Napoleon. But then, Napoleon escaped from his first island. Robby figured he could do the same. For a Vamp with teleportation abilities, it would be easy. And no one would ever know.

Chapter Two

Island of Patmos, three months later . . .

*O*livia Sotiris eased the back door shut. It had to be about one-thirty in the morning, she guessed, but her inner clock was still on Central Standard Time.

Her ferry had arrived in the port of Skala that afternoon, and her grandmother was there, waiting with a young taxi driver who just happened to be single. After driving them the short distance to the Sotiris home in Grikos, the young Greek had stowed her luggage in the guest room, then taken them to a local taverna.

The whole village had gathered there to gawk at Eleni Sotiris's American granddaughter. And according to Eleni, every eligible bachelor on the island was in attendance.

Olivia endured several hours of gentle scolding in broken English from the older villagers. Her crime: not visiting

Yia Yia, her poor grandmother, for six long years. It didn't matter that she saw her every Christmas in Houston, where her family lived and her grandmother migrated for a few months every winter. Olivia was still guilty of breaking her poor old widowed grandmother's heart.

At the time, her grandmother was bouncing across the dance floor with a line of young men, happily yelling *"Opa!"* and breaking plates, so Olivia decided this was one guilt trip she could decline. She drank more wine than usual, hoping it would help her sleep, but here she was, two hours later, wide awake.

And once again she questioned her reason for coming. Her supervisor had insisted she take time off, but part of her argued that running away from a problem never solved it. She should have faced the monster again. She should have told him the game was over. No more sick manipulation. But what if running away just proved he was still pulling the strings?

A chilly breeze swept off the sea and up the rocky bluff to the courtyard of her grandmother's house. Olivia snuggled her white blanket tighter around her green cotton pajamas. She wouldn't think about him anymore. He couldn't find her here.

She breathed in crisp, salty air. It was wonderfully quiet, with just the sound of waves breaking on the beach and the breeze ruffling the tamarisk trees. So peaceful. Except that her feet were freezing on the tile floor.

She padded across the courtyard. It was much the same as she remembered. On her last visit, the summer after graduating from high school, her father had built the arbor that covered a small section on the left. The grapevines had grown, their branches curling like snakes around the wooden frame. In the dark shade of the arbor, she could barely see the familiar wooden table and four chairs.

The rest of the enclosed courtyard had been left open to the sky, and a half-moon shone down, reflecting off the whitewashed walls of Yia Yia's house and the waist-high walls enclosing the patio. Three large clay pots, each one holding a small lemon tree, lined up along the right wall. Around the base of each tree, green clumps of parsley and mint grew. In the far corner, a pot of red geraniums stood guard by the stone steps that wound to the beach below.

Next to the geraniums, she recognized the telescope her father had given Yia Yia for Christmas last year. An excellent present, she thought as she glanced up at the night sky. So many stars. They were never this bright in the cities back home.

She reached the far wall, leaned her elbows on top and peered down at the beach. The moon glittered on the dark sea and gleamed off the white sand.

"You cannot sleep, child?"

Olivia whirled around. "Yia Yia, I didn't mean to wake you."

"I'm a very light sleeper these—" Her grandmother's eyes narrowed. "Are you barefoot?"

Before Olivia could explain that she'd forgotten to pack house shoes, her grandmother scurried back inside, muttering about scorpions. A minute later she reappeared with some bright red booties.

"These are one size fits all, which means they are too big for me." She tossed them on the floor next to Olivia. "Your brother, Nicolas, gave those to me for Christmas. What was he thinking? A woman my age in red boots?"

Olivia smiled as she draped her blanket over the courtyard wall, then leaned against it to pull on the boot-shaped house shoes. Her brother probably thought the same thing everyone in the family thought. Eleni Sotiris never acted her age, unless it got her something she wanted. Her hair might be gray, but it was still long and thick. Right now, it hung in a long braid over her shoulder. She was still active, her eyes still sharp, and her brain even sharper.

Eleni cinched the belt tighter on her blue terry-cloth bathrobe. "Tell me what's troubling you, child."

"I'm fine. Just jet lag and—" Olivia stopped when she felt a flash of anger emanating from her grandmother. "Sorry. I'm used to telling people I'm fine when I'm . . . not."

Eleni sighed. "I understand, but you should know better than to lie to me."

Olivia nodded, relieved that her grandmother's anger had quickly dissolved. She knew all about her grandmother's strange gift, for she was the only grandchild to inherit it. They could both tell when a person was lying. And they could sense people's emotions.

"I've known you all your life, but I've never seen you this . . . frazzled," Eleni continued. "You were happy and relieved when you arrived, then you were annoyed with me during the party."

Olivia winced. "Sorry."

Eleni waved a hand in dismissal. "No matter. That's what family's for. But there is something else troubling you. Something . . . dark. And hidden."

Olivia groaned inwardly. It *was* hidden. She'd been repressing it for months. "There *is* a problem, but I—I don't want to talk about it." She took the blanket off the wall and wrapped it around her shoulders.

"It frightens you," Eleni whispered.

Olivia's eyes welled with tears. *He* frightened her.

Her grandmother looped an arm around her and pulled her close. "Don't be afraid, child. You're safe now."

She hugged her grandmother and squeezed her eyes shut, willing the tears to go away. Yia Yia had always been the one she relied upon, the one she told her secrets to. When she was young and struggling to adjust to her empathic abilities, it was only her grandmother who understood.

Eleni patted her on the back. "Who is frightening you? Is it a man?"

Olivia nodded.

"Did the bastard mistreat you? I could send your brothers after him to teach him a lesson."

Olivia laughed. Her skinny younger brothers would have trouble intimidating a Chihuahua. As usual, her grandmother had chased away the tears.

"You just leave this to me. I'll find a good man for you." Eleni stepped back and tilted her head. "Did you like any you met tonight?"

Olivia groaned. "I'm not looking for a husband."

"Of course you are. What are you, twenty-four? I had three babies by the time I was your age."

Olivia grimaced. "I have a career. A master's degree."

"And I am proud of you. But nothing is more important than family. What did you think of Spiro?"

"Which one was he?"

"The very handsome one. He was dancing on my right."

Olivia thought back, but couldn't remember a man who stood out. They had all congealed into a greasy blob of testosterone. "I can't recall."

"He's a good boy. Goes to church every week with his mother. Very nice body. Does push-ups every morning in his underwear. Not too hairy."

Olivia cocked her head. "And how do you know that?"

Eleni motioned toward the telescope.

With a gasp, Olivia noticed the telescope was not pointed toward the sky. She rushed over and peered through the eyepiece. A whitewashed wall came into view with a large window. "Yia Yia, what have you been doing?"

She shrugged. "I'm old, but I'm not dead. Spiro is a beautiful young man. And he takes good care of his goats. You should go out with him."

Olivia wrinkled her nose. "What on earth would I do with a goat herder?"

"Make little kids?"

Olivia snorted. "I can't get married. I can't even date worth a darn. It always ends up badly. I can tell when the guys are lying, and unfortunately, that's most of the time."

"We just need to find you an honest man."

"I'm afraid those have gone the way of the dinosaur." Olivia pointed the telescope away from Spiro's home. "How did you find Grandpa?"

"I didn't. My parents arranged the marriage."

Olivia winced. "How old were you?"

"Sixteen. I was from Kos." Eleni gestured to the south, where the island of Kos was located. "I met your grandfather here on Patmos at our engagement party. I told Hector right away that he must never lie to me because I would know. And I would make his life miserable."

Olivia blinked. "That didn't scare him away?" Learning that she was a human lie detector had certainly made her high school boyfriend run for the hills.

"Hector was surprised, but then he said we should both be honest, because if I lied, he could make me miserable, too." Eleni chuckled. "And then he said I was the bravest, most beautiful woman he'd ever met. And I knew he was telling the truth."

"Oh." Olivia's heart squeezed. "That's sweet."

"Six months after the wedding, he told me he loved me,

and that was the truth, too." Eleni's eyes glittered with unshed tears.

"And he never lied?" Olivia whispered.

"Once. When your father was young, he fell out of a tree and broke his arm. Hector told me not to worry, that he was certain our boy would be all right. But he was lying. He was scared stiff. So was I."

"That's not much of a lie. He was trying to comfort you."

Eleni nodded. "Not all lies are bad. It is the intent to deceive that is bad. Your grandfather was a good man, may God rest his soul." She crossed herself in the Orthodox fashion, touching her right shoulder first.

Olivia crossed herself, too, an automatic response that had been ingrained in her since childhood.

Eleni blinked away her tears and straightened her thin shoulders. "I'll make you a cup of chamomile tea. It will help you sleep." She hurried back into the house.

Olivia rested her elbows on the courtyard wall and gazed at the beach below. A breeze swept a tendril of hair across her face, and she shoved it aside. Most of her long hair was secured on the back of her head with a big claw clip, but as usual, there were always a few unruly strands that managed to escape.

She took a deep breath, savoring her solitude. There were times, like during the party that evening, when the constant bombardment of everyone's emotions became hard to bear. It would feel like she was drowning, her own emotions submerged under the flood of those around her to the point that she feared losing herself entirely. She'd learned over the years to handle it, but still, every now and then she had to escape the maddening crowd.

Being an empath had certainly helped with her job. Unfortunately, her unique abilities had also caused the monster to become obsessed with her. *Don't think about him. You're safe here.*

A movement far to the left caught her eye. She turned toward a grove of tamarisk trees, but only saw them swaying with a breeze. Nothing strange there.

Then she saw him. A lone figure emerging from the dark shadow of the trees. He was jogging along the beach. At this time of night? He reached a clear, sandy expanse where the moon shone brightly, and Olivia forgot to breathe.

His body was beautiful, and she suspected his face was, too, but it was hard to tell at this distance. Dressed in dark jogging shorts and a plain white T-shirt, he moved quickly and easily along the beach. His skin seemed pale, but that could be caused by the moonlight.

She sucked in a deep breath as he came closer. He was a big man. His T-shirt was stretched across wonderfully broad shoulders, the short sleeves tight around his biceps.

If only she could see his face better. Her gaze drifted over to the telescope. Why not? She rushed over, pointed it in the man's direction, and peered through the eyepiece.

Oh, yeah, he did not disappoint. His eyes looked sharp and intelligent. Pale, though she couldn't tell the color. Green, she hoped, since that was her favorite. He had a straight, strong nose, a wide mouth, and a strong jaw with a sexy hint of dark whiskers. There was a grim expression on his face, but it didn't make him unattractive. Quite the opposite. It added to his aura of masculine power.

He passed by the house, and she admired his sharp profile for a few seconds, then lowered the scope to his body. His chest expanded with each deep breath, and she found herself matching her breaths to his. Even lower, she noted his muscular thighs and calves. His white running shoes pounded on the sand, leaving a steady trail.

He continued down the beach toward the rock known as Petra, giving her a glorious view of his backside.

"*Opa,*" she muttered as she continued to spy on him through the telescope. She'd seen plenty of fit men during her training days for the Bureau, but this guy put them to shame. While their muscles had seemed forced and clumpy, this guy looked completely natural, moving with an easy, graceful control.

She was still focused on his rump when she noticed the attached legs were no longer moving. Did he run out of steam? He hadn't seemed tired. His jogging shorts slowly turned, affording her a long look at his groin. She gulped.

She raised the scope to his chest. Oh dear. That huge expanse of chest was now facing her direction. Surely, he wasn't . . . She lifted the scope to his face and gasped.

He was looking straight at her!

She jumped back, pulling her blanket tight around her. How could he see her? The courtyard was dark and the walls reached to her waist. But then the walls were white-washed and she was cocooned in a white blanket, and the moon and stars were bright. Maybe he *could* see this far. Surely he hadn't been able to hear her? She'd barely spoken over a whisper.

He stepped toward her, gazing at her with intense eyes. Oh God, he'd caught her ogling him with a telescope! She pressed a hand against her mouth to keep from groaning out loud. Apparently, the smallest of sounds was carrying across the beach.

He took another step toward her, and the moon glinted off his hair. Red? She hadn't met any redheaded men at the party. Who was this man?

"Olivia," Eleni called through the open door. "Your tea is steeping."

She strode into the kitchen and waited impatiently for her mug of tea. "There's a man on the beach."

"Are you sure? It's almost two in the morning."

"Come and see. Maybe you know him." Olivia wandered back to the courtyard and peered over the wall.

He was gone.

"He—He was there." Olivia pointed south toward Petra. There was no sign of him anywhere.

Eleni gave her a sympathetic look. "You're exhausted and seeing shadows. Drink your tea, child, and go to bed."

"He was real," she whispered. And the most beautiful man she'd ever seen. *Dear God, please let him be real.*

Bloody hell, she'd better be real. Robby sprinted up the stone steps to Roman's villa. He'd hate to think that three months of forced boredom was causing him to see things. Lovely things like an angel dressed in white, gazing down at him from an ivory tower.

He strode around the pool and Jacuzzi to enter the white-washed house. It was an old house, but thoroughly renovated with all the modern amenities. Carlos was in the family room, lounging on a sofa, watching a DVD and munching popcorn.

Robby waved at him as he passed into the kitchen. He retrieved a bottle of synthetic blood from the fridge and silently cursed his great-great-grandfather.

Angus must have guessed he intended to escape this forced vacation, 'cause by strange coincidence, this house had suddenly become everyone's favorite vacation spot.

Roman Draganesti and his family had visited the last week of August and the first half of September, accompanied by their bodyguards, Connor and Howard. Since Connor and Howard both worked for MacKay Security &

Investigation, they reported straight to Angus. And Robby had been unable to slip away.

Then Jean-Luc Echarpe and his family had stayed for the last half of September, accompanied by their bodyguards, who also worked for Angus. Then Jack and Lara dropped by for a few weeks. Then Ian and Toni, and now Carlos. And of course, they all worked for MacKay S&I.

Jailors. That damned Angus was using his employees as jailors to keep him on his island prison. He stuffed the bottle into the microwave and punched a button.

"What's up?" Carlos wandered into the kitchen with an empty popcorn bowl.

"Nothing." Robby leaned against the counter and folded his arms across his chest.

"Something's up. I've been here two weeks, and every single night, you go out for a run. Then you come back, give me a dirty look, and growl that I should call Angus and tell him you're in great shape and not crazy."

"Did ye call Angus?"

"No. They don't have a clue where Casimir's hiding. You might as well stay here and enjoy yourself."

Robby sighed. Angus could make better progress locating Casimir if he wasn't sending some of his best employees here to babysit.

"Something's different," Carlos continued. "Tonight you came in with no scowling or growling. Why the change?"

Robby shrugged one shoulder. "I'm trying to convince you I'm no' crazy. If I kept doing the same thing when it wasna working, would that no' be crazy?"

"Good point." Carlos rinsed the bowl and placed it in the dishwasher. "So you're trying a new strategy tonight."

Robby removed the bottled blood from the microwave and filled a glass. "Tonight I saw an angel."

Carlos's eyes widened. "And you're still trying to convince me you're not crazy?"

Robby snorted. "No' a real angel. No' unless they've taken to watching the mortal plane with telescopes."

"Ah." Carlos grinned. "You caught a babe, scoping you out. Was she hot?"

She was a goddess, a beautiful Greek goddess, but Robby didn't feel like sharing that news with the Brazilian shapeshifter who could meet people during the day, while he was dead to the world. "She was all right."

"Just all right? I thought she was an angel."

Robby ignored the comment and took a long drink from his glass of synthetic blood.

"Did you talk to her?" Carlos asked. "Get her number?"

Robby frowned at his half-empty glass. "No." He'd heard her whisper in Greek, so he wasn't sure she understood English. "There's no point in pursuing her. My prison term will be over in three weeks."

Carlos rolled his eyes. "You're not in prison, *muchacho*. Besides, a lot can happen in three weeks."

Robby finished his glass. He wasn't the sort of man who could indulge in a casual fling. When he was attracted to a woman, there was nothing casual about it. And he was definitely attracted to this woman.

The minute he'd laid eyes upon her, the world had screeched to a halt around him. He'd forgotten he was on vacation and due to leave soon. He'd forgotten it was the wee hours of the morning and not a proper time to approach a lone woman. He'd forgotten he was a stranger dressed in sweaty gym clothes and likely to frighten her. Hell, he'd even forgotten he was a vampire and had no business getting involved with a mortal. He'd simply been drawn to her.

And then, suddenly, she'd disappeared. He'd sprinted all

the way home, wondering if he'd just imagined her. After all, he'd jogged down that beach every night for the past three months. If she lived in that house, why hadn't he seen her before?

"If you see her again, you should talk to her," Carlos said as he strode from the kitchen. "A beautiful woman might be just the therapy you need."

"I doona need therapy," Robby grumbled. He just needed revenge. Three months of exercise had whipped him back into shape, and he was ready to go. Ready to leave this wretched island and hunt Casimir down.

The angel's lovely face floated back into his mind, erasing the image of his enemy. She had to be real. A mere dream couldn't have affected him this strongly. He had to see her again. Even when there were a dozen reasons why he should avoid her, he'd still try to see her again.

Maybe he did need therapy after all.

It was past three in the morning when Olivia finally fell asleep. Unfortunately, it was Sunday morning, and her grandmother woke her at dawn so they could go to church. Apparently if she didn't go, everyone in Grikos would say bad things about her.

Afterward, Olivia was put to work in the kitchen, helping her grandmother cook an enormous amount of food, and then, surprise! Two of Yia Yia's best friends showed up for dinner with their eligible sons. Olivia was cordial, but disappointed that neither of them had red hair. Luckily, their English was as limited as her Greek, so she didn't have to talk much. Her mind kept wandering back to the man on the beach. Who was he? Would he be back tonight?

By nine o'clock in the evening, jet lag and sleep deprivation caught up with her, and she stumbled off to bed. As she pulled the blanket up to her chin, she told herself she'd only take a short nap. She'd be in the courtyard at 1:00 A.M., waiting for the mysterious jogger to pass by.

She blinked awake when sunlight poured into her window. "Oh no!"

She sat up and looked at her bedside clock. Eight-thirty in the morning? Damn. She slipped the red booties onto her feet and shuffled into the kitchen.

"There you are, sleepyhead." Her grandmother was stirring something on the stove. "I've already been to the bakery. There's fresh bread on the table next to the honey jar. I'll bring you a cup of tea."

"Thank you." Olivia sat down and cut off a thick slice of bread. As she reached for the honey jar, she noticed the narrow vase in the center of the table with a single red rose-bud. "I didn't know you grew roses."

"I don't. You can't eat them." Eleni set a cup of tea on the table and regarded her with a gleam in her eye. "I think you have a secret admirer."

Olivia blinked. "Me?"

"Who do you think he is? Giorgios or Dimitrios?" Eleni referred to the men who'd come over the day before.

"I don't know." Olivia's mind had immediately snapped to the mysterious jogger with red hair and intense eyes. Could it be him? She reached out to touch the soft red petals. "You didn't see who delivered it?"

"No." Eleni planted her hands on her hips and frowned at the flower. "There was no note with it. I swept the courtyard early this morning, and while I was sweeping off the steps I found it halfway down to the beach. It was lying there, pinned down by a rock."

Olivia's heart raced. "Then whoever left it came from the beach." It had to be from *him*.

Eleni gasped. "Of course! It's from Spiro! He lives just down the beach." She clasped her hands together, grinning. "My beautiful Spiro and Olivia together, right here on Patmos. Oh, the beautiful babies you'll have."

"Wait a minute. I'm not so sure it came from Spiro. And I don't want you getting your hopes up about me living here. I specialize in criminals, and I seriously doubt if Patmos has enough of those to keep me in business."

Eleni sat at the table with a huff. "We do have criminals. Last year there was a boy from Hora whose bicycle was stolen. Right in front of the monastery, too. It was shocking."

Olivia shook her head as she drizzled honey on her bread. "Not bad enough."

"Humph. Why do you need criminals? Can't you help normal crazy people? Patmos has plenty of those. There's a goat herder in Kambos who talks to his goats."

Olivia sipped her tea. "It's not unusual for people to talk to their animals."

"Ah, but in this case, his goats talk back. And the solid black goat speaks Turkish."

Olivia stifled a grin. "He's the worst case you've got to offer?"

Eleni tilted her head, considering. "Well, there's the old widower in Skala who was caught peeping in Maria Stephanopoulos's window. His son started taking him to the nude beach at Plaki once a week, so he's much better now."

Olivia nodded. "I'm afraid that Peeping Tom syndrome is contagious. I heard there's a widow woman in Grikos who uses a telescope to spy on a nearby goat herder."

Eleni scoffed. "I'm not a Peeping Tom! I'm just admiring Spiro. He's a work of art. It's like I'm going to the museum. And I've never seen him naked. That wouldn't be right, not when I want him to marry my granddaughter."

Olivia winced, then took a bite of bread. Maybe her grandmother had a point. Not about Spiro, but about her work with criminals. Her life could be so different if she played it safe and lived here.

Who was she kidding? She wouldn't last two months before boredom drove her absolutely bonkers. She thrived on the excitement that came with her work at the FBI. At least she had until her job had brought her into contact with one criminal in particular. The monster, Otis Crump. She didn't have to worry about him sending roses. That sick pervert preferred apples. Big red apples.

"Hmm." Eleni drummed her fingers on the table as she glared at the rose. "I don't like secrets. I want to know who this admirer is."

Olivia sighed. If dreams could come true, her secret admirer wouldn't be Spiro, Giorgios, or Dimitrios. He'd be the mysterious man who jogged along the beach in the middle of the night. Could he have left the rose?

Her heartbeat raced at the thought. One way or another, she'd find out tonight.

Chapter Three

"That's not what you usually wear to go jogging," Carlos commented as Robby strode across the family room.

Robby grunted and headed into the kitchen. He'd already had one bottle of blood when he'd first wakened, so he wasn't really hungry. This was just a precaution in case he actually met the Greek goddess. Sometimes good old-fashioned lust managed to trigger his lust for blood, and he didn't want his fangs popping out and scaring her.

He poured half a glass and warmed it up in the microwave.

Carlos entered the kitchen. "Your hair's damp. You took a shower *before* jogging?"

He wasn't going to jog tonight. He didn't want to arrive at her house all sweaty, especially since a Vamp's sweat tended to be a wee bit pinkish in color, just like their tears. It came from a steady diet of blood, he supposed. "I'm taking a walk."

"Ah. A midnight stroll. Sounds wonderful." Carlos regarded him with a smirk. "I think I'll join you."

"Nay."

"I like to walk on the beach."

"Piss off."

Carlos laughed. "I know you're hoping to see her."

"I know ye know." Robby removed his half glass of blood from the microwave and downed it.

"I also know that a red rose is missing from the garden."

Robby arched a brow. "Ye're keeping inventory on all the flowers?"

Carlos chuckled. "I had my eye on that rose. I was planning to give it to someone, and you beat me to it."

Robby wondered briefly what Carlos was up to, but refrained from asking. Toni claimed he was gay, but Ian disagreed. When they were here on the island, Robby had heard them argue over the matter for ten minutes, then rush off to their bedroom to make up. He'd gone jogging for two hours, and when he returned, they were still making up.

He groaned inwardly. His Vamp friends, Ian, Jean-Luc, and Jack, were deliriously happy with their mortal women, but he doubted he could ever experience such happiness. First, there was the problem of finding a woman who could actually love a creature of the night.

Then there was the matter of trust. How would he know what she was doing during the day? He couldn't bear another betrayal from a woman he loved. What if she tired of him and decided to stake him while he was in his death-sleep?

And then there was the last problem, the one that bothered him the most. Loving a Vamp was a death sentence. He didn't know how his friends could even stomach the thought that one day they would have to literally kill their wives in order to transform them. What kind of love was that?

So what the hell was he doing? He set his empty glass in the sink. "This was a bad idea."

"Dude, don't chicken out now."

He shot Carlos an annoyed look. "'Tis no' fear that's giving me pause. She's an innocent mortal. She deserves better than me."

"Right, because you're a disgusting, slobbering beast who'll rip her throat out and toss her dead body out to sea."

Robby stiffened. "Are ye asking for a bloody nose? I wouldna harm her."

"Exactly. Go see her, *muchacho.*"

Robby glanced down at his clothes. It had taken him fifteen minutes to decide what to wear. He'd finally chosen some worn jeans, a dark green T-shirt, and a navy hoodie lined with the green and blue MacKay tartan. His hair was tied back with a leather strip. "I doona look too casual?"

"You look fine. Go get her, tiger."

Robby snorted. Strange words from a were-panther. He strode from the house before he could change his mind. Rather than descend the stone steps, he simply jumped off the edge of the rocky bluff and landed neatly on the pebbly beach below. Even in the dim light of the three-quarter moon, he could spot the rock called Petra about half a mile to the north. He teleported there, then walked around it to the beach at Grikos.

What was he going to say? He doubted she'd want to hear about his favorite topic—which swords were best suited for different situations. Bugger. He was woefully out of practice when it came to talking to women.

Olivia debated what to wear for fifteen minutes even though her choices were severely limited to the few items she'd packed. She finally opted for a pair of jeans and a soft pullover sweater. Then she trapped her unruly hair in a claw clip on the back of her head.

Her grandmother was sound asleep when she made herself comfortable in the courtyard. She lit a trio of candles on the table beneath the grape arbor. On a chair, she set an old cricket bat Yia Yia used to beat rugs.

She hoped she wouldn't need it to defend herself, but her work at the Bureau had taught her that looks could be deceiving. She'd been surprised the first time she met Otis Crump by how harmless and ordinary he appeared. Underneath the pleasant exterior lurked a monster who had raped, tortured, and murdered thirteen women.

She shoved him out of her thoughts. This was her time to recover and heal. He had been an assignment, nothing more, and she was done with it. Done with him.

She could only pray that he was done with her.

She strode back into the house to make a cup of hot tea. As she exited the kitchen, she grabbed the rose and took it with her. Back in the courtyard, she waited. And waited. She finished her tea and left the cup on the table.

Back at the wall, she smoothed her fingers over the velvet rose petals. The thorns had been pinched off the stem, so her secret admirer appeared to be considerate. She hoped he was the mysterious jogger. But where was he?

Maybe she was too early. Or maybe he had left the island and this rose was his way of saying good-bye. After all, the last week of November was way past the tourist season. Or maybe she'd imagined him. After dealing with the ultimate dregs of humanity in the person of Otis Crump, her subconscious could be trying to compensate by manufacturing a handsome, honorable hero.

She sighed. Too many years of psychology classes had left her with a tendency to overanalyze everything. She just needed to relax and smell the roses. Or one rose in particular. She lifted it to her nose and smiled.

Her attention snapped to a figure coming from the south. She looked through the telescope, and her heart lurched in her chest. It was him! He *was* real.

He wasn't jogging tonight. Instead, he walked toward her with a quick determined stride. He lifted a hand in greeting, and her heart did another flip. Through the telescope, she could tell he was focused entirely on her. He certainly had good eyesight.

She stepped toward the wall and waved a hand to acknowledge his greeting. He immediately broke into a jog, and her heart pounded with each step that brought him closer. His eyes never seemed to leave her. He was checking her out, and that brought heat to her cheeks. Was he excited and attracted? Or was he already regretting his actions? She opened her senses to detect his feelings.

Nothing. In all her twenty-four years, she'd never met a person she couldn't read. She closed her eyes and furrowed her brow with concentration.

Nothing.

She opened her eyes to make sure he was real. Yep, he was almost in front of her. Why couldn't she sense him? She always knew how people felt. She always knew when they were lying.

Good God, this was awful. How would she know where

she stood with this man? How could she trust anything he said? A spurt of panic flashed through her, and she considered escaping into the house.

But then she saw his face. He had stopped on the beach below her, and he was gazing up at her with an intense, searching look as if he didn't know what to think. Well, that made two of them.

She met his gaze, and an instant wave of desire flooded through her. It caught her by surprise, nearly buckling her knees. *Whoa.* She gripped the edge of the wall to steady herself. She didn't usually react like that.

Actually, she wasn't sure how she usually reacted. She'd always concentrated on other people's feelings so she would know how to deal with them.

This was a first for her. She was in the company of another person, but alone with her own feelings. And she'd never realized her feelings could be so . . . strong. Maybe they just seemed that way because they were isolated. Or because this situation was new to her.

Or maybe *he* was the cause.

She swallowed hard. She'd have to be careful. She had no idea what he was feeling. Or if he could be trusted. How did normal women survive like this? It was terrifying.

And incredibly exciting.

He raised a hand. "Good evening."

His low voice carried up to her with the slight stir of a breeze that tickled her neck. She felt giddy with excitement. Almost giggly.

"Do ye speak English, lass?"

She bit her lip to keep from laughing out loud. His accent was adorable. "You're Scottish?"

"Aye. Ye're . . . American?"

She nodded with a growing smile. He smiled back, and

a fluttery feeling started in her stomach. *Careful. You don't know if he can be trusted.*

"I'm Robert Alexander MacKay." He inclined his head, leaning forward.

He was bowing? She stifled a giggle and wondered what the gorgeous Scotsman would do next.

He regarded her expectantly. Green, she noted with great satisfaction. His eyes were green just like she had hoped. And even though his hair was a rich, dark red, his eyebrows and whiskers looked more brownish.

"And you?" he asked.

"Yes?"

His mouth quirked with a half smile. "Forgive the bold assumption, but I thought ye might be in possession of a name I could call you?"

She laughed. Several suggestions flitted through her mind. *Sweetheart, love of my life, center of my universe.* She'd been so busy admiring him, she'd forgotten to introduce herself. "I'm Olivia. Olivia Sotiris."

"Ah. Then I was wrong about you."

"How?"

"I thought you were a Greek goddess."

She snorted. What a smooth talker. And what a shame that she couldn't tell if he was lying. She lifted the rose. "Did you leave this?"

"Aye."

"Where?"

His eyebrows lifted. "I left it on the steps, pinned down with a rock. Why do ye ask?"

Because she needed to know if he was an honest man. She loved the way he pronounced *down* like *dune,* but she'd be a fool to fall for a man just because his voice was like music and his face and body were like a beautiful sculpture. She sniffed the rose. "It's lovely. Thank you."

"Would ye care to walk with me a wee bit?"

Her heart rate sped up. "I—I'd rather stay here. You can join me if you like."

His gaze flitted over the rocky bluff separating them, then his mouth twitched. "I'll take the stairs."

"Be careful. The stairs are steep. And dark." Her heart raced as he disappeared in the narrow stairwell. He was coming up!

She glanced toward the back door. Her grandmother was alone and asleep. What if she'd invited an axe murderer up here? She left the rose on the table and grabbed the cricket bat. It wasn't just her work at the FBI that made her suspicious. She'd learned as a young child to be wary when she'd discovered how often people lied.

He reached the top of the stairs and stopped, motioning to the cricket bat in her hands. "Are ye planning to whack me now?"

He was taller than she'd realized. And his shoulders broader. She flexed her hands around the bat. "I don't usually talk to strangers. I should warn you, I'm a black belt in tae kwon do."

His jaw shifted. "I willna harm you, lass."

"I know. I won't let you."

He studied her a moment, then his mouth relaxed with a hint of a smile. "Ye're as brave as ye are beautiful. That's a rare combination."

Her heart stilled for a moment. Brave and beautiful. That's what her grandfather had said to Yia Yia the day they met. "I don't mean to be rude, Mr. MacKay. A woman has to be careful these days."

"Aye, ye're correct." His gaze moved slowly down her body to her feet. His mouth lifted in a half smile as his gaze roamed back to her face.

Damn. She didn't know whether to whack him or melt into a puddle. Part of her was flustered and flattered. Her skin tingled when he examined her with those gorgeous green eyes. But another part of her was nervous. She tightened her grip on the bat in case he made a lunge at her. It was so hard, not being able to read his emotions. For a second she thought his eyes were darkening, but he turned toward the telescope and peered through the eyepiece.

"So, Olivia, what brings you to Patmos?"

She liked the way her name sounded with his accent. "I'm visiting my . . . relatives. Four uncles. They're . . . big. Professional wrestlers." When his mouth twitched, she figured he wasn't buying her story. "What about you?"

"Vacation. And recuperation. I was . . . injured, so I've been trying to get back in shape."

She glanced at his muscular body. "I would say you definitely succeeded."

"Thank you for noticing."

Her face heated with a blush. "How did you get injured?"

He grew silent, frowning at the tile floor.

"Sorry." She propped the bat against a wooden column of the grape arbor. "You don't have to talk about it . . ."

"It just happened. My job can be dangerous."

"What do you do?" When his frown deepened, she felt a sudden need to comfort him, to make him smile again. "I know! You're a bullfighter."

He gave her a dubious look. "A Scottish bullfighter?"

"Yeah, with a red plaid cape. And little sequins on your kilt. Drives the Scottish bulls crazy."

He chuckled. "Nay."

Her heart expanded in her chest. It felt so good to chase away his frown. She wandered toward the whitewashed wall to stand next to him. "Then you're a lion tamer?" When he shook his head, she continued. "Rodeo clown? Snake charmer?"

"Nay." He grinned, his green eyes twinkling.

"Okay. I'm thinking Navy SEAL."

"I'm thinking seals are black."

She snorted. "You know what I mean. You could be a member of a special, macho, elite force, protecting mankind from insidious evil in all forms, including the triple-decker bacon cheeseburger."

"I can safely say I've never battled a cheeseburger."

"Sure, but have you battled evil?"

He stiffened and looked toward the sea, frowning again.

The skin on the back of her neck prickled. "You *are* some kind of soldier."

His chest moved as he inhaled deeply. "Aye."

"Top secret?" she whispered. "Are you fighting terrorists?"

He hesitated a moment before answering. "Ye could say that."

She nodded. His reluctance to speak on the subject made her fairly certain he was telling the truth. "You're on leave now?"

"Aye." He planted his hands on top of the wall, then drummed his long fingers on the plaster for a while before continuing. "My boss insisted I take some time off."

She blinked. "You're kidding. That's why I'm here. My boss wanted me to take time off, too."

He turned toward her, regarding her curiously. "Why? What do ye do?"

She didn't want to discuss her work with criminals. She was here to get away from all that. And besides, she enjoyed making this gorgeous man smile. "You were right from the beginning. I'm a Greek goddess. Zeus told me to take off a millennium or two."

His mouth tilted and his eyes twinkled. "I knew it. One look into yer eyes, and I could fall at yer feet."

Her cheeks grew warm. She didn't usually flirt like this. Normally, she was too busy analyzing people's feelings. With a jolt she realized she'd always been an observer before, not a participant. This was new and scary, but so much fun.

She lifted her chin. "No groveling allowed. Goddesses find that very annoying."

He smiled slowly. "If I fell to my knees, I'd find something better to do than grovel."

Her face blazed with heat. This was getting too hot to handle. "I work for the FBI," she blurted out.

His eyebrows shot up. "Do ye really?"

"Yes. We're in the same sort of business, Mr. MacKay. Catching bad guys."

He cocked his head, studying her. "Where are ye stationed?"

"Kansas City. You?"

"Wherever they need me. So ye really are a black belt in tae kwon do?"

He'd doubted her? She planted a hand on her hip. "I've been thoroughly trained in self-defense, Mr. MacKay."

A corner of his mouth dimpled. "My friends call me Robby."

Her heart pounded. "Are you calling me a friend?"

"Aye." He reached out and touched a strand of her hair that had escaped from the clip on the back of her head. "Does yer hair curl like this naturally?"

"I'm afraid so. It's impossible to deal with."

"I like it." He tugged on the strand till it was taut, then let go, and it bounced back into its normal corkscrew shape. He grinned. "A man could play with yer hair for hours." He touched her temple.

With a gulp, she stepped back. "I—I should check on my uncles. Would you like something to drink? Some hot tea?"

He lowered his hand. "I'm fine, thank you."

"I'll be right back." She dashed into the house and quickly set some water to boil on the stove. Chicken, she chided herself. She should have let him touch her, maybe even kiss her. But how could she trust him? She was so attracted to him, but as far as she knew, he was simply looking for a little fling to spice up his vacation.

She'd never been the type to indulge in a fling. Growing up with the ability to detect lies had caused her to avoid anything that smacked of insincerity. Besides, she would only be on the island for two weeks. Was that enough time to forge an honest, meaningful relationship? Did she dare even try it with a man she couldn't read? The unknown could be scary, but also very exciting.

She peered through the windowpane in the back door. He was still in the courtyard, amusing himself by peering through the telescope. Robby MacKay, a soldier on leave. She wondered how badly he'd been injured.

She fixed her cup of tea and carried it back to the courtyard. When he smiled at her, her heart stuttered. She was seriously falling fast.

She sat at the table and motioned for him to join her. "Are you sure I can't get you something to drink or eat?"

"I ate before I came." He sat beside her.

She liked the way his red hair glinted in the candlelight. It seemed rather long for a soldier, but it was neatly tied back. "How long will you be on Patmos?"

"About three more weeks." He hesitated a moment, then continued. "I'm ready to go back now, but my boss disagrees. He thinks I was traumatized or some such nonsense."

"Post-traumatic stress syndrome." Olivia sipped some hot tea. "It's very common among soldiers."

He shrugged one shoulder. "'Tis much ado about nothing. I know life is no' fair. There's no point in whining about it."

She gave him a worried look. "Sometimes it's healthier to talk things out. Repression can lead to serious side effects down the road, and I don't just mean emotional outbursts. It can affect your physical health."

He shot her an annoyed look. "I'm perfectly fine. And hell will freeze over before I'll talk to a damned psychologist."

She sucked in a quick intake of air. Her cup wobbled in her hand, and she set it down on the table.

He frowned at her. "What's wrong?"

Everything was wrong. Her heart plummeted into her stomach. She should have known this couldn't last.

His eyes narrowed with suspicion. He jumped to his feet and crossed the courtyard. "Bloody hell," he whispered. He turned back to her, regarding her with a look of horror. "Ye're a psychologist?"

She nodded slowly. "I think hell just froze over." For both of them.

Chapter Four

Robby paced across the courtyard. "Bugger. Bloody hell."

He glanced at Olivia, and a mixture of anger and futility surged through him. Damn it to hell. Just when he had his hopes up, everything came crashing down. For a few minutes he'd actually believed that his future could hold more than revenge and violence, and it had felt *good.*

He'd found a woman who was beautiful, clever, and adorable. She made him laugh. She opened a world of new possibilities, and to his surprise, he wanted it.

Even more surprising, she seemed to like him. He was definitely taken with her. She had soft brown eyes, thick black lashes, a perfect oval face, small straight nose, enticing pink mouth, all framed with a riot of black curls that made him want to dive in.

And she was so much more than a classic beauty. She was brave, witty, and kind. He couldn't recall ever laughing or

smiling so much. For the first time in many years, he'd felt
. . . blessed.

But the last surprise had been on him. He wasn't blessed.
He was cursed.

He stopped at the wall and gazed at the dark sea, his gut
churning like the waves. "Did ye think I wouldna figure it
out? Ye can call Angus and tell him to piss off."

"I don't know Angus."

He whipped around to glare at her. "Of course ye do. He
sent ye here."

She rose to her feet with a skeptical look. "The only
Angus I've ever seen are cows, and they've never told me
where to go."

Robby snorted. "Either Angus or Emma sent ye here.
Ye're probably no' even Greek. Is yer name really Olivia?"

"Yes, it is. And I never claimed to be Greek. I'm American." She planted her hands on her hips, glaring at him.
"And I don't lie."

"Are ye sure? Would ye care to introduce me, then, to yer
four uncles who all happen to be professional wrestlers?"

"I ought to. You deserve the thrashing they'd give you."

He arched a brow. "Bring it on."

She crossed her arms over her chest, scowling at
him. "Okay. It was a slight embellishment, but just for
self-protection. And now that we're being perfectly honest,
I think you should leave."

He stiffened. She was rejecting him? Why was *she* upset?
He was the one who'd been tricked into seeing a therapist.
"Angus willna pay you unless ye do yer bloody therapy."

"I don't know Angus!" she shouted, then winced and
glanced at the house. "We need to keep it down. I don't
want to wake my—"

"Four uncles on steroids?" he growled.

She gave him a bland look. "Believe it or not, I have no interest in being your therapist. You're obviously too stubborn and paranoid to listen to reason."

"I'm no' paranoid!" He wasn't sure he could deny the stubborn part.

"You think there's a big conspiracy that brought me to this island just to be your therapist. That's paranoid, not to mention totally self-absorbed."

"Bloody hell. They sent ye here to insult me?"

"Paranoid," she muttered under her breath. "Who are 'they'? Aliens from another galaxy? Talking Angus cows who demand we eat more chicken?"

"Doona mock me, woman. Angus is my grandfather."

"Woman?"

He scowled at her. "I noticed. A man would have to be crazy no' to. And I'm no' crazy."

She gave him a dubious look. "You think your own family is out to get you."

Bugger. He *was* sounding paranoid. But it was too much of a coincidence that Angus and Emma had wanted him to see a psychologist, and then one magically appeared. "Ye swear Angus dinna send ye here?"

"I swear. I told you, I work for the FBI. I specialize in criminal psychology, so you're of no interest to me." She gave him a wry look. "Unless you're a criminal."

He cocked a brow at her. "Did Sean Whelan send you?"

"I don't know him."

"He works for the CIA."

"So the CIA is out to get you, too?"

He gritted his teeth. "I'm no' paranoid!"

"Maybe you should check the lemon trees," she whispered, pointing in their direction. "They could be bugged."

"Woman—" He paused when her brown eyes flashed.

Lord Almighty, she was beautiful. "Maybe I should strip *you* to check for bugs."

Her cheeks turned a rosy pink. "Maybe you should leave."

He swallowed hard. What the hell was he doing? "I—I apologize. I wouldna strip you." *Tonight.*

She refused to look at him and motioned to the stairs.

He trudged toward them. What a fool he was. Accusing her of working for Angus, insulting her.

The stairwell loomed before him, dark and ominous. He hesitated, suddenly feeling like the stairs descended into the pits of hell itself. Could he return to a life filled with nothing but rage and revenge?

No laughter. No flirtation. No Olivia.

His heart sank with a heavy sense of loss. "I'm truly sorry, lass. I dinna mean to insult you."

He glanced at her and noted the tears in her eyes.

"Doona be sad. 'Twas my fault for reacting so badly to yer job. I'm sure ye're a verra fine psychologist. I just doona want to talk about certain . . . things. I see no point in opening old wounds."

She sighed. "I understand. But it doesn't . . . change anything. You might as well go."

She looked so defeated, and he had no idea why. He hated to see her this way. "Why are ye so sad?"

She rubbed her brow as if her head hurt. "Things never work out for me. They all go."

"Who?"

"Men. Dates. I get my hopes up, then they learn the truth about me and hightail it away as fast as they can."

He studied her curiously. He'd thought he was the one with the dark secret. He inhaled deeply of her scent. Not a shape-shifter. Deliciously sweet as only a mortal could be.

Blood Type A negative. "Ye're verra clever and beautiful. I canna imagine why any man would leave you."

"That's kind of you to say, but . . ." She took a deep breath and released it with a whoosh. "I'm an empath. I can sense people's feelings. I even see them in color if the emotions are really strong."

He winced. "Ye know what I'm feeling?" He'd been fighting a major case of lust all evening.

"It gets even worse," she continued. "I can tell when people are lying, like a human lie detector. Comes in real handy in my line of work, but it's the pits for personal relationships. The minute a guy lies to me, I tell him to hit the road."

Just like she was doing to him. Robby thought back over their conversation. He might have hedged a few times, but he'd actually told her more about himself than he'd originally intended. She'd been so easy to talk to. "I dinna lie to you, lass."

She bit her lip, frowning.

"Since I'm no' a liar, ye must want me to leave because ye think I'm crazy? I'm no' crazy. Yer lie detecting skills should tell you I'm speaking the truth."

She shifted her weight. "I don't think you're crazy. You have some baggage, obviously, that you're dealing with, but we all do."

"Then . . . we should be all right."

She gave him an incredulous look. "Doesn't my gift disturb you? Guys are usually out the door right after I tell them. Some would be halfway to another island by now."

He shrugged one shoulder. "'Tis an odd ability, I grant ye that, but I—I'm no' in a position to cast stones for being different."

She still looked stunned. "You're okay with it?"

"Aye. I'd like to see you again."

"I—I can't. I'm sorry."

It hurt more than he expected. Dammit, why would she reject him? She didn't know he was undead. She didn't think he was crazy. He'd been honest, so she couldn't have caught him in a lie. But if he kept seeing her, wouldn't he have to lie at some point? And then she would know.

Unless . . . A niggling suspicion crept into his thoughts. "What am I feeling now?"

Her eyes widened. "I would say you're . . . annoyed."

Not even close. His heart was aching at the thought of never seeing her again. He stepped toward her. "Ye're no' sensing me, are ye?"

Her face paled. "I'd rather not talk about—"

"Since ye value honesty so much, ye should tell me the truth."

She looked away with a grimace. "Okay. I can't sense you at all. And I don't know why. It's never happened to me before."

Obviously, she'd never met the Undead before. "Ye canna tell if I'm lying?"

"No." Her shoulders drooped. "It's terrible. I've never felt so . . . blind."

"Lass, 'tis no' that bad. We're in the same boat. I canna tell if ye're lying either."

She snorted. "You knew the four uncles was a lie."

He smiled. "I dinna hold it against you. I thought it was understandable and . . . adorable."

Her mouth fell open, and it struck him like an invitation. Lord Almighty, he wanted to kiss her. He took another step toward her.

She stepped back, her cheeks a lovely shade of pink. "I'm sorry, but I can't get involved with someone I can't read."

A spurt of anger shot through him. He was accepting her even though she was a therapist. Why the hell wouldn't she accept him? "Lass, we were having a grand time, joking and laughing. Ye doona need special abilities to recognize how happy we were."

Her eyes glimmered with tears. "I enjoyed it, too. But I can't have a relationship with someone I can't trust."

Of all the complaints to lodge against him, this had to be the absolute worst. "Ye—ye think I canna be *trusted*?" His voice rose to a shout.

Her eyes widened. She moved closer to the grape arbor.

"Bloody hell." He paced away, fighting to control his anger, but it was obvious that he was pissed. She grabbed hold of the cricket bat.

"Lass, I willna hurt you." Damn it to hell. First he'd insulted her, and now he was frightening her. There was no help for it. He would have to explain. Otherwise she would never understand. "I dinna want to tell you this, but . . . I was in battle one night with the enemy. And I was captured."

She drew in a quick breath.

He looked away, ashamed to admit he'd been a victim. "They wanted information about my comrades. When I refused to talk, they . . . tortured me. For two nights."

The bat she was holding fell onto the tile floor with a clatter.

He turned to her. "I told them *nothing*. I wouldna betray my friends. They burned me, cut me, broke my fingers, shattered my feet—"

She covered her mouth with a trembling hand, but a strangled whimper escaped.

He stepped toward her. "I dinna betray my friends. I prayed for death so I wouldna betray them."

"I'm so sorry," she breathed.

"I doona want yer pity, lass."

"But I *am* sorry."

"Bloody hell, I dinna want to tell you." He paced away. "Now ye'll look at me like some poor weakling who was fool enough to get captured—"

"No." She stepped toward him. "Don't you dare blame yourself. It wasn't your fault."

He groaned. There she went with the therapy. "Olivia, I only told you so ye'd understand how much I value loyalty. I would rather die than betray my friends and family. Ye'd be hard pressed to find any man in the world as trustworthy as I."

Her mouth curled up. "Or as modest."

He smiled. "There, ye see. Ye read me quite well, so I doona think ye need yer special powers with me."

She hooked a curly tendril behind an ear. "Maybe. I don't know. This is so . . . strange."

"Ye can trust me, lass. May I see you tomorrow night?"

Her eyes met his with a searching glance. The lust he'd battled all evening returned at full force. He stuffed his fists into the pockets of his hoodie to keep from grabbing her. Lord Almighty, he wanted to kiss away her doubts.

His gaze dropped to her pink mouth. So soft and sweet. Everything was slowly becoming tinted with pink, which could only mean his eyes were turning red. A sure sign that he desperately wanted her. She licked her lips, and he closed his eyes, praying for control.

"All right," she whispered.

Thank God. He opened his eyes and found her gaze drifting over his body. She wanted him. He didn't need any empathic powers to feel the heat coming from her. He could hear her heart pounding. Maybe he could steal a kiss after all. He stepped toward her, lowering his gaze to her feet so his red glowing eyes wouldn't frighten her.

"I'll see you tomorrow." She turned and dashed into the house.

He took a deep breath to calm his raging lust. "Olivia," he whispered, simply because he liked hearing it. He liked the way it rolled off his tongue. She was so beautiful. Unique. Worth fighting for every step of the way.

His eyes slowly returned to normal, and he headed toward the stairs with a growing sense of triumph. She'd tried to reject him, but he'd persevered and emerged victorious. Fate was on his side after all.

By the time he reached the beach, Robby was grinning. He'd see her again. Flirt again. Laugh again.

Life was good. He'd found Olivia.

"I thought you'd never get up." Eleni Sotiris frowned when her granddaughter wandered into the kitchen shortly before eleven the next morning. "Are you still not sleeping well?"

"No, 'fraid not." Olivia yawned. She'd spent most of the night tossing and turning, replaying her meeting with Robby MacKay over and over in her mind. And after re-creating the scene faithfully a dozen times, she'd started fantasizing alternative endings. What if she'd let him kiss her?

She fixed a cup of hot tea while her grandmother sat at the table chopping an onion into tiny bits.

Eleni scraped the onions into a mixing bowl filled with ground meat. "Are you still worried about that bad man? You never told me about him."

"It's not him." That was one good thing about Robby MacKay. He'd completely taken her mind off Otis Crump.

Olivia peered at the contents in the mixing bowl. "Is that hamburger?"

"A little beef, a little lamb. Some tabouli." Eleni peeled some cloves of garlic. "Don't you recognize the stuffing for dolmades?"

Olivia sat across from her grandmother and sipped some tea. She could lie, but her grandmother would know. "I guess not."

Eleni gave her a worried look. "You remember how to make dolmades, don't you?"

"Not really." It had been years since she had tried stuffing grape leaves. Her attempts had always turned out messy and lopsided.

Her grandmother clicked her tongue disapprovingly as she chopped garlic. "How will you make a proper Greek wife if you don't know how to cook? What have you been doing with yourself?"

"I went to college. Got a master's degree. Went to Quantico for training. Been chasing down bad guys." She gave her grandmother a wry look. "You know, the usual girly stuff."

Eleni's mouth twitched. "It'll take a special husband to keep up with you."

Olivia's thoughts immediately snapped to Robby MacKay. He was definitely special. She'd tried to scare him away, but he'd refused to give up on her.

Eleni scraped the minced garlic into the mixing bowl. "I need some fresh parsley." She grabbed a pair of scissors and headed out the back door to the patio.

Olivia sipped her tea and noted that the red rosebud had opened. After Robby had left, she'd returned it to the vase on the kitchen table. Its sweet scent competed with the onions and garlic of Yia Yia's cooking.

She wondered how long the rose could last. And how long a relationship with Robby could last. In two weeks she'd be accompanying her grandmother to Houston for the Christmas holidays. And then she'd be returning to her job in Kansas City. It seemed highly doubtful that she'd ever see Robby again once she left Patmos.

She sighed. Why should she let it bother her? The relationship was doomed anyway. She could never get involved with a man she couldn't read. She would never know if he was being completely truthful.

Still, there were a few facts she could believe. One, he was extremely handsome. Two, she was hopelessly attracted to him. She felt fairly certain that his story was honest. He was a soldier who'd been captured and tortured for two days. That sent a shudder down her spine.

Could he have made up the story to gain her sympathy? Yes. But his reluctance to tell her had seemed real. And the pain in his eyes had seemed real. Too bad there was no computer or Internet at Yia Yia's house so she could run a check on him.

She was tempted to believe him. She wanted to believe him. If he'd really survived being tortured, it explained a lot: his reluctance to admit that he'd been traumatized. His tendency to be suspicious and paranoid.

It wasn't surprising that his family wanted him to see a therapist. And it wasn't surprising that he'd be averse to it. Who would want to relive such an experience? No doubt a big, strong guy like Robby found it humiliating to admit he'd been victimized and totally helpless.

With a gulp, Olivia realized his physical wounds might have healed, but the wound to his pride was still raw. She'd smacked his pride badly when she'd implied he couldn't be trusted.

Eleni marched back into the kitchen with a bouquet of parsley clutched in her hand. "We're having dolmades, spanakopita, lamb, and salad for dinner. I'll need your help." She rinsed off the parsley in the kitchen sink.

Olivia winced. She had a bad feeling about this. "That seems like a lot of food just for the two of us."

Eleni sat across from her and chopped the parsley. "I invited Spiro for dinner. Dolmades are his favorite."

Olivia groaned. "Does he speak English?"

"A few words." Eleni added the chopped parsley to the mixing bowl. "I can tell you're annoyed with me, but don't worry. The language of love doesn't need words."

Olivia snorted, then sipped some tea. She doubted it would do any good to complain.

Eleni dug her hands into the mixing bowl to combine all the ingredients. "We'll be busy for a few hours. Why don't you tell me about the bad man who's got you so worried?"

Olivia sighed. "He can't bother me here." She hoped. "He's in prison."

"Prison? What did he do?"

"He raped and murdered thirteen women."

Eleni made a sound of disgust. "I don't know how you can deal with such terrible people."

Otis Crump was more than terrible. Olivia interviewed lots of criminals, but she'd never felt like she'd come face-to-face with evil incarnate until she'd met Otis. "I'd rather not talk about him." She didn't want her grandmother exposed to all the gruesome details.

Eleni shook her head, making tsking noises as she readied the grape leaves. "All right. Now you watch, so you'll know how to do it." She spooned a dollop of the meat mixture onto a grape leaf, folded over the stem, then the sides, and rolled it up.

Olivia wanted to shove all thoughts of Otis out of her mind, so she took the rose from the vase and held it up to her nose. The scent filled her head, reminding her of Robby.

"You're not watching me," Eleni admonished her. Her eyes narrowed. "Your emotions have suddenly changed for the better."

Olivia smiled as she stroked the velvet rose petals. "Last night I met the guy who left this."

"Your secret admirer? Who is he?"

"His name is Robert Alexander MacKay. Robby for short."

Eleni looked confused. "He doesn't sound Greek."

"He's Scottish." When her grandmother gave her a blank look, she elaborated. "You know, Scotland? Plaid kilts and bagpipes?"

Eleni pursed her lips. "He's from an island?"

"Yes."

"Hmm. Then he can't be too bad." She rolled another grape leaf. "Did he come here? Why didn't I meet him?"

"It was after midnight. You were asleep."

"Why so late? Is he some kind of smuggler?"

"No. He jogs at night. I saw him the first night I was here. And he saw me. From a distance. We didn't talk. Then the next night, he left this rose."

"Hmm." Eleni frowned as she stuffed another grape leaf. "And you talked to him last night?"

"Yes. In the courtyard."

"He didn't try any nonsense, did he?"

"No. He seemed . . . really nice." Olivia returned the rose to the vase. "He told me I was brave and beautiful, just like Grandpa told you."

"That's good." Eleni tilted her head. "Now I'm sensing worry and fear. What's wrong?"

Olivia took her teacup to the sink and rinsed it out. She knew her emotions were waffling back and forth. One minute she was basking in the warm glow of her attraction to Robby, and another, she was backing off in cold fear. "I told him about my abilities."

"How did he take it?"

"He . . . seemed all right with it."

"*Seemed?* Couldn't you tell how he was feeling?"

"No, I couldn't." Olivia strode to the table. "Has that ever happened to you? Have you ever met anyone you couldn't read?"

Eleni shook her head slowly. "No. Never."

A chill tickled the back of Olivia's neck. "Doesn't that strike you as really strange?"

"I suppose. This is . . . making you fear him?"

With a groan, Olivia sat and rested her elbows on the table. "A little, yes. I thought if I told him I could detect lies, he would make a run for it. But he didn't."

"You tried on purpose to scare him away?"

"Yes."

Eleni regarded her with narrowed eyes. "Child, you're not making any sense. Didn't you tell me you have trouble dating because you always know when a man is lying?"

"Yes."

"So you don't want to date men you can read, and now you don't want to date the man you can't read. You have two choices, and you're rejecting them both."

Olivia winced. She hated to admit it, but Yia Yia was making a good point. "I didn't realize I would ever have a choice. Robby caught me completely off guard. I simply reacted emotionally."

"With fear."

"Yes, with fear. It was scary as hell!"

"Watch your language, young lady."

Olivia groaned and rubbed her forehead. "I need to analyze the situation and figure out the pros and cons, so I can arrive at a logical course of—"

"Child," Eleni interrupted her. "Sometimes, you don't need to think."

"I always think things through. I've spent years honing my ability to analyze any given—"

"Do you like him?" Eleni asked.

"Yes, but—"

"You find him attractive?"

"Yes, but—"

"Then, it's settled." Eleni waved a hand in dismissal. "There are no buts."

"There are, too! I don't know if I can trust him. I don't know what he's feeling."

Eleni shrugged and started rolling another grape leaf. "He came to see you because he wanted to meet you. That means he was attracted to you. Did he ask to see you again?"

"Yes. Tonight."

"Then he is still attracted to you. It's not brain surgery, you know."

Olivia slumped in her chair. Was she overanalyzing again? "I won't know if he lies to me."

Eleni arranged her finished grape leaves in the bottom of a pot. "I loved your grandfather dearly, and he loved me. But there were days, bad days when I could feel more anger or resentment from him than love, and it would hurt something terrible."

"I'm so sorry. I didn't know."

Eleni sighed. "I never speak of it because over the years he always stayed faithful. He always found a way to keep on loving me. But it was hard. There were times when I wished

I couldn't tell what he was feeling. So what I'm saying is this could be a blessing for you."

Olivia swallowed hard. "I don't know. I still think it's scary."

"Of course it is." Eleni went back to stuffing grape leaves. "Everything worthwhile is scary."

"You think I should continue to see him?"

Eleni huffed. "I think you should help me with the cooking. I still have my hopes for Spiro. And my friend, Alexia— she's hoping you'll fall for her son, Giorgios."

Olivia smiled and reached for a grape leaf. She didn't care how handsome the Greek men were. They couldn't compare to Robby MacKay.

Robby had said she was brave and beautiful. There wasn't a whole lot she could do about her looks, but she could work on being brave. Tonight she'd see him again. And if he tried to kiss her, she wouldn't chicken out.

Chapter Five

Shortly after sunset, Robby met Carlos in the garden at Roman's villa for their weekly sparring match. Barefoot, bare-chested, and dressed in white martial-arts pants, they bowed to each other on the rectangular-shaped lawn. The nearly full moon shone down on them, casting Carlos's shadow across the green grass, but not Robby's.

At the back of the garden, a row of white stone columns gleamed in the moonlight as they stood guard at the head of the reflection pool. The scent of roses and gardenias filled the air, and Robby glanced quickly at the flower beds, wondering if he should pick a bouquet for Olivia.

His attention snapped back to Carlos as the were-panther began to shift his weight back and forth. Robby had learned not to underestimate him.

"I could beat you easily if I shifted," the Brazilian boasted as he danced around the garden's perimeter.

"I could beat you easily in my sleep. If I slept."

"Too bad you can't dream about your angel," Carlos said, his amber eyes twinkling. "I know her name."

Robby frowned as he pivoted to keep Carlos in view. He didn't recall mentioning Olivia by name. After meeting her the night before, he'd returned to the villa to investigate her on Roman's computer. She was employed by the FBI as a professional consultant and stationed in Kansas City. She'd earned a master's degree at the University of Texas. She was twenty-four and the oldest of three children. Her family resided in Houston, Texas, where her father worked as a geologist for an oil company.

Just as the sun neared the horizon, Robby had finished compiling all the information into one report. He'd clicked on Print, then stumbled off to his bedroom for his death-sleep.

Now, he narrowed his eyes. "Ye looked at my private papers."

"What do you expect me to do all day while you're playing dead?" Carlos feigned an attack, then jumped back, grinning. "I'm a good investigator, too, you know. So out of the goodness of my heart, I decided to help you."

"Hell, no. Stay out of my business."

Carlos shrugged with a nonchalant look. "Fine. I guess you don't want to hear what I learned today."

The bastard. Robby was contemplating how to get Carlos to talk when the wily were-panther suddenly pounced forward with a flying kick.

He dodged it just in time.

Carlos chuckled as he pranced backward in retreat. "Ooh, *muchacho*. That was close."

"Talk."

"Yes, sir. Lovely weather we've been having."

"About Olivia, ye bloody hellcat!"

Carlos laughed. "Well, if you insist." He crouched low as he circled Robby. "I went shopping for supplies around noon, and everyone in Grikos was talking about the beautiful American girl who's come to visit her old widowed grandmother."

So the four burly uncles were actually one frail old woman. Robby swiveled to keep up with Carlos. "Go on."

"The grandmother is Eleni Sotiris, and apparently she has some odd empathic abilities. The rumor is that Olivia shares the same gift."

Robby shrugged one shoulder. "I already know about that."

"Oh." Carlos gave him a sly look. "Then I guess you also know that the grandmother's looking for a nice Greek boy to marry Olivia."

Robby stiffened. The thought of Olivia marrying another man was . . . wrong. More than wrong. It was infuriating. Too late, he realized Carlos had made his move, and he leaped to the side. The kick that would have struck him in the chest landed on his arm.

Bugger. It smarted, but Robby would never admit it. He deserved the pain for letting Carlos distract him.

"One point for me," Carlos announced.

"Aye, though ye had to resort to trickery and lies."

"I'm telling the truth, *muchacho*. If you go to the taverna in Grikos, you'll find them laying bets on which guy will win Olivia's heart. So far, the leading contenders are Giorgios, Dimitrios, and Spiro."

Robby gulped. He was competing with three men? Men who could see Olivia during the day, who could court her while he lay useless in his death-sleep.

A surge of possessiveness grabbed hold of him. Dammit, he wanted her for himself. But what on earth did he have to offer her? Could he in clear conscience woo Olivia, knowing it could eventually be a death sentence for her?

Carlos spun and aimed a roundhouse kick at Robby's chest. With vampire speed, he seized Carlos's leg and hurled him through the air.

Carlos fell on his rump. "Umph."

Robby cocked an eyebrow. "I thought cats always landed on their feet."

Carlos snorted, then rolled onto his back and leaped forward into a standing position. "One point for you, Big Red."

"What do ye know of the three men?" Robby moved forward, forcing the were-panther to retreat toward the reflection pool.

Carlos grinned. "How badly do you want to know?"

"Enough to rip yer arms off if ye continue to play cat and mouse with me."

"You can't blame me for acting like a cat." Carlos feinted to the right, then danced to the left. "I heard the grandmother favors Spiro. He's a goat herder."

"A goat herder?"

"A very good-looking one. I've seen him."

Robby couldn't imagine Olivia being content to live out the rest of her days on an island with a goat herder. Even though he was undead, he could show her the world. He could help her with her work at the FBI. Thanks to Roman's scientific breakthrough, he could even father children. Surely he was better suited for her than a goat herder.

But a goat herder could be with her during the day. Or maybe not. Didn't he have to be with his goats? The more Robby considered it, the more he decided he had a fighting chance.

"I saw her, too." Carlos snuck behind Robby.

He pivoted. "Ye saw Olivia?"

"Oh, yeah. I can see why you have the hots for her." Carlos made sizzling sounds while he wiped his hands on his hips.

Robby's hands curled into fists.

"I saw her and her grandmother coming out of the butcher's shop. Man, what a rack!"

With a growl, Robby lunged forward at vampire speed and seized Carlos by the neck.

"Rack of lamb," Carlos squeaked. "That's what they bought."

Robby eased his grip. "Ye'd better have nine lives, ye mangy cat, for I canna allow you to insult . . . Olivia." With a shock, he realized he'd come damned close to saying "my woman." Somehow in just a few nights, he'd become obsessed with her. He still managed to be realistic, though. There was so much he didn't know about her. What if she couldn't be trusted? An employee from the FBI might be more inclined to kill a vampire than date one. He didn't want to fall in love just to have his heart crushed with betrayal.

Carlos cocked an eyebrow. "How many lives do you have, *muchacho*?"

Robby felt a slight jab in his stomach and glanced down to discover a knife pointed at his belly. "Ye brought a weapon? That's cheating."

"You think a Malcontent's going to fight fair?" Carlos smirked. "I win."

"Nay." Robby gave the were-panther's throat a slight squeeze. "I could have pinched yer head off. I win."

"I would have stabbed you first." Carlos gave him a little poke. "I win."

With vampire speed, Robby seized the knife and tossed it away. Before Carlos could even object, Robby picked him up and dropped him with a splash in the reflection pool.

"*Merda,*" Carlos growled.

"*I* win." With a smile, Robby grabbed the fallen knife and circled the garden, cutting flowers.

"The mighty warrior gathering flowers." Carlos climbed out of the reflection pool, his white pants dripping. "You are so owned." He walked over to Robby, then shook his head vigorously, causing water to fly off his long black hair and shower Robby. "Take that."

Robby continued to smile. He was going to shower anyway before his date with Olivia.

"Did you see him?" Eleni asked as she fixed herself some tea. "Is he coming?"

"Not yet." Olivia shut the back door behind her. She'd just checked the beach, but no sign of Robby.

Eleni yawned. "It's after eleven. Why does he keep such late hours?"

"I don't know." Olivia had mixed feelings about her grandmother's insistence on meeting Robby. No doubt she intended to interrogate him. "You don't have to stay up, you know."

"Of course I do. I have to make sure this young man is a decent sort." Eleni set her mug on the kitchen table with a *clunk*. "He should court you at a proper time."

"He's not courting me."

Eleni snorted. "He'd better be. If he can't see what a prize you are, then—" Her eyes widened. "Is that him?"

Olivia whirled to look out the windowpane in the back door. There was a man in the courtyard, standing with his back to them. Moonlight glinted off his red hair. *Robby*. Her heart began to pound. How thrilling . . . and confusing. She'd just checked the beach and it had been empty. How had he arrived here so fast?

Eleni scurried to the kitchen window and peered out. "*Agios Kyrios*, he's a big man. Looks very strong."

"Yes." Olivia hesitated with her hand on the doorknob. He must be waiting for her to join him. "Can you sense his emotions?"

Eleni tilted her head, concentrating. "No, I can't." She slanted a sly grin at her granddaughter. "I've never met a man of mystery before. How exciting."

Olivia sighed as she peered out the window. He *was* exciting. And so gorgeous. But still a little scary.

"I like his hair," Eleni whispered. "It reminds me of a fiery sunset over the sea."

"Yes," Olivia whispered back. "He's the most beautiful man I've ever met."

Suddenly he turned toward them.

Eleni gasped. "He brought flowers! Olivia, he *is* courting you."

"I don't think so." Her cheeks grew hot.

"Don't just stand there." Eleni smoothed her gray hair into the bun at the base of her neck. "Invite him in."

She opened the door. "Hi, Robby."

"Olivia." He smiled slowly.

She smiled back, completely mesmerized by his green eyes that focused on her so intently.

"Let him in," Eleni hissed, snapping Olivia back to reality.

"Please come in." Olivia stepped back. "Watch your head."

Robby leaned over slightly to keep from hitting the top

of the old, blue-painted door frame. "This is for you." He offered her a bouquet of roses and gardenias as he entered the kitchen.

"Thank you." When she realized the flowers were loose, she grabbed at them with both hands to keep from losing any. Her fingers brushed against his hand, and zings of excitement raced up her arms.

It was the first time she'd touched him. Her cheeks blazed with heat, and she glanced at him, overwhelmed suddenly with a feeling of awkward shyness.

"Ye're so beautiful," he whispered.

Her heart melted, and she held the bouquet against her chest. Once again his gaze captured her eyes. Tingles shimmered down her arms and legs. Oh God, she wanted this man. She was actually falling for a man she couldn't read.

Eleni cleared her throat.

"Oh." Olivia stepped back. "This is my grandmother, Eleni Sotiris."

"Mrs. Sotiris, it is a pleasure." Robby bowed to her. "I am Robert Alexander MacKay."

"Please have a seat." Eleni motioned to the kitchen table and chairs. "Would you like something to drink? Some wine? Hot tea?"

Robby sat at the table. "Some . . . tea would be nice."

"Excellent." Eleni plucked a mug off a cupboard shelf. "So why do you keep such late hours, Mr. MacKay?"

Olivia glanced at him as she arranged the flowers in an old pickle jar. She hoped he didn't mind being interrogated.

He smiled at her. "I'm busy during the day, providing security at a villa on the other side of Petra."

"I thought you were a soldier." Olivia set the jar of flowers on the table.

"I was, but I work for a private company now. MacKay Security and Investigation."

"MacKay?" Olivia sat beside him. "Is it a family business?"

"Aye. My grandfather owns it. 'Tis based in London and Edinburgh, but we have clients all around the world."

"Is your grandfather married?" Eleni asked as she set a mug of tea in front of him.

"Yia Yia," Olivia whispered with a warning look.

She shrugged. "I'm a single woman. And if the grandfather looks anything like this one . . ." She gave Robby an appreciative look.

Robby's mouth twitched. "I'm afraid my grandfather has recently remarried."

"Humph. Well, that's his loss." Eleni pulled on oven mitts, then began removing pans from the oven. "Are you single, Mr. MacKay?"

"Please call me Robby." He slanted an amused look at Olivia. "Definitely single."

"You're in for a special treat." Eleni readied a plate with leftovers. "My granddaughter is an excellent cook."

Olivia shook her head and wrinkled her nose. Robby's eyebrows lifted with a questioning look.

"She's been cooking all day." Eleni plunked a plate on the table. "Try these. You'll love them."

Robby gave the dolmades a dubious look while Eleni went back to the counter to ready another plate. "What are they?" he whispered to Olivia.

"Stuffed grape leaves," she whispered back, then pointed at a messy, lopsided one. "That's one I made."

He smiled and picked it up. "What's inside?"

"Ground meat, onions, bulgar wheat, and spices," Olivia explained. "I suppose that sounds strange."

"Nay. My mother used to stuff minced meat and oats into a sheep's stomach to make haggis."

"Eew." Olivia made a face, then lowered her voice. "You don't have to eat it if you don't want to."

"My granddaughter made all this food," Eleni boasted as she spooned rice onto a plate. "One of her suitors came for dinner. Spiro."

Robby's hand flinched, tightening so hard that the grape leaf squished and the stuffing popped out. It bounced off the pickle jar and splatted on the table. "Sorry." He dropped the mangled grape leaf on the plate.

Olivia stifled a laugh. He was jealous! "Here." She grabbed a cloth napkin and reached for his hand to wipe off the mess.

"Thank you." His fingers curled around hers.

Her heart raced, and she glanced at his eyes. Big mistake. Whenever she looked at his eyes, she felt like she was drowning. And actually enjoying it.

"Well, what do you think?" Eleni plunked another plate on the table, this one filled with lamb, rice, and spanakopita. "Looks delicious, doesn't it?"

He never took his eyes off Olivia. "Yes. I can't wait to have a taste." He continued to hold her hand. His thumb smoothed over her knuckles.

Her skin tingled as goose bumps rushed up her arms.

"You won't find a better cook than Olivia," Eleni announced. "She uses lots of fresh garlic."

His gaze shifted to the plates of food. "Garlic?"

"Yes." Eleni smiled proudly. "Try it. You'll love it."

"I—actually, I ate right before coming here." Robby gave her an apologetic look. "But it looks and smells so wonderful, I wonder if you would mind if I took it home with me to eat later?"

Eleni pursed her lips. "I suppose I could wrap this up."

"That would be great." Robby smiled at her. "Thank you."

"Hmm." Eleni tilted her head, studying him. "Why are you interested in my granddaughter?"

His hand tightened on hers. "I've never met anyone like Olivia before." He looked at her and smiled. "She's beautiful, brave, and clever. I feel . . . at home with her, but at the same time, completely lost."

Olivia was melting inside. The man was practically a stranger, but she didn't seem to care. A deep sense of longing welled up inside her. She wanted to touch him. She wanted to be touched. She wanted him to love her.

She must be losing her mind. She'd always been so sensible before. Always carefully analyzing all available information and options before taking action. Now she just wanted to throw herself at this guy.

"Why don't you two take a little walk?" Eleni suggested. "The moon is beautiful tonight."

"That's a great idea." He stood, releasing Olivia's hand. "Will ye walk with me, lass?"

"Yes." She grabbed her sweater, pulled it over her head, then fixed the clip that held her hair in place on the back of her head.

"No funny stuff," Eleni warned. "I'll be watching with the telescope."

Chapter Six

This was one of those moments, Robby thought as he strolled along the beach with Olivia. One of those rare and perfect moments that he would remember a hundred years from now. If he lived that long. The minute he left this island, he would jump back into the ongoing struggle against the Malcontents. He'd been eager to do that for weeks, but for the first time in many months, he was happy to be exactly where he was.

A nearly full moon shone over the sea, causing sparkles on the dark waves. The moon was also casting Olivia's shadow, so he walked close to a line of tamarisk trees that disrupted her shadow and, hopefully, disguised the fact that his was missing.

The air was crisp and cool, and the breeze caressed his face with the scent of salt and Olivia. He breathed deeply, enjoying her fragrance. Type A negative mixed with rose-scented soap. The scent of wool from her thick knitted jumper. A hint of lemon from her hands. His hands, too, after squashing one of her stuffed grape leaves.

There'd been an awkward moment when Olivia's grand-mother had wanted him to eat real food, but he thought he'd avoided it without looking suspicious. Overall, he'd thor-oughly enjoyed the feisty grandmother's blatant attempts at matchmaking. And he'd enjoyed seeing the close, protective bond between the two women. Even now, when he glanced back, he could see Mrs. Sotiris watching them through the telescope.

The breeze was tormenting Olivia, blowing a curly lock of her hair across her face. She was telling him about her childhood and the family trips here every summer, but the tendril of hair kept wafting into her mouth. She hooked it behind an ear, but the next breeze dislodged it once again.

"Allow me." He smoothed it behind her ear, then let his fingers linger there, outlining the shape of her ear. "Ye're fortunate to have a close, loving family." No doubt they would object to her becoming involved with a vampire.

"What about your family?" She tilted her head slightly as his fingers moved to her neck.

He rested his fingertips on her carotid artery. It throbbed against the pads of his fingers, an erotic sensation that caused his gums to tingle and his groin to tighten. He lifted his fin-gers and stepped back. *Control yerself.* It didn't take much to trigger an onslaught of lust for Olivia, and he couldn't risk glowing red eyes. "My family has passed away, except for my grandfather."

"I'm so sorry. It must be . . . lonesome for you."

His chest tightened with a sudden realization. He *was* lonesome. And although he had good friends, there were some things a man didn't discuss with other men.

Like the need to feel loved. Another guy would laugh and

call that a weakness. Hell, he'd considered it a weakness, too. He'd taken pride in being self-sufficient. He'd played the role of the proud, tough warrior for so long, it was all he knew.

And then he'd found himself entirely helpless and humiliated while the Malcontents tortured him. His self-sufficiency had been nothing but an illusion. His pride had only covered up the deep, gaping loneliness inside.

He glanced at Olivia. She was watching him curiously, but not even attempting to do therapy on him. Even so, it was happening. He was seeing things he'd never seen before. A warm, gentle feeling swelled in his chest, tempering the hard lust that had seized him earlier. Lord Almighty, he truly cared for this woman.

He swallowed hard. How should he go about this? When should he tell her the truth about himself? "I hear there's stiff competition over who's going to win yer heart." *Stiff?* Bad choice of words. He avoided looking down.

She waved a hand in dismissal. "That's my grandmother's doing. I'm not really interested in any of the men here."

"Then I have a chance?"

Her eyes widened. "Are you . . . competing?"

"Aye. Are you . . . interested?"

Her cheeks turned a rosy pink. "Maybe. But you have to understand, I've worked hard to get where I am. I'm not giving up my career."

"I wouldna want ye to." He resumed his stroll, clasping his hands behind his back to keep from touching her as she walked beside him. "What do ye do at the Bureau?"

"Criminal interrogation and analysis, mostly. When I was working on my master's, I interviewed a bunch of inmates at the Huntsville State Penitentiary in Texas. I convinced a guy on death row to confess to some unsolved murders, and it was covered in all the local papers. When the FBI offered me a job, I jumped on it. I've always wanted to use my gift for something important."

"Then ye shouldna stop."

She smiled wryly. "Tell that to my parents. They want me to get a cozy little private practice in a nice suburb and only see the right kind of mentally disturbed people."

He smiled. "There's a right kind?"

"Nonviolent, or rather, people who only harm themselves. Eating disorders or . . ." She gave him a pointed look. "Nice guys suffering from post-traumatic stress."

His smile quickly faded. "I'm no' suffering."

"Robby, you were tortured. That's not something you easily recover from."

"I'm fine."

"How long ago did it happen?"

He shrugged one shoulder. "Last summer."

She halted with a small gasp. "That's no time at all. You said they . . . broke your bones?"

He wiggled his fingers. "All healed." His gaze drifted down her body. "And ready for action."

"Don't make light of this. You've barely had time to heal physically. And mentally—"

"Olivia," he interrupted, then softened his tone. "Sweetheart, I doona want to discuss it. We've all had bad things to deal with. I'm sure ye've seen some verra nasty things on yer job."

She winced, then looked down as she dug the toe of an athletic shoe in the sand. "It's hard, sometimes, to see the horrendous things a person can inflict on a fellow human being. But I guess you know about that firsthand."

"Aye."

She turned her head and gazed into space. Her brow furrowed and a haunted look settled in her eyes.

He touched her shoulder, but she was so far away, she didn't seem aware of him. "Are ye all right, lass?"

"I think so," she whispered. "He can't find me here."

"Who?"

She shuddered, then gave Robby an apologetic look. "It's nothing. I'd rather not talk about it."

"Ah." He recalled her words from the night before. "I've recently heard from an expert that repression can lead to serious side effects down the road. It can even affect yer physical health."

Her eyes narrowed with warning.

His mouth twitched. "Perhaps ye should see a therapist."

She punched him lightly on the arm.

"Och." He rubbed his arm. "I've been traumatized."

She scoffed. "I'll tell you what. I'll do therapy for both of us."

"I'd rather ye hit me again."

She gave him a playful shove. "It won't hurt. It's just a few questions, and you don't have to answer out loud."

"Then ye canna know if I've answered."

"You don't have to answer. Just think about it." She crossed her arms over her cream-colored jumper. "When I was interviewing criminals for my master's, I came up with a list of questions to figure out what makes them tick."

"Ye want to interrogate me like a criminal?"

She looked annoyed. "Let me finish. I discovered the average criminal doesn't have the patience to answer a long list of questions, especially if there's nothing in it for him. So I pared it down to three questions. Just three."

"Let me guess." He stepped closer. "What's your favorite color?"

She shook her head, smiling. "Green. Like your eyes."

His heart expanded. "I like yer eyes, too."

She blushed. "I know what you're doing. You're trying to distract me."

"I'll have to try harder." He touched her cheek.

She stepped back. "Question number one: what do you want more than anything in the world?"

That was easy. *Revenge.* "Next question?"

Her eyebrows lifted. "You're already done?"

"Aye. I know what I want."

She cocked her head, studying him. "It must be very important to you."

"It is. How did ye answer the question?"

A hint of a smile played on her lips. "If you're not telling, neither am I."

"Saucy wench," he muttered.

Her smile widened. "Question number two: what scares you more than anything in the world?"

Failure to get revenge. "Done."

"That was fast."

"Aye." He would have revenge on the bastards who had tortured him. They would pay for every blow, every burn, every break of his bones.

"Okay, then," she continued. "The last question refers back to the first one about what you want more than anything. If you succeed, will it make you a better person?"

He stiffened with a quick intake of air. Bloody hell. He turned and stared at the sea. He didn't want to think about this. He knew his plans weren't an eye for an eye. They hadn't killed him, yet he fully intended to kill them. And what's more—he intended to enjoy it.

Would it make him a better person? He closed his eyes briefly. It didn't matter. They deserved to die. They were evil, and the world would be better off without them.

He curled his hands into fists. He needed revenge. It gave

him purpose. It had incited him to recover physically. With every step he jogged, every weight he lifted, he envisioned himself getting revenge. Killing Casimir. Killing all the Malcontents who had tortured him, who had watched his pain and humiliation. They all had to die.

Would it make him a better person? With a groan, he relaxed his hands. *No.*

"Robby?" She touched his arm. "Are you all right?"

He turned to look at her, examine her, memorize every lovely inch of her face. How could she reach so deep inside him? She made him see things he didn't want to see. She made him want to be worthy of her. "Olivia."

"Yes?"

He could hear her heart pounding, her pulse racing, and he ached to touch her. "How can ye be so young and so wise?"

"I don't feel wise." Her face flushed with rushing blood. "I—I can hardly think at all."

He lay his fingers on her neck and felt the throbbing artery. "I shouldna do this."

"You mean . . . touch me?" She sounded breathless. "It's okay."

"Lass." He cupped his hand around the base of her neck. "I'm only getting started." He pulled her hard against his chest, leaning over to claim her mouth.

She stiffened with surprise, and he halted a mere fraction away from her lips. Her quick breaths feathered his skin, making him desperate to taste her.

"Olivia," he whispered. He was so damned close.

He felt it the minute she surrendered. Her body melted against his. Her eyes fluttered shut. He pressed his mouth against hers, molding her lips, relishing their soft fullness.

He wrapped an arm around her to pull her closer. Even

through the thick wool of her jumper, he could feel her breasts, round and firm. He slanted his mouth, deepening the kiss, coaxing her lips to open.

With a sweet feminine moan, her lips parted, and he teased the small opening with his tongue. She panted, as if trying to catch her breath, her breasts pushing against his chest. With each push, his groin tightened and his passion threatened to strip away the last remnant of his control.

"Robby," she whispered. She wrapped her arms around his neck and rubbed her cheek against his whiskered jaw.

He kissed a trail back to her mouth, and this time she kissed him back, matching the desperation of his desire. His heart soared. He invaded her mouth, tasting her with his tongue. She stroked his tongue with her own, then sucked it.

His groin hardened and pressed painfully against his jeans. He slid his hands down her spine to the delicious curve at the small of her back, then over her sweet round butt. He splayed his hands and pulled her tight against his erection.

She gasped against his mouth, breaking the kiss.

"Olivia." In his vision, her face turned from pink to dark red. He tucked her face against his chest to hide the red glow of his eyes.

She snuggled against him, breathing shallow and fast. He plucked the strange contraption from her hair, and the long curly locks fell free. He grabbed a handful and buried his face in it. It was so soft, so silky against his skin. He willed himself to regain control, a losing battle when he imagined how thick, black, and silky her hair would be between her legs.

Patience. He needed to court her slowly and carefully. Good timing would be essential, or he could lose her.

In the distance, he heard a clanging sound. He turned and

spotted Olivia's grandmother standing by the telescope and banging a large metal spoon against a pot.

"What is that?" Olivia glanced toward the house and winced. "Oh God, I'm sorry. I forgot she was watching."

Robby stepped back, releasing Olivia, and the clanging stopped. "Apparently, round one is over."

Olivia turned to him with a shy smile, but it transformed instantly into a frown. "Are you all right? Your eyes seem a little red."

With an inward wince, he looked away. "I think some sand blew into them." He hated to lie, so he quickly changed the subject. "Do ye want me to take ye home?"

She glanced at her grandmother, then shook her head. "You've endured enough interrogation for one evening. And you should hurry home to wash out your eyes." The wind swept her hair across her face, and she shoved it back.

"Here." He handed her the tortoiseshell contraption he'd removed from her hair, and winced when she opened the claw. "Bugger, look at the teeth on that thing. It doesna poke holes in yer head?"

With a laugh, she twisted her hair onto the back of her head. "No."

He moved closer to observe her attaching the claw.

She slanted him an amused look. "Are you worried about my safety?"

He smiled. "I willna let anything harm a hair on yer head. May I see you tomorrow night?"

Her cheeks bloomed pink. "Yes."

"Good." He pressed a light kiss against her brow. "I'll wait here to make sure ye get home safely."

"Good night." She strode back down the beach.

He observed her graceful walk, her hair piled on the back of her head, and her slender, elegant neck. His gaze lowered to her well-rounded hips, which swayed with every step. He flexed his hands, recalling the feel of her rump. Thank God the bones in his fingers had healed properly. There were times when a man needed nimble fingers.

Olivia woke Wednesday morning with thoughts of Robby. She snuggled under the blankets, closed her eyes, and remembered every delicious detail of the hottest kiss she'd ever indulged in. First he'd pulled her against him like a man losing control, then he'd hovered over her mouth like a man straining to regain control. His struggle had excited her, making her want to push him past the brink.

She didn't need to read his emotions. His desire and passion had been clear with every movement of his lips and every touch of his hands. He'd shown himself to be bold and demanding with the way he'd pulled her tight against his erection. Shocking, but so exciting.

She smiled to herself. There was something sweet about Robby, too. Something trustworthy that made her feel safe, even though her lie detecting skills didn't work on him.

She was beginning to like the fact that she couldn't read his emotions. For the first time in her life she'd been able to kiss a man only feeling her own emotions. Instead of the usual flood of lust pouring out of the guy, drowning her desires with his needs, she'd only felt herself. Suddenly, it had all been about her. Every shudder, every tingle, every heart-pounding sensation—it had all come from her. She liked it. She wanted more.

She wanted Robby.

With a sigh, she sat up. She couldn't call it love. She'd only known the man a few days. She couldn't fall in love that fast, could she?

Why not? An inner voice chided her. Robby MacKay was

a gorgeous, sexy, fascinating man. *And he wants you.* She'd have to be made out of stone not to react to that.

But what if she was simply reacting to his desire? Or maybe she was fascinated with him because she couldn't read him. With a groan, she headed to the bathroom. She was overanalyzing again.

Hopefully, her grandmother was no longer angry with her. Last night, after she 'd climbed the stairs to the courtyard, Eleni had given her a stern look.

"Decent people should be in bed by now," she'd huffed. Then she'd tramped inside the house to her bedroom.

Olivia ventured into the kitchen. Her grandmother was sitting at the table, nibbling on bread, olives, and feta cheese. There was an aura of concern and worry, but no anger that Olivia could detect.

Eleni stood with a smile. "Sit down and eat, child. I'll fix you a cup of tea."

"Thanks." Olivia sawed off a piece of bread, then reached for the pot of honey.

"I went to the bakery early this morning and asked if anyone knew about a house owned by a foreigner on the other side of Petra."

Olivia frowned as she drizzled honey on her bread. "You're checking up on Robby?"

"Of course." Eleni plunked a cup of tea in front of her. "Don't you think you should know something about the man you're kissing?"

"I know a lot about him."

"You know his address?"

Olivia bit off a hunk of bread to keep from having to answer.

"I take that as a no." Eleni sat across from her.

"I know important things about him."

"Like how much he has in his checking account?" Her grandmother popped a morsel of feta cheese in her mouth.

Olivia snorted. "He's employed. And he's a sweet, considerate man."

"He was groping you like a . . . a squid with suction cups attached to your rump."

Olivia laughed.

Eleni huffed. "I wasn't making a joke, young lady. You barely know the man, but you were . . . I hope you don't make a habit of behaving like that."

"I don't. Believe me. I . . . I don't know how it happened. I've never gotten so carried away before."

Eleni's eyes softened. Obviously, she could tell her granddaughter was telling the truth. "Are you in love with him?"

Olivia took a deep breath and exhaled slowly. "I don't know. I feel very strongly for him, but as a psychologist, I have serious doubts a person can actually fall in love this quickly."

Eleni waved a hand in dismissal. "It's not science. It's love."

"There's a certain amount of science involved," Olivia protested. "Chemistry, hormones, pheromones—"

"And how are your hormones reacting?"

Olivia winced. "Off the charts."

"And the chemistry?"

"Highly combustible. We could provide electricity for half the United States."

Eleni nodded knowingly. "You're falling in love."

"It's too fast."

"Then slow it down."

"We're leaving for Houston in two weeks." Olivia drank some hot tea.

"That's plenty of time. Besides, he can come to Houston, too. He'll need to if he's going to ask permission to marry you."

Olivia spewed some tea on the table. "Who said anything about marriage?" She grabbed a napkin to wipe up the mess.

Her grandmother narrowed her eyes. "Surely you're not intending to live in carnal sin?"

"I just met the man."

"You looked well acquainted with him last night."

Olivia ate some more bread. "I am . . . extremely attracted to him. But I still can't read his emotions, so I don't know how he feels about me."

"Child, he was mauling you like a bear. We can safely assume he's attracted to you."

"That doesn't mean he wants to marry me."

"If he wants to climb the honey tree, he'll have to."

Olivia shook her head, smiling. "You make him sound like Pooh Bear."

"Hmm. I hope he's more intelligent than that." Eleni motioned toward the fridge. "He forgot his plate of food."

"I'll give it to him tonight."

"We can take it to him right now." Eleni stood and started clearing off the table. "I found out at the bakery which house he's staying at."

"What else did you find out?"

Eleni placed the cheese and olives in the fridge. "The house is owned by a rich American family, the Draganestis, and they have lots of friends who come and go. No one has seen much of your Robby, but they all know a man named Carlos who is also living there. Now, go on and get dressed, so we can go."

Thirty minutes later Olivia was dressed in jeans and her nicest cashmere sweater and knocking on the door of an elegant villa. Pots of overflowing geraniums flanked the rough, antique wooden door. The house was dazzling bright in the morning sunshine, with a fresh coat of whitewash. The tiled roof looked new, as well as the stone-paved driveway.

Eleni had insisted on coming as a chaperone. She was wearing one of her best black dresses, and she clutched a canvas tote bag filled with foil-wrapped food.

The door cracked, and a young man peered out at them. He flashed a smile as if he recognized them, then opened the door wider and leaned his long, slim body against the door frame.

"Good morning." Olivia suspected this was Carlos. "We're here to see Robby MacKay."

He nodded. "You must be Olivia and Eleni Sotiris."

Olivia detected a slight accent. "Yes, we are. Robby told you about us?"

His grin widened, showing off very white teeth. "*Menina*, everyone on the island knows about you."

Menina. Not quite Spanish, but close. "You're . . . Portuguese?"

"Brazilian. From Rio." He winked. "If you ever want to samba, I'm your man."

"Ah. I'll keep that in mind."

He sniffed, and his gaze shifted to Eleni's tote bag. "Is that lamb? It smells delicious."

"It *is* delicious," Eleni announced. "My granddaughter is an excellent cook."

"Excellent timing. I'm starving." The man stepped back and motioned for them to enter. "Please come in."

"Thank you." Olivia stepped into a narrow foyer, followed by her grandmother. She noted a large icon of the Apostle John, patron saint of Patmos, on the wall. "Are you on vacation, Mister . . . ?"

"Panterra. But call me Carlos. And no." He led them into a large family room. "I'm working here like Robby."

Olivia glanced around the empty room. "Where is Robby?"

"He's not available right now. He . . . had to go to Horos on business."

It was a lie. Olivia stiffened and glanced at her grandmother. By the look on Yia Yia's face, she'd caught it, too. "When do you expect him back?"

"This evening. Sometime after sunset."

That was the truth. Olivia wondered what Robby was doing that took all day. The family room was tastefully furnished, but not filled with expensive artwork or anything else that warranted extra security. "You work for the same company as Robby? MacKay Security and Investigation?"

"Yes. Are you investigating us, Olivia?" He looked back, his amber eyes twinkling.

"I was just hoping to see Robby."

"Believe me, *menina*. He will be very sorry he missed you." Carlos escorted them into a roomy country kitchen, decorated in blue and yellow.

Eleni plunked the tote bag on the kitchen table, then began removing foiled-wrapped packages. "These should go in the refrigerator, and when you're ready to eat, you should heat it up properly in the oven."

"Yes, ma'am." Carlos bowed his head, and his long black hair fell forward, obscuring his face. "We will follow your instructions exactly."

"Hmm." Eleni leaned close to her granddaughter and muttered, "I've never seen so many security guards in need of a decent haircut."

Olivia winced, but Carlos simply chuckled and hooked his black shoulder-length hair behind his ears. A gold stud gleamed in each earlobe.

He picked up the food packages and began stashing them in the fridge. "Is there a message you'd like me to pass on to Robby?"

"Not really." Olivia grabbed the empty tote bag. "I'll come back this evening."

"Good." Carlos smiled as he closed the refrigerator door.

Olivia could sense a great deal of amusement coming from him, but there was something more. Excitement. Anticipation. And underlying it all, a hint of deception.

She and her grandmother left and headed back home. Eleni was unusually quiet as they walked, and Olivia felt an aura of concern radiating from her.

"Are you tired, Yia Yia? I could call a cab."

She shook her head. "I walk like this every day. It's good for me." She grew silent again, frowning at the road.

"It's a shame we missed Robby," Olivia murmured. "Does it seem strange to you that there are two security men at that house? I didn't see anything that needed protecting."

"Carlos lied about Robby," Eleni said.

"I know." What was Robby doing that needed to be kept secret?

"There's something strange about that Carlos," Eleni whispered. "But I can't figure out what it is."

"I'll go back tonight and get some answers."

Eleni cast her a worried look. "Are you sure it's safe?"

Olivia patted her on the back. "I'm fully trained in self-defense. I can take care of myself."

That evening after sunset, Olivia strolled down the Grikos beach, headed for Robby's house. A full moon hung heavy in the sky, casting sparkles on the sea. The breeze was chilly, and she was glad she'd worn a jacket over her sweater. She strode around Petra—or Kallikatsou, as the locals called it—and spotted the house she'd visited that morning. From the back, she could see the extensive garden and stone columns. She surveyed the rocky bluff, searching for steps that would lead up to the house.

A sudden movement caught her eye, a black blur that seemed to fly off the bluff and land with a soft thud on the sand.

Her heart lurched. She blinked her eyes to make sure she was seeing right. A cat. A giant, hulking black cat.

A *jaguar*? On Patmos? It bared its teeth and growled at her.

A chill settled over her, prickling her skin. She could die. She couldn't outrun a jaguar. She had no weapons, and she doubted her martial arts could save her from those vicious claws and gleaming white teeth.

The giant cat watched her with golden eyes; then, with a slow, graceful move of its big paw, it took a quiet, lethal step toward her.

She could only think she'd better not act like prey. She glared at the cat, then screamed as loud as she could. The cat snarled and took another step toward her.

She couldn't retreat without getting caught. She couldn't climb the bluff faster than the cat. She sure didn't want to advance toward it. That left the sea. Cold and treacherous with a strong undertow caused by the full moon.

She could only hope the jaguar didn't like cold water.

Chapter Seven

Robby had just stepped out of the shower when he heard a scream. A feminine scream. He dropped his towel, pulled on a pair of boxer shorts, and strode into the family room. "Carlos, did ye hear something?"

The shape-shifter was gone.

Robby stepped onto the patio. A chilly wind slapped his bare skin and whipped his wet hair across his face. He shoved his hair back and noted the steam coming up from the Jacuzzi. Carlos must have turned it on, but where was he? Robby strode to the edge of the bluff and looked down.

Damn it to hell. He'd found Carlos. And Olivia.

Something must have snapped in the were-panther's head, 'cause for some insane reason, he was terrorizing Olivia. He stalked along the water's edge, a large beast with a shiny black coat and a long pair of canine teeth that made Robby's fangs look downright wimpy in comparison.

Carlos was purposely pushing her into the cold sea. Damn him. Robby could hear her teeth chattering.

"Olivia!" He called out to her. "Hold on! I'll be right there." He sprinted to the stairs. It was tempting to jump off the bluff or teleport down, but he didn't want to cause her further alarm. He didn't think Carlos would actually hurt her. Not if the bastard wanted to live through the night.

"Robby, no!" Olivia screamed. "Don't come down here!"

She was trying to protect him? His beautiful, sweet Olivia was so brave. "I'll be right there!"

"Just call the police," she yelled. "*Please!* I don't want you to get hurt." She moved toward the beach, but Carlos pounced toward her, splashing his front paws in the water. She lurched back, now up to her waist in the chilly surf.

Robby paused at the bottom of the stairs with a sudden realization. Olivia was loyal. He could trust her. After all these years, he'd finally found a trustworthy woman.

He couldn't let her go. He strode onto the beach.

"Robby, no." Her voice cracked with emotion, and he could see the tears on her face. "Go away before it sees you."

Lord Almighty, he could love this woman forever. He stepped closer, and Carlos whipped around, hissing at him.

Robby attempted vampire mind control, focusing all his mental powers on the were-panther. He hit a rock-solid barrier.

Bugger. The shape-shifter had good defenses. That would normally be a good thing since it meant Carlos would be impervious to any control by the Malcontents. But it didn't help the situation now.

"Ye crazy cat," Robby whispered. "What the hell are ye doing?"

The were-panther snarled, showing his gleaming white, sharp teeth. *Attack me, Big Red. Make it look good.*

Robby stiffened. He hadn't realized Carlos was capable of telepathic communication while in cat form. *What are ye doing here?*

Waiting for you to chase me off. Come on, dude. Rescue the fair maiden. Be a hero.

This was a matchmaking scheme? Robby balled his hands into fists. *Ye bloody bastard. Ye're scaring her to death.*

Carlos growled. *That's the thanks I get. Look, if you play your cards right, you'll get lucky. The hot tub's ready—*

"Get the hell out of here!" Robby charged toward him.

Oh, good acting skills. Carlos backed away. *You're looking really pissed.*

"I *am* pissed!" Robby scooped an egg-shaped rock off the beach.

Merda. No need to get violent. Carlos trotted down the beach.

Robby hurled the rock. Carlos yelped when it clipped him on a rear leg. *You big lummox! See if I ever help you again!*

I doona need yer help, ye mangy hellcat! Robby ran into the water to fetch Olivia. A strong wave pummeled her from behind, and she lost her balance. For a few terrifying seconds he saw her go under.

"Olivia!" He reached her just as she broke the surface, sputtering. He swooped her into his arms and charged back to the shore. Her clothes were soaked through. Her hair was dripping wet. And her body shook violently.

Damn you, Carlos. He watched the were-panther as it scrambled up the bluff. *Where the hell are ye going?*

None of your business. The were-panther stopped at the

top of the bluff and peered down at them. *I'll be back by sunrise. Have fun, Big Red. Is it true what they say, that a good Vamp can last all night long?*

Piss off. Robby heard a strange huffing sound that sounded like a feline chuckle, then the were-panther scampered off.

Olivia wrapped a trembling, cold hand around his neck. "How d-d-did a jaguar g-g-get here?"

"Let's get you warmed up." He strode toward the stairs.

"Robby." She touched his face with icy fingers. "Th-Thank you."

She was turning blue. He should teleport straight to the patio. It was the fastest way to get her in the hot tub. And the surest way to provoke some unwanted questions.

Forgive me. He hugged her tight against his chest and invaded her mind with a surge of vampire mind control. Normally, a mortal would feel a blast of cold air when a vampire took over their mind, but in Olivia's case, she was already freezing to death.

Sleep, he commanded.

She went limp, and he teleported them to the patio.

Olivia felt deliciously warm and cozy as she slowly awoke. Someone was stroking her cheek and brushing her hair back from her brow. Soft fingers. A deep, sexy voice.

"Wake up, sweetheart."

Robby. That made her smile. Her eyes opened and there he was, his handsome face shrouded in mist. Unfortunately, her mind was just as foggy. She was up to her neck in hot churning water? "Where am I?"

"Ye're in the Jacuzzi of the villa where I'm staying. Ye needed to warm up as quickly as possible."

Her sleepy brain fumbled for an explanation, then she remembered and sat up with a jolt. "There was a jaguar! On Patmos! How on earth did it get here?"

"I—well—"

"I thought I was a goner." She pressed a hand to her chest, then gasped when she felt bare skin. Good God, she was only wearing her bra and underwear. "Where did my clothes go?"

"Over there." He motioned with his head, and she spotted a heap of wet clothes on the stone floor next to a chaise lounge.

"I don't recall taking them off." And what the heck was she doing on his lap? She lurched to the other side of the hot tub and glared at him. "What did you do to me?"

His jaw shifted. "I took off yer wet clothes."

"Did I give you permission?"

"Nay, ye were unconscious. And turning blue. I was trying to save you."

Heat invaded her cheeks. She wasn't used to men seeing her without her clothes on. And here she was in her boring white cotton bra and panties. Damn, if only she'd worn her black lace undies.

She winced inwardly. She'd come close to getting mauled by a jaguar, and all she could think about was the sexiness factor of her underwear? She must be in shock. Or suffering from hypothermia. Or fuzzy-headed from being unconscious. She rubbed her forehead. She was overanalyzing again. "I apologize. You did the right thing."

A corner of his mouth lifted. "It was a tough job, but someone had to do it. I could say that I refrained from leering or drooling, but that would be a lie."

Her blush grew hotter. "Well, thank you for your honesty. And your bravery. I can't believe you chased away that huge jaguar. You were incredible."

He shrugged one shoulder. "I couldna let it harm you."

Her gaze dropped to his broad shoulders, and then his bare chest. He'd run down to the beach in his underwear to rescue her. "You saved me."

"Ye tried to stop me," he whispered.

Her gaze lifted to his eyes and her heart fluttered in her chest. "Well, there was no sense in both of us getting mauled to death."

"Ye wanted to protect me."

The look in his eyes was so intense, she was starting to tingle all over. Now she felt strangely overdressed.

His eyes darkened. "Ye were willing to face danger alone in order to keep me safe."

She squirmed on the molded seat. She shouldn't have left his lap. She could be touching him right now. He could be touching her. "I—I assume you called the police about the jaguar?"

He hesitated.

She sat up. "You didn't call?"

"Ye were unconscious. I couldn't let go of you."

She stood. "We have to call. Right away."

"I—" His gaze shifted downward.

She glanced down. Her wet cotton bra had molded to her like a second skin, clearly showing her nipples, which were now reacting to the cold air. She ducked into the water up to her chin. "Can you make the call, please?"

A hint of red glimmered in his eyes, and he rubbed them. "I'll be right back." He surged out of the Jacuzzi, water dripping from his body and black boxer shorts.

She watched as he strode to the house. There was something odd about his eyes. They seemed to get irritated easily. Her gaze wandered over his broad shoulders and strong back, then zeroed in on his backside. The wet black cotton was glued to his buttocks, clearly showing the muscles at work with each step he took.

She licked her lips. "Could you bring me a glass of water?"

He glanced over his shoulder as he opened the door. "Aye. Just a minute."

She moved across the tub so she could see him through the large plate-glass window. His back was still to her as he talked on the phone. He'd left the back door open, so she was able to catch most of his conversation.

"Does anyone there speak English?" he asked after connecting with the police. "Good. I need to report a—an incident. 'Tis a wee bit strange, and ye may find it hard to believe—aye, I am speaking English."

Olivia chuckled. Then Robby turned slightly, and her jaw dropped. Good God. The front of his boxer shorts was protruding.

"There was a jaguar on the beach at Petra. A ja-gu-ar," he repeated slowly. "No, no' the car. The cat. A black panther. Nay, it wasna a big house cat. 'Twas a panther."

Robby raked a hand through his long hair, inadvertently giving Olivia an excellent profile of his washboard abs. She gulped. His flat stomach made the swelling in his underwear look even bigger.

"No, I'm no' high on any drugs," Robby growled. "And I can tell the difference between a bloody goat and a panther. Hello? Hello?" He hung up and walked out of her view.

With a grimace, Olivia settled back into the Jacuzzi. The police thought it was prank call. Who could blame them? How on earth could a jaguar get on a Greek isle?

And where was it now? She looked about nervously. She'd seen the cat scamper up a rocky bluff not far from here. What if the Jacuzzi was his favorite watering hole? She'd look like a yummy morsel, floating in the middle. She needed to relocate fast.

Robby heated up a bottle of synthetic blood in the microwave. He needed to take the edge off his appetite before returning to Olivia. He smiled to himself as he fixed her a glass of ice water. Carlos was right. If he played his cards right, he could get lucky. Hell, he'd been lucky ever since he'd met Olivia. She was the best thing that had happened to him since . . . he thought back. Lord Almighty, since he'd been transformed in 1746.

He needed to be careful so he wouldn't lose her. Or frighten her away. He glanced at his swollen groin and winced. He looked like he'd been playing the old bagpipe.

The microwave dinged, and he guzzled down half the bottle of warm synthetic blood. It was just as well the police in Skala hadn't believed his panther story. He sure didn't want them roaming the island with rifles, looking for Carlos.

Maybe he'd been too hard on the shape-shifter. There was a full moon tonight, so Carlos might have been forced to shift. Still, he shouldn't have terrorized Olivia just to help Robby have a hot date. He recalled how good she had felt in his arms, how she managed to look both sexy and innocent in her white brassiere and knickers. And she was waiting for him in the hot tub. His groin stiffened just thinking about her all hot and wet.

Bugger. He couldn't go back to her looking like this. He grabbed the glass of ice water and dumped half of it on himself. "Oy! Bloody hell."

"Are you all right?"

He spun and discovered Olivia standing in the kitchen doorway. He froze for a few seconds as he looked her over. She was clutching her wet clothes to her chest, effectively hiding the parts he really wanted to see. Still, he enjoyed seeing her bare arms and lovely long legs. His gaze wandered to her face, and he realized she was giving him a similar examination.

Her eyes widened at the sight of his groin.

Water dripped from his wet boxers, the droplets plopping onto his feet. Bugger. He must look like he'd just peed on himself. The blood he'd recently ingested rushed to his face, giving him a rare blush.

" 'Tis naught but water, ye ken." He winced. His embarrassment was causing his accent to thicken. He lifted the glass so she could see it was half full. "I used some of yer ice water to . . . minimize a growing concern."

She made an odd strangled sound that sounded suspiciously like a stifled giggle. With pink cheeks, she focused on the counter behind him. "I thought I'd be safer in the house, since there's a jaguar out there."

"I see." So much for making love to her in the hot tub. "Did ye want this water? I can refill it for you."

"That's okay." She looked at the bottle in his other hand. "I'll just have whatever you're having."

"Nay! Ye-Ye wouldna like it." He quickly emptied the rest of the synthetic blood in the sink. " 'Tis flat."

She watched him curiously. "It was wine, right?"

"Would ye like some wine? I can pour you a glass."

"That would be lovely, thank you."

He set the glass of water on the counter and retrieved a wineglass from an overhead cabinet. Then he located a bottle of merlot in the fridge that Carlos had opened earlier when he'd eaten the leftovers that Olivia and her grandmother had left. He filled the glass , then handed it to her.

"Thank you." She shifted her clothes to one arm so she could take the wineglass. Her wet jeans slipped from her grasp and tumbled onto her feet. "Oops."

"I'll get it." He leaned over to grab her jeans, then noticed how close he was to her bare legs. He straightened very slowly, enjoying the view. By the time his eyes reached her face, her cheeks were pink again.

She cleared her throat. "I need to get out of my wet clothes."

"That would be nice. Ye want to do it now?"

"I need a towel to dry off."

"Of course." He grabbed a clean kitchen towel and handed it to her.

She gave him a dubious look. "That won't cover up much."

"Works for me." He tossed it back onto the counter. "I'll bring you a bath towel."

"Could you find something for me to wear?"

"Aye." Maybe a handkerchief.

"Is there a dryer in the house? I need to rinse out my clothes and dry them."

"Aye, right through there." He motioned to a door by the refrigerator.

"Great. Thank you." She headed to the utility room.

He waited for her to pass so he could see her from behind. Her wet panties clung to her rump, wedged into the crease and molded to each rounded cheek. Lord Almighty, he wanted to touch her. Kiss her. Make her shudder and scream.

She cleared her throat.

He glanced up. "Yes?"

She'd paused just inside the utility room to glare at him. "I need those jeans."

"Of course." He strode to the doorway and tossed her wet jeans into the sink next to the washing machine. "I'll be back with some clothes and a towel."

"Thank you." She shut the door after he left.

He dashed to his bedroom to change clothes. He glanced at his bed and smiled. The night was still young, and like Carlos said, a good Vamp could last all night long.

Chapter Eight

Olivia was relieved to find a stack of clean beach towels on the dryer. She rinsed her sweater in the sink, then laid it on the counter on top of a beach towel. After rinsing the rest of her clothes, she tossed them in the dryer. She glanced at the closed door. Hopefully, Robby would knock first. She quickly stripped off her wet underwear, rinsed it out, and threw it in the dryer.

A knock sounded at the door.

"Just a minute." She grabbed a beach towel and wrapped it around herself. "Okay."

The door cracked open, and Robby peered inside. "Och, ye found a towel."

"Sorry to disappoint you."

He grinned. "Lass, ye could never disappoint." He set a bath towel and some clothes on the counter next to her sweater. He was still barefoot and bare-chested, but he'd traded in the wet boxer shorts for a pair of white martial-arts pants. "Come out when ye're ready." He closed the door.

Ready for what? She grabbed the wineglass off the counter and gulped down a swallow. *Relax. You don't have to do anything you don't want to.* But that was the problem. Where Robby was concerned, she found herself wanting the whole shebang. And she'd only known him a few days.

She turned on the dryer, then examined the clothes he'd given her. They were definitely for a woman, so she assumed they must belong to the wife of whoever owned the villa. They were summer pajamas: a blue tank top and a pair of cotton shorts that were blue with white fluffy clouds.

The shorts fit, although they seemed a bit baggy around the legs. The top was a snug fit that left little to the imagination. With a grimace, she wrapped the bath towel around her shoulders like a shawl. As soon as her clothes were dry, she'd put them on and hurry back home. Or could she? She didn't dare walk home with a jaguar out there. Maybe Robby had a car. Or maybe she'd have to spend the night with him.

She snorted. Her grandmother would never believe the jaguar excuse.

She took another sip of wine for fortification, then left the utility room. The lights in the kitchen had been turned off, but enough light filtered in from the family room that she was able to find her way. She reached the arched entrance to the family room and stopped.

A fire blazed in the hearth. Spare pillows and an afghan from the couch had been spread on the rug in front of the fireplace. She swallowed hard. Robby's intentions were clear. He meant to seduce her.

He blew out a match he'd just used to light a candle on the coffee table. "Would ye like more wine?"

"I'm okay." *I'm in deep trouble.* She perched on one end of the couch and set her wineglass on the coffee table.

"Are ye warm enough? The only clothes I could find were summer ones that Shanna left behind."

"Who's Shanna?"

"Shanna Draganesti. She owns this house, along with her husband. Several houses, actually." He sat in the middle of the couch and shifted sideways to face her.

She noted how muscular he looked, and how the hair on his chest was more brown than red. He'd tied his damp auburn hair back into a ponytail. "Where is *your* home?"

"Scotland, a few miles south of Inverness. I have about twenty acres next to my grandfather's land. I have my own house, but he always expects me to stay in his castle."

She blinked. "A real castle?"

"Aye. 'Tis a wee bit drafty for my taste. My house is cozier, but I'm rarely there. I'm usually on assignment."

"What kind of assignments?"

He rested an elbow on the back of the couch. "Security and investigation."

She nodded. Even though her lie detector skills didn't work with Robby, she believed he was being honest. The physical signs were correct. He was facing her, keeping eye contact with her and looking comfortable. What's more, she had a strong feeling that he wanted her to trust him. He'd claimed from the beginning that he was trust-worthy. He'd endured torture without betraying his colleagues. So why shouldn't she trust him? He'd confronted a huge jaguar in order to save her.

"You were working for your grandfather's company last summer when you were captured?" she asked. "What kind of assignment was that?"

He rubbed his jaw. "Sometimes MacKay S and I gets involved with some sensitive security issues."

She sat back. "You mean national security? That's how you know people in the CIA?"

He nodded. "We were trying to locate a group of domestic terrorists."

"Where? How come I never heard about this?"

He shrugged one shoulder. "'Tis a secret."

She took a deep breath. "And these terrorists are the ones who tortured you."

"Aye, but I'd rather no' talk about it. 'Tis over and done with."

"Is it really?" She turned to face him, resting a bent leg in front of her on the couch. "Can you honestly say that you never think about it?"

His jaw shifted. "I think about it every day."

"When you answered my first question about what you wanted more than anything, what was your answer?"

His gaze lowered to her leg.

"Do you want to get even, Robby? It would be understandable if you did."

He leaned forward and tugged gently on her big toe. "If I tell you, ye'll have to give me yer answers, too."

She bit her lip. "Okay. It's a deal."

He wrapped his hand around her ankle and squeezed. His green eyes locked on hers, glimmering with emotion. "I want revenge. My worst fear is that I willna get revenge, and no, it willna make me a better person."

She swallowed hard. "So you still intend to do it?"

He nodded slowly. "Do ye think that makes me a bad person?" He trailed his fingers up her calf.

She watched his hand as it slowly approached her knee.

Oh, he could definitely be bad. And she'd like it. "I think it means you're human. And you suffered more than physical injury."

"It was humiliating," he whispered as he stroked the tender crease behind her knee.

She was having trouble concentrating. "There's a famous saying by Eleanor Roosevelt. I—I can't recall the exact words, but it's something like, no one can make you feel inferior without your permission."

He sat back, withdrawing his hand from her leg. "I like that. Thank you."

"You're welcome."

He slanted her a curious look. "For someone who dinna want to be my therapist, ye're doing a great job."

She grinned. It was about the best compliment she could ever receive. "It's a good thing I'm not your therapist. Otherwise, it would be totally unethical for me to be involved with you."

With a smile, he touched her hair. "So ye want to be involved with me?"

Heat rushed to her face. "I think I already am."

His smile widened and he coiled one of her curls around a finger. "Yer turn now. What do ye want more than anything?"

"A long, happy life. I'm not quite sure what that would entail, though."

"A *long* life," he murmured, and released her hair. "And what was your greatest fear?"

This was the part she didn't want to talk about. She turned to face the fireplace. "Apples."

"The fruit?"

"Yes." She drew her legs up in front of her, hugging her knees. "He sends me apples. Big red ones in a box. First he sent them to my office. Then he sent them to my apartment. I moved to another apartment, but he found me."

"Who is he?"

She shuddered. "Otis Crump. I even moved to a safe house, but the apples still came."

Robby moved closer to her on the couch. "He must be following you."

"He can't. He's in Leavenworth Federal Penitentiary. In solitary confinement."

"He's ordering the apples from prison?"

"There's no record or proof of that."

"Then how can ye be sure he's the one sending them?"

She closed her eyes briefly. *Don't make me explain it. It's too awful.* "Believe me, it's him."

Robby touched her shoulder. "I believe you. He must have an accomplice."

She rubbed her forehead. "That's what I thought, but my supervisor thinks I'm . . . overreacting. That's why he sent me away, so I could calm down. Regain some perspective."

"Ye were a wee bit vocal in stating yer opinion?"

"More than a 'wee' bit. I was told I was being paranoid."

Robby smiled. "Och, we have so much in common."

She snorted. "Thanks."

"I still think yer prisoner has an accomplice."

"I agree, but I don't know how. He's been in solitary for two years. They monitor all his mail. I've questioned him about it, but it's hard to tell now when he's lying. He scatters just enough truth and half-truths into everything he says, that I can't tell what's what anymore. He—he enjoys playing with me."

"Does he know about yer gift?"

"He figured it out after the first few times I caught him lying. He . . . he finds me fascinating."

"Bugger," Robby muttered, then rose to his feet. He paced toward the fireplace, then turned. "Doona see him again."

"If I'm ordered to—"

"What crime did he commit?" Robby interrupted.

"He raped and murdered at least thirteen women."

Robby grimaced. "He's a bloody monster. Why did ye ever see him?"

"He was convicted on three murders, but we suspected he'd committed other homicides in several states. It was my job to get him to confess. He'd been in solitary for so long, he really looked forward to our meetings. He kept dropping hints that he would tell me more if I continued to see him."

"He was manipulating you."

Olivia sighed. "I know. We all knew, but my supervisor wanted me to play along. Otis is very proud of what he did." She shook her head, wishing she could block out the images. "We knew he'd want to brag about it eventually."

Robby sat next to her on the couch. "What happened?"

She focused on the fire in the hearth. "He promised to tell me everything if I would just bring an apple to our next meeting. A big red apple and a paring knife. He watched from behind the glass while I peeled it. And he . . ."

How could she admit that the monster had ejaculated in her presence? Or that he'd described to her in great detail how he'd tortured the girls, using a paring knife just like she had.

She covered her face, but the gruesome images still haunted her. Tears burned her eyes. "That's how I know he's the one sending the apples. He wants me to go back to see him. He—he's obsessed with me."

"Olivia." Robby scooped her into his lap and wrapped his arms around her. "Sweetheart, ye're safe now. I willna let anyone harm you."

She buried her face against his shoulder and let the tears go. She'd held them in for so long, always trying to be strong on the job. She cried for the girls who had died. She cried for the perversion she'd been forced to endure. She cried for the torture Robby had suffered.

He continued to murmur sweet things as he rubbed his hands up and down her back.

She rested her head against his chest, listening to the steady beat of his heart. "I got the confession like I was supposed to, but I felt so *dirty*."

He took her by the shoulders. "Sweetheart, ye're an angel. Ye canna be tainted with that man's evil."

She smiled and touched Robby's cheek. His whiskers were prickly and sexy, but above the whiskers, his skin was baby soft. He was the sweetest man she'd ever met, and God help her, she wanted him with an ache that squeezed her heart till she could hardly bear it.

"I think we should modify that quote of yers. No one can make ye feel dirty without yer permission."

The tears returned to her eyes. "Thank you."

He smiled. "We're good for each other." He wiped her damp cheeks with his fingers. "Enough sad tears." He kissed her cheek. "We should be happy."

She smoothed a hand over his temple and into his hair. "You make me happy."

"Lass, ye fill every dream in my head and every desire in my heart. I'm falling in love with you."

She was speechless. She was lost. She opened her mouth to speak, but simply stared at him.

He pressed a kiss against her lips, then sat back.

"Robby." Her heart cracked open, and she knew he was the one. The one she'd waited for all her life. She flung her arms around his neck and squeezed him tight. "I want to be with you forever."

"We can do that." He rose to his feet, still holding her in his arms, then skirted the coffee table. He dropped to his knees on the rug in front of the fire, neatly depositing her on the afghan and pillows.

She pulled him close for a kiss, and he claimed her mouth with a hunger that thrilled her. He stretched out on the floor, half on top of her. She smoothed her hands down his back and arched against him. She'd never felt so desperate before. Or so bold.

A small voice in her head reminded her that she'd only known Robby a few days. It was all happening too fast. She didn't know him well enough.

But she knew he was the one. Wasn't that what mattered? She needed to stop overanalyzing and enjoy this. She wrapped her arms around his neck and kissed him back. He groaned and rolled onto his back, pulling her on top of him. She dusted his cheeks and closed eyelids with kisses.

His hands slid underneath her tank top. Abruptly, he shifted her onto her rump and whisked the top over her head. She gasped, but before she could react, he'd pushed her onto her back.

"Robby." She struggled to catch her breath, painfully aware that each breath caused her bare breasts to heave. And he was watching, his eyes downcast.

"Ye're so beautiful." He rested a hand on her rib cage, then slowly moved it up to cup the underside of a breast.

Her nipples pebbled, and she closed her eyes, feeling suddenly shy and embarrassed. She shivered when Robby nuzzled her neck and nibbled on her ear.

"Yer nipples are growing darker," he whispered. "They

were a lovely shade of pink, but now they're turning red. Do ye think they're more sensitive now?"

She jolted, her eyes flying open, when he tweaked a hardened tip.

"Och, I was right."

She watched as he lowered his head and circled his tongue around her nipple. With his free hand, he cupped her other breast and teased the nipple with his thumb. She moaned. She'd never felt anything this good before.

He sucked her nipple into his mouth.

She jerked in response. Oh, now this was even better. She'd never felt anything this wonderful. Her fingers dug into his back. Her toes curled.

He was doing something incredible with his tongue. And it was making her squirm. Making her feel wet.

He released her nipple and she stared at it, shocked that it could be so red and distended. He moved to her other breast and clamped down on the nipple. All the itchy, wiggly sensations started again. They prickled her skin and sent waves of heat straight to her vagina.

With a moan, she squirmed and pressed her thighs together.

His hand skimmed over her pajama shorts. Her heart lurched. *Yes.* She lifted her hips just as his hand cupped her.

She gasped. She lowered her hips to the floor and held her breath. She'd never gone this far before. The one time she'd come close, she'd caught the guy lying and she'd stopped him.

But now all she could feel were her own sensations, and Robby was making it so good. He suckled her breast gently and started pressing his hand against her core, massaging her in a circular motion. Her nervousness melted away and

she was able to breathe. Her breaths matched the movement of his hand. It felt like her whole body was in sync
with his hand.

She moaned and rocked her hips in rhythm with his hand.
This was definitely the most incredible thing she'd ever felt.
Her whole body was tingling and tensing.

He released her breast and blew on it. She shuddered.
Then suddenly, the slow, languid circles weren't enough.
Her fingers dug into his back. "Robby."

"Yes, love." He slipped his fingers inside the baggy hem
of the pajama shorts and stroked the damp hair.

She whimpered. Something intense and amazing was
building inside her.

He hooked his fingers around the crotch of her pajama
shorts and pulled them down her legs.

She'd never been completely naked with a man before,
but instead of feeling awkward, she was desperate. "Robby,
please."

He seemed to understand she was past the point of gentle
coaxing. He slid a finger inside her wet passage, then pressed
his thumb against her clitoris.

She cried out as her orgasm shot through her. She pressed
her legs together as her spasms squeezed his finger.

She pressed a hand against her chest as her breathing
slowly returned to normal. She noted his eyes looked red
again. Strange, but maybe it was just a reflection from the
fire. His smile was decidedly smug.

She grinned. He had good reason to be proud. "You were
incredible. I've never felt anything so wonderful before."

His mouth twitched. "Are ye sure?"

"Yes."

He moved between her legs and pressed a kiss into her
belly. "Are ye really sure?"

Her mouth fell open as he trailed kisses down her belly, into her pubic hair, and then between her legs. She jolted at the feel of his tongue teasing her clitoris. Good God, he was right. This was even more wonderful.

She let her legs fall open wide so he could lick and suckle all he wanted. She squirmed while the tension coiled within her. "Oh, Robby."

He inserted a finger inside her, waggling it while he flicked his tongue. A second orgasm crashed over her, and she clenched him between her thighs as she cried out.

"Oh my God, Robby." She struggled to catch her breath.

He loosened the drawstring around his waist. "Olivia, I'm dying to be inside you."

She swallowed hard. Should she tell him now about her virginity or let him discover it later?

"I want ye to know how serious I am about this. Once I've taken you, I willna want to lose you. Ever."

She sat up and touched his cheek. "I wouldn't be here if I didn't love you."

"Och, Olivia." He cradled her face in his hands. "I've waited so long for you."

A loud knock sounded on the front door.

Chapter Nine

Robby groaned. *Bloody hell, not now.* "Just ignore it."

Olivia glanced toward the foyer. "Could it be the other guy who lives here?" she whispered. "Carlos?"

"Nay. He wouldna be knocking."

"Oh, right. He probably has a key." She fumbled through the pillows and located her pajamas.

"Sweetheart, we're no' finished." They'd better not be finished. His erection had reached painful proportions.

A banging noise echoed through the house as the unknown visitor pounded on the door.

Olivia jerked the pajama shorts up to her waist. "Who could it—"

"Police!"

She gasped. "Oh no!" She pulled on the tank top.

"Bugger," Robby muttered.

"What are they doing here?" she whispered.

"It must be about the jaguar."

"I thought they didn't believe you."

Robby stood and winced at the bulge in his pants. What a way to greet the local police. "I'll take care of it. Wait here." He headed across the room.

"They might want to check the grounds. And if they look through the windows . . . this could be bad."

He turned and saw her tossing the pillows back onto the couch. A twinge pricked at his gut. "Ye shouldna be embarrassed." Or ashamed. He couldn't bear to go through that again.

"I need to get dressed." She dashed toward the kitchen. "If they see me like this, the whole island will hear about it, and my grandmother will be mortified."

Would you be mortified? He wanted to ask, but she'd already run into the kitchen. He heard the door to the utility room shut, then more banging on the front door.

"Bugger." He trudged into the foyer, then cracked open the front door and peered out, making sure his swollen groin was hidden behind the door frame.

"Police," a portly, middle-aged man said with a thick accent and the hoarse voice of a habitual smoker. There was a badge pinned to his khaki uniform. "You telephoned about the panther?"

"Yes. Did ye find it?" He hoped Carlos was all right.

"We thought you were drunk, so we did not look for it. Then we get a call from Spiro. His goats were very loud, so he goes outside. The big cat is there, scaring the goats. He tries to shoot the panther, but it runs away."

So Carlos had wanted goat for dinner. Robby aimed a surge of psychic vampire control at the police officer. *There is no panther. Spiro was mistaken. So was I. We had too much to drink. If ye see anything that looks like a panther, ye willna shoot at it. Ye willna try to harm it. Do ye understand?*

The police officer nodded with a blank, glassy stare. "I understand."

Ye will leave and no' return here. "Thank you for stopping by," Robby added out loud.

The officer looked confused as the mind control faded away. "Oh. Okay." He stepped back. "I will go, then."

"Good night, officer." Robby shut the door. The policeman would subconsciously follow his orders, so hopefully, Carlos would be safe.

Robby wandered back into the family room and glanced at the rug where just moments ago he'd brought Olivia to climax. Twice. She'd been so passionate and responsive, so sweet and loving. Tonight should have confirmed their future together, but a small doubt had weaseled into his heart. What if she couldn't handle the truth about him being a vampire? What if she found it ugly or shameful?

No, he rejected that thought. Olivia was not like his wife. She would never betray him. His wife had put her own interests first, but Olivia was different. She'd wanted to face the panther alone rather than put him in danger.

"Did you get rid of the police?" she whispered from the darkness of the kitchen.

"Aye, they're gone." He strode into the room and noted with dismay that she'd dressed.

She avoided looking at him. "I—I left the sweater. It was still wet. And my shoes are still on the patio. I'm sure they're wet, too."

"It's all right. We can wait. No one knows ye're here."

"My grandmother knows. And if I don't return soon, she'll be sending the police back here." She looked at him now, her eyes sad. "I'm sorry. I know you . . . expected more."

"Sweetheart." He touched her cheek. "Ye're far beyond anything I ever expected. I never thought such a beautiful and brave lass could care for me."

"Robby." Her eyes filled with tears. "I don't know how this can be happening. How can I fall in love so fast?"

"There's no need to question it."

"But that's what I do. I analyze feelings and situations. When people fall in love this quickly, how can you trust it to last when times get—" She stopped when he placed his fingers on her lips.

"Do ye believe in love?"

She nodded.

"Do ye believe in faithfulness and loyalty?"

"Yes." She took his hand in hers and smiled. "And I believe good will overcome evil. I believe in family and friendship, kindness and respect. Just don't ask me to believe in unicorns and the Tooth Fairy."

He chuckled. "Nay. But I will ask you to believe in me."

"I want to. I really want to."

"Then do it." He kissed her brow. "I wish ye would stay with me." *Forever.*

"I need to go for now." She placed a hand on his chest. "But I could come back tomorrow night."

"Tomorrow?"

"Yes." She smoothed her hand through his chest hair and over his nipple. "Can you wait till tomorrow?"

"I could wait forever for you." He slapped himself mentally. "But I doona want to wait that long. I'm ready for you now."

She glanced down and winced. "I noticed. Would it help if I threw more ice water on you?"

"Cruel wench," he growled, then smiled at the sound of her giggle.

"Can you give me a ride home? I don't want to walk with a panther out there."

"Aye. I can do that." Robby gathered the car keys and his ID. The evening hadn't gone completely as he'd hoped, but over all, he couldn't complain. He'd given Olivia pleasure. He'd felt her shatter in his arms.

He'd confessed his love, and she'd surrendered her heart. She might not quite realize it yet. She was putting up a wee bit of resistance, but there was no denying it. She was falling in love with him.

Tomorrow night he would lay full claim to her. And then nothing would ever part them.

It was almost noon by the time Olivia woke on Thursday. She'd tossed and turned most of the night, waffling between anxiety and elation. Elation because she was falling in love with the sweetest, most gorgeous, most heroic man she'd ever met. Anxiety because she'd known him less than a week. And she was seriously considering losing her virginity to him tonight.

For the first time in her life the term "madly in love" was making sense. The overwhelming rush of passion and desire was causing her to do crazy things. But it felt so good. The things he'd done to her with his hands, his mouth—he was incredible. And she didn't need her empathic powers with him. She could feel his love with every touch, every glance, and every word he spoke to her.

She dressed and wandered into the kitchen. "Good morning, Yia Yia."

"Morning?" Eleni snorted as she tossed some olives and feta cheese into a salad. "It's time for lunch, child."

"Sorry." Olivia checked the kettle on the stove. The water inside was still hot. "I didn't sleep well."

"No one will sleep well until they catch that nasty jaguar," Eleni grumbled. "Just as well you missed breakfast. I didn't dare go to the bakery for fresh bread."

"What's the latest news?" Olivia retrieved a mug from an overhead cabinet. She'd told her grandmother about the panther after Robby had driven her home the night before. Of course she'd avoided letting Eleni know how close she'd come to being attacked by the wild animal.

"Alexia called this morning. She heard that a goat was killed near Horos. The goat herder said a huge black cat like a panther did it, but the police are saying there is no panther. No one has seen it all day."

Olivia nodded as she fixed a cup of tea. "It may be nocturnal."

"I don't think you should go out tonight."

"I'll be fine. Robby said he'd pick me up."

Eleni heaved a huge sigh. "I had such high hopes for Spiro. But this Robby seems like a nice boy. He sent you a nice box of fruit this morning."

Olivia's breath hitched. Her hand trembled and she set the mug on the counter. "Fruit?" She turned to face her grandmother. "What kind of fruit?"

"Apples. Next to the—child, what's wrong?" Eleni hurried over to her.

Olivia stumbled back against the counter. *No, no, it couldn't be him.*

"What's wrong?" Eleni touched her shoulder. "There's a dark aura of . . . terror surrounding you."

"Where?" she whispered. "Where are the apples?"

"On the counter by the refrigerator."

Olivia forced herself to walk, one step at a time, around the kitchen table to the fridge. There was a deafening noise in her ears, the thundering beat of her heart. Her grandmother was right beside her, still talking, but her voice seemed fuzzy and far away.

She spotted it. The familiar brown box with the green logo. He always sent six apples. Red ones nestled in green Easter grass. Inside would be a note. Typed.

Previous messages flitted through her mind. *Dearest Olivia, I'll never let you go. Dearest Olivia, you are mine forever. Dearest Olivia, you are the only one worthy of me.*

Her hand shook as she opened the lid. Six red apples. Green grass. She stepped back as a sob escaped her mouth. Why did he keep doing this? Did he intend to terrorize her for the rest of her life?

"Easy, child." Eleni patted her back.

"How did he find me here? The bastard's in solitary. Damn him!" Olivia grabbed the note and tore it open. The words were neatly typed.

Dearest Olivia, I will always find you.

"Dammit!" She wadded the note in her fist and threw it.

"Calm down," Eleni said in a soothing voice. "It can't be that bad."

"It *is* bad. He knows I'm here. This was supposed to be my safe place. My sanctuary." Tears filled her eyes. "I was supposed to be safe with you!"

"Shhh, child. We'll be all right."

"With a mass murderer sending us gifts and a panther outside the door?" Olivia paced across the room. "I have to leave. *We* have to leave. I'm not leaving you here alone."

"We *are* leaving. Eleven days from now."

"We're leaving today," Olivia announced. When her grandmother started to object, she raised a hand. "You don't understand how serious this is. Otis Crump is behind this, but since he's in solitary, he must have someone helping him."

"A friend, maybe, but that doesn't mean we should run away in fear."

"I'm not sure this is just a friend," Olivia explained. "Otis hinted that he might have had an accomplice for the murders, but I could never get a name from him. If this accomplice exists, then he knows where we are. It's not safe for you here. I'll feel better if you're with Dad in Houston."

Eleni sighed. "Very well. I'll go with you, but mainly because I don't like to see you so upset."

"Fine. I'll get busy making the travel arrangements. You start packing."

"Let me call Alexia first. She can help us get the house ready. You start bringing in the table and chairs from the courtyard."

Three hours later the furniture was covered with bedsheets, the blue-painted shutters were firmly closed over the windows, and the food, including the apples, had been given to Alexia. A cab picked up Olivia, her grandmother, and their luggage and took them to the port.

As they boarded the ferry, Olivia's heart sank at the thought of leaving Robby. She'd left a note for him with Alexia. She hoped he would understand.

She stood on deck with a chilly breeze whipping her face as the island of Patmos grew smaller and smaller on the horizon. Tears ran down her cheeks. Damn that Otis. The monster had defiled her sanctuary. He'd put her grandmother in danger. And he'd caused her to leave the man of her dreams. She could only hope that somehow, someday, she would see Robby MacKay again.

"Och, good. Ye're still alive," Robby said as he crossed the family room to the kitchen. At dawn, Carlos hadn't returned yet, so Robby had fallen into his death-sleep not knowing if the were-panther had survived his night out.

Now the sun had set and Robby was newly awakened and hungry for breakfast. He padded into the kitchen and grabbed a bottle from the fridge. Type A negative to remind him of Olivia. After breakfast he needed to shower and change. He was supposed to pick her up at her grandmother's house at nine.

He heard footsteps behind him and glanced back as he stuffed the bottle into the microwave. Carlos was shuffling in with a frown on his face.

"I'm afraid I have bad news, bro." He leaned against a counter and folded his arms across his black T-shirt.

Robby took a wineglass from the cabinet. "Let me guess. Ye have a stomachache from devouring a whole goat."

"No. I only had a few bites before the goat herder started shooting at me. I've never seen such a dedicated bunch of herders in my life. It's bloody hard to get a meal on this island."

"How sad." Robby poured his bottle of warm blood into the glass. "Remind me to cry for you later."

"Save your tears for yourself, Big Red. I went to the taverna an hour ago to eat and listen to the latest gossip on the mysterious panther." Carlos chuckled. "The police say I don't exist, but Spiro's telling everyone that I do. And no one can figure out where the hell I came from."

"Hell being the operative word." Robby guzzled down his glass of blood.

"Very funny. But there were two big topics of gossip today. The panther who has mysteriously disappeared, and your girlfriend who has mysteriously run away."

Robby gulped the last swallow of blood. "What?"

"The tavern owner's wife, Alexia, told me all about it. She helped Olivia and Eleni close up the house for the winter. She's Eleni's best friend, so she always keeps an eye on the house, waters the plants, and so on."

"Wait." Robby set his glass down. "Are ye saying Olivia left the island?"

"A little slow on the uptake, bro. Yes, she's gone. Her grandmother, too."

"She canna be gone. I'm supposed to pick her up at nine."

"The house is closed. I went by it on the way home to make sure."

Robby stared at Carlos, speechless. Completely gob-smacked. She was gone? Why would she leave? Had he pushed her too fast? Bugger. She'd complained about it all happening too quickly. He should have taken it slower. "Why would she leave?"

Carlos shrugged. "Maybe you're a lousy kisser."

"Maybe ye'd like two black eyes to match yer black heart."

Carlos grinned. "Easy, Big Red. I asked Alexia that same question. She said something had Olivia really scared. A man."

Robby swallowed hard. Had he frightened her away? She hadn't seemed that scared last night.

"Alexia was upset about them leaving," Carlos continued. "She wanted Olivia to stay and marry her son Giorgios."

"Anything else?" Robby grated. Now that he'd adjusted to the shock, he was becoming angry. Olivia shouldn't have run away. She'd admitted she was falling in love. You didn't run away from the man you loved. Not if you were loyal and trustworthy.

"I asked Alexia if she knew where they were going,"

Carlos said. "The grandmother always goes to Houston to spend Christmas vacation with her son there. So they're probably headed to Houston."

Robby nodded and strode from the room. Damn it to hell, he didn't even have Olivia's cell phone number. He hadn't expected her to run away. He went into his bedroom and dressed quickly in a pair of jeans, T-shirt, and hoodie. Then he headed out the back door onto the patio.

"Wait up!" Carlos yelled.

Robby didn't wait. He jumped off the bluff and landed with a thud on the sand below. He stalked toward Petra, tempted to rip the giant rock apart with his bare hands.

"Wait!"

Robby glanced back when he heard a thud. Carlos had leaped off the bluff, holding a jacket in his hand. "I doona want company."

Carlos walked toward him as he slipped on his black leather jacket. "Where are you going?"

"Running." Robby broke into a sprint.

Carlos ran alongside him. "Are we going to her house?"

Robby ignored him and kept running. Maybe he would go to her house. It was better than staying at home all alone. *Lonesome.* His pace slowed to a walk.

"I'm sorry about how things turned out, *muchacho.*"

Robby grunted. He motioned toward the moon, which was still fairly full. "Why don't ye shift and go away? The goat buffet is waiting for you."

"Actually, I had intended to shift tonight so I could terrorize Spiro's goats again." Carlos grinned. "Just trying to upset your competition, bro. But there's no point in shifting since your bird flew the coop."

Robby ground his teeth. How could she leave him? It didn't make sense. And something Carlos had said didn't make sense, either. "Ye intended to shift, but ye changed yer mind?"

"That's what I said. You're a little slow tonight, bro."

"Ye have control over yer shifting?"

Carlos hesitated. "Yes."

"Then ye're like an Alpha wolf? Ye can shift without a full moon?"

Carlos grimaced. "Please. Don't compare me to those drooling dogs. Cats are naturally superior creatures."

Robby snorted. "Ye're both shifters."

"Our cultures are completely different. Wolves huddle into packs and follow the commands of their pack master like well-trained little puppies. A panther obeys no one."

"I think Phil would disagree with yer assessment of werewolves. He broke away from his pack."

"Phil is all right." Carlos smirked. "For a dog."

Phil had found his true love, Robby recalled. A lot of his friends had recently found their mates. He thought he'd found his.

He trudged past the area where Olivia had asked her three questions.

What do you want more than anything in the world? Without hesitation, he'd answered revenge.

What scares you more than anything in the world? Robby halted with a jerk. *Losing Olivia.*

A sharp pain pierced his heart. How could he lose her? Somehow, in just a few nights, she'd completely overturned his thoughts and feelings. What did he want more than anything? *Olivia.* He still wanted revenge, but it was no longer the driving force in his life.

He wanted Olivia. Now when the sun went down and his heart jolted back to life, pumping blood into his brain, his first thought was Olivia. At sunrise, when his heartbeat faded away and his thoughts dissolved into nothingness, the last image in his mind was Olivia.

With revenge as his goal, he'd lived in order to hate. Now he wanted love. More than anything, he wanted love.

And yes, it made him a better person.

His heart ached. He couldn't lose her. She was a part of his heart and soul.

"Don't give up, bro," Carlos whispered. "I tell myself that every day. Never give up."

Robby nodded.

"So are we there yet?" Carlos muttered.

Robby pointed at the Sotiris house in the distance. "That's it."

"I'll race you." Carlos took off at a fast pace.

Robby focused on the courtyard and teleported there.

"Show off!" Carlos shouted from the beach.

Robby surveyed the courtyard. The telescope and table and chairs were gone, probably taken indoors. He examined the house. Blue shutters boarded up the windows. The back door was locked, and the windowpane was covered with another shutter.

Footsteps sounded behind him as Carlos jogged up the stairs to the courtyard.

Carlos paused by one of the lemon trees and broke off a sprig of mint that grew around the base. "Place is locked up, bro." He chewed on the mint.

"I'm going to teleport inside."

"Are you sure that's wise? You could end up part of a sofa."

Robby placed a hand on the door and focused on moving himself just inside. He materialized by the door, unlocked it, and opened it. "Come on in."

"What are we looking for?"

"I'm no' sure. Something wrong."

Carlos pivoted as he looked around the kitchen. "Everything's wrong. The countertops need replacing. That stove is ancient. There's no water dispenser in the refrigerator door. This place needs a major makeover."

"Go check the rest of the house," Robby growled. When his annoying companion headed into the parlor, Robby examined the kitchen. It looked fine to him. But then he'd grown up in a one-room stone hut with a thatched roof.

The fridge was empty; the pantry nearly so. All the dishes had been washed and put away. The flowers he'd given Olivia were in the litter bin. Not a good sign.

He ventured into the parlor. It was dark inside with all the windows shuttered. Still, his superior vision allowed him to see the small room. The furniture had all been covered with bedsheets.

"I got it!" Carlos entered the parlor from a hallway. "I found something of vital importance in Olivia's bedroom."

"What?"

With a smirk, Carlos dangled some blue cotton bikini underwear from his fingertips. "A little memento for you, bro."

Robby snatched the underwear away. "That is no' what I was referring to."

"Oh." Carlos's mouth twitched. "In that case, I'll put them back."

"Piss off." Robby stuffed the underwear into his jeans pocket and stalked back into the kitchen. Something white snagged his attention. A wad of paper underneath the kitchen table.

He leaned over to fish it out.

"What did you find?" Carlos asked.

"I'm no' sure." Robby smoothed the paper out. It was a card with a message typed on it.

Dearest Olivia, I will always find you.

"This is it," Robby whispered. "This is what scared her."

"A note?" Carlos leaned close to read it. "Who sent it?"

"A bastard who's stalking her from prison." Robby stuffed the note into his hoodie pocket. Part of him was relieved it wasn't him that had scared Olivia. But another part was still angry. Angry that Otis Crump was terrorizing her. And angry that Olivia had run away. She should have stayed and let him help her. She should have trusted him to protect her. "Did that woman in the tavern mention any apples?"

"No. But she did mention taking some food from here."

"I need to talk to her."

"No problem." Carlos headed out the back door. "I'll take you."

They locked up the house, and then ten minutes later they strolled into the taverna in Grikos. Robby was surprised when the locals greeted Carlos like he belonged.

"This is Alexia." Carlos gave a gray-haired woman a kiss on each wrinkled cheek. "If she wasn't still in love with her husband, I'd steal her away."

Alexia laughed and swatted Carlos on the shoulder. "You silly boy. You just come here for the moussaka."

Carlos looked properly chastised. "What can I say? You are the best cook on the island."

Alexia beamed. "And who is this friend of yours?"

Robby inclined his head. "A pleasure to meet you. I'm Robby MacKay."

Her smile vanished and a wary look glinted in her eyes. "What would you boys like to drink?"

"I'd like to ask you a few questions, if ye doona mind," Robby said. "About Olivia Sotiris."

Alexia lifted her chin. "Olivia would have been perfect for my son, Giorgios. It was a shame she had to leave so quickly."

"Did she leave you some apples?" Robby asked.

"Yes. A box of very nice apples."

Robby nodded. It was just as he thought. "And did she mention me at all?"

The wary look flitted over Alexia's face once again. "Why would she?"

Robby focused a blast of vampire mind control at the old woman. She stumbled back, her face going blank.

Carlos grabbed her arm to steady her. "What are you doing, bro?"

"Getting answers." *Did Olivia say anything about me before she left?* Robby asked telepathically.

"Yes." The woman pulled a small envelope from her pocket. "She left a note for you."

"Thank you." Robby stuffed the envelope into his jacket pocket, then released Alexia from his mind control.

The woman shook her head with a confused look. "What—oh, I was going to get you drinks."

"A beer for me." Carlos checked his pockets. "Oops, forgot my wallet. Looks like you're paying, bro."

"Fine." Robby reached into his jeans pocket and dug out a few coins. When he pulled out his hand, Olivia's bikini underwear slipped out and tumbled to the floor.

Alexia gasped.

Carlos snickered, then gave Alexia a wistful look. "I just can't take him anywhere."

She sniffed. "Olivia would be much better off with my Giorgios."

Robby stuffed the underwear back into his pocket and handed the coins to the old woman. "I'll be going now." He stepped outside and ripped the envelope open.

Dear Robby, I'm sorry I had to leave so suddenly. You can contact me at the FBI office in Kansas City. I'll miss you and remember you always. I hope to see you again. Love, Olivia.

She still loved him. His heart swelled with relief. *I love you, too, sweetheart. You will see me again.*

Chapter Ten

One week later . . .

Olivia stepped off the elevator onto the second floor of the FBI Field Office in Kansas City and strode toward her work area. She passed empty desks. Most of the special agents were out, working on assignments. A few remained, catching up on paperwork. They glanced up and smiled.

She waved and kept going before anyone could stop her. Most of them hated paperwork and would have welcomed an interruption, but she wasn't in the mood for chitchat.

How was your vacation? they'd ask. *Ruined by a serial killer.* She could only hope her relationship with Robby wasn't ruined, too. It hurt more than she'd expected to be separated from him. There was a constant ache in her heart, as if she'd lost her best friend, along with a nagging fear that she'd never see him again.

The family reunion in Houston had not gone well, so she'd left early. Her parents were upset with her, claiming she'd brought a psychotic killer into their lives. She'd assured them that Otis Crump was securely behind bars, but she could hardly refute the fact that he was successfully stalking her.

Her parents wanted her to resign, but how could she? She loved this job. And she'd worked hard to be accepted as a contributing employee. At first she'd suffered a bit of an inferiority complex, surrounded by all the special agents. She hadn't met the qualifications to be "special," since she'd joined straight out of college and didn't have the required years of work experience. Officially, she was labeled as a criminal psychologist on the professional staff. The FBI wasn't about to admit they'd hired her for her secret paranormal abilities.

She reached her work station, stashed her handbag in the bottom drawer, and glanced over the cubicle wall to see if J.L. was at his desk. Nope, gone. She wouldn't have minded talking to him. He was her best friend at work. Unlike most of the special agents here who had worked previously as lawyers or accountants, J.L. Wang had been hired for his linguistic abilities. They'd both felt like the odd ducks, so they quickly bonded.

She smiled at the plaque hanging next to her monitor. J.L. had proudly presented it to her on her twenty-fourth birthday. With his love for initials, he'd come up with the plaque's message: OLIVIA SOTIRIS, APA, FBI, HLD, WACC. He'd translated the last two acronyms for everyone. Human Lie Detector, Weird-Assed Crap Consultant.

After that, everyone in the building had decided it was perfectly acceptable to ask her about any weird-assed crap that popped up on their assignments. Finally, she belonged.

Dammit, she didn't want to quit.

"Olivia!" Yasmine Hernandez rushed toward her. "What are you doing here?"

"Gee, that makes me feel welcomed." Olivia smiled wryly.

Yasmine waved a dismissive hand. "I just meant you're not supposed to be back till after Christmas."

Olivia shrugged and gave a purposely vague response. "Stuff happens." Yasmine was a wonderfully competent office manager, but unfortunately she was equally talented at snooping into everyone's personal life.

"Didn't you go to Greece?" Yasmine asked.

"Yes." When Yasmine opened her mouth to dig for more information, Olivia quickly added, "I need to talk to Barker. Is he in?" She glanced at the glassed-in corner office of her supervisor, Patrick O'Shea Barker. The door and the window blinds were closed, but the light was on inside.

"He's in a meeting right now." Yasmine's mouth thinned. "With Special Agent Harrison."

Olivia nodded. She felt a brief spurt of anger from Yasmine, no doubt caused by Harrison, who could be overbearing and rude. Yasmine's emotions were usually steady and cheerful, and Olivia had always sensed that her nosiness was not caused by malice but rather by curiosity and a sincere desire to help. Harrison, on the other hand, took pleasure in being a jerk.

"Why do you need to see Barker?" Yasmine asked. "Is something wrong?"

"Just something I need to discuss." Like how on earth did Otis Crump find her on Patmos? This stalking had to stop. It had been bad enough when it was focused just on her, but Olivia was worried that he'd broadened his scope to include her family, especially her grandmother, who lived alone most of the year. Otis was locked away, but what if he had an accomplice who was free to harm her loved ones?

A spurt of alarm emanated from Yasmine. "You're not thinking of transferring, are you? We don't have enough women in this office as it is. You can't leave."

"I don't want to leave." Olivia kept an eye on Barker's door, wondering how long his meeting would last.

Yasmine gasped with a sudden thought. "I know what will cheer you up! A package came for you this morning."

Olivia stiffened. "Not apples."

"No, no, of course not." Yasmine waved her hands, then lowered her voice dramatically. "We don't accept any mail from you know who."

"Is he still sending mail here?" Olivia asked.

Yasmine shook her head. "Not for several months. He gave up when it was all returned."

"Do you remember what return address he used?" Olivia always checked that. The last few times she'd received apples, the return address had been a post office box that had turned out to be bogus.

Yasmine frowned. "I think it was his address at Leavenworth. But that was months ago." A wave of curious excitement rolled off her. "Are you still getting stuff from him?"

Olivia didn't want to discuss it further. "You said there was a package for me?"

"Oh, right. I'll get it." Yasmine hurried off, her low-heeled pumps clicking on the wooden floor.

Olivia booted up her computer to check her e-mail. For the hundredth time she chastised herself for not leaving her e-mail address in the note to Robby. Or her cell phone number. The island seemed so far away now. The memory of her time with Robby seemed magical. Not quite real.

She suspected there was a part of her that hadn't wanted to

make it easy for him. She'd had her doubts that two people could fall in love in less than a week, so maybe now she wanted proof. She wanted to know if he'd make the effort to find her and contact her.

She glanced up when Barker's door opened and her supervisor exited with Harrison. At six-foot-six, Barker was easy to spot. He murmured something, then slapped the special agent on the shoulder. Harrison laughed before heading toward his work area.

Olivia jumped to her feet and approached her supervisor. "Excuse me, Barker. Do you have a minute?"

"Sotiris, I didn't know you were back." Barker's brown eyes narrowed. "Are you supposed to be back?"

"Not till after Christmas, but there was something important I wanted to discuss with you in person."

"All right." He motioned for her to enter his office. "Take a seat."

She perched on the edge of the black leather and chrome chair and gripped the armrests.

Barker approached his desk slowly, studying her. "I sent you away to relax, but you still look tense."

"I—" She lifted her chin. "I want to take another look at the Otis Crump files."

Barker closed his eyes briefly with a weary look. "Olivia, we went over this before. He was tried and convicted for three murders, and he's serving three life terms. Thanks to you, he confessed to ten more murders, but at this point it's a waste of taxpayer money to prosecute him. He's not going anywhere. Ever."

"I believe he may have had an accomplice."

"Not for the murders. Our forensic team went through all the evidence with a fine-tooth comb. He worked alone."

"He hinted to me several times—"

"He was playing you." Barker planted his hands on his desk and leaned forward. "The man is desperate to keep you on a leash. He'd tell you little green men helped him if it got you to heel. The case is closed, and frankly, I'm getting worried about your obsession with him."

"I'd get over it if the bastard stopped stalking me!" Olivia took a quick breath to calm herself.

Barker straightened. "You're still getting apples?"

"Yes." She jumped to her feet and paced to the window. "He sent them to my grandmother's house on Patmos. My grandmother! I had to rush her over to my dad's house in Houston to make sure she'd be safe."

Barker winced. "I can see why you're upset."

Olivia paced back to the chair. "There has to be someone helping him. Someone's mailing the apples for him."

Barker crossed his long, lanky arms over his gray pin-striped suit jacket. His frown made his long, lean face appear even longer. "I agree he has an accomplice now."

"It could be someone close to him," Olivia suggested. "If we reopen the investigation, we can interview all his friends and family."

"Or it could be a groupie. The serial killers always ac-quire a few of those." Barker rubbed his chin. "Does your family understand the importance of keeping this quiet? We don't want the media turning this into the latest fashion. Next thing you know, every prisoner in the country would be stalking their favorite officer of the law."

"And Otis would love the publicity," Olivia grumbled. "Don't worry. My family thinks this is awful enough al-ready. They're not going to make it worse."

Barker frowned at his desk, deep in thought, while she paced about the office.

"I want to go back home a few days for Christmas," she

murmured. "I'd like to be able to tell my family that we found the accomplice, and that it's all over."

Barker nodded. "This person was able to track you to a remote Greek island. There could be a different explanation for this."

"Like what?"

"Not an accomplice, but an employee. Crump may have managed to hire a P.I." Barker leaned over his desk once again. "Think, Olivia. Did you see anyone on that island who could have been a private investigator?"

She halted with a jerk. *MacKay Security & Investigation.* The room swirled around her, and she grabbed onto the back of a chair. *No. It couldn't be.* But there hadn't been any other P.I.'s on the island.

"It would most likely be a man who was visiting the island and keeping a low profile," Barker continued.

A shudder racked her body. *No, not Robby. Anyone but Robby. Carlos? But they worked for the same company. They were probably on the same assignment.* She pressed a fist to her mouth. What if the assignment had been her?

"Hey, are you all right?" Barker skirted his desk.

"I—I need to go."

"But we're not—"

"I have to go!" She wrenched open the door and lurched outside. Heads turned her way. No, she couldn't think about it. It was too awful. She couldn't fall apart here.

She dashed into the hallway to the women's restroom. *No, not Robby. He couldn't have done that to me.* She shoved the stall doors open. Empty. She caught a glimpse of herself in the mirror. That pale, panic-stricken face was hers. Could she have been duped? Had she fallen in love with the enemy?

With a sob, she ran back and locked the restroom door.

A long keening cry escaped, ripped from her soul, and she slapped a hand over her mouth. She couldn't let anyone hear.

Her knees gave out and she slid down the door to plop onto the linoleum floor. Oh God, she should have known. Maybe a part of her had always known. He couldn't have fallen in love with her so fast.

Tears streamed down her face. What a complete fool she'd been! The first time in her life that she couldn't detect lies, and she'd fallen for such terrible deceit.

No! She shook her head. She still wanted to believe. She wanted love to be true.

"Robby," she cried. She didn't want to lose him, didn't want to lose the dream, the magic, the glory of his love. She leaned her head onto her knees and wept.

Oh God, the last time she'd cried like this, she 'd been in Robby's arms. He'd held her and comforted her. Then he'd made love to her.

A twinge of nausea twisted in her gut, and she breathed deeply to get control. She was at work, dammit. She needed to get a grip. She could fall apart later when she was alone in her apartment.

She stumbled to a sink and splashed cold water on her face. She leaned over the sink, reluctant to even look at herself. She didn't want to see living proof of how badly her heart was breaking.

The door shook as someone tried to open it. Then she heard a knock.

"Olivia?" Yasmine asked quietly. "Are you all right?"

She took a deep breath. "I'm fine." She glanced at the mirror and winced. Her eyes were red and puffy, her nose pink and runny.

"Do you want to talk?" Yasmine asked.

No. Olivia trudged toward the door and unlocked it. Yasmine slipped inside with a large brown package hugged to her chest. She took one look at Olivia and gasped.

"I'm not feeling well." Olivia yanked a tissue from the dispenser and blew her nose.

"Man trouble?" Yasmine whispered. "Don't worry. I won't tell anyone. I'll say you caught a bug on vacation. Happens all the time."

"Thanks."

Yasmine sighed. "It's so hard to find a good man these days. I should know. I've looked everywhere."

Olivia's tears threatened to flow again. "I should go home."

"Of course." Yasmine patted her on the back. "You still have some vacation days, so stay home and take it easy."

Olivia glanced at the mirror and winced. "I'll have to cross the office to get my handbag."

"I'll get it. You wait here." Yasmine moved toward the door, then stopped. "Oh, I forgot. Here's your package." She handed it over and left.

Olivia's heart lurched when she read the return address. It was from Grikos. Her fingers trembled as she ripped open the sticky flap on the supersized bubble envelope. Inside, she spotted cream-colored yarn. Her sweater. She'd left it at Robby's house.

She dropped the envelope on the vanity between the two sinks and stepped back. Memories of that night flooded her mind. She'd lain naked beside him. She'd let him touch her and kiss her everywhere. She'd felt so much love and desire for him, she'd been ready to give up her virginity.

She doubled over as her heart squeezed painfully in her chest. How could she have fallen in love so fast with a complete stranger? She should have followed her first instincts and stayed far away from a man she couldn't read.

Yasmine strode back into the restroom. "Oh my gosh, are you all right?" She dropped Olivia's handbag on the floor and rushed to her side.

Olivia took a deep breath and motioned to the package. "There's a sweater inside. Would you like it?" She and Yasmine looked similar in size.

"Are you sure?" Yasmine slipped the sweater out of the package. "It's very nice."

"Take it. Please."

Yasmine frowned. "Is it from him? He has good taste."

"It was mine. I don't want to see it again."

"Well, okay." Yasmine peered inside the package. "There's something else in here. A note." She pulled out a small envelope. "It has your name on it."

Olivia swallowed hard. She took the envelope, and her hand trembled when she saw the bold, masculine handwriting. *Robby.* A surge of love rose inside her, still clinging hopelessly and desperately to a dream that now appeared false. Before she could weaken, she ripped the envelope in two, threw the pieces in the toilet, and flushed it down.

"Whoa." Yasmine's eyes grew wide. "That bad, huh?"

Her eyes blurred with hot tears. "It's very bad. The worst ever."

Yasmine wrinkled her nose. "You deserve better than him."

Olivia sighed. Part of her still believed there was no one better than Robby. No man could ever touch her heart like Robby had.

No wonder this hurt so damned bad.

Chapter Eleven

Two weeks later . . .

Robby hesitated at the open doorway. He dreaded this evening, but everyone expected him to be here. No one ever missed the Christmas Ball at Romatech Industries. The partitions from eight large meeting rooms had been pulled back to make one huge ballroom. The band, the High Voltage Vamps, was onstage, playing a waltz. Normally, he would enjoy the lyrical music, but tonight it was just noise.

Shanna Draganesti had outdone herself this year. Instead of the usual fifteen-foot Christmas tree, there were four of them, one in each corner of the ballroom. Giant ice sculptures in the shape of reindeer adorned the buffet tables. By the looks of their shrinking antlers, they'd been in place for several hours.

The party usually started at four in the afternoon, with

tons of mortal food and a mortal band for the unsuspecting human employees who worked at Romatech during the day. By six-thirty the last of them were shooed away, and a subtle change came over the ballroom.

All the buffet tables but one were cleared of mortal food. Huge tubs of ice were hauled in, each one containing bottles of Vampire Fusion Cuisine. Roman Draganesti had used his scientific genius to mix synthetic blood with beer, whiskey, chocolate, and champagne, resulting in Bleer, Blissky, Chocolood, and Bubbly Blood. For those who overindulged, there was Blood Lite, synthetic blood with low cholesterol and blood sugar.

Robby watched the couples happily twirling about the dance floor and decided to partake liberally of the Blissky. It would be the best way to survive the night. Hell, it was the only way.

As he trudged to the Blissky table, he spotted Howard Barr dressed as Santa Claus and sitting on a throne. Howard had a baby in his lap, a little girl with curly black hair. That had to be Sofia, the youngest Draganesti child. Her older brother, Constantine, was dressed as an elf, and he bounced around the throne, trying to make the bells on his pointed shoes jingle. Shanna had chosen well, having Howard look after her children. The were-bear would be ferocious if anyone threatened his charges.

Two little girls ran up to join Constantine. Robby recognized them as Bethany, Jean-Luc's stepdaughter, and Lucy, Maggie's stepdaughter. That could only mean that Jean-Luc and his wife Heather were in attendance, along with Maggie and her husband, Pierce O'Callahan.

Robby groaned inwardly. Just what he needed, an evening surrounded by happily married couples. He yanked a bottle of Blissky out of a tub of ice. There were glasses on the table, but he didn't bother with them. He unscrewed the top and jammed the bottle into the microwave.

Why didn't she call? Olivia should have received the package by now. He'd double-checked the tracking information, so he knew her jumper had arrived at the FBI office in Kansas City. He'd included a note, telling her how much he missed her and wanted to see her again. He'd written his cell phone number down so she could call him.

She never called. How could he interpret that except that she didn't feel the same way he did? He'd returned to New York two nights ago, his prison term over. If Angus and Emma had expected him to return all cheerful and full of energy, they were in for a big disappointment.

If anything, he felt worse. At least before, when he was consumed with anger, he'd had a purpose. His quest for revenge had motivated him and filled him with passion. Now, he just felt like an empty shell, quietly enduring each night, doing his duties and trying not to check his cell phone every five minutes for missed calls.

He opened the microwave and burned his fingers on the hot bottle. "Bugger." He'd left it in too long.

Some giggles sounded behind him, and he turned to find Constantine, Bethany, and Lucy watching him.

Bethany lifted her chin with a prissy look. "You said a naughty word."

"Aye, that I did." Robby inclined his head. "My apologies."

"You're wearing a kilt," Constantine announced.

"Ye're verra observant." Robby swallowed some hot Blissky. It sizzled painfully down his throat, and he liked it.

"Go ahead," Constantine whispered to Bethany, nudging her with an elbow. "I dare you."

"Eew!" Bethany made a face and ran back to Howard, followed by a giggling Lucy.

"Tino." Robby arched a brow. "What are ye up to, lad?"

Constantine assumed an angelic look, easily done with his blond curls and big blue eyes. "I was just wondering if you do like Uncle Angus. I heard he doesn't wear any underwear. So I dared Bethany to look under your kilt."

Robby took another swig from his bottle. "First, ye shouldna be frightening the young lassies. Ye could end up old and alone." *Like me.* He gulped down more Blissky. "And second, ye shouldna be spending all yer time thinking about a man's private parts."

Tino's mouth dropped open. "I—I don't. I was just teasing Bethany. Really."

Robby nodded. "Ye're a good lad. And I know what to get you for Christmas now."

Tino grinned and bounced, causing his shoes to jingle. "What? What will you get me?"

"A kilt."

A look of horror flashed over the boy's face before his training in etiquette kicked in. He attempted a wobbly smile. "Thank you, Robby." He ran away, his shoes jangling. "Mom, Mom!" He dashed around, looking for his mother.

Robby guzzled down the last of the Blissky. A comforting warmth spread through his chest and fizzled up to his brain. He stuffed a new bottle into the microwave just as Tino located his mother. With his superior hearing, Robby caught the conversation.

"Tino, what's wrong?" Shanna leaned over her son.

"If Robby gives me a kilt, do I have to wear it?"

Shanna grinned. "I think you would look adorable in a kilt."

"Agh!" Tino scurried back to Howard to tell him the terrible news.

Robby sighed as he removed the bottle from the microwave. He was certainly doing his share of spreading Christmas cheer. He saluted the dripping reindeer sculpture and took a long drink.

"Is it true, Robby?" a female voice asked behind him.

He spun around and saw double for a moment. Two Shanna Draganestis wearing matching red gowns. "Och, Shanna. A lovely party, as always." He bowed and watched her four feet transform into two.

"I heard some disturbing news," she said, thankfully with one voice. "I hope I can change your mind."

He straightened, and the room swirled around him. "I willna buy the lad a kilt if it fashes him."

"Not about that." Shanna waved a hand. "I heard you took your name off the Secret Santa list. You don't intend to deliver presents this Christmas eve?"

"I'm no' feeling verra celebratory this year."

"That's exactly why you should do it," she insisted. "It'll make you feel better."

He groaned. Why did every woman want to fix him? Correction, every woman except the one he wanted. He guzzled down more Blissky.

Shanna planted her hands on her hips. "Getting drunk is not going to solve your problems."

"Aye, but 'twill make me no' give a damn." He upended the bottle and finished it.

"Robby, please, you need to see a therapist. Emma and I were discussing it last night, and you're clearly—"

"No' another therapist. The last one nearly killed me."

Shanna's eyes widened. "You saw a therapist? When? Where?"

"On Patmos. But she ran away." He yanked a third bottle from the tub of ice.

"She?"

"Aye."

Shanna gasped. "Then it's true."

He stiffened. "I'm no' crazy. I never was."

"No, I mean Carlos was right. He told us you were love-sick, but we didn't think you'd met anyone . . ."

"That damned Carlos," Robby muttered. "I told him to keep his trap shut."

"Well, who is she?" Shanna asked.

"A Greek goddess." He gestured dramatically with his bottle. "To know her is to worship her. To love her is to spout bad poetry till the end of time."

Shanna's mouth twitched. "That sounds very promising."

"Nay." He pressed the bottle against his chest. "She's no' interested in me."

"Oh dear," Shanna murmured.

"Oh bloody fucking hell," he corrected her.

She winced. "Try not to pass out under the table. It might scare the children."

"As ye wish, madam." He unscrewed the bottle and drank the Blissky cold.

"Oh, look." Shanna's face brightened. "Darcy and Austin have arrived. Did you hear their good news?"

"Nay, but I have a terrible feeling I will—"

"You know how Darcy's eggs all died when she was a vampire?"

"I wasna personally acquainted with her eggs."

Shanna snorted. "She borrowed some eggs from her sister, and Roman used Austin's sperm to fertilize them. And it worked! They're pregnant!"

Robby slanted a bleary look at Austin. "He doesna look verra pregnant." When Shanna slapped his shoulder, he stumbled to the side.

She shook her head disapprovingly. "At least you know about Jean-Luc and Heather, don't you?"

"Nay. I was shuffled off to a remote island for four months. I believe that's what mortals do with their unwanted Christmas fruitcakes."

"We all came to visit you," Shanna protested. "Anyway, when Jean-Luc and Heather came back from Patmos, they told Roman they wanted to have children. So he did his little magic trick, and it worked!"

"Och, that's good." Robby was truly happy for Jean-Luc. Roman had found a way to use live human sperm, but erase the donor's DNA and replace it with a Vamp's. Thanks to Roman's procedure, Jean-Luc's child would actually be his. Just like Constantine and Sofia were really Roman's children. They weren't quite human, though.

Maybe it was just as well that Olivia hadn't called. He doubted she'd want to marry a vampire and give birth to half-vampire children.

"Well, guess what?" Shanna's excited voice interrupted his thoughts. "They're going to have twins! Isn't that exciting!"

Robby nodded. "Aye. I can barely contain myself."

She gave him a wry look. "You should try to be happy for your friends."

"I am. I'm delighted that everyone but me is happily married and multiplying like bloody rabbits."

"Not everyone here is married. Lady Pamela and Cora Lee are over there at the Chocolood table. They'd probably love for someone to ask them to dance."

"No thanks." They weren't Olivia.

"How about the famous models, Simone and Inga?" Shanna motioned toward the Blood Lite table. "You know them, don't you, from your days in Paris?"

"Aye. That's the problem. I know them. If vanity and shallowness were virtues, they'd be named saints."

Shanna grinned as she peered around the room.

"Ye doona need to play matchmaker," Robby told her. "I'll be fine."

"Are you sure?" She gave him a dubious look.

"Aye. Go on. Enjoy yer party."

Shanna patted him on the shoulder. "Merry Christmas, Robby." She headed in the direction of her children.

From what Robby could hear, Constantine was getting a lecture from Angus on the benefits of wearing a kilt, while Roman listened with an amused expression. Shanna drew Emma aside to whisper to her.

Bugger. Maybe the Blissky hadn't been such a great idea after all. It had loosened his mouth too much. Now everyone would know about his sad love life.

He turned to look at the dance floor. The band was playing a slow tune, and couples were swaying with their arms around each other. Bloody hell. Would the night never end? He took a long swig of Blissky.

"Robby, my lad." Angus strode up to him and slapped him on the back.

He stumbled forward and caught himself on the table. He looked to his left and saw Emma eyeing him with a frown. He looked to his right and found Angus scowling at him. He checked the left again, but the room swirled, so he widened his stance to keep from swaying. Emma's frown deepened.

He sighed. "Och, to what do I owe the pleasure of yer cheerful companionship?"

Emma yanked the Blissky bottle out of his hand. "Shanna told me you were getting drunk."

"She's wrong," Robby said. "I'm already drunk. I'm feeling a verra nice buzz right here." He attempted to tap his temple with a finger, but missed and hit himself on the nose. "I'm no' on duty tonight, so it shouldna fash you."

Angus's scowl softened. "I'm no' vexed with you. I'm worried about you."

Emma touched his shoulder. "Do you need to talk about it?"

"Nay."

"What's her name?" Emma pressed.

"What's the latest news on Casimir?" Robby asked, attempting to change the topic.

Angus took the bait. "We have a lead that he's hiding in Bulgaria. Zoltan and Mikhail are checking it out."

"Why is it taking so long?" Robby asked. "Casimir and his followers like to kill after feeding. Ye should be able to track them down by following the trail of dead bodies."

"Aye, normally that would work," Angus agreed. "But apparently he's hiding alone right now. He doesna trust anyone. And we believe he's cut back on the killing in order to stay hidden."

"Must be hard on the bastard," Robby muttered.

"Right now, we're more concerned about you, lad," Angus said.

"Is there anything we can do?" Emma asked.

"Ye can give me the bottle back." Robby reached for it.

Emma plunked it on the table. "What's her name?"

"Olivia." Robby grabbed the bottle. He started to drink,

but set the bottle down. The thrill was gone, and the pain was still there. "I'll be all right. Go, dance, have fun."

"We'll be in New York through Christmas if ye need us," Angus said.

Emma patted him on the shoulder. "Merry Christmas, Robby. May all your dreams come true."

"Merry Christmas." He watched them wander off to the dance floor.

May all your dreams come true. His dream would be Olivia calling on his phone. Nay, Olivia lying in his bed. He might as well dream big. Her hair would be loose, and the black curls would fan out across his pillow. Her arms would reach for him, her legs would wrap around him, and he would plunge inside—

"What's so funny, bro?"

Robby was ripped back to the present. "Funny?" He glared at Phineas.

"Yeah, you were standing there with a big grin on your face." Phineas yanked a bottle of Blissky from a tub of ice. "Don't tell me. You were thinking about a woman."

Robby groaned. "Is it that obvious?"

"Only to me, bro. I'm supersensitized to all matters involving love and the fairer sex." Phineas shoved his bottle into the microwave. "And Carlos mentioned in passing that you're lovesick over a hot babe."

"That damned cat."

"Chillax, bro. This is your lucky night. The Love Doctor is in the house and at your service. Feel free to partake of my expertise by directing all your romantic queries in my general direction."

Robby snorted, then thought, Why not? "She dinna call."

"You asked her to call you?" When Robby nodded, Phineas continued, "How many times?"

"Once. I wrote her a note."

Phineas scoffed. "*Once?* Dude, you're barely getting started. After you've asked about twenty times, then you can get worried."

"Twenty times? That wouldna be a wee bit like stalking?"

Phineas shrugged. "Take my situation. I'm madly in love with LaToya Lafayette. I know she's the one for me."

"But is she no' the one who tried to poison you with hot sauce?"

"A minor speed bump on the road to love, bro." Phineas removed his bottle from the microwave. "You can't expect true love to be easy. Afterward, she said she was sorry and that she didn't mean for it to hurt that bad. So you see, she really does care."

"So she's going out with you now?" Robby asked.

"Well, no. All of a sudden, she moved back to New Orleans."

"That sounds like a no."

"Dude, that sounds like a challenge. Only wimps give up." Phineas gulped down some Blissky. "So guess where I'm going for Christmas?"

"New Orleans?"

"You got it. I'm gonna surprise LaToya." Phineas took another swallow of Blissky. "Hot damn. It's gonna be good!"

Robby had his doubts that LaToya would ever accept Phineas. Still, the Love Doctor was making a valid point. True love was worth fighting for.

One note wasn't enough. Robby had sent the package to Kansas City, but Olivia could still be in Houston. "She might no' have received the note."

"Right. It could have ended up in Timbuktu." Phineas held up his bottle of Blissky. "You see this, bro. You gotta say the bottle is half full. You gotta believe there's hope."

Robby nodded. He needed to trust Olivia, trust that she'd come through for him. "Ye're right. I'm going to write her again. I love her. I willna give up."

"That's the ticket!" Phineas grinned. "All in a day's work for the Love Doctor."

Chapter Twelve

*O*livia was glad when the holiday season was over. The added stress seemed to be the tipping point for a lot of people. She and her colleagues at the Bureau had been busy nonstop with murders and abductions, usually committed by a so-called loved one. At least her loved ones were no longer angry with her. She'd spent Christmas with them in Houston, and no apples had arrived.

It was a bitterly cold Tuesday morning toward the end of January when things finally settled down from a frantic pace to the normal hectic one. She draped her coat and scarf on the back of her chair, then opened the bottom drawer of her desk to drop her handbag inside. The letters were still there, a constant reminder of the pain and confusion she felt toward Robby.

He was mailing her a letter every week, and she didn't know what to make of it. She sat at her desk and placed the three envelopes in front of her. They all had the same return address in the corner, a place called Romatech Industries in White Plains, New York. Should she write back? And say what? *Leave me alone. Don't leave me alone.*

She smoothed her fingers over her name, written by his hand. She still missed him something awful. The pain of his betrayal had still been too strong when she 'd received a second letter. She'd thrown it in the trash.

When the third letter arrived, it made her wonder. Would a guilty man continue to write? Maybe. Otis was guilty as hell, and he loved to interact with her. A part of her, deep down in her gut, rebelled against the idea that Robby could ever be like Otis. Robby was noble and brave. He'd risked his life to save her from the panther.

But she was afraid to trust her instincts. Blind faith could get a girl killed. All of Otis's victims had believed in him before learning he was a sadistic murderer.

She'd dropped the third letter in her bottom drawer un-opened. Since then, two more weeks had passed and two more letters had arrived. Chicken, she chided herself. *Why don't you open them?*

Because they could be full of lies. They could be full of emotional pleas that would tear at her heart. She dropped the letters back into the drawer and shut it. If she opened them, she'd be opening herself up to the possibility of get-ting hurt all over again. She had to keep her emotions out of this, because where Robby was concerned, she was an emotional wreck.

Her heart ached for him, but her logical mind warned her to be cautious. She'd known him less than a week and she'd been unable to read his feelings or gauge his sincerity. She simply couldn't trust him or her feelings toward him. And her penchant for overanalyzing everything was driving her crazy. What she needed was cold hard facts. Facts she could trust.

Three weeks earlier, after the third letter had arrived and her doubts had bubbled to the surface, she'd initiated an investigation of Robby MacKay. The website for MacKay Security & Investigation was surprisingly bare, offering nothing more than an address in London and Edinburgh and a contact button to e-mail them for information. She hadn't e-mailed 'cause she didn't want to alert the company that she was snooping about.

Things had been so hectic at the office, she'd resorted to coming in an hour early every day to squeeze in time for her investigation. Three weeks of research, and she still had zilch. There were hundreds of Robert MacKays, scattered all over the planet.

She'd started with the three Robert Alexander MacKays she'd found in Scotland. One was a sixty-four-year-old physician in Aberdeen, one was a thirty-five-year-old fisherman on the Isle of Mull, and the last one was an eight-year-old student in Glasgow. Dead end.

She recalled that he'd mentioned owning property in Scotland, but her search there hit another dead end.

The simpler name of Robert MacKay yielded a much longer list of names, but none of those panned out. She broadened the search to the entire British Isles, but still no luck. She discovered an interesting article about an investigator named Robert MacKay who had captured a notorious serial killer in London, but that had happened in 1921. Another dead end.

She thought she might have found a reference to Robby's grandfather. A medal of valor and knighthood had been awarded to an Angus Alexander MacKay at the end of

World War II. No mention of him again. Another dead end.

She booted up her computer and examined the notes on her legal pad. There were numerous Robert MacKays in Australia and New Zealand, a few in South America and South Africa, and many more in Canada. Since the return address on the envelopes had cited New York, she was now investigating possibilities in America.

"How's the Great Robby Hunt going?"

She glanced up to see J.L. Wang leaning his forearms on the top of her cubicle wall. She'd told him several weeks ago that she suspected a guy she'd met on Patmos to be in league with Otis. Since then, J.L. had kept up with her research, calling it the Great Robby Hunt.

She sighed. "One hundred and twenty-four down and about three trillion to go."

"Could be worse," J.L. muttered his favorite phrase. "He could have been named John Smith."

She groaned with frustration. "I've been at this for three weeks. I've never seen anyone so hard to trace."

"Too bad your guy doesn't have a more distinctive name, something like . . . Willoughby Gallsplat."

Olivia snorted. "Yesterday, I located a twenty-seven-year-old Robert Alexander MacKay in Kentucky. An ex-soldier, awarded the Purple Heart."

"Sounds good."

"Yeah, he sounds like a great guy. He's a star player on the local wheelchair basketball team."

"Oops. I gather your Robby had legs?"

"Yes." And a wonderful chest. Broad shoulders. Handsome face. Soft auburn hair. Lovely green eyes.

"Did he have a fully functional brain?"

She shot J.L. an annoyed look. "Yes."

"I'm just saying it would take a moron to let someone like you get away."

"Well, that's kind of you, but I'm getting worried about all the dead ends I keep running into. It's not normal." She frowned at her notes. What if he'd lied about his name? What if he'd lied about everything?

"Yeah, this is weird." J.L. drummed his fingers on the partition. "With all the information we have at our disposal, you should be able to trace him. A person would have to purposely work at not showing up anywhere."

She swallowed hard. What kind of person had no past? In this day and age, it was virtually impossible to erase every trace of yourself. "Do you think he's into covert operations?"

"Maybe. Or maybe he gave you a false name." J.L. held up a hand. "I take that back. You would have caught him if he'd lied."

She winced. "That's the problem. I couldn't read him. My grandmother couldn't, either, and that's never happened before."

"Never? Shit. He could have been lying about a lot of things. Maybe he's had special training in deception."

Her chest tightened. "Then you think he's the one helping Otis to harass me?"

J.L. regarded her sadly. "I think we need to get to the bottom of this. I can't sense emotions like you, but even I can tell this is causing you a lot of pain."

She inhaled a shaky breath. "I need to know the truth." She needed to know if Robby had been sincere. He'd said he was falling in love with her. He'd made love to her so sweetly. It had to have been real. It was just too awful to think otherwise.

"You want him to be innocent, don't you?" J.L. whispered.

She nodded. Tears gathered in her eyes, and she blinked them away.

"Okay, let's assume he is innocent. If he didn't send the apples—"

"Then someone else did," Olivia finished his sentence.

"Who knew you were going to Patmos?" J.L. asked.

"My family. You."

He affected a shocked look. "I'm innocent, I swear. I've been a good boy my entire life."

She scoffed. "I'm detecting a little deception."

"Shit. I knew I shouldn't have robbed that bank."

She grinned. J.L., bless him, always had a way of cheering her up.

"And I shouldn't have kicked Mickey Mouse in the balls at Disney World."

She sat back. "You're telling the truth now."

"Damn, you're good."

"Why did you kick Mickey?"

J.L. shrugged. "I was only three years old. Imagine the horror of meeting a smiling rodent that's bigger than you. Besides, I think he wanted my ice cream."

She laughed.

"Who else knew where you were going?" J.L. asked.

"A few people around here." Her smile faded, and she exchanged a worried look with him.

J.L. glanced over his shoulder, then lowered his voice. "What did Barker tell you?"

"He agreed that Otis could have an accomplice, but he ordered me to stay out of it. He told Harrison to look into it." She rose to her feet. "I'll see if he's done."

They walked over to Harrison's work area. In most ways, Frank Harrison appeared completely normal: average height, average weight, brown hair, hazel eyes. Olivia tended to agree with J.L's assessment. Harrison acted like a jerk so he would stand out from the crowd.

"Have you got a moment, Harrison?" she asked.

He slanted an annoyed look her direction, then went back to studying his monitor. "I'm busy. In case you didn't know, the Morehouse case is still open."

Olivia nodded. Tyson Morehouse was a postal worker suspected of embezzlement. He claimed to know nothing about the missing money, but Olivia had interviewed him the day before and knew better.

"He was lying," she said. "It was in my report."

Harrison snorted. "Like we needed your input. We already figured the guy's guilty. Saunders is trailing him while I trace all his bank accounts." He glanced at Olivia. "Why don't you save us some time and use your weird-assed powers to locate the missing money?"

"I'm not a psychic, Harrison."

"Oh. Too bad." He went back to studying the monitor. "I thought all that paranormal crap was the same."

Olivia sensed anger about to boil over from J.L., so she gave him a warning look.

He gritted his teeth. "Look, Harrison, we were wondering if you'd checked on the Otis Crump situation."

"Another waste of my time," Harrison muttered as he scribbled some notes. "I went to Leavenworth last Friday and talked to the warden. He had a guard check the log-in book. The only visitors Crump has had in the last eight months is me and you, Sotiris."

"And his mail?" she asked.

"It's all checked, coming in and going out. Nothing about apples." Harrison glanced at her, and she could feel his growing irritation. "You've got the wrong guy. Someone else is messing with you."

She frowned. Apples would have significance only to Otis. Or someone else who knew all the details about his case. Maybe an admirer? Some sick person who had studied Otis and wanted to harass the criminal's enemies out of a twisted sense of loyalty? "I need a list of everyone who's communicated with him."

A spurt of anger rolled off Harrison, and he glared at her. "Forget it, Sotiris. The case is over."

"It's not over as long as Otis keeps sending me apples."

"So you're getting some fruit," Harrison growled. "So what? If you can't take the heat, get out of the fucking kitchen."

"Hey," J.L. protested. "Don't talk to her like that."

"It's none of your business, Jail," Harrison replied, using his nickname for J.L.

"Hold it, you two." Olivia raised her hands. She returned Harrison's glare. "I'm not calling the case closed, because you didn't do a thorough job. Since you can't be bothered, I'll do it myself."

Harrison made a sound of disgust. "You're freaking obsessed with the guy. You two deserve each other."

J.L. muttered something rather nasty-sounding in Chinese, but Olivia hushed him with a slight shake of her head. She focused on Harrison. "How many times have you seen Crump?"

Harrison turned back to his monitor. "Just a few times. I hate seeing that asshole."

"When did you see him last?"

"I don't remember."

She stiffened.

"Now buzz off and let me get back to work," Harrison grated through clenched teeth.

Olivia opened her mouth, but J.L. grabbed her arm and hauled her away.

"Come on, Sotiris, you heard the man," J.L. said loudly as he dragged her across the room. "Let him work."

"I wasn't done," she whispered. "He—"

"Shh." J.L. shot her a warning look and whispered back, "We need to activate the cone of silence."

"We don't have a cone of silence."

"We'll improvise." He glanced around the open work area. "Go to Yasmine's office. She's out today. I'll meet you in five minutes."

"Fine." Olivia headed right, while J.L. veered left toward the hallway.

She slipped inside Yasmine's office and turned on the light. The supply closet was attached, so she could always claim she was getting paper clips or staples if anyone asked what she was doing there.

She paced across the office, her heart racing as the severity of her new suspicions hit home. Why would Harrison lie about meeting Otis? What was he hiding? It seemed too far-fetched, too awful to imagine a special agent helping a criminal to harass her. But there was no mistaking the truth. Harrison had lied. And he'd tried to convince her that Otis wasn't the one responsible for sending her apples. She knew that wasn't true.

She continued to pace, her thoughts growing increasingly alarmed. She spotted the sweater she'd give Yasmine, neatly folded on a shelf. Thank God Yasmine had never told anyone about her meltdown in the restroom. She wondered where the office manager was, and stopped by her desk to check her calendar. A doctor's appointment.

The door opened, and J.L. strode inside with a bag of chips from the hallway vending machine. He locked the door. "Okay, let's talk."

"Harrison was lying," she whispered.

"I know. Whenever you hear a lie, you get all stiff and prickly looking."

She stiffened. "I do?"

"Yeah, just like that." He opened the chips and the smell of nacho cheese filled the room. "So we're thinking the same thing? Harrison's the one sending you apples?"

She winced. "It's a terrible accusation to make. We can't assume he's guilty just because we don't like him."

"Okay, emotions aside, let's look at the facts." J.L. removed a chip from the bag. "He lied to you. He knew where you were vacationing. He's had opportunity—that's contact with Otis. And he has motivation." He popped the chip into his mouth.

"What motivation? I know he doesn't like me—"

"It could be more. You're the one who took Otis's latest confessions. They might be trying to make you look unstable so no one will believe you." J.L. offered her a chip.

She shook her head and paced across the room. "Otis was already convicted before he met me. I don't think making me look crazy will help his appeal."

J.L. bit into another chip. "What would help his appeal?"

"He would have to appear innocent." She halted in midstep. "He could swear that an accomplice did the murders."

J.L. winced. "And you've been insisting that he has an accomplice."

"Because of the apples, yes. But if he can convince everyone there was an accomplice during the murders . . ." Olivia groaned. "He's playing me. The bastard's using me."

"It looks that way." J.L. stuffed another chip into this mouth. "We need to be careful about this."

"We need proof." Olivia pressed a hand to her stomach. Just the idea that a federal agent could ally himself with a serial killer—it was a nauseating thought.

"I'll check on Harrison," J.L. offered. "Don't worry. I'll be discreet."

Olivia nodded. "I'll step up my investigation on Robby." She would contact MacKay S&I. If Robby MacKay was secretly sending the apples, she'd uncover it. She'd prove his innocence.

And then she'd be free to love him.

Chapter Thirteen

I don't know why *you* have to take me," Constantine grumbled.

Robby didn't know, either. Usually, Roman took his son, but for some reason he was unavailable tonight. Connor, too. Shanna had called Robby to the waiting room of her dental office at Romatech and informed him that Tino needed help getting to school. Then she'd hurried off to an examination room, leaving him alone with Tino.

It had to be a conspiracy of some sort. Robby smiled to himself when he pictured Olivia calling him paranoid.

Constantine puffed out his wee chest. "I could teleport myself."

"'Tis a long way to the school." Robby wasn't sure of its exact location since that was a heavily guarded secret, but he knew it had to be several hundred miles from Romatech. "'Twould be verra dangerous if ye got lost on the way."

Tino's bottom lip jutted out. "I wish everyone would stop

treating me like a baby. Sofia's the baby. I'm almost three."

"Och. 'Tis a wonder ye havena cut yerself shaving." Robby opened his cell phone and punched in the number Shanna had given him.

"Dragon Nest Academy," a female voice answered.

She sounded vaguely familiar, but Robby dismissed that thought since he'd never been to the school before. "Just a minute." He covered the phone with his hand and gave Tino a questioning look. "Dragon Nest? Is that the right place?"

Tino nodded. "Mom named it that because our last name is Draganesti." He hung his head and kicked at a chair leg. "But there aren't any dragons there."

"What a shame." Robby uncovered the phone. "Could ye keep talking a wee bit? I need yer voice to know where to teleport to."

"Sure. Are you bringing a student with you?"

"Aye. Constantine." Robby scooped the boy up in his arms. "Keep talking." He would use the woman's voice as a beacon to ensure he arrived at the right place. After this, the location of the school would be embedded in his psychic memory, and he'd no longer need a beacon.

"Okay," the woman said. "I'm Constantine's teacher. I know he may seem a little young for kindergarten, but he's doing very well. I only have three students in the class, so they get a lot of individual attention."

Robby materialized in a classroom with two short round tables encircled with little chairs. The shelves along the walls were neatly stacked with supplies. A little girl with long black hair sat at one of the tables, coloring a picture of a ball with the word written underneath. With a quick sniff, Robby could tell she was a shifter. Or she would be once puberty set in. He figured she was one of Carlos's orphans from Brazil. A were-panther.

Tino squirmed out of his arms and ran to the table to take a seat. "Hi, Coco."

The little girl grinned at him. "Hi, Tino."

Robby closed his cell phone and dropped it into his sporran.

"Thank you for bringing Tino." A pretty young woman with reddish-blond hair approached him with a shy smile.

Bugger. His conspiracy theory had been correct. Shanna was playing matchmaker. His eyes narrowed. He'd met this woman before. He thought back. "Wolf Ridge?"

Her smile widened. "You remember! I'm Sarah. Sarah Anderson." She extended a hand.

"Robby MacKay." He shook her hand. "How are you?" The last time he'd met this woman, he'd used vampire mind control to help her regain some painful memories. She'd been one of the imprisoned girls at Apollo's compound, and he'd helped Jack and Lara rescue them.

"I'm okay." She nodded her head slowly. "I love my job here. And I love the children."

"That's good." Robby shifted his weight. Apparently, Shanna thought he'd hit it off with this mortal lass.

"I'll be so happy when you guys finally defeat Casimir," Sarah added.

"Aye, 'twill be a good day." Robby knew this lass had good reason to hate Casimir. The bastard had used vampire mind control to subdue her and rape her.

Sarah stepped closer and lowered her voice. "Shanna told me what he did to you. I'm so sorry."

He nodded. Shanna must have figured he'd be attracted to Sarah since they'd both suffered under the hands of Casimir. They did have that in common, but it seemed like a miserably sad basis for a relationship. And the torture wasn't something he wanted to be reminded of anymore. Olivia had shown him there was more. She'd brought joy and laughter back into his life.

"Hey, Sarah! Everything okay?" A young man rushed into the classroom. From the alarmed look on his face, Robby guessed the young woman already had a serious admirer.

"Oh, hi, Teddy." Sarah gave him a reassuring smile. "Everything's fine. This is Robby MacKay. He brought Tino to school."

"I could have brought myself," Tino grumbled.

"I'm Teddy Brockman." The young man shook hands with Robby. "The headmaster of Dragon Nest Academy."

"Teddy's very supportive," Sarah explained. "He comes by every night to make sure I have everything I need."

Robby nodded. "I'm sure he does." He gave the young male mortal a pointed look. "Good luck to you."

Teddy's eyes shifted to Sarah, then back to Robby. "Thanks."

A form wavered, then materialized. It was Jean-Luc Echarpe, holding his stepdaughter Bethany in his arms. He set her down, and she skipped over to the table to greet her classmates.

"I need to get started now," Sarah announced. She glanced at Robby with a smile. "It was nice to see you again."

"I'll see you guys later." Teddy waved at Robby and Jean-Luc and rushed out the door.

Jean-Luc greeted Robby with a slap on the shoulder. "*Mon ami*, stay for a while. I'm teaching a fencing class in thirty minutes. You can help me warm up."

"Verra well." Robby accompanied the Frenchman into the hallway. "I could use some practice."

Robby had been Jean-Luc's bodyguard for years, first

in Paris, and then in Texas. A few years ago he'd helped Jean-Luc defeat his archenemy, Lui. Since then, the job had become too routine and boring for Robby's taste, so he'd requested a transfer.

Jean-Luc was a master swordsman, and he could usually take care of himself, so Dougal Kincaid had been given the job as his new bodyguard. Dougal had lost his right hand in a battle in New Orleans.

"How is Dougal?" Robby asked.

"He's doing well. He's learning to fence left-handed." Jean-Luc led Robby to a wide staircase with ornately carved wooden balusters.

As far as Robby could tell, the school was housed in an old mansion. The wooden steps creaked under their feet. "I heard ye and Heather are having twins."

Jean-Luc laughed. *"C'est incroyable, non?* Me, a father?"

Robby shrugged one shoulder. "I think ye'll be a great father. Ye're certainly verra good with Bethany."

"Merci, mon ami." Jean-Luc paused when they reached the landing. "So when is Jack's wedding?"

"April." Robby grimaced. "I'm the best man."

Jean-Luc's eyes twinkled with amusement. "You don't look very happy about it."

Robby stifled a groan. "It just seems like everyone is getting married." *Everyone but me.*

Jean-Luc nodded and headed down the stairs. "There's a rumor going about that you're lovesick."

"Bugger. People should mind their own business."

Jean-Luc smiled. "We're not people, *mon ami.* We're family."

They reached the bottom of the stairs. The ground floor, Robby guessed. The foyer was grand, with a black and white marble floor laid out in checkerboard fashion. A huge wrought-iron chandelier hung from the ceiling three stories up. The front entrance consisted of two heavily carved wooden doors with a Gothic arch.

"'Tis verra fancy," Robby murmured.

"Oui." Jean-Luc motioned toward a hall to the right. "The gymnasium is outside. It was the old coach house."

They headed down the hall. A door opened and two women emerged. The first one's purple hair made her instantly recognizable. Vanda Barkowski.

Robby jerked to a halt when he saw the second woman. A cold chill sifted along his skin. He reached over his shoulder for his claymore, but he'd neglected to bring it.

She stopped, her eyes widening. "Robby," she whispered. "You're all right?"

No thanks to you. Anger erupted inside him. "What the hell is she doing here?"

The woman flinched.

Vanda stiffened. "Where do you get off, talking to my sister like that?"

Robby clenched his fists. He'd never hit a woman before, not even his wife when she'd betrayed him, but Marta Barkowski deserved it. "What is she doing here?"

"We live here," Vanda snapped. "I'm the art teacher, and Marta's working as Teddy's secretary."

"Angus must be out of his mind!" Robby yelled. He fumbled in his sporran for his cell phone.

Jean-Luc touched his arm. "Calm down, *mon ami.*"

"This is a serious breach of security," Robby growled. "That woman canna be trusted."

"I'm not a Malcontent anymore!" Marta shouted with a thick accent. Her eyes glistened with tears.

"You're upsetting her." Vanda glared at Robby.

He glared back. "Has she ever told you how she assisted in my torture?"

"Please!" Tears rolled down Marta's face. "I'm so sorry, Robby. I didn't want to do it."

"Ye were smiling!" Robby shouted, raising a fist. His hand shook as he struggled for control.

"She was brainwashed and abused," Vanda explained. "She's a victim as much as you."

Jean-Luc pulled Robby back. "You two go on."

Vanda and Marta rushed toward the stairs, Vanda looping an arm around her crying sister.

Robby glared at them, his fists still clenched, his breath hissing through gritted teeth.

"You probably set Marta back a few months in her recovery," Jean-Luc murmured.

"Ye think I care? The woman is a Malcontent. She canna be trusted."

Jean-Luc sighed. "She's trying to start over and lead a good life."

"She doesna deserve it," Robby grumbled.

"Everyone deserves a second chance."

Robby turned and stalked down the hallway. He'd tried for months to forget the details of his torture, but seeing Marta brought it all back. Casimir had left her alone with him to touch him and get him physically aroused, just to make Casimir's whipping more painful. More humiliating. "She shouldna be here. No' with the children. She canna be trusted."

"Robby." Jean-Luc grabbed his shoulder to stop him. "I know you suffered. But you need to give her a chance."

"Nay," he hissed. "She'll betray us."

"Not all women are like your wife," Jean-Luc whispered.

Robby stiffened. In the years that he'd worked as Jean-Luc's bodyguard, they'd become good friends. Robby had confided a great deal about his past. About his wife.

He'd tried to return to her after Culloden, but Mavis had rejected him in horror. He'd stayed nearby, hiding in a cave during the day and working the farm at night. He hadn't known what she was doing during the day until it was too late. She took up with the enemy, took an English soldier as her lover, one of the same English that had killed him and his friends on the battlefield.

Robby had been forced to leave when the Englishman swore to find him during the day and kill him. He'd tried to keep in touch with his daughter over the years. She'd grown up, treated like a servant until she ran away at the age of fifteen to marry a local boy. Then they'd taken a ship to America, and he never knew what had happened to her.

Robby took a deep breath and let it out slowly. "'Tis difficult to trust women. They can rip yer heart in two."

"I know." Jean-Luc opened the door at the end of the hall, and an icy breeze swept inside. The courtyard outside was dark, with snow piled around the perimeter. "Come. You can work off your anger with some swordplay."

Robby stepped outside onto the brick pavement, and icy cold air stung his face. His breath vaporized as he exhaled. He followed Jean-Luc toward the gymnasium. He didn't feel angry anymore. He just felt weary and tired. And so alone. *Olivia, why do ye no' call me?* If it were possible for a woman to be loyal and true, it would be her. He wanted it to be her.

The cell phone in his sporran rang, and he halted with a jerk. Was it her? He reached in the sporran, grabbed the phone and opened it. "Hello?"

"Robby, I'm calling from London." Emma MacKay spoke

briskly. "Something came up that I thought you should know about."

"You have a lead on Casimir?" Robby asked.

"No, an e-mail came through the MacKay S and I website. Someone from the FBI is requesting information about you."

His chest tightened. "Who?"

"It was signed O. Sotiris."

His heart lurched. "'Tis Olivia."

"The woman you met on Patmos?" Emma asked.

"Aye." Robby grinned. If she was investigating him, then she hadn't given up on him.

"Shall I send her some information?" Emma asked. "I could make you sound really good."

"I'll take care of it. Forward the request to me at Romatech."

Emma chuckled. "All right. Good luck." She rang off.

Robby snapped his phone shut, still grinning.

"Let me guess." Jean-Luc smiled. "You need to return to Romatech right away."

"Aye, I do."

Jean-Luc slapped him on the shoulder. "Go get her, *mon ami.*"

Chapter Fourteen

Robby sat at the desk in the security office at Romatech, frowning at his MacKay S&I file on the computer screen. What information should he send to Olivia? He could disclose some of his recent activities, but most of his personnel file was off limits.

Birth: October 21, 1719. Scotland.

Death: April 16, 1746. Culloden, Scotland.

Transformation: Sired by Angus MacKay.

There was no way around it. He'd have to send Olivia a pack of lies.

Phineas McKinney lounged in a chair, watching the wall of security monitors. "I'm bored." He propped his feet up on another chair. "At least I have something to do tonight. I'm supposed to meet Stan the Snitch in twenty minutes. You want to tag along?"

"Nay, I'm busy." Robby began typing his response to Olivia, using the generic MacKay S&I e-mail address.

"Are you kidding?" Phineas asked. "I thought you hated Stan. You could threaten him with bodily harm and watch him squirm. It'll be fun, bro."

Robby shrugged one shoulder. " 'Tis Casimir I really want to kill. Stan is more useful as an informant." He glanced up. "Have ye learned anything from him?"

"No. The Russians in Brooklyn don't know squat. Stan and I usually have a few Bleers while he gripes about how crazy their leader Nadia is." Phineas yawned. "He's an okay dude once you get to know him."

The door opened and Connor strode inside. "How's it going?"

"Boring," Phineas muttered. "Casimir needs to get his act together, so we can kick some ass again."

Connor arched a brow. "When is the last time ye practiced yer fencing? If ye want to kick ass, ye need to stay prepared."

"You want to rumble, Scotty?" Phineas sat up. "I'll take you on. Name the time and place of your humiliating defeat."

Connor's mouth twitched. "Three A.M., the back garden, claymores. The practice ones, of course. I doona wish to do ye permanent harm."

Phineas smirked. "Bring it on, dude. I've been practicing with Jack."

Connor shrugged. "I can beat Jack with one hand tied behind my back."

"Ha!" Phineas scoffed. "I heard Jack cut your little pony-tail off with his foil."

Connor chuckled, then turned to Robby. "How about you? Ye want to fight the winner? Which would be me, of course."

Phineas snorted.

"I'm busy." Robby frowned at the monitor.

"He's romancing a hot babe," Phineas whispered loudly.

"Piss off," Robby muttered.

Connor's eyes narrowed. "Are ye serious? Ye're no' involved with a mortal, are ye?"

"None of yer business." Robby typed a few more words, then changed his mind and deleted them.

"It *is* our business if ye intend to tell her our secrets," Connor grumbled.

Robby glanced at him. "Maybe ye enjoy being alone for yer entire miserable existence, but I'd like to find someone to share my life with."

Connor groaned. "Another hopeless romantic. And for yer information, I doona consider myself miserable."

Phineas snorted. "Show of hands. Who thinks Connor's a miserable old gasbag?" He waved his hand in the air while giving Robby a pointed look.

Robby smiled and lifted his hand.

Connor rolled his eyes. "I could insult ye both now, but I'll just wait till I have ye pinned to the ground, begging for mercy."

"We'll see who does the begging, bro," Phineas said.

Robby drummed his fingers on the desk. He didn't know what age he should claim. "How old would ye say I look?"

"I'd say . . . thirty-three." Phineas winced when Robby made a face. "I meant thirty. Not a day over thirty."

"How old were ye when Angus changed you?" Connor asked.

"I was twenty-seven." Robby gave Phineas an annoyed look. "Life was tougher back then. Everyone aged faster."

"Just make up a number, bro. How would she ever know the truth?"

Robby groaned inwardly. Sooner or later he would have to tell her the truth. "I'll say I'm twenty-nine." It sounded better than thirty, and he wouldn't appear too much older than Olivia.

Phineas rose to his feet and stretched. "Well, I've got to grab a few Bleers and meet Stan."

"I'll go with you," Connor offered.

The two Vamps strode from the office. Peace, at last. Robby went to work, finishing his message to Olivia.

Olivia arrived at work an hour early so she could continue her extracurricular research. She was still scouring the Internet, looking for any reference to Robert Alexander MacKay. The day before, she'd e-mailed MacKay S&I for information. All day long she'd checked her e-mail, anxious for a response. Nothing.

She'd called the warden at Leavenworth, and he agreed to send her a list of everyone who'd had contact with Otis Crump. The fax arrived in the afternoon, and she and J.L. had examined the list. The only people who had visited Otis were Harrison and herself. A number of people had mailed letters to him: his mother, his brother, and a few female admirers. The mother lived over a hundred miles away in Missouri. J.L. offered to go with her the next weekend to interview the woman. All Olivia needed to do was ask the lady if she was sending her apples. She would instantly know whether the mother was telling the truth.

Olivia downloaded her e-mail while she stashed her handbag in the drawer. Her breath caught when she saw the response from MacKay S&I. She clicked on it.

Dear O. Sotiris,

Thank you for contacting us. MacKay S&I is a premier investigative firm and provider of security for select clients worldwide. Founded in 1927, its headquarters are located in London and Edinburgh.

Robert Alexander MacKay is one of our most valued employees. He's an expert in firearms, martial arts, and fencing. He has recently served as head of security for Jean-Luc Echarpe, and is currently providing security for Romatech Industries in White Plains, New York. Age: 29. Height: 6'2". Weight: 220.

We would be hard pressed to find anyone as trustworthy as Robert MacKay.

Olivia sat back and read the last line again. It seemed almost identical to something Robby had told her on Patmos. She checked the e-mail address: *info@mackays&i.com.*

She read the entire message again. It was a favorable report where Robby was concerned, but she couldn't shake the feeling that he'd written the last line himself. In fact, he could have written the whole damned thing.

His grandfather owned the organization. He could have passed her request straight to Robby. She gritted her teeth. Dammit. Now she felt like a fool. Did he really think she wouldn't figure this out?

She hit Reply, then typed a message. With a grim smile, she hit Send. *Take that, Robby.*

All day long she checked for a response. Nothing.

By the time she left work that evening, she was beginning to doubt her initial conclusion. If Robby was behind this, he would have responded by now.

Robby woke that evening in his small room in Romatech's basement. One whole wing of the complex's basement had recently been transformed into guest rooms for the Undead. He quickly dressed, grabbed a bottle of synthetic blood

from his minifridge, and dashed up to the MacKay security office. While his e-mail downloaded, he drank from
the bottle.

He smiled when an e-mail from O. Sotiris appeared. He
clicked on it, and his smile faded.

> *We regret to inform you that we may have wasted your time.
> The Robert MacKay we're looking for doesn't quite match up
> to your specifications. We believe he is older and quite a bit
> heftier than the one you mentioned.*

"What?" He didn't look older than twenty-nine. And he
sure as hell wasn't fat. He punched Reply.

> *Robert MacKay is in peak physical condition!*

He clicked on Send, then winced. What if Olivia had figured out that he'd sent the original message? She could have
laid a trap, and like a fool, he'd jumped right into it.

He finished his bottle, glaring at the screen. She'd probably left work for the day. He'd have to wait till tomorrow
night for her response.

"Damn it to hell." Sometimes being a vampire was a
bloody nuisance.

The next evening he dashed upstairs to check his e-mail.
Sure enough, she'd responded that morning.

> *We at the FBI are willing to concede that Robert MacKay is in
> excellent physical condition. However, we are experiencing
> some major concerns regarding his mental faculties. He may
> not be the brightest lightbulb in the pack.*

"What?" Robby slammed his bottle of synthetic blood on the desk. He hit Reply.

I'm smart enough to know when you're toying with me, you saucy wench!

He hit Send. "Take that, Olivia."

The next evening, he rushed to the computer. She'd responded to his last message from a new e-mail address that looked like a personal one. That was a good sign. It was Friday night, so maybe she was planning to correspond with him from her home. Maybe he wouldn't have to wait so long for her reply.

He clicked on her response.

And I'm smart enough to know when I'm being punked! Admit who you are, Robby. This wench is too saucy for you.

He snorted. She'd known all along it was him. A grin tugged at his mouth. What a clever lass she was. It was a good thing she'd moved from her business address to her personal one. His grin widened. Their correspondence was about to get very personal.

In her tiny apartment in Kansas City, Olivia lounged on the love seat in her pajamas. A half-eaten bowl of soup rested on the coffee table in front of her, next to an open package of saltines, her notes, and her laptop. The television was on, tuned to a news channel with the volume turned down to a soft drone.

The three letters from Robby sat on the cushion next to her. She'd brought them home so she could open them in private. She spread the letters out and scolded herself for waiting so long to open them. There was nothing sinister inside. Robby had written that he missed her, and he'd given her his phone number. Simple and to the point. No flowery purple prose with claims of everlasting love. No threatening remarks that indicated an alliance with Otis.

All her instincts told her that Robby was innocent and could be trusted. Still, she'd feel a lot better if she could find the actual person who was helping Otis.

Hopefully, she would tomorrow. She dragged her computer into her lap and clicked on Maps. Then she checked her notes for the address of Otis's mother.

The town in Missouri came up, and she wrote down some quick notes. J.L. had offered to drive, and he was going to pick her up in the morning. His car was equipped with a GPS navigation system, plus every other modern gadget known to mankind, so the trip should go smoothly. Thanks to her lie-detecting skills, she would know instantly if the mother was telling the truth.

Olivia clicked on her e-mail, and her heart did its usual flip when she spotted a new message from the MacKay S&I e-mail address. She checked the time. Why did Robby e-mail only at night? She'd had a good laugh when he'd called her a saucy wench. It sounded so old-fashioned, but maybe it was normal speech for a Scotsman. With her heart racing, she opened his latest message.

> *Aye, this is Robby. I have tasted you, wench, and you weren't too saucy. I thought you were perfect.*

She gasped. *That . . . that . . .*

She clicked on Reply, typed *Pig!*, and hit Send. How dare he joke about their most intimate moment? Her cheeks blazed with heat. Memories flooded back of Robby kissing her all over and giving her the biggest orgasms of her life. Thank God she'd taken this conversation off her official FBI address.

A new message popped up. So fast. Her heart pounded. She grabbed her glass of ice water off the coffee table and gulped down a few swallows. Then she opened the message.

Good evening, sweetheart. I have missed you.

"Oh, Robby." Now he was making her heart melt. She sent a message back: *I missed you, too.*

Within a few seconds, a new message appeared. *May I have your phone number?*

Her mind raced. Was she ready to get involved with him again? She hadn't found the guilty party yet who was helping Otis, so she couldn't swear with one hundred percent certainty that Robby was innocent. And it was so strange that she couldn't find any trace of him over the Internet.

What did she know about him, really? He'd been the one to send the information from MacKay S&I. He could be telling her all sorts of lies, and she had no way of determining the truth.

But how could she get to know him better if she refused to talk to him? With trembling fingers, she typed her cell phone number and pressed Send.

She jumped when her phone rang. Don't be silly, she chided herself. *What did you think he'd do with the number?*

She set her laptop aside and strode to her handbag she'd left on the console by her front door. The phone rang again. She retrieved it from its pocket inside her handbag and opened it. "Hello?"

"Och, 'tis good to hear yer voice again."

She bit her lip to keep from moaning out loud. The soft lilt of his accent and the deep timbre of his voice made a lethal combination. Her knees actually wobbled as she headed back to the love seat.

"Olivia? Are ye there?"

She collapsed on the love seat. "Yes. I'm here." Her heart swelled with a flood of longing. God help her, she still loved this man.

Chapter Fifteen

Robby covered the phone with his hand and glowered at Phineas. "Go on with you."

Before dialing Olivia's phone number, Robby had told the young Vamp to do a security check of the grounds, but Phineas was loitering by the office door, grinning at him.

"You might need some assistance from the Love Doctor." Phineas motioned to himself. "I can provide the right words for romancing and entrancing your hot babe."

"I've got it covered," Robby whispered. "Go."

"Tell her she's sizzlin' hot. And bootie-licious."

"Piss off!"

"Excuse me?" Olivia asked on the phone.

"No' you," Robby told her, then made a face at Phineas as the young Vamp left the office, laughing. "My apologies. I needed to get rid of someone in the office, so we could have some privacy."

"You're at work?" she asked.

"Aye. I work at night."

"So that's why you e-mail only at night?"

"Aye."

"And you're working at Romatech Industries, the place that manufactures synthetic blood?"

"I work for MacKay S and I. My current assignment is Romatech." He frowned. This was not the fun, flirtatious conversation he'd hoped for. Why was she interrogating him?

"I read that two Romatechs were bombed last summer. Apparently, domestic terrorists were responsible?"

"Yes. Olivia, did ye receive yer jumper and the letters I sent?"

"You—you mean the sweater?"

"Aye."

She hesitated before mumbling, "Yes, I did. Thanks."

Something was wrong. Instead of her usual cheerful friendliness, she seemed a bit suspicious and guarded. "Ye left Patmos without warning. I was worried about you."

"I needed to take my grandmother to my father's house as quickly as possible. I was concerned for her safety."

"Because of the apples?"

She drew in a sharp breath. "How did you know about that? I didn't mention them in the note I left for you."

"Basic investigation. Ye told me about the bastard who's harassing you. I asked the woman at the taverna why ye'd left so suddenly, and she said something had frightened you. I asked her if ye'd received apples, and she said yes."

"Oh."

"I wish ye had stayed, Olivia. I'm an expert in security and investigation. I could have helped you."

"I—I'm used to taking care of myself. And I needed to get back here where I could check things out."

He gritted his teeth. Had it never occurred to her that

he would want to help? Didn't she understand how deeply he cared for her? "So have ye discovered who sent the apples?"

"No. But I hope to make some progress this weekend. J.L. and I are driving to Missouri to interview Otis Crump's mother."

Robby's grip on the phone tightened. "Who is J.L.?"

"J.L. Wang. A special agent from the office. He's helping me get to the bottom of this."

"He?"

"Yes. He's a good friend. Oh . . ." She paused. "Are you . . . jealous?"

"Nay." Robby winced. "Yes, dammit. I should be the one helping you." He was tempted to teleport straight to her, but that would only cause more problems at this point. "I thought ye understood how much I care for you."

"I—I want to believe it."

She didn't believe him? Damn, that hurt. He grabbed a pen and a pad of paper. "I *will* help you, Olivia. Tell me everything ye can about this Otis."

"I—don't worry about it. I've got it covered."

"Ye doona want my help?"

"I . . . appreciate the offer, but I'll take care of it."

He ground his teeth. Why would she reject him? She didn't mind accepting help from J.L. "What has happened, Olivia? Why can ye no' trust me?"

"I want to. I really do. But it's hard when I can't read you, and it seems foolish for me to go on blind faith."

He rose to his feet. There was nothing he hated worse than being considered untrustworthy. "Ye were happy on Patmos. Ye trusted me. What has changed?"

She hesitated, then made an exasperated, groaning sound. "The apples came. Whoever sent them knew where I was."

He tossed the pen onto the desk. "Fine. Who knew ye were on the island?"

"My family, a few people at the office."

"If yer family is as loyal and protective as yer grandmother, ye can safely rule them out. Is there anyone suspicious at yer office?"

"There is someone who lied to me. J.L. is checking him out."

J.L. again. Robby groaned inwardly. "What about this J.L.? Wang, was it? Could it be him?"

"Oh no. He's always been honest with me. I can read him easily."

And she couldn't read him because he was Undead. Robby kept a tight grip on his growing irritation. "So ye're going to check Otis's mother? How would she know ye were on Patmos?"

Olivia sighed. "I don't know. I'm clutching at straws now."

"There has to be another explanation." When she didn't respond, he knew she was holding back on him. "Tell me."

"I can't. It'll upset you. It upset me something awful."

"Tell me!"

She groaned. "My supervisor thought Otis might have hired a professional to follow me."

"With yer training, I think ye would have picked up on someone trailing you."

"Maybe," she whispered. "Unless he was so good at hiding in plain sight that he had me completely fooled."

The quivering sound of her voice sent a chill down Robby's neck. Had she met someone on Patmos who could have fooled her?

He stumbled back as if he'd been suddenly struck in the chest. Bloody hell. "Ye thought it was *me?*"

"Robby, think about it," she said quickly. "You're a professional. We knew each other less than a week—"

"We bared our souls to each other! How could ye—" He screamed inside his head. His heart twisted in his chest.

She thought he'd betrayed her? *Him?* He'd never betrayed anyone in his life. He dropped the phone on the desk and clenched his fists.

"Bloody hell!" He slammed a fist through the wall behind him.

Breathing heavily, he scowled at the gaping hole in the Sheetrock. He didn't usually lose control like that, but dammit, how could she suspect him? Was it always to be this way? Would no woman ever believe in him? Or stay loyal to him?

"Dammit!" He grabbed a napkin off the credenza where the day guards kept their coffee machine and pressed it against a cut and bloody knuckle.

"Robby? Robby, are you there?" Olivia called from the phone.

He groaned. No doubt the other MacKay employees would notice the hole. They would have fun tormenting him.

"Robby!"

He collapsed in the chair and picked up the receiver. "I'm here."

"Are you are okay?" Her voice trembled, and he wondered if she was crying. "I heard a terrible crash."

"I was . . . redecorating." He glanced at the hole. "I believe it's called an art niche."

"I heard you cursing. Are you all right?"

"Nay. I'm bloody well angry. I canna believe ye suspected me. I would never harm you."

"I was afraid it would upset you. That's why I didn't want

to tell you. I know how much it hurts. It nearly killed me when I first thought about it."

He tossed the bloody napkin in the litter bin. "Why would ye think of it at all?"

"My supervisor asked me if I'd met anyone on Patmos who could be a P.I. It made sense—"

"Nay! Olivia, I would never betray you. Ye must know how much I hate betrayal."

She sniffed. "I didn't want to believe it. I cried and cried. My heart was breaking."

"If it hurt so badly, why did ye consider it? What did I do to make ye doubt me?"

"It wasn't you. It was me. I was freaked out because I couldn't read you. I've never had to rely solely on instinct before, and I was afraid I couldn't trust it. And I just had trouble believing that someone like you could actually fall in love with me in less than a week."

"Are ye kidding? I canna understand why every man in the world is no' in love with you. Ye're beautiful, clever, brave . . . ye're everything I've ever wanted."

She made an odd, strangled sound that sounded like a stifled sob. "Oh, Robby."

"Olivia." It took all his self-control not to teleport to her and pull her into his arms. He heard a sound in the distance. She was blowing her nose.

"That's why I didn't answer your letters. I—I threw the first two away. It hurt too much to see them."

"And that's why ye dinna call." He took a deep breath and let it out. "So how do ye feel now?"

"I believe you." Her voice shook with emotion. "I heard your reaction. It sounded like the pain I went through. Robby, I'm so sorry."

"It's all right, sweetheart. We'll be fine." Until the next

disaster. Sooner or later he'd have to tell her the truth about himself.

Not now. Their relationship was too young and fragile. First, they'd had to survive an abrupt separation, and now a crisis of doubt and suspicion. He didn't want to test their relationship any further at this point. He needed time. Time to prove how well he could be trusted, and how much he loved her.

Their romance had happened so fast, Olivia hadn't gotten a chance to know him well enough. Even though he was tempted to teleport straight to her and sweep her off her feet, he knew he needed to proceed slowly. She needed time to get to know him and trust him. The physical attraction was strong, but it wasn't enough. He couldn't reveal his secret until she'd gained a complete trust in him.

"I don't want to lose you, Robby," she whispered. "I've never felt this way about anyone before."

"Ye willna lose me, sweetheart." He collected the pen and paper. "Now tell me everything ye know about Otis, so I can help you."

For the next thirty minutes he took notes and asked questions. She promised to call the next evening to let him know what had transpired.

She yawned. "I'd better get to bed. J.L.'s picking me up early."

Robby gritted his teeth and made a note to check out J.L. Wang, too. "All right. Stay safe, sweetheart."

"You, too. Thank you for understanding." She paused. "I wish I could touch you."

He closed his eyes. "I wish I could kiss you."

She sighed. "I'll call you tomorrow. Good night." She rang off.

Robby set the phone down in its cradle. He'd come so

close to losing her. How would she take the news of him being a vampire?

He dropped his head into his hands. She might accuse him of lying to her. And she would be right. He was purposely withholding the truth while he courted her. If he told her now, he would lose her. If he waited, he could still lose her. She might not be able to forgive his deception.

He groaned. *Damned if you do, damned if you don't.*

Robby was relieved when Olivia called him Saturday night as promised. She reported that Otis's mother had passed the lie detector test. Mrs. Crump knew nothing about the apples, but she was delighted to meet Olivia. Otis had told her that he and Olivia were in love and destined to be together forever.

"Did ye tell her the truth?" Robby asked.

"I tried to, but I don't think it registered. She's convinced Otis is innocent and that he'll be set free someday. She's in major denial."

"Well, it may be the only way she can cope," Robby suggested. "Who would want to admit that they'd raised a psychotic serial killer?"

"Exactly," Olivia muttered. "Anyway, when the mom didn't pan out, we decided to try the brother. He lives in Indianapolis."

"So ye drove there?"

"Yeah. We saw him about an hour ago. He was so full of rage, his aura was bright red tinged with black. He was angry at us, angry at his mother, angry at the whole world. Afterward, I called the local police to warn them to keep an eye on him. The guy's about to explode, and I think he's capable of being extremely violent."

Robby winced. This was bad. If the brother blamed

Olivia for Otis's incarceration, she could be in danger. "Did he know anything about the apples?"

"Zilch. He knew nothing, and it was the truth. As raw as his emotions were, he was very easy to read."

"Are ye still in Indianapolis?"

"Yep. It was getting late, so we checked into a hotel. We'll drive back tomorrow."

He gritted his teeth. "Ye're in a hotel room?"

She laughed. "Separate rooms. So did you make any progress on your end?"

"I have a few ideas. First off, we have to assume everyone in yer office knew ye were on Patmos. The few who did know could have talked to others. So, ye need to check everyone, from yer boss to office workers to the night janitor."

"Okay."

"I'm going to check on Otis's lawyer," Robby continued. "He may have received long range instructions from Otis years ago. And we need to figure out if Otis has a way of communicating with the outside world that the prison doesna know about. Could he possibly be psychic?"

"You think he's communicating telepathically?"

"I think we need to consider every possibility, no matter how bizarre." Robby talked to her for another ten minutes, then rang off when she wanted to shower and go to bed.

He decided that since she was obviously away from home, this was the perfect time to visit her apartment. He called her home phone number, and when the answering machine kicked on, he used her voice as a beacon. Within seconds he materialized in her dark apartment. His eyes quickly adjusted, taking in the small living room. It contained a green love seat, a coffee table, and a television set on a small entertainment console. A table for two was tucked into a tiny eating area next to the kitchen.

He made sure the blinds and curtains were all shut before turning on a light. Then he retrieved the bug detector he'd stashed in his sporran. He doubted Otis or his alleged accomplice had managed to bug Olivia's apartment, but he wanted to make sure.

He checked the living room and kitchen, then ventured into her bedroom. He couldn't look at the queen-sized bed without imagining Olivia lying naked on the cool blue sheets. Now that he'd teleported to her apartment, the location was embedded in his psychic memory. It would be awfully tempting to pop in at night to join her in bed. Unfortunately, the popping in part would probably make her more frightened than romantic.

Her bedroom, bathroom, and closet all checked out. No bugs. He turned off the lights and peered out a window. He was on a second floor, overlooking a landscaped area and parking lot.

He spotted a dark, shadowy area where the bushes were overgrown, and teleported to it. Now, the next time he returned, he would have the option of arriving outside her apartment.

He retrieved his cell phone from his sporran and called Olivia's work number. He materialized in the FBI building in Kansas City. Before the night guards could become aware of him, he teleported away, going back to Romatech.

He felt much better now with all three locations in his psychic memory. If Olivia needed him, he could be there within seconds. He'd only started his investigation the night before, but had learned enough to be worried.

Otis Crump was sick and dangerous, a truly evil man. And even though Crump was apparently locked away for life, Robby knew that evil should never be underestimated.

Chapter Sixteen

As the month of February wore on, Robby stayed in contact with Olivia, either by phone or e-mail. She told him all about her job. They were busy investigating an adoption scam that had her working overtime. Then, in March, a series of drug-related kidnappings and murders monopolized her time.

Her investigation of Otis had to be postponed, but she claimed it didn't matter since she hadn't received any apples since November. Her supervisor had insisted Otis would stop harassing her if she ignored him. It looked like it might have worked.

She admitted that sometimes her job left her completely exhausted and frazzled. She was bombarded with the painful emotions of victims and their families. She could even feel the stress and angry frustration of her fellow colleagues. Since she couldn't feel anything from Robby, talking to him was like taking a vacation. She looked forward to it at the end of every day.

By mid-February they both installed webcams on their laptops so they could see each other as they talked. Robby knew she was stressed from work, so he did his best to cheer her up. He told her about his friends—how Jack threw a rowdy bachelor party and the police had come to shut it down, and now he was marrying the pretty police officer. How Phineas was in love with a girl who had slipped hot sauce into his drink. Seeing Olivia and hearing her laughter was the highlight of Robby's evening. Of course, he left out the pesky fact that some of his friends were Undead.

A few times their late night conversations turned sexy and flirtatious, but Robby tried to keep that to a minimum. He would always take his laptop and webcam to a nearby conference room, since there was no privacy in the office at Romatech. Even so, the guys enjoyed barging into the room to tease him. He couldn't afford to get too excited, or he'd be stuck trying to do his job all night with a conspicuous lump in his trousers.

Even so, it was hard not to get turned on. Olivia was so damned beautiful. More than once she had peered closely at the monitor and asked if his eyes were turning red.

"'Tis the camera," he'd tell her. "My eyes are always looking red in photos." Luckily, she accepted that excuse.

One more good reason, he thought, for keeping their relationship long distance for a while. If he went to visit her, his eyes would be glowing red within three minutes.

He verified that J.L. Wang was trustworthy, and he found nothing wrong with Otis's lawyer. When he mentioned he was the best man in Jack and Lara's wedding in April, Olivia insisted on hearing all about it.

"What does the wedding gown look like?" she asked.

Robby thought back. Lara had shown him a picture. "'Tis . . . white."

Olivia snorted. "That's real descriptive. Is it bright white or cream? Is it floor length? Is there a train? Does it have beadwork or lace? Is she wearing a veil?"

Robby frowned, trying to recall the picture. "'Tis white." When Olivia groaned, he added, "I'll e-mail you the picture."

He ended up e-mailing all sorts of things that Olivia was curious about, even the menu that the mortals would be eating at the reception. Since she was so fascinated with the wedding, he was sorely tempted to invite her, but he rejected the idea. How could he explain the Bubbly Blood— synthetic blood mixed with champagne—that he and his friends would be drinking at the reception? No doubt she would want to do some sightseeing, too, and she'd wonder why he was completely unavailable during the daytime.

He needed to tell her the truth soon, but figured it should be done in private. A wedding was not the right place to break the news.

The wedding took place in mid-April at the Romatech chapel. While Robby listened to the couple reciting their vows, his thoughts kept returning to Olivia. Could she marry a vampire? It involved more than just accepting him as Undead. If she wanted to stay with him over the centuries, she would have to become a vampire, too.

The conference rooms were opened up to make a ballroom for the reception. The bride and other mortals enjoyed a gourmet meal, while the Vamps celebrated with Bubbly Blood.

The High Voltage Vamps began playing a waltz, and Jack

escorted Lara to the dance floor, leaving Robby alone with LaToya at the bridal party table. LaToya had flown into town two days earlier to be Lara's maid of honor.

When the waltz was over, other couples joined Jack and Lara on the dance floor.

LaToya suddenly jumped to her feet and grabbed Robby's arm. "Come on, dance with me."

"As ye wish." He stood, then noticed Phineas hurrying toward their table.

"LaToya, will you dance with me?" he asked.

"Sorry. Robby asked me first." LaToya tugged on Robby's arm. "Come on."

He gave Phineas an apologetic look, then led LaToya to the dance floor. It was a slow dance, which made it easier to talk. "Ye canna avoid him all evening."

LaToya frowned as she placed her hands lightly on Robby's shoulders. "Why doesn't he give up?"

"He's crazy about you."

She glanced to the side where Phineas stood watching her with a lovesick expression. "Crazy is right. I can't scare the guy away. I practically killed him with hot sauce. He came to see me in New Orleans, and I threatened to shoot his ass. Somehow he thought that was romantic."

Robby shrugged one shoulder. "He believes in love. He has a big heart."

"He has a *dead* heart. Dead as a bloodsucking mosquito caught in a bug zapper."

Robby winced. "He's alive now."

"And what kind of weird shit is that? I mean, you're alive at night, but dead during the day? Sheesh, make up your minds. Either be alive or be dead. How can you be both? It's just wrong."

"So ye're still upset about us being vampires?"

She heaved a sigh. "I promised to keep my mouth shut, if that's what you're worried about. I don't want any of you creepy guys erasing my memory, not when my memories of Lara would end up erased, too."

"She is fortunate to have a loyal friend like you."

LaToya glanced at the bride, who was beaming with joy as she swayed to the music in Jack's arms. "I want her to be happy. I guess she is, but I don't see how it can last."

"There's never any guarantee." Robby thought back to his own failed marriage. His wife, Mavis, had rejected him for being Undead. Just because Shanna, Heather, Toni, and Lara were able to love Vamp men, it didn't mean all women could. Would Olivia be able to handle it?

"My mother's on her third husband," LaToya grumbled. "She's never had a marriage that lasted more than five years. And you Vamps think you can stay married for centuries? You're out of your half-dead minds."

Robby smiled. "Maybe so."

LaToya chewed her bottom lip. "Though I have to admit, the thought of being around for a few centuries is kinda appealing. And staying young forever—that's not bad."

"Aye, there are some advantages." Maybe she was learning to accept them, after all. "We're no' so bad once ye get to know us. When I was captured last summer, a lot of the Vamps in this room risked their lives in order to rescue me."

She nodded. "Yeah, Lara told me about that."

"Phineas was one of them. He's known us for only a few years, but he's demonstrated over and over again how loyal, brave, and trustworthy he is."

LaToya scoffed. "He was a drug dealer. I checked him out, you know. There's an outstanding warrant for his arrest."

"He's come a long way since then."

"That doesn't mean he shouldn't pay for his crime."

"He did pay," Robby insisted. "With his life. He deserves a second chance."

LaToya huffed. "I'm not sure I can be that forgiving."

Robby glanced at Marta Barkowski, who was sitting at a table with Vanda and Phil. "I dinna think I could be forgiving, either. But sometimes there's just no point in prolonging everyone's suffering."

With a small shock, Robby realized he was changing. His time with Olivia was healing his heart and soothing his wounds. He still wanted to kill Casimir, but it was no longer the top priority in his mind. And when it came to Vamps like Marta or Stanislav, he now understood that they'd been victimized, too.

"Can I cut in?" Phineas tapped him on the shoulder.

Robby released LaToya and stepped back. "That depends on the lady's wishes."

Phineas extended a hand to LaToya. "Sweetness, will you dance with me?"

She gave him a wary look. "I guess I could finish this one with you."

"Great!" With a grin, Phineas wrapped his arms around her.

The music ended.

"Oops. Dance is over." LaToya stepped away.

"No, it's not." Phineas pulled her back.

"Yes, it is!" She stomped a stiletto heel on his foot.

With a yelp, Phineas released her.

"So long, sucker." She strode away, flipping her long curls over her shoulder.

Phineas tried putting weight on his sore foot and winced. "Ouch."

"Sorry about that," Robby murmured.

Phineas gave him a wry look. "Yeah, it hurts, but at least I didn't turn emo and punch a hole in a wall."

"I fixed it," Robby grumbled. He'd taken a lot of ribbing over that hole.

Phineas turned his attention back to LaToya, who was ordering a drink at the bar. He smiled slowly. "It's happening, bro. She's falling under my spell."

"How can ye tell? She attacked you again."

"Yeah, but this time she didn't threaten to kill me." Phineas smoothed a hand over his short black hair. "Oh yeah, baby, the Love Doctor is hard to resist."

It was the end of April when the pace at work finally slowed down. Olivia had spent the morning finishing up paperwork. "Ready for lunch?" she called over the partition to J.L.

"Almost," he replied. "Give me five minutes."

This was the perfect opportunity to check her personal e-mail account. She grinned when a message from Robby popped up.

> *Good morning, sweetheart. After we talked on the phone last night, I received a message from Jack and Lara in Venice. They sent some pictures from the wedding. I've attached them for you.*

Olivia clicked through the photos, delighted to finally put faces to the names she'd been hearing about for the last two months. Her heart swelled when she saw a photo that included Robby. He looked dashing in his formal black jacket, white shirt, and black tie that matched his black and white plaid kilt. There was a twinkle in his green eyes and an amused tilt to his wide mouth. She could have gawked at him for hours, but there were a bunch more photos to see. She clicked through some more.

"Hey, Liv. Here's that report you wanted." Yasmine set a file on Olivia's desk, then glanced at the monitor. "Are those wedding pictures? I love wedding pictures!"

"Let me show you the bride." Olivia clicked on Lara's photo.

"All right." J.L. leaned his elbows on the partition. "I'm ready for lunch now."

"Wow, she's beautiful," Yasmine whispered.

"I know," Olivia said. "Can you believe she was a New York cop?"

"Hello?" J.L. waved at them. "Lunch?"

Yasmine ignored him. "I didn't know you went to a wedding. Are you friends with the bride?"

"I didn't go," Olivia replied. "I'm just friends with the best man."

"Just friends?" J.L. scoffed. "He's all you ever talk about anymore. I can't eat my lunch without getting the latest 'Robby' update."

Olivia made a face at him. He'd laughed at the stories, too.

"Who's Robby?" Yasmine asked.

"He was the best man. Here, I'll show you." Olivia clicked on a group photo.

Yasmine snorted. "Who's the big guy in the skirt? And what's that? A purse?"

Olivia stiffened. "That's Robby."

"He's wearing a skirt? I've got to see this." J.L. peered over Yasmine's head at the monitor, then snickered.

Olivia glared at him. "Robby's Scottish. That's why he's wearing a kilt and a sporran."

"Where on earth did you meet a Scotsman?" Yasmine asked.

"Look, guys," J.L. interrupted them. "I'm starving. If you want to keep drooling on those photos, I'll bring lunch back here."

Olivia's glare switched to a smile. "That would be great. I'll take a turkey sandwich."

"Me, too," Yasmine said.

J.L. walked away, muttering about the female fascination with weddings where poor saps got shackled for life.

"Well?" Yasmine asked. "Where did you meet the handsome Scotsman?"

"On Patmos last November."

"A Scotsman on a Greek island?" Yasmine laughed, then abruptly turned serious. "Oh my gosh, Liv, he's not the one who made you cry, is he?"

Olivia's cheeks warmed with embarrassment. "That was just a misunderstanding. We're okay now."

"You're dating him?"

"Sorta. We talk and e-mail every day. I wish I could go see him, but I'm out of vacation days."

Yasmine shook her head slowly. "I had no idea you were involved with someone. How serious is it?"

Olivia bit her lip. Yasmine could be annoying sometimes with her constant curiosity about everyone's personal affairs, but Olivia was dying to tell someone her news. "Last night Robby told me he was taking some vacation time in June so he could come for a visit. He said he had something really important to discuss with me and he needed to do it in person."

Yasmine gasped. "Do you think he's going to propose?"

Olivia grinned. She was so excited, she'd hardly slept at all last night. "It sounds that way, don't you think? I mean, he wouldn't come all this way to break up with me, would he?"

An aura of anxiety swirled around Yasmine. "Are you seriously considering this? You can't really know him that well."

"We've had lots of long talks. I can tell him anything, and he understands. He makes me laugh. I make him laugh."

"Girl, he made you cry last December. You were hurting really bad. Maybe you should rethink this. Or at least slow down."

Olivia shrugged. The last thing she wanted to hear was something bad about Robby. He was the sweetest, most gentle man she'd ever met.

"Here, I'll show you the rest of the photos." She clicked through them, and her eyes were invariably drawn to Robby whenever he appeared in a photo.

Was he really planning to propose to her? She couldn't imagine anything else of importance that he would need to tell her.

There was, however, something important she needed to tell him. She'd meant to tell him before, but the appropriate time had never come up.

How was yer day? he would ask on the webcam.

Great. We arrested a kidnapper, and by the way, I'm a virgin. That would have been too strange.

But surely it didn't matter if Robby was unaware of her secret. Why would any man object to it?

Two weeks later, on a Saturday afternoon, Olivia returned to her apartment after running errands. She dropped her handbag and keys on the console by the front door, then carried her bag of groceries to the kitchen.

As she passed the breakfast nook, she noticed something

on the dinette table. A brown cardboard box. The logo on top was unmistakable.

Apples.

Her heart lurched up her throat. The box was in her house. Not on the front porch, left by a delivery man. *In her house.*

She set her tote bag of groceries on the floor and moved quietly to her bedroom. All her senses tingled high on alert. She might not be alone in the apartment. She was good at martial arts, but she'd feel a lot safer with her gun in her hand. She reached her bedside table and removed her side-arm from the top drawer.

With a quick glance, she verified that the pistol was loaded. She flipped the safety off, then quickly checked the bathroom and closet. She did a more thorough check of her bedroom, looking underneath the bed and behind the curtains. Then she checked the living room and kitchen. Empty. The box on the table wasn't clicking like a bomb, but she wasn't taking any chances opening it.

She examined the front door. No sign of forced entry. She called the apartment manager and asked if they'd let anyone into her apartment. No.

Someone has a key. Her heart thundered in her ears.

She called J.L. "The box was in my apartment. The bastard's been inside my house!"

"Calm down," he told her. "I'll be right there."

She hung up. *Calm down?* Someone could enter her apartment at will. She wasn't safe in her own home.

Damn that Otis. How long was she supposed to put up with his stupid game? Her supervisor, Barker, had told her to leave him alone and stay away from Leavenworth. Once Otis realized she wouldn't play his game, he'd leave her alone. But it wasn't working. Otis was not giving up.

She was tempted to go tell him once and for all to buzz off. Of course, that was what he wanted. He wanted her to visit. He wanted to keep a connection between them.

She groaned with frustration. There had to be a way to stop this. She was ready to rip her hair out. Instead, she called Robby. Since he worked nights, his phone would be turned off during the day while he slept, but she could still leave a message.

"Robby, another box of apples came. I went out to run some errands, and when I came back, they were in my apartment! Sitting on the kitchen table. The accomplice wants me to know he can enter my house whenever he damn well pleases. And you know what? I'm not running away this time. I've had it! I'm staying here, and if that bastard dares to come back, I'll—"

Beep. The allotted time for the message ran out.

She snapped the phone shut. Just stating her thoughts out loud had left her feeling stronger and more empowered. She wasn't going to take it anymore.

A knock sounded on her door, and she immediately grabbed her gun. *Get a grip.* The bad guy didn't need to knock. He either had a key or knew how to pick a lock.

"Olivia!" J.L. yelled through the door. "Are you there?"

"Yes." She opened the door.

He slipped inside and looked quickly about. "Are you planning to shoot me?"

"No." She set the gun down on the console. "Sorry about that."

"Don't apologize. I'm packing, too."

She locked the door, then groaned. "Why do I even bother? The bastard can come in whenever he likes."

"We'll get a new lock put in today." J.L. walked toward

the kitchen table. "So this is it. The infamous apple box. No postage or delivery markings. You checked the rest of the apartment?"

"Yes, everything else is normal."

"Look inside your closet or chest of drawers. He may have taken a souvenir."

Olivia shuddered at the thought. "Okay." Everything appeared normal in her closet. She rifled through her drawers and noted one thing missing—a pair of red lace panties. Damn, now she really felt violated.

"The scumbag swiped a pair of—" She froze at the bedroom door. J.L. was standing an arm's length away from the cardboard box while he used a spatula from her kitchen to open it.

"Stay back," he warned her.

So he'd purposely managed to make her leave the room while he opened the box. It was heroic of him, but not the smartest move if he actually suspected the box would explode if opened.

"There's never been anything dangerous about the apples," she reassured him. Still she held her breath when he flipped the box open. Nothing.

He scooped an apple out, and it bounced onto the table, then rolled off the edge to land on the floor. "Have you ever had the apples tested for drugs?"

"The first time, yes. They were normal." She watched a second and third apple plummet to the floor. "They're just meant to be a threat to my peace of mind. It's a psychological game."

"Yeah." J.L. flipped the rest of the apples out of the box with his spatula. "But criminal behavior can escalate over time, when the creeps need a bigger thrill."

"So far he hasn't shown a desire to hurt me." Olivia approached the kitchen table. "He just wants to manipulate me and keep a connection between us."

"Because you two are destined to be together forever," J.L. repeated what Otis had told his mother. "If he ever realizes you're not agreeable to that plan, he'll turn on you in a second."

"I know."

With the spatula, J.L. dug around in the green plastic grass that had cushioned the apples. "It seems all right, but we should still take this to Forensics and see if they can lift any prints off it. The creep obviously wanted to scare you by putting it inside your apartment, but it may have been a big mistake for him to deliver it himself."

"I think he must be watching the apartment. He knew when I had left."

"Good point." J.L. tapped the spatula on the tabletop while he considered. "Let's see if he'll come back."

Olivia and J.L. made a show of leaving the apartment, locking the front door, and driving off in his car. Then, a few blocks away, Olivia exited the car and J.L. proceeded to a nearby hardware store to buy a new lock.

She jogged back and hid behind a Dumpster to watch the apartment. No one approached. She sighed. It could be that the accomplice's job was done and he'd left.

J.L. returned and installed the new lock while she finally put away the groceries she'd bought earlier. Wearing latex gloves, she returned the apples to the box and wrapped it up in a trash bag. They took it to the forensics department, then picked up a pizza on the way back. Even with the new lock, J.L. refused to leave Olivia on her own.

They sat on the love seat, eating pizza and discussing options. As the sun went down, Olivia finally decided on a course of action, but J.L. didn't approve because it required a trip to Leavenworth to see Otis. He finally relented when she agreed to let him accompany her.

"You realize you're doing exactly what he wants you to do," J.L. warned her as he jammed the last bite of pizza into his mouth. "He sends the damned apples to lure you in."

"I can't threaten him without seeing him," Olivia said. She jumped when a knock sounded on the door.

"Expecting anyone?" J.L. strode to the door while he un-snapped the shoulder holster containing his sidearm.

"No." Olivia grabbed a napkin to wipe the pizza grease off her fingers, then rushed to the console where she'd left her weapon.

J.L. peered through the peephole in the door. "Well, I'll be damned."

"What? Who is it?" She envisioned a UPS man with fifty boxes of apples. Or maybe Otis's enraged brother with a shotgun. She aimed her weapon at the door.

J.L. gave her a wry look. "Is that any way to treat your boyfriend?"

She blinked. "My what?"

He grinned. "Robby MacKay is on your front porch."

Chapter Seventeen

Right after hearing the message Olivia left on his phone, Robby made arrangements for Phineas and Connor to take over at Romatech. Then he teleported to the shadowy, overgrown area next to the parking lot. Now, on the front porch of her second floor apartment, he could hear her and a man talking inside. His heart sped up at the sound of her voice.

The door opened and a tall Asian American greeted him with a wary look. "You must be Robby."

Robby shook hands with him. "Ye must be J.L."

"Robby!" Olivia grinned at him.

"Olivia." He strode into the apartment and pulled her into his arms. His heart swelled with joy when she wrapped her arms around his neck and squeezed him tight.

He enveloped her, burying his face in her hair, breathing her sweet scent. She felt so right in his arms. In his life. What a fool he'd been over the last few months, courting her from afar. Now that he had her in his arms again, he never wanted to let her go.

"Whoa! Is that a sword on your back?" J.L. asked.

Robby lifted his face from Olivia's curls. "Aye. I brought it for protection."

Olivia leaned back in his arms. "I guess you got the message I left? You must have caught the next available flight."

Robby knew she would assume he'd flown there. "I came as quickly as I could. How is everything?"

"You traveled with a sword?" J.L. asked, still eyeing the scabbard on Robby's back. "What kind of sword is that?"

"A claymore." Robby slipped the halter off his shoulders. He'd dressed in a black T-shirt and black jeans, to be less noticeable teleporting in. He offered the scabbard to J.L. "Would ye like to see it?"

"Whoa! It's heavy." J.L. unsheathed the sword. "Sweet! This is massive!"

"Are ye all right?" Robby turned back to Olivia and touched her face. "I was worried about you."

"I'm fine. J.L. changed the lock." She motioned toward the front door. "I should be safe here now."

Robby shook his head. "There are ways to get past a locked door. Where are the apples?" He glanced about the room. The kitchen table was bare, and an empty pizza box lay open on the coffee table.

"We took the box to Forensics." Olivia winced when J.L. swiped the sword through the air. "Careful with that! You nearly slaughtered the ceiling fan."

"This is so awesome!" J.L. made a jab at an imaginary opponent. "I've got a Chinese sword and a samurai at home, but they're not nearly as big as this."

"Ye know how to fence?" Robby asked.

"Sure." J.L. ran a hand along the flat of the blade. "I took fencing in college, but there's not much demand for it at the Bureau."

Olivia snorted. "They have this bizarre notion that guns might be more effective."

J.L. rolled his eyes. "A sword like this is a piece of art." He sheathed the sword and lay the scabbard on the table.

"I'll be happy to spar with you sometime," Robby said. "I could loan you a claymore."

"You're on." J.L. motioned for Robby to join him at the table. "Dude, if you hurt Olivia, it'll be more than a sparring match."

She huffed. "I heard that. I don't need big male protectors who like to play Conan the Barbarian."

Robby smiled at her. "Even so, ye have two." He rested a hand on J.L.'s shoulder. "I appreciate everything ye're doing for Olivia. Ye're a loyal friend."

J.L. blushed. "Well, I meant what I said. You hurt her, and I'm coming after you."

She groaned. "I can take care of myself."

"I would never want to hurt her," Robby confessed quietly as he looked at her. "I love her."

She drew in a sharp breath and her eyes misted. "Oh, Robby," she whispered.

"Okay." J.L. grabbed his jacket off the kitchen chair. "I can tell when three's a crowd."

Olivia dashed over to hug him. "Thank you so much for everything. I don't know what I'd do without you."

"If you need me, call," he whispered. He glanced at Robby. "I wasn't going to leave her alone tonight."

"I'm staying," Robby announced. "But I need to leave shortly before dawn."

"You have to go back to New York?" Olivia asked.

He nodded. "They're expecting me." She would assume he was catching an early morning flight. He hated misleading her, but didn't think this was a good time to reveal his secret. She'd been through enough stress and turmoil today.

"Liv, I'll check on you tomorrow morning." J.L. fished his keys out of his jacket pocket as he headed for the door. "Good to meet you, Robby."

Olivia gave J.L. another hug before he left, then locked the door. She turned to face Robby. "Well?"

Alone at last. His fingers curled with a sudden desire to grab hold of her. Her gaze wandered over him, and he could hear her heart rate speeding up. The apartment seemed suddenly smaller and warmer, as if a hot, humid cloud of desire had descended on them. His own heart rate increased, even though he tried to stay calm. He didn't want his eyes to start glowing.

Think about something else, something not sexy. "I forgot how beautiful ye are." No, that didn't help.

She smiled. "I thought the same thing when I saw you in those wedding pictures." Her cheeks flushed. "You looked very handsome in your kilt."

She was taking on a pinkish tint, and he didn't think it was all due to her blush. He glanced down and rubbed his eyes.

"Are you tired from your flight? I can't believe you came all this way. It was so sweet." She rushed to the coffee table and folded the empty pizza box. "Sorry about the mess."

"'Tis all right."

She scurried into the kitchen with the box. "Can I get you something to eat or drink?"

"I'm fine. Thank you."

She came out of the kitchen with two glasses of ice water.

"Pizza makes me so thirsty." She set the glasses on coasters on the coffee table. "Are you sure you're not hungry? I've got chips and ice cream and—"

"I'm fine. But if ye wish to eat, please go ahead."

"I'm full." She clutched her hands together. "I'm just . . . nervous. It's been so long since we were in the same room together."

"I shouldna have stayed away so long."

"It's all right." She perched on the green love seat. "I've really enjoyed our talks. I feel like I got to know you a lot better, and that's important. If we had met in person, we might not have . . . talked so much."

No, he would have been making love to her. "That is true."

Her cheeks bloomed a brighter pink. "I'd forgotten how strong the . . . chemistry is."

Chemistry? "Is that a nice word for wanting to throw you on a bed and rip yer clothes off?"

She drew in a sharp breath. "I suppose."

He sat beside her. "Do ye remember our last night together?"

"Yes!" She jumped to her feet and strode to the door to check the lock. "It was very sweet of you to come tonight."

"I dinna feel verra sweet when I heard yer message. Ye were so upset."

"The box was *in my house.* I felt violated. And the creep took a pair of my underwear for a souvenir. Can you believe it?"

Unfortunately, he could. He still had a pair of her underwear stashed under his pillow at Romatech. "The bastard," he muttered. "Would ye like me to speak to Otis for you? I could convince him to leave you alone."

"How?"

Vampire mind control. "I can be verra convincing." Though the mission would require a lot of planning, since he'd have to erase security tapes and the guards' memories.

"I appreciate that, but I have my own plan." She paced across the room. "I'm going to see him Monday."

Robby winced. "I'm no' sure that's a good idea. I investigated the man, and he's verra dangerous. I could take you away, if ye like, and hide you someplace he would never find you."

"I'm not running away. I did that before when my supervisor insisted on it, but it didn't work. And I'm not going to spend the rest of my life in hiding. I'm confronting him Monday. My mind's made up."

"And how are ye planning to make him stop harassing you?"

She explained her plan as she continued to pace. "Don't worry. J.L. is coming with me."

Robby frowned. "I'm glad ye have such a loyal friend, but it vexes me that he's here for you, and I'm no'."

"You're here now." She sat beside him once again. "And that means a lot to me." She touched his cheek.

He took her hand and kissed the pad of each finger. "Ye've changed me, Olivia. I've seen people the last few months, people who aided and abetted the man who tortured me. Before, I would have wanted to kill them."

"And now?"

He kissed the palm of her hand. "Now I realize they were victims, too. I want a second chance in my life, and I know 'tis wrong to deny others that same chance."

"What do you want your second life to be like?"

He smiled. "Ever the therapist. I want it to be full of joy and laughter." He smoothed a hand across her cheek. "I want it to be with you."

"Yes." She closed her eyes as he leaned closer. He pressed his mouth lightly against hers.

"Yes," she whispered again.

Her eyes popped open when he scooped her up and set her in his lap. He scooted to the center of the love seat.

"What are you—this can't be very comfortable for you." She squirmed in an attempt to get up, but he held tight as her wiggling rump incited a delicious agony in his groin.

He moaned.

"I knew it. I'm too heavy for—"

He cut her off with a kiss. Not a gentle peck this time, but a thorough, demanding kiss. For a second she stiffened, then she melted, becoming limp in his arms.

He invaded her mouth, exploring and tasting. His first taste of pizza. So much more spicy and flavorful than the steady blood diet he'd consumed since 1746.

She broke away from the kiss, gasped for air, then kissed him again. Evidently the limp phase had passed. She was now more aggressive, digging her fingers into his hair to pull him closer. She invaded his mouth and stroked his tongue. Her boldness made his groin swell and his heart pound with sudden urgency.

He'd waited too long for this. He slipped his hands under her T-shirt. Her skin was warm and smooth, and her back arched when he pressed against the sweet curve of her spine. He found her bra strap and unhooked it.

She continued to kiss him as he slipped his hands underneath her loose bra. The bottom curves of her breasts were so soft and full. When he palmed one of her breasts and squeezed, she gasped, breaking the kiss. Her breath puffed softly against his cheek as he drew circles around her nipple. The tip hardened, and he rubbed it between his thumb and forefinger.

She moaned, her head falling back. Her neck was exposed, the carotid artery throbbing. He nuzzled his face against her neck, inhaling the scent of her blood. Thank God he'd drank two bottles of synthetic blood before coming. He could resist the temptation of feeding, but the scent of her blood and the throbbing of her veins added to his sexual hunger.

He dragged his tongue along her carotid artery, knowing his saliva would heighten her sensitivity. She shuddered.

"Please," she breathed.

"I will please you," he whispered in her ear, then tickled it with his tongue. "All night long."

"Yes." She reached for the hem of her T-shirt.

"Let me help you." He pulled the T-shirt over her head and tossed it onto the coffee table.

She slipped off the bra and threw it on the floor.

He paused a moment to look at her breasts. The nipples pebbled and darkened before his eyes. "Lord Almighty," he whispered. "Ye're so beautiful."

Her eyes glimmered with tears. "Robby, I'm in love with you."

"Olivia." He kissed her briefly. "Sweetheart, I love you, too."

"Will you make love to me?"

"I thought I was." He brushed a thumb over her hardened nipple.

She drew in a sharp breath. "It feels so good. I can't think when you're—" She groaned when he took her nipple into his mouth.

"Robby." She sounded breathless. "We . . . we should talk before—" She shuddered when he flicked his tongue.

He suckled her and teased her relentlessly. He didn't want to talk, dammit. He knew he should tell her he was a vampire before making love to her, but if he told her, there wouldn't be any lovemaking.

He released her nipple and smiled grimly at the distended bloodred tip.

"Robby, wait a minute." She gasped when he took her other nipple into his mouth. "I—I should tell you I'm on the pill. I started it at Quantico when all the exercise was messing up my period, and I wanted to be regular."

"Hmm." He continued to suckle.

"I just thought you should know that I have about a two percent chance of getting pregnant."

More like zero percent on account of his dead sperm. "I understand." He blew on her wet nipple.

She shivered. "But I do want to have children someday."

"So do I." He unfastened the top button of her blue jeans.

"Wait. I have to know if you have any diseases."

He paused with his hand on the zipper. "Diseases?"

"Sexually transmitted ones. I can't continue with this unless I know you're . . . healthy."

"I'm verra healthy." Except for the part about being dead during the day.

She bit her lip. "We'd better use a condom just to be safe."

She thought he had the pox? He stiffened with indignation. "I havena been sleeping with prostitutes."

"You can get a STD almost anywhere. To be perfectly safe, it's best to require a medical report prior to engaging in certain activities."

He blinked. Since when had lovemaking become a business transaction? "I can e-mail you a report tomorrow."

"Oh. Okay." She frowned. "I guess I can trust you."

"Thank you. That's verra kind of you. And while we're completely destroying the romantic mood, how do I know if ye're healthy? Do ye keep yer medical report in yer bedside table so ye can whip it out at the appropriate time?"

"No, of course not."

He arched a brow. "I guess I'll have to trust you."

"You can. I—I've never done anything to get a STD."

He shrugged one shoulder. "Neither have I."

She gasped. "You're a virgin?"

He scoffed. "Do I look like an inexperienced pup?"

Her cheeks turned pink. "No."

He smiled and kissed her nose. "Can we get on with this now? I'm dying to bury myself deep inside you and feel ye shudder—"

"I'm a virgin," she blurted out.

He blinked. He couldn't have heard that right. "Ye . . . what?"

"I'm a virgin."

"Nay. Ye're sitting half-naked in my lap. Ye were naked and screaming with orgasms on Patmos."

"I have some experience, yes. Mostly with you." She moved off his lap and sat on the love seat beside him. "But I've never had intercourse."

"Ye've never . . . what is wrong with modern men?" He winced at the slip. He was supposed to be modern, too. "They must be blind! They should be lining up at yer door."

"A lovely thought," she muttered. "I could have them take a number."

"I just meant they must be incredibly stupid if they canna see what a treasure ye are. How could such a thing happen?"

She shot him an annoyed look. "I finished a master's degree by the age of twenty-three, so I was really busy. And then there's the human lie detector thing. A few guys tried to get me in bed, but the minute they lied to me, I showed them the door."

She's a virgin. Robby stood and paced across the room. He'd never suspected this. Olivia had reacted to his love-making on Patmos with such free abandon. His wife had been a virgin on their wedding night, and she'd acted shy and fearful, refusing to completely undress.

He'd loved Olivia's boldness. She'd been so responsive to his every touch, squirming and screaming.

Lord Almighty, how could he take her virginity? She was so young, so alive, and he was close to three hundred years old. He was bloody dead half the time. No woman should have to lose her virginity to a bloodsucker.

He would have to tell her the truth, that he was a vampire, because once he made love to her, he wouldn't want to give her up. Ever. She deserved to know the truth before she ended up straddled with one man for all eternity. He grimaced. How could he live up to that?

"Great," she muttered. She grabbed her T-shirt off the coffee table and pulled it over her head. "I didn't realize this would be a problem for you."

"Olivia—"

"And to think I actually hoped you might be flattered." She rose to her feet, her face pale. "I can't believe this."

"I—I'm no' sure I should accept such an honor."

"Honor?" She scoffed. "Yeah, I feel real 'honored' that you would reject me for being too innocent."

"I doona wish to reject you."

"But you don't want to be bothered with my pesky virginity!" She strode toward the front door, her breasts bouncing beneath the T-shirt. "Don't let it worry you, okay? I'll just run down to the local bar and get rid of it. After all, the guys will line up for it, right?"

He winced. "That's no' funny."

"Who's being funny? I'm dead serious." She stalked back to the coffee table and grabbed a glass of water. "I'll just make sure I get their attention." She poured the water over her chest, and the wet T-shirt glued itself to her breasts and distended nipples. "Now I'm ready. With any luck, I can get the service for free."

His hands curled into fists. "Ye canna do this."

"Watch me." She strode back to the front door to collect her handbag and keys. "I should be back in fifteen minutes or so, minus a hymen."

He dashed to the door, ripped her handbag from her hands and tossed it on the floor. "Bloody hell, woman. Ye think I'd let anyone else touch you?"

She shoved at his chest. "Go away! I hate you for thinking my virginity is a problem."

He grabbed her wrists and pinned them against the door. When she squirmed, he pressed his body against her, letting her feel his erection. "Ye love me, sweetheart, and doona worry. Yer virginity will no' be a problem for long."

Chapter Eighteen

Olivia glared at him. "I'm not going to bed with you. I'm mad at you."

"Ye'll get over it."

She tugged at her wrists, but he tightened his grip. When he attempted to kiss her, she turned her head so his mouth landed on her jaw.

That didn't deter him. He nibbled a path along her neck, teasing her with his tongue. Her skin tingled. It took all her concentration not to moan out loud.

"Ye were begging me earlier," he whispered in her ear. "Ye were saying, 'Please make love to me.'" He traced the contour of her ear with his tongue.

Her knees nearly buckled. "That was before I realized what a big . . ." She searched her mind for a good insult, but it was hard to think with him nuzzling her neck.

"Aye. Big." He rubbed his erection against her.

She fought an urge to press back, to wrap her legs around him and pull him into her core. She ached with emptiness, as if she would scream if he didn't fill her up.

But dammit, she was still mad at him. There was no way she was going to beg. "Maybe you didn't want to take my virginity 'cause you're not *up* to the task."

He lifted his head from her neck. "Are ye trying to insult me now?"

She smirked. "You'll get over it."

"Unzip my pants and see if I'm *up* to it." He released her wrists.

Now that she was free, she tried to move away from him, but he grasped her shoulders and kept her pinned to the door.

"Go ahead, lass. I dare you."

Her cheeks burned with heat. "Fine. Let's see what you're made of." Pure titanium alloy, most probably. Damn him.

She fumbled with the button at the waistband of his jeans. "I should remind you that I'm thoroughly trained in martial arts." She jerked the zipper down. "My hands are lethal weapons."

He chuckled. "And I should remind you that whatever ye do to me, I'm doing to you."

"Damn. There goes my plan for the kitchen knife."

He growled deep in his throat, and it sent a quivering sensation through her belly. When she lifted her hand to find the waistband of his underwear, she accidentally brushed against a huge protuberance.

He closed his eyes and moaned.

She hooked a finger in the waistband of his black cotton briefs, close to his hip. "I can't seem to find it. It must be awfully small."

He snorted and slid her hand to the center. Her finger bumped into a rock solid column of . . . pure titanium alloy.

Her breath caught. He was so swollen, he was spilling out. He yanked his underwear down, and his penis slammed against her hand.

She gulped. It was definitely *up*. And big. Too big. Good Lord, it was a battering ram. She winced. "This is going to hurt."

His mouth twitched. "Ye'll get over it."

"Oh, really?" She wrapped her hand around him and squeezed.

"Easy with that." He tried to pull her hand away, but she held tight. The jerking motion made him gasp. "Lord Almighty, woman, do ye want me to embarrass myself?"

"You'll get over it."

He arched a brow at her, and she gasped, releasing her hold on him.

"Your eyes are red!"

He muttered a curse. "'Tis a medical condition." He swooped her up into his arms and strode toward the bedroom.

She studied him, frowning. "I've never heard of a medical condition like that."

"Doona fash."

"Fash?"

"Upset yerself." He grimaced as he entered her bedroom. "Bugger."

"What? Are your eyes hurting?"

"Nay. My pants are falling off."

She laughed.

He stopped by the side of the bed and smiled at her. "Does this mean ye're no longer angry at me?"

She gave him a sly look. "My final judgment will be based purely on job performance."

He snorted. "Ye're a virgin. How would ye know a good job from a bad one?"

"If you're done in five minutes, then roll over and start snoring, I'll be very angry."

His eyes twinkled. "Ye'll get over it."

She punched him in the shoulder.

He chuckled and dropped her on the bed. She propped herself up on her elbows, opening her mouth to complain when she noticed his pants had indeed fallen to his ankles and his erection was still . . . erect.

Her jaw dropped farther when Robby pulled his black T-shirt over his head, displaying a lean six-pack and broad, muscular chest. The curly brown hair narrowed into a thin line that ended in a thick thatch around the . . . battering ram.

"If ye open yer mouth a wee bit wider, I could fit it inside." Her jaw snapped shut, and he winced. "Ouch."

She looked down, embarrassed by her reaction. He was kicking off his shoes. Good idea. She slipped her shoes off and dropped them on the floor.

Her gaze landed on his calf and she gasped. He had a knife strapped to his leg. He'd slung his jeans and underwear to the side, so he was standing by the bed, completely naked except for the knife.

"You're certainly well-equipped."

"Thank you. I've wanted you a long time."

Her gaze flitted to his erection. "I wasn't referring to . . . although it is rather imp—" She halted when he slipped the knife from its sheath. "What are you—" She gasped when he pointed the knife at her throat.

"Doona fash." He nicked the neck of her T-shirt, then dropped the knife to the floor. He grasped the cut edges of her T-shirt in his fists and ripped the shirt in two.

Her jaw dropped open. "What are you—"

He pushed her back onto the bed. "I told you I wanted to throw you on the bed and rip yer clothes off. I believe ye called it chemistry."

She glanced down at her ripped T-shirt. "I liked this shirt."

"Ye'll get over it." With a gleam in his red eyes, he yanked her jeans and panties down her legs and threw them on the floor.

He stretched out on the bed beside her, and she moved to the center to make more room for him. Her heart pounded in her ears. This was it. Maybe she should get under the comforter. She felt so exposed lying here with only a ripped T-shirt. Maybe she should go to the bathroom to freshen up. Maybe she should shave her legs really fast. Maybe she should turn off the light in the living room. It was filtering into the bedroom, making it possible to see.

Maybe she was overanalyzing again. She glanced at him. He was propped up on one arm, looking at her. "Is something wrong?"

He smiled. "It seems right to me."

Her heart expanded in her chest. It *was* right. The man she loved was going to make love to her. "I'm so lucky I found you."

"I'm the lucky one. I had lost my way till ye found me."

She touched his face. He had shaved, and his cheeks were smooth. "I love you, Robby MacKay."

He kissed her brow. "I will love you forever."

Tears gathered in her eyes. She believed him. Even without her lie detecting skills, she believed him.

When his mouth met hers, she opened for him. She wrapped her arms around his neck and sank into a slow, languid world of sweet sensation. She loved the gentle movement of his lips, the soft stroking of his tongue, and the way his fingers caressed her face and neck. She smoothed her hands down his back, enjoying the feel of his skin and the ripple of muscles.

The kiss continued in a leisurely fashion until she felt wonderfully relaxed. Her fears melted away. She knew he would take it slow and easy. He was such a gentleman.

He kissed a path to her neck. She shivered when he tickled her with his tongue. Suddenly, she became intensely aware of her private parts. The more he tickled her neck, the more she tingled.

She gasped when his tongue dragged up her neck. Good God, she'd felt a delicious throb in her vagina. "Robby?"

He licked her again, and she jolted. Her fingers dug into his back. Her thighs squeezed together.

Suddenly she didn't want a gentleman anymore. *"Robby?"*

He made a low growling sound in his throat that sent a shiver down her arms, prickling her skin with goose bumps. Without warning, he cupped her between the legs. She gasped. He pressed against her as he licked her neck again.

She cried out.

He applied pressure again. "Ye're already wet."

She whimpered. She didn't know how he'd made her so desperate so fast.

He moved down to her feet. "Open yer legs."

She let her knees sag open a bit, then gasped when he spread her feet wide. "What are you . . . ?" She bit her lip. She'd never been so exposed before. He was actually sitting between her legs, studying her.

As embarrassed as she was, she still felt strangely turned on. Her skin itched, desperate for him to touch her.

"Ye're glistening," he whispered. "Ye're like a pink rose covered with dew."

She felt more moisture seeping from her core. "Robby, if you don't touch me, I'm going to scream."

He smiled. "Ye're going to scream anyway."

"I'll get over it." She jerked when his fingers traced the wet folds.

He slowly inserted a finger inside her. "Ye're verra tight. I'll try to loosen you up a wee bit."

"Oh, oh my . . ." She gripped the comforter in her fists. She was never going to last. It felt too damned good.

He slipped two fingers inside and waggled them about. "Ye're dripping now. Growing more red and swollen. I can smell yer scent, and it makes me want to taste you."

"Then do it! I'm dying here. I—" She squeaked when he pinched her clitoris.

He stroked the inner walls of her vagina while he fondled the highly sensitive nub. Tension sharpened inside her, ready to snap. Suddenly, his fingers were moving incredibly fast, and she was spiraling out of control. Her whole body jolted. She screamed. Her vagina squeezed his fingers with powerful spasms that made her shudder all over.

Moments later when she was still trying to catch her breath, she realized he'd shifted his position. He was now poised over her. He lowered himself onto his elbows.

"Are ye all right?"

She nodded, still breathless. His eyes were redder than ever, actually glowing. It was wrong, but she couldn't seem to make herself care.

"Wrap yer legs around me."

She did. She shuddered when she felt his thick shaft nudging her.

"I'll try to make it as painless as possible." He nuzzled her neck. When he kissed her and tickled her with his tongue, she felt a tingle in her core.

"How do you do that?" she whispered. Even though she was inexperienced, she knew that couldn't be normal.

He didn't answer, just suckled on her neck. It made her throb and ache for him. He pushed into her, stretching her tight until he bumped into her hymen. She felt a twinge of discomfort, then he licked her again, and a frisson of pleasure vibrated through her core.

"Ready?" He lifted his head from her neck. Beads of perspiration dotted his brow, and he grimaced as if in great pain.

"Are you all right?" she asked.

"Hard . . . to control," he grated out between clenched teeth. He seized one of her decorative pillows and jammed it up against her neck.

"What—ack!" She stiffened with pain as he ripped through her barrier.

He shouted, too, and buried his head in the pillow at her neck.

She froze. He was inside her. She was no longer a virgin. The pain seeped away, leaving her with the pleasant sensation of being stuffed to the gills. She giggled.

He grunted, and she giggled again. A seed of joy burst in her chest and brought tears to her eyes. She was so glad she had waited, that it was Robby who was inside her.

She patted him on the back. "Thank you. I'll always remember this. It was just perfect."

"Are ye going somewhere?" he mumbled into the pillow.

"No. I live here."

"Good." He lifted his head from the pillow. His face seemed pale and strained. "Because we're just getting started."

"Really?" She sucked in a breath when he dragged his erection out.

"Really." He thrust back in. "I'm no' hurting you, am I?"

"No, it's—" She moaned when he rubbed himself against her clitoris.

"Ye're so beautiful, so tight." He withdrew and pushed into her again. "And ye're mine."

"Yes." She wrapped her arms around him and kissed his face all over. He quickened the pace, and once again she felt the delicious coiling sensation, driving her up and up toward a breaking point. She raised her hips to meet him, wanting him deeper and deeper inside her.

He reared back onto his knees and lifted her hips to meet his. She gasped at the strength of his thrusts. The coil shattered inside her, and she screamed. He ground himself against her, then with a hoarse shout, he collapsed on the bed beside her.

She pressed a hand to her chest as her breathing and heart rate finally slowed. "Oh God, that was so good."

He moaned.

She turned onto her side to face him. "Are you all right?"

He moaned.

"You're not going to roll over and snore, are you?"

He opened his eyes. "I don't snore."

She smiled. "Your eyes look much better. The redness is gone."

He snorted. "Not for long."

"It's a recurring problem?"

"When I'm with you, yes."

She frowned. She was causing the problem with his eyes? She knew eyes could get red and irritated, but not the way his were doing. "Are you allergic to me?"

"I'm in love with you." He sat up. "Are ye all right, sweetheart? Are ye sore?"

She moved her legs. "A little. I think I'll take a hot bath. Would you like to join me?"

"Maybe later." He climbed out of bed and put on his clothes. "I'm going to do a perimeter check of the area to make sure I'm guarding you properly." He kissed her brow and smiled. "Don't go away. We still have round two."

Round two? She winced with soreness as she sat up. "I'm not sure I can take any more."

He chuckled as he strode from the room. "Ye'll get over it."

She snorted. "If you're going outside, take my keys with you."

"I'll lock you in. And I'll be right back."

"Okay." She heard the front door open and shut, and the sound of a key turning in the lock.

She glanced at the wet spot on her comforter. There was some blood mixed in. Proof her virginity was gone. Her gaze landed on the decorative pillow Robby had pressed up against her neck.

How odd. She picked it up. There were two puncture holes in the blue satin material.

She tossed it back onto the bed. She shouldn't have washed it last week. The cheap material was falling apart.

She padded into the bathroom and turned on the water. She wasn't going to let anything detract from the most glorious night in her life. No thoughts about apples or red eyes or ruined pillows. She'd just been bedded by a wonderful lover. Robby MacKay loved her.

Life didn't get any better than this.

Chapter Nineteen

Life didn't get any tougher than this. Robby dashed down the stairs and across the parking lot to the overgrown bush where he'd hidden a small ice chest. He yanked a bottle of synthetic blood out of the ice and unscrewed the top.

He'd drunk two bottles before coming to Olivia's apartment, so he wouldn't be hungry, but he hadn't counted on spending so much time with his mouth on her neck, and her throbbing carotid artery just millimeters away from his fangs.

He guzzled down some bottled blood. Thank God he'd brought an emergency supply. He hadn't expected her to be a virgin. Years ago, when he'd had to feed to survive, he'd learned how to ease the pain of a bite and make the whole experience pleasurable for the donor. He'd used the same technique tonight to lessen Olivia's pain and heighten her pleasure, but the cost had been high.

He'd nearly died, fighting the compulsion to bite her. And the struggle hadn't ended there. He'd had to make sure the sex was good, too.

He strode around the perimeter of the parking lot, looking for anything suspicious. The parked cars were empty. He studied the apartment building while he finished the bottle of blood. If a mortal was hiding in the shadows, he'd be able to hear a heartbeat. Nothing.

He walked over to the Dumpster and tossed his empty bottle inside. There was still another bottle in the ice chest. He might need it before the night was over.

He ran a hand over his hair, pushing back the strands that had come loose during lovemaking. A virgin. He hadn't expected that. And he'd taken it.

He shouldn't have done it. It would be harder now to tell her the truth about himself. No woman would want to hear that she'd lost her virginity to a night creature.

No doubt she was hoping for a normal life. She would want to share normal activities during the day with a normal husband, and give birth to normal children. He could never give her that. He should have been honest with her before taking her to bed.

But dammit, what choice had she given him? He'd had to stop her from throwing herself at a stranger. And he'd tried his damnedest to deflower her with as little pain and as much pleasure as possible.

Stop lying to yourself. He had wanted to do it. He'd wanted Olivia since the first night he'd spotted her on Patmos. He could pretend he regretted behaving in a dishonorable fashion, but the truth was, he was doing exactly what he wanted. He loved her, and he was going to fight for her.

He climbed the steps to her apartment. Round two was about to begin.

* * *

A ringing telephone jerked Olivia from a deep sleep. She rolled over and winced. Muscles she never knew she had were sore. She blinked at the sunlight filtering through the edges of her closed blinds. The clock radio on her bedside table beamed 10:16. Good God, she'd slept late.

But then she'd fallen asleep late. Memories of marathon sex flitted through her mind. She glanced at the pillow beside her. Robby was gone. She had a fuzzy memory of him kissing her good-bye at some point.

The phone jangled again, and she fumbled for the receiver. "Hello?"

"Olivia," J.L. said. "Thank God. I tried calling your cell phone and you didn't answer."

"I didn't hear it. I guess it's in the living room."

"Did I wake you?"

"Well . . . yeah. But I needed to get up." She struggled to sit up and the bedsheet slipped down to her waist. Sheesh, she was still naked. She vaguely remembered putting on a sexy nightgown about 2:00 A.M. Robby had admired it, then promptly removed it for what he called round three.

"Are you all right?" J.L. asked.

"Yeah, I'm fine." What was the appropriate term . . . thoroughly shagged?

"I'll be over in about an hour." J.L. hung up.

She eased out of bed and stumbled toward the bathroom. She winced at the sight of herself in the mirror. Her hair was a wild mess, her eyeliner was smudged, and what were those red things on her neck? She peered closer. Good God, they were huge hickeys. She had a matching set. This was embarrassing. She'd have to wear a scarf.

She grinned. Robby had certainly taken on the role of her lover with great enthusiasm.

She took a long shower, and her thoughts went back to round two. She'd just finished her shower when Robby had returned from his perimeter check. He'd ripped the towel off her and tossed her on the bed. He'd kissed her wet and slippery body all over, flipping her over to nibble on her bottom, then flipping her back so he could dive between her legs and wreak havoc with his tongue.

One climax hadn't been enough. He'd slid her to the edge of the bed where he was standing, and raised her hips so he could plunge into her. She hadn't thought she could climax again, but he'd proven her wrong. Several times.

What an insatiable man, she thought with a grin. She dried off from the shower and pulled on a clean pair of jeans and a T-shirt. She glanced at the stained comforter and bed-sheets. It looked like she'd be doing laundry today.

She padded into the living room and noticed that it had been straightened up. Her handbag and keys were back on the console. Her laptop and legal pad were stacked on the coffee table. A folded note on yellow legal paper rested next to them with her name written on it.

She sat on the love seat and opened the note.

Good morning, Olivia. I was sorry I had to leave you so early. You looked so beautiful in your sleep, I hated to wake you.

I know you'll have some questions. We need to talk. Please remember that no matter what happens, I love you. I will always love you. I want to spend my life with you.

Robert MacKay

With a smile, she lounged back against the love seat. He loved her. He wanted to spend his life with her. That was perfect because she felt exactly the same way.

She read the note again and her smile faded. This time the words "we need to talk" jumped out at her. What was there to talk about?

I know you'll have some questions.

Her hands trembled as she folded the note. Dammit. She didn't want to think about it. Denial was so much better. Last night had been glorious. Perfect.

But this was the morning after. She couldn't deny it any longer. Every time they'd made love, his eyes had glowed red. Medical condition, he'd said. There was no such thing.

Tears gathered in her eyes. He'd lied to her. Knowing how much she hated dishonesty, he'd still lied. What was he covering up?

And then there was his lovemaking. Granted, she had been woefully inexperienced, but even so, she suspected there'd been something unusual about it. Unusually fantastic, she thought with a snort. She'd be crazy to complain about that.

But she might complain about the blue satin pillow that now had two holes in it.

She set the note back on the coffee table. Her heart lurched with a sudden thought. He'd taken the sheet of paper from her legal pad, and it was full of notes from the Great Robby Hunt. She grabbed the legal pad and thumbed through it. He must have seen how hard she'd worked to locate information on him. He knew she hadn't found squat.

I know you'll have some questions.

Damn. She threw the legal pad down and headed for the kitchen. She needed a strong cup of tea. She halted at the kitchen entrance. All the discarded clothes and towels from the bedroom were neatly piled in front of the washer/dryer combo. The sink was empty. She checked the dishwasher and found the glasses from last night inside. Even the trash and the pizza box had been taken out. Hadn't Robby slept at all? He must have done all this while she was sleeping.

A man who voluntarily cleaned up? So what if she had a few questions? The man was worth his weight in gold. And he loved her. She loved him. Whatever the problem was, they'd work it out. They'd certainly resolved her virginity problem with satisfactory results.

She started a load in the washing machine while her water heated on the stove. Her tea was steeping when she heard a knock on the door.

"Olivia, it's me!" J.L. yelled.

She peered through the peephole to make sure, then froze. The door was locked. Robby must have locked it when he left. She glanced at the console where her new key rested, attached to her key ring. This was . . . odd.

She opened the door.

J.L. strode inside, smiling. "I brought breakfast." He showed her a white paper sack full of doughnuts.

"The dead-bolt lock you put in—it came with two keys, right?" Olivia asked.

"Yeah." He strode over to her kitchen table and set the bag on top.

"Where's the second key?"

He gave her a sheepish look. "I kept it. Just in case I needed to get in here someday."

In case she was attacked or incapacitated by Otis Crump's buddy. Great. She frowned at her key ring on the console. How had Robby managed to lock her door without a key?

I know you'll have some questions.

That evening, Olivia set up her laptop and webcam at the usual time for her daily talk with Robby.

He appeared on screen and smiled. "How are ye, sweet-heart?"

She smiled back and touched the monitor. "I wish you were here. Thank you for straightening up. You must not have slept at all."

He shrugged one shoulder. "I'm used to working all night." His smile widened. "Though last night was definitely more pleasure than work."

Her cheeks grew warm. "You must have been exhausted by the time you got back to New York."

"Aye." His mouth twisted with a wry look. "I slept like the dead."

"You're back to doing security at Romatech tonight?"

He nodded. "The danger here is greater at night. The terrorists who attack the Romatechs always strike in the dark."

"What have they got against Romatech?" she asked. "Synthetic blood must save thousands of lives."

"Aye, it does, but these . . . people doona approve of the cloning of blood." He glanced to the side. "Piss off, Phineas. I doona need any more advice."

Olivia heard some laughter in the background.

Robby turned back to her with an exasperated look. "Sorry about that. The guys are giving me hell tonight."

Olivia sighed. She knew the feeling. J.L. had pretended to gag when she'd carried her bedsheets into the kitchen to stuff them in the washing machine. "Isn't Phineas the one who calls himself the Love Doctor?"

"Aye. He offered to lend me a book for educational purposes. It shows thirty different positions displayed in photographs."

She laughed. "I think we went through half of them last night."

He grinned. "I'm afraid the other half would require us both to be contortionists."

"Ouch. So what kind of advice is the Love Doctor giving you?"

Robby's grin faded. "I should make sure ye know how much I love you."

She touched the screen. "You're doing well on that."

A frown creased his brow. "And I should tell you . . . everything."

She took a deep breath. "You were right in your note. I do have questions."

He nodded but didn't say anything.

She swallowed hard. "Have you been lying to me?"

He winced. "I always try to be honest. I know it's important to you. There are times, though . . ." He shifted in his chair. "Sometimes I canna explain things."

"Like the red glowing eyes."

A pained expression flitted over his face. "I will explain. But I need to do it in person."

"What was wrong with last night?"

"I—" He ran a hand through his hair. "I thought ye'd been through enough trauma for one day."

She sat back. Telling her the truth about himself would be traumatic?

"And then I . . . I became a bit single-minded," he continued. "I wanted to make sure ye enjoyed losing yer virginity."

"Yeah." She gave him a wry smile. "You made sure of that about ten times."

He shrugged one shoulder. "I got a bit carried away. Will ye be free next weekend?"

"Yes." That would be the first weekend in June. "You're coming back?"

He nodded. "We need to talk."

A chill skittered down her arms. "How did you get out of the apartment this morning and lock the door?"

He looked away, frowning. "I'll explain it next weekend."

"Isn't there an easy explanation? Like you took my key to an all-night hardware store and had a copy made while I was sleeping?"

"That would be an easy explanation." He grimaced. "But it would be a lie."

"Oh God." She leaned back against the love seat cushions.

"Olivia, are ye still planning to see Otis Crump tomorrow?"

"Yes." She sat forward so she'd be back in camera range.

"Is there any news from Forensics regarding the box?"

She shook her head. "Not on a Sunday. We might get some results tomorrow."

"Let me know what happens. I'll be happy to deal with him myself, but it would take some planning."

What kind of planning? "I'll update you tomorrow night."

He nodded. "And I'll see you Friday night, so we can talk." He gave her a searching look. "Remember I love you."

"I love you, too." Why did he look so worried? "Can you spend the whole weekend here?"

"Possibly. It . . . depends."

"Depends on what?" she asked.

He touched the screen. "You."

She opened her mouth to ask what he meant, but the screen went blank.

He was gone.

Chapter Twenty

We're here to see Otis Crump." Olivia showed her FBI badge to the security guard at Leavenworth. "The warden has authorized it."

The guard studied her badge, then J.L.'s. "Sign in, please." He slid a clipboard across the counter.

Olivia signed in, noting the log-in sheet was just for that Monday. "Last time I was here, I signed into the book."

The guard nodded. "Change in procedure. We'll add this page to the book tonight. We get all kinds of visitors—wives, girlfriends—it protects the prisoners' privacy if their visitors don't know who else is coming to see them."

"I see." He was telling the truth. Olivia passed the clipboard to J.L.

The guard stepped back and yelled into an adjoining room. "Hey, Joe, you need to move Crump into the visitation room. Some FBI agents want to see him."

"Harrison again?" Joe shouted back.

Olivia exchanged a look with J.L. He'd told her a month ago that his investigation had cleared Harrison.

"No," the guard replied. He looked at the sign-in sheet. "J.L. Wang and Olivia Sotiris."

The second guard, Joe, peered out of the adjoining room. Even though he kept his face blank, Olivia could sense a frisson of alarm sizzle through him.

"Is there a problem?" she asked.

"No," Joe said quickly. "I'll get Crump ready." He slipped back inside the adjoining room, and they heard the banging sound of a metal door shutting.

"It'll be a few minutes," the guard told them.

"We understand." J.L. dragged Olivia across the waiting room. "You stiffened up," he whispered.

"The other guard lied," she whispered back. "And he's seriously freaked out about us being here."

"That's . . . interesting." J.L.'s eyes narrowed.

Olivia could sense his growing concern. "Are you sure Harrison checked out?"

"Yeah. I came here a month ago and asked to see the videotapes of every interview he had with Crump. The last one, he threatened to do some nasty things to Crump if he didn't leave you alone."

"That's all?" When J.L. nodded, she continued, "Then why did Harrison lie about seeing him?"

J.L. shrugged. "His threats weren't exactly ethical behavior for a special agent. And I don't think he wants you to know that he was standing up for you."

Olivia sighed. "Why was that guard upset that we're here? I've been here before, so it's not that strange."

"But it's been a long time." J.L. rubbed his chin while he considered. "I might have made a mistake asking to see only the Harrison videos. I should have asked to see yours."

"Mine? Believe me, you don't want to see them."

J.L. walked back to the counter. "I need to see all the interview videotapes of Ms. Sotiris and Otis Crump."

"Just a minute." The guard retrieved the log-in book from beneath the counter and set it down. He thumbed through a few pages at the back of the three-ring binder and shook his head. "Ms. Sotiris declined to have her last interview taped."

"What?" Olivia strode to the counter. She'd always had her interviews taped, and yet she could tell that the guard was telling the truth. "What date was that entry?"

"Last Monday."

Her breath hitched. "Let me see that." She rotated the binder and found her name listed on last Monday's sign-in page. The signature resembled her own. "This wasn't me."

The guard's surprise and confusion was genuine. "We always check IDs before anyone signs in."

"Were you working the desk when this woman signed in?" J.L. asked.

The guard frowned and studied the log-in sheet. "It was after eleven. I was on lunch break. It would have been Joe."

Olivia's heart rate sped up. "We need to talk to him."

The guard nodded and punched a button on a walkie-talkie. "We need Joe Kitchner at the front office."

"Look at this." J.L. had flipped back a few more pages in the log-in book. Four weeks earlier someone calling herself Olivia Sotiris had signed in. He kept turning pages. Every four weeks, Olivia had supposedly visited Crump.

"Check November," she said.

J.L. found an entry for the eighteenth of November. "You weren't even in the country. Harrison should have caught this. The moron spent more time threatening Otis than actually investigating."

Olivia motioned to the surveillance camera in the corner. "Whoever impersonated me was recorded when she signed it."

The guard groaned. "It'll take a while to find the right tape."

"We've got all day," J.L. muttered.

The guard's walkie-talkie made a clicking noise. "Crump is ready," a voice declared. "He's in Visitation 3."

"Is that you, Chip?" the guard asked over his walkie-talkie. "Where's Joe?"

"I don't know," Chip replied. "He told Bob and me to move Crump, then he left. Do you need me to escort the visitor?"

"I know the way," Olivia said.

J.L. dragged his gaze away from the log-in book. "Do you want me to come with you?"

"I'll be okay," she said. "You find out who's been impersonating me."

"I think I already know." He grimaced. "I hope I'm wrong."

Olivia hoped she was wrong, too. No doubt she was suspecting the same person. There was only one woman in the office who had access to her ID and her signature.

She strode to the visitor door and waited to be buzzed in, then walked down the plain hallway, her steps echoing on the shiny linoleum floor. She halted outside the door labeled VISITATION 3 and took a deep breath.

Otis Crump was a master at detecting weakness and exploiting it for his own sick pleasure. She needed to be calm and stay in control. If all went well, she'd never have to see the bastard again.

He was standing in the small room, plain walls on all four sides and a fortified Plexiglas wall dividing his half of the room from hers. There was a metal door behind him, and beside him, a plain metal chair was bolted to the floor.

The guards had started the videotape and agreed to wait outside. They could watch what transpired on the monitor in the hallway.

Otis must have been using the prison's fitness room, for he'd put on some muscle. His jumpsuit was clean, his hair combed; his face shaved. In his narcissistic way, he'd always considered himself exceptionally handsome.

Olivia had always found his features too mellow. No doubt it was his soft look that had encouraged his victims to trust him. Brown hair, brown eyes, average height, good bone structure. But there was nothing striking about him. Nothing overtly masculine and memorable.

He made up for that with his personality.

He smiled as she entered the divided room, and she could sense he was genuinely happy to see her.

"Come in, Olivia. Sit down." He sprawled in the metal chair. "I've been expecting you."

Predictable. He'd started off with commands in an attempt to establish dominance.

"I'll make this short." She strode inside and stopped beside the metal chair in her half of the room. "I have a few questions—"

"And I have all the answers," he interrupted her with a smirk.

"I expect your full cooperation."

"Really?" He rubbed a hand up and down his thigh. "What can you give me to make it worthwhile?"

"I can make sure you stay alive."

He grinned. "Oh, a threat. I like it. Strong women are so much more fun. They fight back and struggle till their last breath. Makes the final victory much more satisfying." He held up a hand. "Don't worry, darling. I would never hurt you. We're destined to be together."

She could point out that he was serving three consecutive life terms, but he never seemed to grasp that concept. "Since you're so fond of me, I expect you to answer my questions honestly."

"And I expect something in exchange. A token of your affection for me." He lowered his hand to his crotch. "I want an eight-by-ten glossy of you so I can masturbate to it."

"You're wasting my time." She strode back to the door.

"Wait." He jumped up and followed her on his side of the glass. "Don't go, Olivia. It's been so long since I've seen you."

She paused at the door, sensing his desperation. His emotional attachment to her always made her queasy in the stomach. "Are you ready to answer my questions?"

He smiled slowly. "You've learned to play the game well. I'm a good teacher, don't you think?"

He was such a narcissist. Even when she took control, he took credit for it. She sauntered back to the center of the room to force him to follow her.

He did. "Did you enjoy your vacation on Patmos?"

"I'm asking the questions." She rested her hands on the back of her metal chair. "Who is your accomplice? Who's sending the apples?"

He lounged in the chair. "Don't you enjoy the apples? You had so much fun peeling them for me. You could make it all around the apple in one long spiral." He rotated a finger in the air. "I had to go through several women before I mastered that technique."

She was careful not to show any emotion, but she could tell he was aroused. "Who is your accomplice?"

He smiled. " 'Quid pro quo, Clarice.' "

"This isn't a movie."

"It should be." He stood and walked toward the glass. "Who do think should play me? Brad Pitt, maybe?"

"Who is your accomplice?"

He pressed his hands against the glass. "Nobody. She means nothing to me. She's just a way to keep up with you. You're the one I love."

"Who is she?"

He stepped back from the glass. "I answered. Now quid pro quo. My turn to ask a question."

His gaze wandered over her and lingered on her linen pants. "The first time you came to see me, you were wearing a tight black skirt, and your legs were bare. You would sit on that chair and cross your legs, and I thought I'd gone to heaven. I would have told you anything to keep you coming here in those tight-assed little skirts."

The queasy feeling in her stomach grew. She'd sensed from the beginning that he lusted for her, and she'd used it to lure him into a trusting relationship. When he'd offered to tell her everything if she'd simply peel an apple for him, she'd gone along with it. And he had confessed to torturing and killing ten more women.

Otis planted his hands on the glass wall and leaned toward her. "It nearly killed me when you stopped wearing skirts. You know how much I love your legs."

She'd started wearing pants when he'd told her what he liked to do to his victims' legs.

"When you peeled that apple for me," he continued, "I knew you were the one. No one understands me like you do. You can tell when I'm lying or being naughty, but you keep coming back to see me. Admit it, Olivia. You find me fascinating. When you fuck other men, you're thinking about me."

She swallowed hard at the bile in her throat. "You didn't ask a question."

He chuckled. "Fine. Tell me, did you peel the apples I sent you? Did you slide the knife just under the skin and hear that little pop when the blade breaks through? Did you skim the knife around and—"

"No. I threw the apples away." She stepped toward the glass. "My turn. The name of your accomplice."

"I'm afraid you'll have to rephrase that in question form."

"Who is your accomplice?"

He shrugged. "Darling, you already know. Now if you would just admit that we belong together, I wouldn't have to take advantage of the poor, stupid sluts who want to help me in my time of need."

"The game's over, Otis. You won't be manipulating anyone. I'm getting the D.A. in Texas to prosecute you for the murder you committed there."

"You do that, darling. I would enjoy a trip to Texas. I can use the opportunity to escape so we can be together."

"You'll be convicted there, and I will come to see you."

He grinned. "That's my girl."

"I'll be a witness when they give you the needle."

His smile faded.

"Death penalty, Otis. How do you like them apples?"

His face hardened with a cold stare. "While you stand here making idle threats, my accomplices are getting away."

"We'll get them." She strode toward the door. As usual, she felt like going straight to a shower.

"Olivia!" Otis called to her.

When she glanced back, he pulled something from the chest pocket of his uniform. It was red and lacy. *Her missing panties.*

He rubbed them against his cheek. "Till we meet again, darling."

Her stomach twinged, and she quickly left the room. She rushed back to the front office.

J.L. was behind the counter with the guard. "We've got her, Olivia." He turned the monitor so she could see.

The woman appeared to be about the same height and weight as Olivia. She was wearing dark sunglasses, and her dark hair was covered with a baseball cap. Joe was the guard. She showed him an ID and signed in.

Yasmine. Olivia's heart sank. She'd hoped it wasn't her, but it had just made too much sense. "She made a copy of my ID."

J.L. nodded. "And she knows where you stash your handbag. She probably made a wax imprint of your house key. It would only take a few seconds."

Olivia pressed a hand to her stomach. It was bad enough to deal with Otis, but to discover that Yasmine had betrayed their friendship—it made her feel physically ill. "Did you call Barker?"

"Yes. They've put an APB out on her."

"She wasn't in the office?" Olivia asked, then realized what had happened. "Joe must have warned her."

"Looks like it. He's disappeared, too." J.L. skirted the edge of the counter. "How did your meeting with Otis go?"

"He wouldn't divulge her name, but he admitted to using her." Olivia made a face. "How could Yasmine do this? Doesn't she know what a monster he is?"

"You never felt any sort of deception from her?" J.L. asked.

"No! She never lied. She was always nosy, but as far as I could tell, her friendship was real."

"She knew about your gift, so I guess she was always careful around you."

Olivia groaned. How could she not have known? Detecting deception was supposed to be her specialty.

J.L. escorted her toward the door. He glanced back at the guard. "You can expect some special agents here this afternoon to interview all the guards. Meanwhile, if you hear anything about Joe, call the number on the card I gave you."

"Will do." The guard looked worried as he watched them leave.

J.L. led her across the parking lot to his car. "Are you all right? You look really pale."

"I trusted her," Olivia whispered. Her thoughts wandered to Robby and his red glowing eyes. If she'd been deceived by Yasmine, then she could have been deceived by Robby. "I feel sick."

"I'll drive you home," J.L. offered.

"No. I want to keep working." If she stayed home all day, she'd have too much time to think. Too much time to nurse some terrible suspicions about the secrets Robby was hiding. Had she been wrong to fall in love with him?

That evening, like most evenings, Robby set up his laptop and webcam in the conference room across from the security office. As soon as Olivia's face appeared on the screen, he knew something was wrong. There was a sadness in her eyes and a weary droop to her expression.

"Sweetheart, what's wrong?"

She told him about her trip to Leavenworth, and how J.L. had discovered that their office manager, Yasmine Hernandez, had impersonated her in order to visit Otis Crump. She'd been assisted in her deception by a guard at the penitentiary.

"Have they been arrested?" Robby asked.

Olivia shook her head. "We're looking for them, but they've both disappeared."

"At least now ye know who was sending the apples," Robby said. "Ye should feel good about that."

A pained look crossed her face. "I thought Yasmine was a friend. I trusted her. I joined the FBI so I could use my lie detector skills to catch bad guys, and there she was, right under my nose, and I never saw it."

Robby leaned forward. "Ye shouldna doubt yerself. Ye always believed there was an accomplice, and ye were right about that. And did ye no' use yer abilities to get Crump to confess to more murders?"

There was a glint of moisture in her eyes. "I should have known. I should have sensed deception from her."

"Ye canna blame yerself. 'Tis normal to be feeling bad right now. Someone ye care about has betrayed you."

She glanced at him with a wary look. "Are you still coming here on Friday?"

"Aye. I should be there a little before nine."

She blinked, as if she were trying not to cry. "I wish we'd never left Patmos. It was so . . . magical there."

"We'll go back someday. Just you and me." If she could accept him as a vampire.

She closed her eyes briefly. "Be honest with me. Have you been deceiving me?"

He inhaled sharply. Pretending to be a normal human was a deception. "Olivia—"

"Forget it." She held up a hand to stop him, then shook her head with a wry expression. "If you've been lying to me, why would you admit it now? I don't even want to hear it. One betrayal a day is more than enough."

She was doubting him again? Bloody hell. But could

he blame her? He'd already admitted there were things he hadn't told her.

"Olivia, listen to me. When I say I love you, that is the truth. When I say I think about you every waking minute, that is the truth. When I say ye've changed my life, that before my heart was filled with vengeance and now it is filled with love, that is the bloody truth."

A tear rolled down her cheek. "I love you so much, Robby. It'll kill me if you betray me."

He swallowed hard. He could only pray she wouldn't interpret his hiding the truth as an act of betrayal.

"Yo, Robby!" Phineas barged into the conference room.

"This is a bad time," Robby told him.

"Yeah, it's bad," Phineas replied. "We just went on red alert."

Robby tensed as he turned back to the monitor. "Olivia, I have to go. I'll talk to you tomorrow."

She frowned. "What's wrong?"

"I'll let you know later. I love you, sweetheart." He disconnected and rose to his feet. "What is it?"

Phineas led the way across the hall to the security office. "Angus and Emma just teleported in. I got an emergency message from Stanislav about five minutes ago. Casimir and his little band of merry bloodsuckers are on the move."

"Do ye know where they're headed?" Robby asked as he entered the security office. Angus, Emma, and Connor were there.

Angus gave him a worried look. "According to Stanislav, they're somewhere in North America."

Chapter Twenty-one

Within minutes the security office at Romatech was overflowing with MacKay S&I employees. The mortals and shape-shifters were teleported in by the Vamps.

"We have to locate Casimir and his followers as quickly as possible," Angus told them.

"It shouldna be difficult once they start leaving a trail of dead bodies in their wake," Connor grumbled.

Emma winced. "Hopefully, we'll find them before any innocent people die."

With a scowl, Connor crossed his arms over his chest. "If they're here, the killing has already begun."

"We need to check every place Casimir has teleported to before," Robby said. "One of those places would have been his point of entry."

"I agree." Angus nodded. "We know he liked going to

Apollo's compound in Maine." He turned to Jack. "Ye're familiar with the place. Teleport there. Take Lara, Zoltan, Mikhail, Austin, and Darcy."

"Yes, sir." Jack led his team into the armory at the back of the office so they could select weapons. He vanished, taking Lara with him.

A few seconds later the phone rang. Connor punched the conference call button.

"We're here," Lara said. "It appears quiet . . ." She continued to talk while Zoltan and Mikhail fixed on her voice. They teleported, taking the mortals Austin and Darcy with them.

"Casimir also teleported to the coven house in New Orleans," Angus said. "They should be warned."

"I'll go," Phineas offered.

Robby snorted. He knew why Phineas was eager to go to New Orleans.

"Go ahead," Angus said. "Call us if ye need help. And stay in touch with Stanislav in case he hears anything."

Phineas grabbed some weapons from the armory and teleported away.

"Ian and Toni." Angus regarded them. "I want you to take Shanna and the children to Dragon Nest. Stay at the school. Keep all the children safe."

Ian's jaw shifted with an annoyed look. "If there's a battle, ye'd better call me."

"We will," Angus assured him. "We'll need every available warrior. In fact, we may need some of Phil's young lads." He turned to the Alpha werewolf. "How is the training going?"

"Two of the oldest boys have achieved Alpha status," Phil replied. He'd been living at Dragon Nest Academy with Vanda. While she taught art, he'd been coaching the young werewolves he'd found in Wyoming. "They're ready to fight."

"Good." Angus glanced at Dougal, who'd teleported in from Texas. "I'm leaving you and Howard in charge here. This could be a primary target if Casimir decides to blow something up."

Dougal nodded. "We're on it."

"That leaves South Dakota," Robby said. Casimir had teleported there last summer with a small army of Malcontents. He'd taken Robby there to torture him.

"Emma and I are going there now," Angus replied. "Connor and Carlos, ye're with us." He gave Robby a speculative look. "And ye can come, too, if ye're up to it."

"I am." Robby's heart rate quickened as he strode into the armory. After all these months of waiting, his quest for revenge was drawing near.

Ten minutes later Robby and his companions materialized at a campground south of Mount Rushmore. It was here that the Vamps had caught the Malcontent army by surprise. Many Malcontents had died. Many more had fled.

Sean Whelan from the CIA Stake-Out Team had assisted with the cleanup. The Malcontents had attacked innocent campers, holding them prisoner and feeding off them till they were all dead. Whelan had released a cover story to the media, blaming the deaths on a fictitious neo-Nazi group of fanatics.

This camp was a cursed place for mortals, Robby thought as he and his comrades searched the small wooden cabins. No people inside, but the clothing and toiletries left behind indicated they were in use.

" 'Tis a bad sign," Robby muttered as they strode toward the main lodge.

Carlos halted suddenly with a grimace. "I can smell death."

They dashed into the lodge, their weapons drawn. Too late. Eight bodies lay on the floor, completely drained of blood and their throats slashed to disguise puncture wounds.

"Oh no." Emma pressed a hand to her mouth.

Connor knelt down to check a man's body. "He hasna been dead for long."

"Casimir could still be in the vicinity," Emma said.

Angus had already retrieved a cell phone from his sporran and was making a call. "Jack, we need you and yer team here."

Robby called Phineas in New Orleans. Within a few minutes their number had more than doubled.

"Spread out," Angus ordered. "If ye find them, back away and call us. We'll fight them together."

Robby zoomed at vampire speed toward the cave. What poetic justice it would be if he could kill Casimir in the same place where the bastard had tortured him. He paused at the entrance to retrieve the flashlight he'd packed in his sporran. Even with his superior night vision, he could use some extra light in the cave.

Emma and Angus dashed toward him and stopped.

"We had a feeling you'd come straight here," Emma id.

Angus frowned at him. "Doona take him on by yerself."

Robby shrugged one shoulder. "I havena found him yet."

Angus took a flashlight from his sporran and clicked it . "Lead the way."

They proceeded down the main shaft. Torches made of eds lay extinguished on the stone floor. When the path vided in two, Robby went left and Angus and Emma went ght.

The caves appeared empty. There were no lit torches. No voices murmuring and echoing in the distance. Robby headed straight for the small room where the Malcontents had held him prisoner.

The circle of light from his flashlight moved along the stone walls. The scent of blood still lingered in the air. His beam of light landed on the chair. The wooden frame was rickety and lopsided from his violent struggles to free himself. Silver chains dangled from the rungs of the chair's back, spilling down onto the stone floor. Those chains had held him to the chair, burning his flesh and preventing him from teleporting away. Blood—his blood—stained the floor a dark burgundy.

Dark memories flashed through his mind. All the pain, all the humiliation and despair, came careening back as if it had just happened last night. The flashlight beam wobbled as his hand trembled with rage.

"I thought ye'd be here," someone said softly behind him.

He whipped around to find Connor at the narrow entrance.

"The cave is empty," Connor announced. "The campground, too. Casimir and his minions have moved on to another feeding ground."

"I'm going to kill him," Robby whispered. "If ye find him, I have to be the one to drive a sword through his black heart."

"Ye need vengeance. I understand that." Connor's eyes took on a sad, haunted look. "Be careful, lad. Vengeance can drive a man to do terrible things. Ye willna feel better if ye lose yer soul in the process."

"I doona intend—" Robby stopped talking when Connor left the room. He glanced back at the rickety wooden chair. "I *will* have my revenge."

* * *

Olivia was getting ready to leave work Thursday evening when Barker opened his office door and shouted, "Harrison, Wang, Sotiris—in my office now!"

She exchanged a questioning look with J.L. as they hurried into their supervisor's corner office.

"What's up?" Harrison asked.

"Some news just came in from a county sheriff in Nebraska. Some folks complained that no one in a nearby farming community was answering their phones, so he went to check it out." Barker sighed and shook his head. "Everyone there is dead."

Olivia gasped. "How many people?"

"About ten, I believe," Barker replied. "There's no airport nearby, so we'll be driving. We may be gone a few days, so pack whatever you need, then let's hit the road."

"I keep an overnight bag in my car," Harrison said.

"And I've got one here," Barker told him. "I'll meet you in the parking lot in five minutes. You can drive."

"Gotcha." Harrison rushed out of the office.

Olivia winced. She didn't keep an emergency bag ready, since she'd never gone on a field assignment like this with the special agents. "I'll have to swing by my apartment to pick up a few things."

"I'll take you," J.L. offered. "Then we can drive together. I have a bag in my trunk."

"This is where we're going." Barker handed J.L. a sheet of paper with some information on it. "Olivia, I'm sure you're wondering why I want you on this case. The fact is, something bizarre is going on here. All the people are dead, but there's no sign of any struggle."

"Weird," J.L. muttered.

"You can say that again." Barker gave Olivia a wry

look. "And when it comes to weird-assed crap, you're the expert."

She smiled grimly. "Thanks."

Forty-five minutes later she dropped an overnight bag in the trunk of J.L.'s car. She set another case containing her laptop and webcam on the backseat. The webcam was just wishful thinking, she realized. Most probably she would miss the usual nine o'clock meeting with Robby. Just as well. He'd missed the last two nights.

"Let's go." J.L. climbed into the driver's seat.

She slid into the passenger seat and buckled up as J.L. took off. Robby had called briefly on the phone the last two nights. He'd sounded rushed and admitted something urgent was happening at work, but he wouldn't explain what. He'd confessed that he might not be able to come see her Friday night after all.

Now it looked like she was in the same boat. "Do you think we'll be back by tomorrow night?"

J.L. shook his head as he pulled onto a freeway. "I doubt it."

She sighed and called Robby on his cell phone. As usual, he didn't pick up, so she left a message. "Robby, I've been sent out of town on an assignment. It doesn't look like I'll be home tomorrow night. Call me, so we can work something out. Love you. 'Bye." She hung up.

J.L. glanced at her. "You had a big date planned?"

"Yeah." She slipped her cell phone into its pocket inside her handbag. "He was going to tell me something important."

"About himself?"

"I guess." She set her holster containing her sidearm in her handbag. It felt awkward, wearing it in the car. She was glad she'd worn one of her more comfortable pantsuits today. The linen pants and jacket were navy blue, and her

T-shirt was white with little red stars, making her look patriotic. In her apartment, she'd exchanged her navy pumps for a pair of black Nikes.

"So Robby has a deep, dark secret." J.L. zoomed past a car on the freeway. "How interesting."

She scoffed. "What makes you think it's deep and dark? Robby is a sweet guy."

"He carries a freaking claymore on his back, Liv. And he's built like a bulldozer."

"Thanks."

J.L. shrugged. "Could be worse. He could be hiding something bad, like he's a kleptomaniac."

"I don't think so."

"Nymphomaniac?"

She snorted. Though J.L. might have a point, if Robby made a habit of always going three rounds.

"I've got it! He escaped from a mental ward."

She shook her head.

"From the zoo?"

She punched J.L. on the shoulder.

"Hey, watch it. I'm driving."

"You're speeding."

"We've got a long way to go." J.L. passed another car. "I want to get there while it's still daylight."

"What's the latest news on the missing guard and Yasmine?" Olivia asked.

"There is no news. They did a good job of disappearing." J.L. glanced at her. "Did you learn anything useful?"

"No." She'd spent the last two days interviewing the other guards at Leavenworth. They all insisted they had no idea Joe was helping someone sneak in to see Otis Crump. And they were all being honest.

She yawned. She hadn't slept well the last few nights. She was still upset about Yasmine's betrayal and still worried about Robby.

"Do you need some sleep?" J.L. asked.

She yawned again. "Don't you want me to navigate?"

"I've got my handy GPS. Go ahead and rest. I have a feeling we're going to be up really late tonight."

She removed the clip from her hair so she could lean back against the headrest, then closed her eyes.

Sometime later J.L. shook her shoulder. "Hey, you want a hamburger, fishburger, or chickenburger? Those are the choices."

She blinked awake and realized they were in the drive-through lane of a small fast food restaurant. "Uh, chicken." She glanced at the digital clock. It was 7:38. "Are we in Nebraska?"

"Yep. We're not in Kansas anymore, Toto." J.L. lowered his car window and placed their order. He reached for his wallet.

"I'll get it." Olivia rummaged in her handbag and passed J.L. a twenty dollar bill. "How much farther?"

"We should be there in about thirty minutes." J.L. paid for the food, handed the paper sacks to Olivia, then set their drinks into the cup holders. "I passed Harrison and Barker on the highway about fifteen minutes ago, so I figured we had a little time to spare."

They exited the parking lot and in a few minutes, they'd left the town behind. Fields of corn flanked the road. Olivia estimated the plants were about five to six feet tall. She finished her chicken sandwich, and the view hadn't changed. She shared some of J.L.'s fries and sipped her drink. The cornfields stretched on and on.

"Lots of corn," she muttered.

"Yep." J.L. drank some cola. "It was starting to make me sleepy. I needed some caffeine."

Shortly after eight, they arrived at the small town where Barker had reserved some rooms. Olivia and J.L. checked into the motel just as Harrison and Barker pulled up.

Olivia used the bathroom and tossed some cold water on her face. In five minutes they were on their way to the cluster of farmhouses where the dead bodies had been discovered. Barker had called the sheriff, requesting that he meet them there.

They turned onto a dirt road that dissected two large cornfields. Olivia noted the sun nearing the horizon. They would end up doing some of their investigation with flashlights.

"There's the sheriff's car." Olivia pointed as J.L. sped past it.

He pulled into a driveway that led to an old wood-frame farmhouse, and they exited the car. Olivia strapped her holster around her waist and wedged her flashlight under the belt. She wound her hair on the back of her head and secured it with the clip.

As they walked back to the sheriff, she noticed there were four farmhouses, two on each side of the road. Farther down the road she spotted two red barns. Each farmhouse was two stories high and painted white. Each house had a wide front porch. Their only distinguishing feature was the color of the shutters. One had black shutters, one had dark green, and the other two were slate blue and maroon. Each house had a big shade tree in the front yard. Surrounding the cluster of farmhouses and barns, green cornfields stretched for miles. The sun hovered on the horizon, painting the sky with shades of pink and gold.

Harrison had parked behind the sheriff's car, and Barker

was already discussing the case with the local officer. J.L. and Olivia introduced themselves.

"I'm telling you it's downright strange," the sheriff said. "I can't make any sense of it. These were good, God-fearing people. Who would want to kill them all?"

"Let's have a look," Barker said.

"Come on." The sheriff led them to the nearest house on the right, the one with slate blue shutters.

A breeze ruffled the cornfield as Olivia passed by. When she heard the rustling sound, she realized how quiet everything else was. No farm equipment being used. No mothers calling the family home for dinner. No sounds of a television filtering through the open windows.

Inside the house, the sheriff showed them the bodies. A man and a woman were stretched out on the wooden floor in the family room. Their throats had been slashed, but there was no pool of blood beneath them.

Olivia swallowed hard. She wasn't accustomed to working the actual crime scene. She usually stayed at the office where she could interview suspects to see who was lying.

"They must have bled out somewhere else," Harrison said. "Then the killer moved them here."

J.L. paced around the bodies. "There's no sign of them being moved. No trail of blood. No scuff marks from their shoes. And I bet there was more than one killer."

Olivia pressed a hand to her stomach. She shouldn't have eaten that chicken sandwich.

Barker leaned over for a closer look. "No defense wounds. They didn't fight back."

She turned away from the gruesome sight and noticed the toys in a plastic crate by the television. Oh God. "Are there more bodies here?"

"Nope, this is it," the sheriff replied. "You want to see the other houses?"

Outside, they decided to split up since they were quickly losing sunlight. The sheriff and Harrison crossed the road to the farmhouse there. Barker, J.L., and Olivia went to the second house on the right side of the road.

Just like the first house, they found a dead couple lying on the floor, throats slashed but no sign of blood. They found an elderly woman in the kitchen, same story.

They went upstairs to check the bedrooms there.

"Come and look," Olivia called from a bedroom.

"Another body?" Barker asked as he and J.L entered the room.

"No." She motioned to the floor where toys were scattered about. "The first house had toys, too."

"Damn." J.L. grimaced. "Where are the children?"

"I don't know." She pulled back the Priscilla curtains and peered out the window. The last rays of sunlight illuminated a small backyard with an old rusty swing set. Behind it, fields of corn went on as far as she could see. "I can't sense any emotions other than our own and the guys across the road."

"Maybe the kids escaped," J.L. suggested. "If a murderer came to my house, I'd run and hide in the cornfield."

Olivia shuddered. The killers might have kidnapped the children.

"I'll see if I can track any of them." Barker grabbed a child's discarded T-shirt off the floor. "You two stay here." He left the room and clambered down the stairs.

Olivia and J.L. exchanged questioning looks. They heard a door bang shut.

"There he is." Olivia pointed out the window. Barker was holding the T-shirt to his face as he strode into the cornfield.

"What's he doing? He could get lost in the corn. It's like an ocean."

"Weird," J.L. muttered.

Olivia watched as Barker disappeared and the last of the sunlight died away. Darkness enveloped the house. She reached for her flashlight, but then a bright light went on in the backyard.

"Great." J.L. looked relieved. "They have automatic outdoor lighting. If Barker gets lost, he can just head for the light."

She nodded. "Let's see how Harrison is doing."

They went to a bedroom at the front of the house and peered out the window. Outdoor lighting gleamed in front of each farmhouse, but a dark abyss separated each home.

"Creepy looking," J.L. whispered.

Olivia shivered. She didn't even want to think about the terror these poor people had gone through before dying. And what if the killers were still nearby? They could be lurking in a field or in the barns. "You told me once that if our lives were ever in danger, you would tell me what your initials stand for."

"We're not in danger."

"Are you kidding? There's a mass murderer around here somewhere. Maybe several murderers."

"I think they're gone," J.L. said. "They did the job and moved on."

She sighed. "I hope the children are all right."

"Look." J.L. motioned to two lights emerging from a house across the road. "That's got to be Harrison and the sheriff."

"It is." Their emotions were so intense, Olivia could feel them from a distance. The sheriff was devastated, for he was mourning people he had known. Harrison was pissed.

The two men walked back to the road, using flashlights to light their way.

"Let's go meet them." J.L. headed for the bedroom door.

"Wait." In the distance she saw two more lights. "Someone else is here."

"What?" J.L. returned to the window and peered out.

The two lights came closer, passing in front of the first farmhouse, and thanks to the outdoor lighting, Olivia could make out the forms of two men. She gasped.

"What the hell?" J.L. whispered.

The two men were wearing kilts. They stopped in the middle of the road. Harrison and the sheriff walked toward them, then stopped.

"Are they talking?" J.L. asked.

"I don't think so. I don't see their mouths moving." Olivia realized all of a sudden that she could no longer sense any emotions from Harrison or the sheriff. They'd gone completely blank. And she couldn't sense anything from the men in kilts.

The sheriff strode past the kilted men, climbed into his car, and drove away. Then Harrison drove away, too.

J.L. made a noise of disbelief. "What the hell?"

The kilted men turned toward them. Olivia and J.L. quickly plastered themselves against the wall on each side of the window. A beam of light shot through the window as one of the strangers aimed a flashlight in their direction.

Olivia held her breath. Her heart raced. Who were those men? She recalled a photo she'd seen of Robby in a kilt. There couldn't be any connection. He was in New York. But on the other hand, she couldn't read him. He was blank like the two kilted men in the road.

J.L. flipped open his cell phone and punched a number. He waited, then whispered, "Harrison, leave your phone on, dammit. And why did you drive off like that? Get back here now." He hung up and jammed the phone into his suit pocket.

"Harrison turned his phone off?" Olivia asked. Why would he do that? Why would he abandon them? She ventured a glance out the window. The men in kilts were coming down the road, headed in their direction.

J.L. drew his weapon. "Don't worry, Liv. Everything will be fine. I know it."

She swallowed hard. J.L. had just told a lie.

Chapter Twenty-two

*O*livia took a deep breath and removed her automatic from its holster at her waist.

"Two against two," J.L. whispered. "Let's find out who these guys are." He led the way quietly down the stairs.

The stairwell was dark, but they didn't dare turn on their flashlights. They crept toward the living room at the front of the house and peered out the window.

J.L. pointed, then lifted his finger to his lips.

She didn't need the warning to stay quiet. The two kilted men were now in the front yard. She could see them well in the outdoor lighting, and neither one was Robby. The man in the red and green plaid kilt had a brighter shade of red hair. The guy in the blue and green kilt looked similar to Robby, with the same dark auburn hair.

J.L. touched his back, then his right calf, signaling to her that the two men had swords on their backs and knives in their right knee socks. A bad sign when the two bodies in the next room had slashed throats.

She wished Barker would come back. She'd feel better if it was three against two.

The kilted men removed cell phones from their sporrans and made calls. A man suddenly materialized in the front yard. Olivia covered her mouth to stifle her gasp. She blinked, not believing her eyes. Then another man appeared. And another.

She struggled to breathe. More people were appearing, and they were all armed with swords and pistols. She thought she detected a woman and a few more men in kilts.

J.L. grabbed her arm and motioned with his head to the back door. She moved quietly with him through the family room and into the kitchen. Her heart pounded in her ears. They slipped out the back door just as they heard the front door creaking open.

They ran for the cornfield. Immediately, she was enveloped in a sea of green. It grew so dark, she could barely make out J.L.'s form. She bumped into him when he suddenly stopped. He grabbed her by the forearms and lowered her into a crouch beside him. She could hear his quick breaths and sense his alarm.

"Those guys materialized like it was a sci-fi movie," he whispered. "What are they—aliens?"

"I don't think aliens wear kilts."

"You're right. And they'd be armed with lasers instead of swords."

She shook her head. "I can't believe we're having this discussion."

"Whatever they are, they've got us seriously outnumbered."

"And they have swords, knives, and guns," she mumbled.

"Could be worse. They could have machine guns and bazookas."

"Thanks. I feel so much better."

"Sorry." He grew quiet.

She glanced back at the farmhouse. She could only see the upstairs, but lights were flickering in the windows. What were they doing? Were they searching for something?

She opened her senses to get a feel for their emotions. Nothing. They were completely blank. Like Robby.

"My first name is Jin," J.L. whispered.

She winced. Did this mean he was afraid they wouldn't get out of this? "That's a nice name."

"Not if the guys in school keep calling you Jennifer."

"Oh. I'm sorry."

"The L stands for Long."

"Jin Long . . . Wang." She smiled. "Sounds very masculine."

He snorted. "Now you know why I go by J.L. But it could be worse. They named my brother L.H.—Lo Hung Wang."

She covered her mouth to keep from laughing.

His teeth flashed white in the dark as he grinned. "I just made that part up. I don't have a brother. But you probably already detected that."

She had. And she'd also realized he was trying to cheer her up.

"So here's the plan," J.L. said. "We move through the corn and get as close to the car as possible. We make a dash for it, drive into town, and get the sheriff and Harrison. And we call for backup."

She nodded. "What about Barker?"

"We'll find him. Let's go."

They moved as quietly as possible through the corn. They

were behind the first house when J.L. abruptly halted and reached out to stop her. He pressed a finger to his mouth to warn her to stay quiet, and she remained perfectly still. Then she heard it. A rustling in the corn.

They were not alone.

She pivoted, searching for the source of the noise. She spotted the swaying plants. Whoever it was, he was moving straight toward them.

J.L. raised his pistol.

The corn in front of them rustled, then out trotted a dog.

Olivia's knees nearly buckled with relief.

J.L. holstered his weapon. "Good boy," he whispered.

It was a huge dog. An Irish wolfhound with long lanky legs and a long thin face. He sat on his haunches and regarded them curiously.

She raised her hand slowly to let him sniff her, then patted him on the head. "Aren't you a big boy."

The dog seemed to grin.

She smiled. She felt safer with him there.

"Let's go." J.L. led the way through the corn, with Olivia and the wolfhound following. They skirted the farmhouse and ventured into the field that extended up to the dirt road. They stopped when they spotted the car in the driveway about thirty yards away.

"You wait here." J.L. handed Olivia the car keys. "I'll find Barker. If we're not back in fifteen minutes, leave."

"I'm not leaving without you."

"Liv, we're outnumbered. You can bring the sheriff and Harrison back and alert the state patrolmen. Okay?"

She nodded reluctantly. "Okay."

J.L. dashed off with the Irish wolfhound trotting along beside him. She was grateful he wasn't alone.

She sat between two rows of corn and pushed the button on her watch to make the digital time light up. This was going to be a long and lonely fifteen minutes.

She took long breaths to calm her racing heart. She considered calling Harrison on her cell phone, but it wouldn't do any good if he'd turned his phone off. Why had he left after speaking to the kilted men? Had they told him to turn off his phone? She considered calling Robby, but he was far away in New York. It would take him hours to get here.

After a few minutes she crept close to the edge of the cornfield. She spotted the guys who had materialized earlier. They'd divided into smaller groups and appeared to be searching for something. Most of them were way off by the barns. When one of them located a storm cellar in the distance, they gathered around it and went inside.

With most of them in the cellar, it seemed like a good time to dash to the car. She glanced at her watch. Fourteen minutes had passed. Still, she was reluctant to leave without J.L. and Barker. On the other hand, she would be more helpful to them if she brought back reinforcements.

She groaned inwardly. She was overanalyzing again.

A car engine roared in the distance. Someone was approaching fast. Maybe Harrison or the sheriff was coming back? She hurried down a corn row till she was close to the road. A black sedan pulled over and parked. It looked like a government car. Three people emerged—a middle-aged man, a younger man, and a young woman. The men were tense and high on adrenaline. The woman seemed reluctant and afraid.

The middle-aged man barked out some orders. "Garrett, check the houses on the left. I'll check the ones on the right. Alyssa, look over the grounds."

Garrett clicked on his flashlight and shone it around. "I don't see Connor anywhere."

"He's here," the older man growled. "And he won't be alone."

Alyssa shuddered. "I don't understand why we had to involve them."

"They're better at killing Malcontents than we are," the older man grumbled. "If you see any of them, keep your distance. And keep your psychic guards up. Especially you, Alyssa. They prefer to target young women."

"I know," she said quietly.

Olivia felt sorry for the young woman. She was clearly terrified. The young man, Garrett, was excited, and he sprinted to the houses on the left. The older man strode toward the houses on the right. He'd mentioned Malcontents. Was that a gang? Were they the ones who'd committed the murders? And what was the deal with psychic guards?

Alyssa remained close to the car, swinging her flashlight back and forth. "Great," she muttered. "You just stay here, all alone, with a bunch of murdering Malcontents close by."

Olivia wanted to know who these people were, so she stepped out of the cornfield and moved slowly toward the woman. "Alyssa?"

The woman squealed and dropped her flashlight.

"I'm sorry." Olivia held her hands out so the woman could see they were empty. "I didn't mean to scare you."

Alyssa drew her gun. "How did you know my name? Are you one of them? Did you read my mind?"

Olivia raised her hands higher. "I heard your conversation with the other two men, and they used your name. I'm with the FBI. Would you like to see my badge?"

"You're FBI? You're not one of them?"

"Who are they?" Olivia assumed she was referring to the men who had teleported in. "Are they the Malcontents?"

"Alyssa?" The middle-aged man came running back. "I heard you yell." He spotted Olivia and drew his weapon. "Who the hell are you?"

She cursed silently. She should have remained hidden in the corn. "I'm Olivia Sotiris, FBI. Who are you?"

"CIA." He moved closer. "Show me your badge."

She did, and squinted when he beamed his flashlight in her face.

"Ms. Sotiris, what you are doing here?"

What did he think? She was on a picnic? "I'm investigating a multiple homicide. May I see your badge, please?"

"I don't have time to fool with this." He holstered his weapon. "We're taking over this investigation, Ms. Sotiris. You may leave."

His attitude was seriously annoying her. "This is an FBI matter. The local sheriff requested our help."

"I don't care," the CIA man snarled. "Get the hell out of here."

"I don't take orders from you, Mister . . . ?"

"Whelan." He stepped closer to her. "And you will do as I say. We're a special presidential task force assigned to this mission, so you have no jurisdiction here."

She lifted her chin. "I suggest you rethink the situation. You could use our help. There are only three of you, and there are about a dozen of . . . I don't know who exactly they are."

Alyssa inhaled sharply. "Did you see them?"

"If you're referring to the guys who magically materialized in the front yard over there, yes. They're heavily armed with guns and swords."

"Did they see you?" the CIA man asked.

Whelan, he'd said his name was. Somehow that sounded familiar. "No," Olivia answered. "Who are they? Did they commit the murders?"

Whelan snorted. "No. They're hunting the murderers. But don't make the mistake of thinking they're innocent. Do yourself a favor and get out of here before they see you."

"I can help—"

"Forget it, Ms. Sotiris. You'll have no defense against them. They can take over your mind and make you do whatever they want."

She gulped. Was that what had happened to Harrison and the sheriff?

"They're dangerous," Alyssa whispered. "We've lost two members of our team because of them."

Olivia winced. No wonder this woman was so afraid. "I'm sorry for your loss."

"Oh, they weren't killed," Alyssa said. "They're just . . . gone."

A shiver skittered down Olivia's back.

"Get a grip, Alyssa," Whelan growled. "And you, Ms. Sotiris, you've wasted enough of my time."

Olivia stumbled back a step when a spurt of heat shot across her brow. Her mind went fuzzy, then sharpened with a sudden compulsion to leave. "I must leave." She wandered down the road to the driveway.

What was she doing? She glanced back and saw Whelan and Alyssa following her.

Keep going. Leave.

She shook her head. This wasn't her decision.

Go to your car and leave. Now.

She turned onto the driveway. Dammit, what was wrong with her? She kept walking toward J.L.'s car. She glanced toward the cornfield, wishing he and Barker would emerge.

She looked in the other direction and spotted the mysterious men who had materialized earlier. They were leaving the barns and the storm cellar. They were headed in her direction.

She veered toward the cornfield so they wouldn't see her.

No. Go to the car. Leave now.

Her steps slanted back toward the car. Damn! What was she doing? She felt exposed.

She pulled J.L.'s keys from her pocket and hit the unlock button. The car's headlights flashed. She winced. Those guys would see her for sure now.

Hurry up. Leave.

She walked up to the driver's side door.

"Olivia?" someone shouted.

She froze. *Robby?* She turned and saw a man break apart from the group that had materialized. He sprinted toward her, passing through the light of the second house.

"Robby," she whispered. It was him. He was wearing a kilt that swished about his knees as he ran toward her.

"Ms. Sotiris, leave now!" Whelan yelled.

She saw the CIA man and Alyssa walking up the driveway. It was Whelan who was making her leave. Somehow, he was projecting commands into her head.

A hot blast seared her brow, and she flinched.

Get in the car and leave.

She reached for the door handle.

"Olivia!" Robby called.

She paused, and suddenly he was there.

"Olivia." He touched her arm. "What are ye doing here?"

"I must leave."

He peered closely at her. "Are ye all right?"

She shook her head. "I must leave."

"Back away from her, MacKay!" Whelan yelled.

Robby glared at the CIA man. "Release her. Ye have no right to control her."

Whelan snorted. "Better me than you. You know this woman?"

"Aye. Release her now, or I'll do it."

"Fine," Whelan growled. "But you leave her alone."

"I willna harm her," Robby said between gritted teeth.

"Right," Whelan snarled. "Just like no one's harmed Shanna or Emma."

A hot wind swooshed through Olivia's mind, and she swayed. Her keys tumbled to the ground.

Robby grabbed her forearms to steady her. "Are ye all right now?"

"Robby." She wrapped her arms around his neck. "Thank God you're here." She shot an angry look at the CIA man. "He was trying to control me."

"You idiot!" Whelan shouted. "I was trying to protect you."

Robby hugged her tight. "'Tis all right, sweetheart."

"Shit," Whelan muttered. "Another woman compromised."

"He seems to actually care for her," Alyssa said.

Whelan slanted a suspicious look at her. "Go back to the car and wait for us."

As Alyssa walked away, Whelan crossed his arms and scowled at Robby. "Why can't you bastards pick on your own kind?"

Robby rubbed a hand up and down Olivia's back. "Go on about yer business, Whelan, and leave us alone."

Whelan. Now Olivia recalled where she'd heard the name. Robby had mentioned it on Patmos. As her mind continued to clear from Whelan's control, she realized that Robby was one of the guys who had magically appeared.

She stepped back, pulling out of his arms. "What's going on, Robby? What are you doing here?"

"Great," Whelan grumbled. "Now she starts thinking. A little too late."

Robby gave the CIA man an annoyed look, then turned back to Olivia. "Ye know I work for an agency that specializes in investigation. We're working with the CIA on this case."

Whelan snorted. "That's a cleaned up version."

Robby scowled at him. "Ye called Connor an hour ago about this place. Ye wanted us to come here first."

"I thought the Malcontents might still be here," Whelan said. "Are they?"

Robby shook his head. "They've already left."

"Who are the Malcontents?" Olivia asked. "And how did you magically appear in the front yard?"

Robby stiffened.

Whelan chuckled. "Yeah, try explaining that to your girl-friend."

Robby's jaw shifted. "The Malcontents are the terrorists I told you about."

"The ones who tortured you?" she asked.

"Aye. We believe they murdered these people."

"Stop sanitizing the truth," Whelan snarled. "They drained every drop of blood from these people, then slashed their throats to hide the bite marks."

Olivia stepped back and bumped into the car. "Bite marks?"

"Did you find any blood around the victims?" Whelan asked.

She shook her head no.

"Whelan, enough." Robby glowered at him. "I need to talk to her in private."

"You haven't told her yet?" Whelan scoffed. "Typical. You bastards are never honest about yourselves."

Olivia swallowed hard. As much as she disliked Whelan, she was afraid he had a point. Robby had materialized out of thin air. And then, there were the other things, like red glowing eyes and leaving her apartment without unlocking the door. She realized with a jolt that he might have simply vanished. "What—what are you?"

Robby regarded her sadly. "I was going to tell you. Tomorrow night."

"Vampires!" Whelan blurted out.

Robby winced.

Olivia blinked. "What?"

"Vampires," Whelan repeated.

Robby's green eyes glittered as he glared at Whelan. "For God's sake, man, go away and let me handle this."

A cold chill teased the back of Olivia's neck. "There's no such thing as vampires."

"Think about it, Ms. Sotiris," Whelan said. "The victims were drained of all blood before their throats were slashed. They were manipulated with vampire mind control. That's why they have no defensive wounds. They never fought back 'cause they were completely controlled."

Vampire mind control? She didn't want to believe vampires existed, but Whelan's description of the crime scene was too accurate. Why would anyone steal a person's blood? Unless they needed it to survive. "How do you know what the crime scene looks like? You never went inside the house."

Whelan shrugged. "I've seen it before. They always use the same M.O."

She looked at Robby. He wasn't denying any of it. He was simply watching her with a worried expression. "Is it true? Do vampires really exist?"

He nodded. "Some are evil, but some are good."

She rubbed her forehead. This was crazy. She might as well believe in leprechauns and fairies. Vampires. Bloodsuckers. They'd slashed the victims' throats to hide bite marks. That meant fangs. A shudder skittered through her. Vampire mind control.

She flinched and looked at Whelan. "You controlled my mind." She moved closer to Robby, and he wrapped an arm around her shoulders.

Whelan rolled his eyes. "Oh come on. I'm not the vampire. I'm the one who told you about them."

"Leave us," Robby whispered. "Let me tell her."

Whelan snorted. "You'll just control her and make her stay with you, the same way Roman does to my daughter."

A chill settled on Olivia as memories flashed through her mind. Red glowing eyes, puncture marks in her pillow. Robby never answered the phone or e-mail during the day. She never saw him during the day. Never saw him eat or drink. And could never read his emotions.

She jumped back and stared at him. "No," she whispered. "No."

"Olivia, I can explain."

"Can you deny it? Can you tell me you're *not* a—" She couldn't even say it.

He stepped toward her. "Ye know I love you."

She stepped back farther and shook her head. He wasn't denying it. She couldn't believe it. He wasn't denying it.

"There's no need to be afraid," he said quietly. "We can talk about it."

A strange sound escaped her mouth, a cross between disbelief and despair. This was the important thing he'd wanted to tell her.

She glanced to the side. The people who had materialized earlier were gathered together by the road. They were keeping a distance and pretending not to watch, but they were casting worried glances at her and Robby and scowling at Whelan.

Vampires. They were all vampires. The murderers were vampires. And Robby.

"No!" She turned and ran into the cornfield. Green leaves swished at her. She batted them away and kept running. Vampires? No. It was ridiculous. It was crazy.

It made sense. It explained everything.

She charged through the field behind the houses. She needed J.L. and Barker. She needed real people.

"Olivia?" J.L. emerged onto the corn row she was running down. "What's wrong?"

"J.L.!" She sprinted toward him.

Barker joined him.

"Oh thank God. You're both okay." She ran into J.L.'s arms and hugged him.

"We were headed back to you," J.L. said. "Are you okay?"

"No." She stepped back, still breathing heavily from her run. And the shock. "You're not going to believe it. It—it's unbelievable."

"You figured it out?" J.L. asked.

"Yes." She pressed a hand to her chest.

"Wow," J.L. muttered. "I had no idea till Barker led me back to his clothes."

"What?"

"Then you don't know?" J.L. looked at their supervisor. "Maybe you should tell her."

"What?" Olivia repeated.

Barker sighed. "I'm a shape-shifter."

"What?"

"I was the Irish wolfhound. I shifted to try to track down the children, but I couldn't trace their scent."

She stared at him. "No."

"Yes," Barker replied.

She stepped back. "No." Her boyfriend had fangs, and her boss was a dog? Her world was tipping upside down. Where had all the normal people gone? She shivered. The normal people were the dead ones in the farmhouses.

She glanced suspiciously at J.L. "And what are you? Do you turn into an animal, too?"

"I wish. I think I'd be a dragon. That would be cool."

"No." She retreated another step. "Not cool." She heard swishing sounds behind her.

"Olivia?" Robby called.

She spun around. Dear God, no. He was coming after her.

"Is that Robby?" J.L. asked. "What's he doing here?"

"Vampire," she whispered. "They're all vampires."

"Holy cow," Barker muttered.

The dog speaks, she thought faintly. Green corn plants swirled around her, and she saw dancing stars.

"Olivia." Robby pushed through some plants into their row.

She stumbled back, and Barker caught her. She lurched away from him, and Robby made a grab for her. God, no. She was stuck between a vampire and a man-dog. The cornfield swayed, and everything went black.

Chapter Twenty-three

Robby swooped Olivia up in his arms. A surge of guilt shot through him. He should have told her the truth weeks ago. But was there ever a good time to tell someone you were a bloodsucker? The poor lass had run away in horror, and now she was in a dead faint.

"Wait a minute." J.L. regarded him suspiciously. "Why was she talking about vampires?"

"She just met one." Robby caught the scent of the tall man beside J.L. "Ye're a shifter?"

The man stiffened. "You know about shifters?"

"Aye. Are ye a wolf?"

"Wolfhound. I'm Patrick O'Shea Barker. FBI."

"Och. Ye're Olivia's supervisor. She's mentioned you before. In a favorable way, of course. I'm Robby MacKay of MacKay Security and Investigation. We have a few shifters in our employ."

"Really? That's interesting."

"Stop!" J.L. held up his hands. "Rewind. I don't think we sufficiently covered the vampire thing. Are you freaking telling me vampires are *real*?"

"Aye." Robby held Olivia close and strode along the corn row, headed toward the farmhouses.

"Where are you going with her?" J.L. followed closely behind.

Robby sighed. She probably didn't want to see him when she awoke. "Do ye have a safe place to take her?"

"We have rooms at the motel in town," Barker said.

"Good." Robby reached the backyard. The two FBI men flanked him and watched him warily.

"Aren't you one of the guys who materialized here?" J.L. asked. "How the hell did you do that?"

Robby winced. They hadn't realized they'd had an audience. He started down a worn path between the two farmhouses. "Does the car in the driveway belong to one of you?"

"It's mine," J.L. said. "Harrison and the sheriff left."

"What?" Barker gave J.L. an incredulous look. "Harrison left? Why did he do that?"

"Beats me." J.L. glared at Robby. "They met some guys in kilts, and the next thing we know, they're driving off."

Robby sighed inwardly. That would have been Connor and Angus. They'd been the first to arrive. They'd called the local sheriff's office and teleported there. Then, using vampire mind control, they'd persuaded the operator to call the sheriff's car radio. They'd erased memories and teleported to the sheriff's car, using the radio as a beacon.

"Yer companions were told to leave," Robby admitted.

"Why would Harrison do what some strangers told him to do?" Barker asked. "I'm his boss, and he doesn't obey me half the time."

"Vampire mind control." Robby spotted his colleagues

gathered by the road. Their number had dwindled. Some must have teleported away.

Barker motioned toward them. "Those guys over there are vampires?"

"Aye, but doona worry. They willna harm you."

"Whoa." J.L. halted with a jerk. "Then you're a vampire, too?"

Robby groaned inwardly. "Aye." Olivia stirred in his arms, so he hurried toward the car.

Barker kept up with him. "You bite people?"

"Nay. I drink synthetic blood."

"And you materialized here?" J.L. asked.

"We teleported."

"What other powers do you have?" Barker asked.

"Superstrength and -speed, superhearing and -vision, a prolonged life, levitation, mind control."

"Cool," J.L. whispered.

"Nay." Robby stopped beside the car. " 'Tis no' cool when it is used for evil. The Malcontents used mind control to render those puir mortals helpless. They died in terror, unable to defend themselves."

"Who are the Malcontents?" Barker asked.

Robby launched into a quick explanation of the Malcontents, Vamps, and the CIA Stake-Out Team. He stopped when Olivia moaned. "Hurry, open the door. The keys are on the ground there."

J.L. picked up the keys while Barker opened the back door. Robby deposited Olivia on the backseat.

"So basically you're the good vampires, and the Malcontents are the evil ones?" Barker asked.

"Aye." Robby shut the back door.

"What's the deal with the skirts?" J.L. asked. "I thought you guys were more into capes."

Robby gave him an annoyed look, then noticed Olivia was waking up. "I'll need you to keep this a secret. 'Tis imperative that the mortal world no' know."

J.L. snorted. "Like anyone would believe this." He climbed into the driver's seat.

"You can trust us." Barker circled to the other side of the car. "I don't want my secret to come out, either." He folded his long frame into the front passenger seat.

J.L. started the engine, and Robby stepped back. Olivia sat up in the backseat and looked around with a dazed expression. She spotted him, and her eyes widened with horror.

His heart twisted in his chest.

The car backed down the driveway. As it turned onto the road, Olivia peered out the window at him.

He raised a hand. Was this good-bye? Would she ever agree to see him again? She had to. He couldn't let her go without a fight.

The car sped off, and he was left looking at a cloud of dust.

"Are ye all right, lad?" Angus walked up to him.

He swallowed hard. "I may have lost her."

"She could still come around." Angus patted him on the back. "Give her some time."

"What did I miss?" Robby changed the subject. It hurt too much to dwell on the horrified look on Olivia's face. And he knew he'd missed some of the strategy meeting while he'd chased after her.

"Casimir is clearly moving south, but we doona know his final destination. Phineas teleported to New Orleans to warn them, in case Casimir is headed there. Dougal went to Jean-Luc's home in Texas to warn him."

Robby nodded. "Maggie and Pierce live in Texas, too. We should warn them. And we should tighten security at the

Romatech in Texas." Casimir had blown it up last summer, but production had started again.

"We're going to spend the rest of tonight checking all the storm cellars in the vicinity." Angus sighed. "'Tis a waste of time, most likely. They could be far away by now."

Robby glanced at the farmhouses. "And the people who died? Is Whelan going to take care of the cover story?"

"Aye." Angus chuckled. "He's threatening to have you arrested for assault."

"Let him try, the bastard." After Olivia had run off into the cornfield, Robby had walked up to the smirking Whelan and punched his face.

His friends had applauded.

"He'll get his comeuppance," Angus said. "One of these days he'll find out his grandchildren are half Vamp."

Robby smiled. He didn't know how Roman could stand having Sean Whelan for a father-in-law. His smile faded. He could end up with some angry in-laws, too, if Olivia ever agreed to marry him.

Olivia took a shower, but it didn't wash away the shock. She took two aspirin, but it didn't take away the pain. She lounged on the lumpy bed in the motel room in her pajamas, staring into space. The television was on with the volume turned down low. The old familiar sitcom helped her believe the world was still normal. Even though it wasn't.

Vampires. The word repeated over and over in her mind. Vampires were real. And Robby was one of them.

She recalled how much attention he'd given to her neck when they'd made love. Two giant red hickeys below each ear. But he hadn't broken the skin. Instead, he'd bitten her decorative pillow. She shuddered, remembering the twin punctures. Robby had fangs.

He was never available during the day. Robby was dead. Or Undead. It was all rather confusing.

She'd caught him drinking something in the villa on Patmos. She'd thought it was a glass of wine, but now she knew better. It must have been blood.

She groaned. She didn't want to think about vampires anymore. She grabbed the remote control to access the movie channel on the television. Tonight's feature was . . . a vampire movie. Great. She flipped the channel to HBO. A vampire series was showing. She switched to the History Channel. A documentary on the history of . . . vampires.

"Dammit!" She turned the television off and sprawled across the bed. It was a conspiracy.

A knock sounded at her door, and she sat up with a jerk. *Please don't be Robby.* She couldn't handle that yet.

"Liv, it's me!" J.L. yelled. "I've got pizza!"

Like she really wanted food after an evening of dead bodies and shocking revelations. But she didn't want to be alone. "Just a minute." She checked her long flannel pajama bottoms and baggy sweatshirt and decided she was decent enough. She opened the door.

"How's it going?" J.L. strode inside, his arms loaded down with a pizza box and a plastic bag of food. He set it all on the table by the window. "Come on, let's party."

She shut the door and locked it. "What's there to party about?"

He reached inside the bag, grabbed a diet cola and passed it to her. "We're still alive. That's something."

She unscrewed the top off the bottle. "I suppose."

"Yeah. Could be worse." He opened a cola and drank a few gulps. "We could be dead."

"Or Undead," she muttered, and sat in one of the two chairs that flanked the table.

"And guess what?" J.L. opened the pizza box. "Harrison drove all the way back to Kansas City, so we don't have to share our food with him. Isn't that a lucky break?"

"What's he doing in Kansas City?"

J.L. selected a pizza slice, then sat in the other chair to eat. "Barker called him at his home, and he doesn't even remember coming here. He knows nothing about this assignment. Isn't that weird?"

Olivia sipped from her bottle. "How did that happen?"

"The vampires zapped him with some mind control." J.L. took a big bite of pizza.

She frowned, recalling how frustrating it had felt when Whelan had controlled her mind. "What about the guy from the CIA? He tried to control my mind and make me leave."

J.L. nodded with his mouth full. "The CIA guys are members of the Stake-Out team. Robby told us about them. They have psychic power so they can resist vampire mind control."

"When did Robby tell you that?"

"While we were walking to the car." J.L. took another bite. "You were unconscious at the time. Robby was carrying you."

She winced. She couldn't believe she'd fainted like that. She never fainted. But then she didn't usually spend her evenings surrounded by dead bodies while she discovered her boyfriend was a vampire and her boss was a dog.

She took another drink. "Where is Barker?"

"He's in his room. He didn't think you were up to seeing him just yet."

She sighed. "It's so strange. I had no idea. I mean his name is a major clue, but people can be named Wood without it meaning they can shift into a two by four."

"Yeah." J.L. stuffed more pizza in his mouth. "But it does explain a few things."

"Like what? His special fondness for fire hydrants?"

J.L. snickered. "No. I mean he never questioned your abilities. When the other guys in the office thought you were crazy or a sham, he believed in you. In fact, he requested you."

"Really? I never knew that."

J.L. nodded. "He already knew weird-assed crap was for real."

She plucked an olive off the pizza and popped it in her mouth. "You believed me from the beginning."

"Well, sure, but I'm a really smart guy."

She smiled. "Yes, you are."

Her cell phone rang and she flinched. Was it Robby? She stared at the phone. She'd left it on the bedside table between the two double beds.

J.L. rose to his feet. "You want me to get that?"

"Not really." The phone rang again.

"What if it's Robby?" J.L. walked over to her phone.

"I don't want to talk to him."

"Because he's a vampire?"

"Yes."

"Oh, come on, Liv. Nobody's perfect."

"I'm not expecting perfection. I just think a heartbeat would be nice." The phone rang again.

J.L. frowned at her. "It really could be worse, you know. He could be like a . . . zombie who eats your brains."

She grimaced. "That's not helping."

J.L. opened her phone. "Hello? Oh, hi, Robby." He gave Olivia a pointed look. "So what's up? Are you out biting people?"

There was a pause, then J.L. covered the phone. "He says he drinks synthetic blood from a bottle, the kind they make at Romatech."

Romatech. She snorted. That would be a favorite place for vampires to hang out.

"Okay," J.L. said into the phone, then looked at her. "He says he wants to talk to you."

She shook her head. "I don't want to talk to him. Not yet. Maybe after a few days. Or weeks."

J.L. sighed. "Sorry, dude. She's not ready to talk to you yet."

Robby suddenly appeared in the room. "She'll get over it."

Olivia jumped and spilled diet cola down her sweatshirt. "Damn!"

"Whoa!" J.L. snapped the phone shut. "Dude, what a way to make an entrance."

Olivia set her bottle on the table. "I'm not ready for this. I assume you can leave the same way you came in?"

Robby frowned at her. "We need to talk."

J.L. put her phone back on the bedside table. "I guess I should leave you two alone."

"No!" Olivia jumped to her feet. "Don't leave me."

Robby stiffened. "Do ye think I would harm you, lass? Have ye forgotten how much I love you?"

"I remember." She crossed her arms over her damp shirt. "I also remember talking to you for months, and you never told me the truth about yourself."

"I was going to tell you tomorrow night."

"That's a little late, don't you think? You should have told me *before* taking me to bed!"

He stepped toward her. "I hesitated, remember? Ye thought it was because I dinna want you, but it was because I knew ye deserved the truth first. But ye wouldna wait! Ye forced my hand."

She snorted. "I forced you to have sex with me?"

"I'm seriously outta here." J.L. grabbed the pizza box.

"You don't mind if I take this, right? Barker wanted a few slices, and I'm guessing you're not into it."

"Ye can take it," Robby muttered.

J.L. glanced at Olivia. "If you need me, call."

"Fine." She plopped down in her chair and scowled at the worn carpet.

The door shut, and she was alone with Robby. Anger simmered deep inside her, along with hurt.

He sat on the bed across from her. "I realize ye're in shock."

"I think I'm over the shock and denial stage."

"That's good."

She glared at him. "And I'm rapidly moving into the royally pissed stage."

He winced. "How long does that one last?"

"As long as I want it to." She stood and paced across the room. "You should have told me. You know how much I value honesty. You should have been honest with me from the beginning."

He turned in his sitting position to face her. "Be honest with yerself, Olivia. If I had told you the truth up front, ye would have refused to see me again."

"We talked for months and you never told me. You purposely deceived me."

"I fell in love with you. That was no' a deception."

She didn't want to talk about love. It had happened so quickly on Patmos, as if it were magical. She'd thought she was falling for the perfect man, but now she realized she didn't even know him. "Who—what are you exactly? Are you dead or alive or something in between?"

"I'm alive right now. My heart is pumping blood. My mind is thinking how beautiful ye are. My eyes have noticed ye're no' wearing a bra."

She crossed her arms and winced at the feel of her damp, sticky sweatshirt. "And during the day, when you never call or e-mail, are you sleeping or unconscious?"

"I'm dead."

She gave him a dubious look. "Seriously . . . dead?"

"Aye." He nodded slowly. "'Tis a major drawback to my condition."

"I should say so."

"When I doona respond to yer messages during the day, 'tis no' because I'm being rude or neglecting you."

"Right. You're not emotionally unavailable. You're just dead." She rubbed her brow. "Is that supposed to make me feel better?"

He frowned. "'Tis no' all bad, being a vampire. We have some excellent perks. A prolonged life—"

"How old are you?" she interrupted.

"I was born in 1719."

Her knees buckled and she sat on the other bed. He was almost three hundred years old. He didn't age. And she did. This was terrible. "What other . . . perks?"

"I have superior strength and speed. Heightened senses. I can levitate, teleport, or use mind control."

She stiffened as her anger flared back to life. "Some of your friends used mind control to make Harrison and the sheriff leave."

"Aye."

"Harrison drove all the way home, and he has no memory of ever coming here."

Robby nodded. "We can erase memories if we need to."

Her anger escalated to a boil. "So you manipulate us mere mortals whenever you feel like it?"

His jaw shifted. "We doona do it unless we have a good reason."

Like making sure a woman fell in love really fast?

She jumped to her feet, glaring at him. "Did you ever use mind control on me?"

His mouth thinned. "Aye."

She cried out with rage. "You bastard!"

He stood. "Let me explain."

"*No!* I knew I fell for you too fast. You—you were making me—"

"Nay! I only controlled you once. Ye were in the sea and freezing to death. I told you to sleep so ye wouldna see me teleport you to the patio—"

"You teleported me?"

"Aye. So I could put you in the hot tub. I was trying to save you."

And she'd been so grateful, so impressed, so ready to fall completely in love. But what if he'd manipulated the whole thing? "Did you arrange it all? Did you know about the panther?"

"I dinna know Carlos was planning to frighten you."

"Carlos?"

Robby winced. "Carlos Panterra. He's a shifter."

She stumbled back a step. "Carlos was the . . . ?"

"Panther, aye."

"He's a cat?" And her boss was a dog. She shook her head. Was her next door neighbor a goldfish? "He scared the hell out of me. Why?"

"He was playing matchmaker. He thought if I rescued you—"

"*What?*" Her anger exploded again. "I was never in any danger? I thought you'd save my life. You tricked me!"

"I did save you. Ye were freezing to death."

She paced away, her hands clenched. Was nothing the

way she'd thought it was? She whirled around to face him. "Was any of it real? Can you swear that you never manipulated my thoughts or feelings?"

"Never. I wouldna want yer love if it was false. Yer feelings were yer own. And they have always been real."

Tears gathered in her eyes. "What would you know about my feelings? I've gone through hell and back because of my feelings for you!"

His eyes glimmered with pain. "I have, too. I love you, Olivia. I have always loved you."

She covered her mouth to keep a sob from escaping. Damn him. She walked away, headed for the vanity area of the motel room. She spotted herself in the mirror, her eyes glistening with tears and her mouth twisted in pain.

She jerked to a stop. Robby wasn't there. She spun around. He was there. She glanced back at the mirror. He had no reflection. He wasn't a real person.

She doubled over as pain stabbed her gut. She'd fallen in love with an illusion. She could never have a real life with Robby. All her dreams of a future with him were gone.

"Olivia, sweetheart." He took hold of her shoulders.

"No." She pulled away as tears streamed down her face. "I wanted it to be real. I wanted to love you forever."

"Ye can. Sweetheart, we can work this out."

She collapsed on a bed and covered her face.

The bed shifted as he sat beside her. "We'll be all right, Olivia."

She sniffed. "I'm not angry anymore."

"Then ye've accepted me?"

She shook her head. "No. I'm . . . in mourning. I've lost the future I thought we would have together."

He sighed. "If I could be a normal man for you, I would."

She sat up and pulled at her sticky sweatshirt. "I can't sleep in this. And I didn't pack another shirt."

"No' a problem." He vanished.

She started. "Damn." She looked around the room. He was really gone.

And she was really in love with a vampire. How could this ever work out? A few minutes later he reappeared with something clutched in his hand.

"You went to my apartment?"

"Aye. I brought you something to wear." He handed it to her.

It was the nightgown she'd put on that he'd promptly removed the night he'd taken her virginity. Her eyes misted with tears. What was she going to do? It hurt too much to just reject him. She needed to learn more about him.

She took a deep breath. "Tell me everything."

He told her about his job, and how he and his friends were battling the evil Malcontents. A vampire named Casimir was their leader, and he was the one who had tortured Robby.

"Casimir murdered the people at the farmhouses?" she asked.

"Aye. He and his minions."

"How many . . . minions does he have?"

"Just a handful, we believe. He needs to replenish his army. He'll either find more vampires or make them."

She grimaced. "Why didn't he change the people at the farmhouses into vampires?"

"They were probably good people. Good people turn into good vampires."

"Like . . . you?"

Robby nodded. "Death doesna change a person's nature."

She thought about that a moment, then inhaled sharply.

"The children! Oh my gosh, with everything that's happened, I forgot."

"What children?"

"There were children living in those farmhouses, and they've disappeared."

Robby grew pale. "Bloody hell. Casimir must have taken them."

"Why? Why would he take innocent children?"

"They're lighter and easier to teleport with. They're an easy food source."

Olivia gasped in horror. "They're snack food?"

Robby stood. "I need to go."

She rose to her feet, too. "Can you find them?"

"We'll do our best." He touched her cheek.

She stepped back. "Don't. Please. I've had a lot thrown at me in one night. I'm not sure I can handle this."

He gave her a wry look. "Ye'll get over it."

"How can you be so sure?" Her heart felt so heavy, so burdened with pain.

"Because ye love me." He vanished.

Chapter Twenty-four

The next evening, Olivia busied herself at her apartment, cleaning and doing laundry. She even cooked some moussaka. Anything to keep from dwelling on the fact that this was Friday night, the night she'd thought Robby was going to propose.

Now she knew better. He'd planned on telling her he was a vampire.

She was sick of hearing about it. On the drive back to Kansas City that morning, J.L. and Barker had talked endlessly about vampires. J.L. thought their powers were awesome. Barker was grateful there were good ones to combat the bad ones. They'd spent a good thirty minutes speculating on what the Malcontents would do next, then another thirty minutes wondering how the CIA would cover up what had happened.

Olivia had been ready to scream by the time they arrived at the office. At least the afternoon had been spent on something different. She and J.L. had interviewed some of Yasmine's relatives. One of Yasmine's sisters admitted that she'd seen her two days earlier. She claimed not to know where Yasmine was hiding, but she'd loaned her debit card to her sister.

After more investigation they learned the debit card had been used at an ATM machine on the Kansas side of Kansas City. They canvassed the neighborhood but didn't find her.

Olivia was exhausted by the time she made it home that evening, but she still kept busy. If she stopped for a moment, her thoughts would return to Robby, and the pain would rush back.

How could she have a relationship with a vampire? He could never share a day with her. Or a meal with her. He would never grow old. And what would it mean to her? Would she continue to age until she lost him? Would she never have children? Would she be lured into a dark world and become one of them?

She shuddered. Love should bring a person joy and life, not darkness and death.

She watched the news while she ate her supper of salad and moussaka. Her fork froze halfway to her mouth when she recognized the scene on the television. A helicopter was flying over the farmhouses in Nebraska. The reporter claimed ten people had died from a new deadly strain of the flu. The public was warned to stay away from the area. It was believed to be the same strain of flu that had recently caused eight deaths in South Dakota.

Olivia set her fork down. The Malcontents were leaving a trail of death down the center of the country. She prayed the children would survive.

When the sun went down, she closed all the blinds and wondered where Robby was. Was he waking up from the dead? Would he spend the night hunting for Casimir and the Malcontents?

She was washing dishes when her cell phone rang. She quickly dried her hands. Part of her hoped it was Robby. Part of her dreaded that it would be. "Hello?"

"Liv, turn on the news," J.L. said. "Hurry."

She went to the television. "If this is about that cover story, I already—" She gasped.

There was a picture of Leavenworth Federal Penitentiary on the screen. A headline read: EIGHT INMATES ESCAPE.

"Do you see it?" J.L. asked.

"Yes." She turned up the volume.

The news anchor reported a strange incident at Leavenworth. Eight of their worst inmates had simply disappeared from their prison cells. The guards had no idea how it had happened.

"Are you thinking what I'm thinking?" J.L. asked. "What if it was teleportation?"

Olivia sank onto the love seat. "You mean the Malcontents teleported in and took them." She closed her eyes briefly. Robby had said that Casimir needed to expand his army. And if he couldn't find evil vampires, he would make them. What better place to find evil people than a federal prison?

The news anchor continued with his report. "This just in. We are now able to identify the eight inmates who escaped. If you see any of these men, notify the authorities immediately. Do not approach them. They are extremely dangerous."

He recited names while the prison photos were flashed on the screen. "And the last prisoner—Otis Crump."

Her heart plummeted into her stomach.

"Shit!" J.L. shouted. "Olivia, get out of the apartment now. Go straight to work. I'll meet you there."

She froze, staring at Otis's photo on the television screen. He was free. Not only free, but if Casimir had freed him, he might soon be a vampire. Otis's claim that they were destined to be together forever took on a sinister new meaning.

He would come after her. And if he succeeded, she would end up either dead . . . or undead.

"Liv!" J.L. yelled on the phone. "Are you there?"

She jerked out of her stunned trance. "I'm here. I'm leaving. See you soon."

She ran into her bedroom to put on some socks and her athletic shoes. Then she strapped on her holster and sidearm over her blue jeans. Her heart pounded. Otis could be on his way to her apartment right now. If he was alive, he might be driving. If he was already a vampire, he might be able to teleport straight into her living room.

She threw on a jacket and stuffed an extra clip of bullets into the pocket. How fast could someone become a vampire? She had no idea. Could her bullets kill a vampire? She hoped she wouldn't have to find out.

She rushed into her living room just as a form suddenly appeared. Her heart lurched.

"Oh God, Robby!" She pressed a hand to her chest. "You scared me to death."

"Ye're in grave danger."

"Yeah, I know." She hurried past him to the console by the front door. "Otis Crump could be on his way here."

"I've come to take you to safety."

"No thanks." She collected her handbag and keys.

Robby strode toward her. "Ye must let me protect you."

"I don't think so." She opened the door and stepped onto the front porch.

"What are ye doing?" His eyes were wide with shock. "Ye canna leave on yer own."

"Watch me." She closed the door in his face and locked it. She hurried down the stairs, stifling a grin. That had felt surprisingly good.

As she strode toward her car, her stride hitched a bit when he appeared in the parking lot. He wasn't wearing a kilt tonight. His black cargo pants and black T-shirt hugged a muscular body. Leather straps across his chest probably meant his claymore was on his back. His brow was furrowed with fierce determination.

Damn, he was good looking. And as much as she chafed against his he-man tendencies, she had to admit there was a raw masculinity to him that made her bones melt. She forced herself to look away and headed for her car.

He followed her. "Perhaps ye doona understand the gravity of the situation. We know it was Casimir and his minions who helped the prisoners escape."

"I already figured that out." She pressed her keypad to unlock her car.

"Then ye should know the Malcontents could be transforming the prisoners into vampires right now, including the bastard who's obsessed with you."

"I know." She reached for the door handle.

He leaned against the car door, blocking her. "I can take you to a safe place where no vampire can get to you."

"Including you?"

His jaw shifted. "Ye have no reason to fear me. I would never harm you."

"Tell that to my breaking heart," she muttered.

His eyes glittered an intense green. "There is no reason

for you to suffer. We could be together. Ye only have to accept me for what I am."

"I can't do that right now. Please move, so I can go."

"Bugger," he muttered, and stepped back. "Dammit, woman. If ye love me, ye will stay loyal to me. Ye willna stab me in the back with betrayal."

She flinched. He was accusing her of wrongdoing? How dare he? "If you loved me, you would have been honest with me!"

His face paled and a glint of pain flickered in his eyes. Her heart clenched in her chest. Damn, she hadn't realized he was hurting as much as she was. She usually knew exactly what other people were feeling.

With a trembling hand she opened the car door.

"Where are ye going?" Robby asked as she climbed inside.

"Work." She shut the door and turned on the engine.

She backed out of her parking space, then hit the brakes with a lurch when Robby suddenly materialized in the passenger seat. "My God, would you stop scaring me? What are you doing here?"

He removed the sheath from his back. "I have to protect you."

"I don't need your protection."

"No one can protect you from a vampire as well as another vampire." He settled back in the seat and put on his seat belt. "Where exactly are we going?"

"FBI building, and I didn't invite you."

"Och, I could teleport you there in a second. 'Twould save you time and gas."

She ignored him and stomped on the accelerator. Traffic was light at this time of night, so she was able to make good time.

"Whelan and his team are at Leavenworth," Robby said as

she passed another car. "And Angus and Connor are there. If there are any clues to be found, they'll find them."

She sped up to catch a yellow light.

"The safest place for you is the silver room at Romatech," Robby continued. "'Tis completely lined in silver so no vampire can teleport in or out."

"You can't teleport through silver?" The minute the question left her lips, she slapped herself mentally. She'd meant to completely ignore him. It irked her that he assumed she would need saving. She wasn't a stupid weakling. She could save herself.

"That is how they were able to hold me prisoner last summer," Robby explained. "They tied me up with silver chains. We canna teleport through it. And if it touches our bare skin, it burns away the flesh."

She grimaced. Poor Robby. And he hadn't been able to save himself. Damn. His fear that she might need saving wasn't an insult. He was simply being realistic.

"I could teleport you to Romatech in a second," he continued. "Ye would be safe there."

"I'm not running away. I'm not hiding." She cast an annoyed look at him. "And I'm not allowing you to take over my decisions."

He crossed his arms, scowling. "I'm trying to keep you alive."

She snorted. "Are you sure about that? Don't you intend to change me over someday?"

He remained quiet a moment, then turned toward her. "Are ye saying ye intend to stay with me?"

She winced. "It was a hypothetical question. I haven't made any decisions yet."

"Och, well, becoming a Vamp would be yer decision as

well. I would hope we could have children first, and ye need to be mortal for that."

She shot him an incredulous look. "Wouldn't *you* need to be mortal for that?"

He quickly explained a procedure that Roman Draganesti had invented to allow the Vamp men to father children.

Olivia drove in stunned silence. She could have children with Robby. He wanted to have children with her. He described Roman's children as mostly mortal. They were awake during the day and ate real food. They just possessed a few special gifts.

That didn't disturb her. She'd grown up with a special gift herself, and had always known her children could inherit it. Even so, she remained quiet until they reached the FBI building.

When they walked inside, she warned him, "They're not going to let you in here with that giant sword."

"We'll see." He slid the claymore off his back and plunked it down on the security officer's desk.

"What the hell?" The officer eyed him suspiciously, then his face suddenly cleared. "Go on through the metal detector, sir. I'll pass your umbrella to you on the other side."

"Thank you." Robby slanted her a smug look.

She glared back, then handed her sidearm to the officer. She walked through the metal detector, then he handed her gun back to her. As she snapped it back into the holster, Robby sauntered through the metal detector. It went off.

The officer calmly turned off the buzzer and handed the sword back to Robby. "Have a nice day."

"Thank you." Robby swung the claymore onto his back.

"I thought you only used mind control when you had a really good reason," she whispered.

"I had one. I'm no' leaving yer side." He strolled toward the elevator. "Ye're on the second floor, aye?"

She punched the up button. "How do you know?"

"I've been here before." The elevator doors opened, and he motioned for her to go first.

She pushed the button for the second floor. "What are you packing that made the metal detector go off?"

He shrugged one shoulder. "It could be the dagger strapped to my leg or the jackknife in my pants pocket. Or the silver chain in the other pocket."

"Wouldn't it burn you to take out the chain?"

"I have a pair of gloves in another pocket. If I get a chance to capture Casimir, I'm no' going to let him teleport away before I can kill him."

"You still want revenge."

"Aye."

She sighed. "Why don't you go hunt for Casimir? Wouldn't you rather do that than babysit me? I'm safe here."

His eyes glimmered with emotion. "I'm no' leaving you."

Was he putting aside his quest for revenge in order to protect her? *He really does love you.* She looked at him, and a bittersweet ache of longing filled her heart. Oh God, she still loved him. She'd always loved him.

A hint of red glittered in his eyes.

"Why does that happen?" she whispered. "Why do your eyes turn red?"

The elevator doors swooshed open, and he turned away, closing his eyes briefly.

She exited, and noticed his eyes were back to normal when he followed.

The office was bustling with activity. Every available special agent had been called in.

J.L. rushed toward her with a relieved grin on his face. "Thank God you're here." He shook hands with Robby. "Thank you for watching out for her. Come on, Barker will want to see you." He led them to the supervisor's office.

Olivia was irked that both J.L. and Barker were delighted that Robby had graced them with his presence. They were full of questions, and Robby explained how the Vamps and CIA Stake-Out Team were at Leavenworth. The Malcontents hadn't bothered to erase any videos from the surveillance cameras, so they knew, without a doubt, that Casimir and his minions were responsible for the jailbreak.

Angus and Connor were questioning the guards. Sometimes, with vampire mind control, a Vamp could help a mortal retrieve lost memories. They hoped to find something useful.

"If Casimir changes the prisoners into vampires, how long will that take?" Barker asked.

"They would be in a coma the first night," Robby answered. "Then the next night they awake as vampires."

"There's no telling when they'll do the change," Olivia said. "They might spend this first night finding a good place to hide."

"Any idea where they might be?" J.L. asked.

"If we did, we would have already attacked," Robby said wryly. "With teleportation, they could be anywhere. Our best bet is to check any mortals the prisoners know and trust. Vampires need a dark place to hide during the day, and they prefer to have some mortals nearby to protect them."

Barker motioned to the large room outside his office where special agents were busily at work. "I have two men assigned to each of the escaped convicts. They're going through all contacts and coordinating with the local police."

"Otis might ask Yasmine to help them," Olivia said. "Or the missing guard, Joe Kitchner."

"I'm watching the debit card she's using," J.L. said. "If she spends any money, I'll know about it."

"At some point Otis will come after Olivia." Barker looked at her. "Do you mind if J.L. and I spend the night in your apartment?"

She shook her head. "What do you want me to do?"

"Stay safe." Barker packed up his laptop. "Stay with Mr. MacKay."

"She will," Robby said.

She frowned as Barker and J.L. left the office. "I'm not going to sit here and do nothing."

Robby glanced at the couch at the back of Barker's office. "I could think of a way to pass the time."

She snorted. "I'm going to work." She went to her work station, and Robby followed her. The other special agents glanced warily at him as he passed by.

He grabbed J.L.'s chair, rolled it into her cubicle, and sat beside her. At first she found it distracting to have him so close, but as they went through her notes on Yasmine and Joe, she grew more accustomed to him. He was thoughtful and thorough.

At one point he brushed back one of her curls and hooked it behind her ear. She stiffened, but he just smiled and said it was blocking his view of her desk.

J.L. called to report that nothing was happening at her apartment. They'd found the pan of moussaka in the fridge and finished it off.

After an hour of dead ends regarding Yasmine, Olivia and Robby turned their attention to Joe. According to some neighbors who lived close to Joe's brother, he had been seen a few times there. The brother wasn't well liked in the neighborhood since he enjoyed hosting loud parties that dragged on all night.

"He might have thrown a 'congratulations on breaking out of jail' party," Robby said, and he called the number. It rang six times, then an answering machine picked up.

"We could drive there," Olivia suggested.

"Teleporting is faster."

She gave him a wry look. "I never quite mastered that skill."

"I have all the skill ye need." The corner of his mouth tilted up. "I can transport you to another world."

Her cheeks grew warm. "I'll take the car."

"Come with me. I dare you."

The last time he'd dared her, she'd ended up with a handful. And a night of glorious sex.

He leaned close. "We canna do it here where people might notice. We need to be alone."

Her face blazed hotter. Damn him. He was seducing her all over again. "Barker's office."

"Good." He grabbed the sheet of paper with the brother's phone number and led her back into Barker's office. He punched the number into his cell phone.

"Okay, it's ringing." He motioned for her to come closer.

She inched toward him.

He wrapped his arm around her and pulled her close. She gasped at the feel of his hard body against hers. Her heart raced.

He lowered his head and grazed the tip of his nose against her temple. "Put yer arms around me."

"Do I have to?"

"Do ye want to get lost on the way?"

She threw her arms around his neck. "Are you sure this is safe?"

His mouth twitched. "Safer than yer driving."

"What? I—" She stopped when she noticed the red glint in his eyes. "Why do your eyes keeping turning red?"

"It—" He glanced at his cell phone. "The answering machine picked up. Hang on tight."

She did, then everything went black.

Chapter Twenty-five

Robby knew something was wrong the minute he materialized in the dark room. He could smell blood. He held onto Olivia with one hand, and with the other he punched Angus's number on his cell phone.

"Angus," he whispered, knowing his great-grandfather would hear him. Unfortunately, if Casimir was here, he might hear it, too. "Need backup now. Hurry." He passed the phone to Olivia. "Keep talking."

"What?" she whispered. "What's going on? I can't see anything."

"Don't move." Robby drew his sword. His eyes had adjusted quickly to the darkness.

They were standing in a small foyer. A small amount of moonlight filtered through the half-closed blinds on the living room windows, just enough so he could see the bodies on the living room floor. He moved slowly toward a lamp sitting on an end table next to a sofa.

"Hello? Angus?" Olivia spoke into the phone. "Robby, there's no one there."

"I'm here," Angus replied next to her.

She gasped.

"I'm here as well," Connor added.

Robby heard the metallic slide of swords being drawn. He turned on the lamp.

Olivia gasped again.

Robby estimated at least twelve dead bodies.

"The devil take it," Angus muttered. "Let's check the house and grounds." He and Connor dashed off at vampire speed.

Olivia's eyes widened. "That was fast." She drew her sidearm. "You think the Malcontents are still here?"

"I doubt it. They would have attacked us by now." Robby motioned to the dead bodies. "We were right. There was a party to celebrate the jailbreak."

She grimaced. "Not my idea of a party."

He retrieved his phone from her and pushed the button for another contact. "Whelan, this is MacKay. We've found more dead bodies." He recited the address, then rang off.

He noticed Olivia looked a little green.

"I can teleport you back to the office, if ye like."

She squared her shoulders. "I'll be all right."

He ventured into the living room to get a better look at the victims. "This is clearly the work of both vampires and mortals. Some of the dead have been drained dry. Their throats are cut to disguise the bite marks, but there was no blood left to drip out."

He pointed at a man. "This one was killed by a vampire."

"That's Joe Kitchner," Olivia whispered.

"Others were murdered by mortals—the escaped prisoners, no doubt." He gestured to a blond woman with a knife still embedded in her chest. "So much spilled blood. A vampire would never waste blood like that."

Olivia covered her mouth and looked away.

Robby couldn't detect a heartbeat. All twelve of the victims were gone. He shook his head. He was almost three hundred years old, but he still couldn't fathom how a man could do such a thing. They weren't men. They were monsters.

He spotted a woman in a short skirt with multiple stab wounds all over her abdomen. Her legs were a bloody mess. "Whoever killed her is obsessed with knives."

Olivia glanced at the body and turned deathly pale. "That's Otis's handiwork. He likes to keep souvenirs."

Robby walked toward her. "I willna let him near you."

Her eyes glittered with tears. "I hate these bastards."

"We'll get them."

"They were already disgusting as mortals, but when I think about them becoming vampires and acquiring super powers—" She shuddered.

He drew her into his arms, and to his relief, she didn't pull away. He held her tight.

"They're gone," Angus announced as he zoomed back into the room.

"Aye." Connor followed him. "They've probably gone into hiding somewhere so they can transform the prisoners."

Angus gave Olivia a curious look. "So ye're the one who's captured Robby's heart."

"This is Olivia Sotiris," Robby said, still holding her.

Angus slapped him on the back. "She's a real beauty, lad."

"She can hear you," Robby muttered.

"You're Robby's grandfather?" she asked.

"Great-great-grandfather, actually. I'm verra proud of Robby. He's a fine young man."

"I doona need a sales pitch," Robby grumbled.

"Aye, this is all verra romantic," Connor said with a wry look. "Especially with the dead bodies in the room. Did ye notify Sean Whelan?"

"Yes," Robby replied. "He's on his way."

Connor frowned at the bodies. "More victims for Whelan's deadly flu. The idiot thinks he's being clever, but he's going to cause panic among the mortals."

"If you two can stay here," Robby said, "I'll take Olivia back."

"Stay in touch." Angus patted him on the back. "And good work, both of you."

Robby wrapped his arms around Olivia and teleported back to Barker's office. She stumbled, and he steadied her.

"Are ye all right? Ye look deathly pale. Do ye need any food?"

"God, no. Who could eat after that?" She slumped in a chair and called Barker to catch him up on the latest news. Then she set her phone down and closed her eyes.

Robby swung his claymore off his back and set it on Barker's desk. "Ye're tired."

"It's been a rough few days. I haven't been sleeping well."

"Go lie down on the couch. I'll watch over you. Ye'll be completely safe."

"With a vampire?" She smiled. "Maybe I'll just rest my eyes for a little while." She trudged over to the sofa.

Robby dimmed the lights. Within minutes she'd fallen asleep. He sat at Barker's desk and watched her. He felt fairly certain that she still loved him. If he could just keep her safe, she would eventually accept him.

A sudden thought made him stiffen with alarm. If Otis was still mortal the next day, he might come for her. He might plan to capture her first, so they could be transformed together the following night.

And Robby was dead during the day. He couldn't protect her. Or maybe he could.

Olivia woke slowly from a deep sleep and stretched in the big comfy bed.

Bed? A lightning bolt of alarm skittered through her. She sat up and looked around the dimly lit room. The light was coming from an adjoining room, a bathroom. She spotted her holster and jacket on a table. She was still dressed, except for her shoes.

"Robby," she breathed with relief when she saw him lying on the other side of the king-sized bed. "Where are we? Where have you taken me?"

He just lay there with a peaceful look on his face. He was wearing plaid pajama bottoms and a white T-shirt. Since he'd changed clothes, she assumed this could be his bedroom, wherever that was.

"Robby?" She tapped him on the shoulder. No response. "Come on, Robby, wake up." She gave him a nudge.

His chest wasn't moving. He wasn't breathing.

"Oh my God!" She scrambled out of bed. She'd been sleeping with a dead man.

"Ms. Sotiris?" a booming voice said, and she jumped.

"What?" She pivoted, looking around, then spotted a surveillance camera in a corner by the ceiling.

"Ms. Sotiris, don't be alarmed. This is Howard Barr. Robby asked us to keep an eye on you."

She noticed a light switch by the door and ran over to turn it on. The room was a fairly typical bedroom. Chest of drawers, easy chair, table and lamp, big bed with a dead body on it. She winced. Poor Robby. At least the light she'd turned on wouldn't disturb him.

"Ms. Sotiris, I'm sending Carlos down to get you," Howard Barr announced.

She realized his voice was coming from the intercom by the door. She pushed the talk button. "Where am I exactly?"

"The basement of Romatech Industries," Howard responded.

Her breath hitched. "I'm in New York City?"

"White Plains."

She looked at her watch. It was almost eleven. She recalled falling asleep in Barker's office about 3:00 A.M. Robby must have teleported her while she slept.

She didn't know whether to be annoyed or grateful. If Otis was still alive and looking for her, he'd never find her here. But Robby shouldn't have done this without her permission. She was supposed to be at work today.

There was a knock on the door, and she opened it.

"Menina." Carlos grinned at her. "It is good to see you again."

"Hello, Carlos." She stepped into the hall, then slammed him against the wall. "I know it was you who chased me into the sea. Don't ever terrorize me again."

His amber colored eyes twinkled. "I guess the cat's out of the bag."

She snorted and released him.

He led her upstairs to the MacKay security office and introduced her to Howard Barr.

"This is where Robby works at night?" she asked. She looked at the wall of monitors and spotted the camera in Robby's room.

"We don't usually watch him sleep," Howard said from his chair behind the desk.

"That's for sure," Carlos agreed. "It's not like he's going to do anything."

"He asked us to keep the camera on so we would know when you woke up." Howard pushed a box of doughnuts toward her. "You must be hungry."

She munched on a bear claw while she called Barker.

He wasn't surprised. Robby had left a note on his desk, telling him where she would be.

"I'll get him to teleport me back as soon as he wakes up," she told her boss.

She spent the rest of the day getting a tour of Romatech and hanging around the security office. She met Shanna Draganesti and her children about supper time, and they invited her to eat with them at the Romatech cafeteria. They were a lovely family, but she was painfully aware that the father wasn't with them. He was currently dead, like Robby.

An hour later J.L. called. "Good news! Yasmine used her debit card last night about three-thirty A.M. She rented two units at a climate-controlled storage facility."

Olivia related this news to Howard and Carlos.

"Sounds like a good place to hide vampires during the day," Carlos said. "They're all locked up safe and secure with no windows."

"Barker and I are going to check it out," J.L. told her.

"Be careful." Olivia groaned inwardly. She should be with them, but she was stuck at Romatech until Robby woke up. "Why don't you take Harrison and Saunders with you?"

"We thought about that," J.L. said. "But if we find any vampires, we'll stake them, and we don't want anyone from the office to see that. Don't worry, Liv. It's still daylight here. The vampires will be dead."

"Okay." She supposed they would be all right as long as

it was daylight. The sun was already nearing the horizon in White Plains, but it would still be up in Kansas City.

She knew the instant the sun had set. On the monitor, she saw Robby's body jerk, then his chest expanded with a deep breath. "I should go see him."

"Give him a few minutes," Howard said. "The Vamps are always very hungry when they first wake up."

They thought he might bite her? She watched on the monitor as Robby sat up and looked at the spot where she'd slept. Then he climbed out of bed and hurried to a small refrigerator. He removed a bottle of blood and stuffed it into a microwave.

"How many bottles do they need every night?" Olivia asked.

"They can get by on a minimum of two," Howard said. "But they prefer more."

"And sometimes they drink for fun," Carlos added. "I've seen them drink lots of Blissky and Bleer."

Howard chuckled at Olivia's confused look. "That's synthetic blood mixed with whiskey or beer."

"Oh." She watched Robby guzzle down the entire bottle. Then he grabbed some clothes and went into the bathroom. "I'll go to his room now."

"I'll show you the way." Carlos led her downstairs. "There are about ten bedrooms down here in the basement. You wouldn't want to venture into the wrong one. Connor, Angus, and Emma stayed here last night, too."

That surprised Olivia. "Wouldn't it make more sense for them to stay close to where the action is?"

"You mean in Kansas City?" Carlos shrugged. "Teleportation only takes a few seconds, so the distance doesn't matter. Besides, they have a strategic advantage by staying here. They're already awake. They'll be fed, armed, and ready to go before the bad guys even wake up."

Carlos opened a door and peeked inside. "This is it." He winked. "Have fun."

"We're just going to talk."

Carlos chuckled as he strode away.

Olivia eased inside and locked the door. She could hear the shower running in the bathroom.

She was sitting in the easy chair when Robby emerged from the bathroom. His hair was wet and loose. He had on a pair of jeans, unbuttoned at the waist, and was drying his damp chest with a towel.

All the memories of the night she'd lost her virginity came rushing back to her. He'd far surpassed any fantasy lover she'd ever imagined. He had been both gentle and strong, both giving and demanding.

He froze when he saw her. "Good evening."

"Good evening," she whispered.

"Did ye sleep well?" He dropped the towel, then slowly fastened his jeans. His eyes glimmered with a reddish tint.

"Why do your eyes turn red?"

He glanced at the surveillance camera and made a cutting motion. The light went off. He sat on the edge of the bed. "A Vamp's eyes glow red when he wants to make love."

Her mouth dropped open. "Are you kidding me? Your eyes are always turning red."

His mouth tilted up. "True."

Her face grew warm. "Then all that stuff about the webcam, or the sand in your eyes, or the reflection from the fireplace—that was all lies?"

He winced. "Olivia, I never wanted to lie. I just never knew how to explain things without scaring you away. The closer I got to you, the more I knew I needed to tell you the truth, but the more I fell in love with you and couldna bear to lose you."

She nodded slowly. "This is a big decision for me. I can't make it lightly."

"I understand."

She studied her hands in her lap a moment, unsure what to say next. When she glanced at him, he was watching her with the red glint in his eyes. Her heart rate quickened. He wanted to make love to her.

He was tempting, so very tempting.

Her cell phone rang. *Saved by the bell.* She stood to retrieve it from her jeans pocket. "Hello?"

"Olivia," Barker said in a rushed voice. "Have you heard from J.L.?"

"No. I thought he was with you." She motioned for Robby to come over and listen.

"Damn," Barker muttered. "He must have gone back."

"What happened?" Olivia asked.

"We went to the storage facility to check out the two units Yasmine rented. We heard crying behind one of them, so we opened it up and found the children."

"Oh thank God!" Olivia cried. "Are they all right?"

"They're very weak. We called ambulances and took them to the hospital. There are eleven of them. I had six in one room where I was questioning them. The vampires were controlling their minds, so they don't remember very much."

"That might be a blessing." Olivia's heart ached for the children. They would have to learn that their parents were dead.

"J.L. was supposed to be interviewing the other children," Barker continued. "I went to see how he was doing, but he was gone. He left the kids with a nurse. I've tried calling him, but he doesn't answer his phone."

"He must have gone back to check the other unit," Olivia said. "Is it still daylight there?"

"Yeah, but the sun is setting. I'm going to drive back to the storage unit." Barker sighed. "It's rush hour traffic around here. It may take a while to get back."

"Let us know when you arrive." Olivia hung up and looked at Robby. "I hope J.L. hasn't done anything stupid."

"He probably wanted to stake some vampires. They won't give him any trouble when they're dead." Robby pulled on a T-shirt. "But he'd better not be anywhere near them when they wake up." He pulled on some socks and shoes.

Olivia fastened her holster and slipped on her jacket.

Five minutes later she was back in the security office. This time, Robby, Connor, Angus, and Emma were there, along with Howard and Carlos.

"This could be it," Robby said. "Casimir and his followers could be in the other storage unit."

"The escaped prisoners, too," Olivia added.

"If we get there right at sunset, we could catch them by surprise," Connor said.

They made plans. Howard was to remain behind to keep Romatech secure. Robby downloaded contact numbers for five more Vamps in Olivia's cell phone so she could call for backup if necessary. They armed themselves. Robby slipped some wooden stakes into her jacket pocket and wedged a long dagger under her belt.

They called Barker from the speakerphone so all the Vamps could use his voice as a beacon.

"I'm just getting off the freeway," Barker told them. "Damn. The sun's going down."

"Let us know the second ye arrive at the facility," Angus said.

They all waited, tense with excitement.

"It's dark now," Barker reported. "I'm about a mile away."

Olivia prayed J.L. was all right. The minutes seemed to drag on like hours.

"Okay! I'm pulling into the parking lot," Barker said. "I see J.L.'s car."

Olivia held onto Robby, and everything went black. They arrived in a dark parking lot. Connor had brought Carlos. Angus and Emma arrived together. Barker exited his car and joined them.

"Let's go." Angus dashed forward.

Olivia found herself with the two shape-shifters, running to try to keep up with the Vamps. Inside the facility, she heard screams of terror. The Vamps drew their swords as they zoomed toward the noise.

She heard the clashing of swords in the distance. The battle had begun. She arrived at the storage unit with her gun ready. It was a huge room with too much movement and mayhem for her to get in a clear shot. She recognized the faces of the escaped convicts. Some of them were hissing with long fangs as they clumsily wielded swords. The Vamps made short work of them, stabbing them in the heart. They turned to dust.

A few escaped prisoners screamed when they were stabbed. They fell to the floor, writhing in pain. She spotted bite marks on them. They'd been kept mortal to provide food for the vampires.

"Olivia, help!"

She spotted Yasmine at the back of the unit. The poor woman looked terrified. Blood seeped from punctures on her neck.

"Hang on!" Olivia drew her dagger and eased into the room.

A vampire made a grab for her, and she slashed at him with her dagger. He hissed and lunged, then turned to dust as Robby stabbed him through the heart.

She rushed toward Yasmine, but a vampire grabbed the woman from behind and teleported away.

"Olivia, darling."

She turned to see Otis coming toward her. He smiled, and his pointed fangs were stained with blood.

"No!" Robby pulled Olivia behind him.

"Well, hello, Robby." A vampire with black eyes moved next to Otis. "So good to see you again."

"Casimir." Robby pointed his sword at him. "'Tis time for you to die."

"If you come after me, my new friend here will attack the woman," Casimir said.

"She's the one I told you about," Otis whispered to Casimir. "She'll be mine for all eternity."

Robby shifted his sword to Otis. "Ye'll never have her."

"You will, dear friend." Casimir seized Otis by the arm. "But not tonight." He vanished, taking Otis with him.

Robby lunged forward, but it was too late. "Dammit. Bloody hell!"

Olivia glanced around. There were piles of dust on the cement floor and the writhing bodies of wounded mortals. The other Vamps were still fighting, but the Malcontents were starting to teleport away. She spotted Barker and Carlos in a far corner and headed toward them.

Her heart lurched when she realized they'd found J.L. He lay unconscious on the ground, trussed up in ropes. Carlos cut through them with his knife.

She fell to her knees beside J.L. and grabbed his wrist

to check his pulse. Usually, she would check a pulse at the neck, but J.L.'s neck was punctured with bite marks and stained with blood. More blood was clotted along his temple where he'd been bashed in the head.

"He must have thought there were only vampires in here," Barker whispered. "He thought it would be safe as long as the sun was up."

"The mortals in here must have attacked him," Carlos added. "They tied him up so the vampires could feed on him when they woke up."

"He's still alive," Olivia cried. "Call an ambulance."

Robby knelt beside her. "I'm so sorry."

She flinched. "He's not dead yet!"

Connor crouched on the other side of J.L. "He hardly has any blood left in him. He'll never make it to a hospital."

"We have to do something." Olivia's hands trembled as she took hold of J.L.'s limp hand. Hot tears stung her eyes. "We can't just let him die."

"We could transform him," Angus suggested as he approached.

"Nay." Robby shook his head. "We canna force such a change on him without his permission."

"He'll be all right with it," Olivia insisted. "He thinks your powers are awesome." She grabbed Robby's arm as tears ran down her face. "Please. You have to help him."

Robby's face paled. "I—I've never done it before."

"If ye doona do it, I will," Angus said. "We need all the good men we can get."

"Ye'd better be quick about it," Connor said. "We're losing him fast."

Olivia squeezed Robby's arm. "*Please.* Save him."

His eyes glimmered with unshed tears. "All right."

Chapter Twenty-six

Robby feared he would lose Olivia forever. He couldn't guarantee J.L. would survive the transformation. Sometimes human bodies rejected the change, and if that happened now, he would be responsible for killing her friend.

And regardless of the outcome, wouldn't Olivia be repulsed by the gruesome act he was about to commit?

"Give him some room." Connor shooed everyone back.

"Ye should step into the hallway," Robby told Olivia. "Ye doona want to see this."

She shook her head, and a tear rolled down her cheek. "I'm not leaving."

Robby was tempted to argue, but there wasn't any time. He leaned over her friend, closed his eyes, and breathed deeply the scent of blood. The primitive urge was always there, usually well-controlled, but this time he surrendered to the lust for blood. His gums tingled. With a hissing sound his fangs sprung out.

He was barely aware of Olivia's gasp. He sank his teeth into J.L.'s neck. He drained the last of J.L.'s blood from his body, and then, instead of stopping, let his vampire saliva seep into the wound.

Angus had described the process to him before, but Robby had never had occasion to use it. He could only hope he was doing it right. If he was, J.L. would defy death and slip into a vampire coma.

"Ye did it, lad." Angus touched his shoulder. "He's in a coma."

Robby sat back with a relieved sigh. He glanced at Olivia, and her eyes widened with alarm. Bugger. His fangs were still out. He *was* repulsing her. He wiped the blood from his mouth and focused on making his fangs retract.

"What happens now?" she asked.

"He'll either come out of the coma or he'll die," Angus told her bluntly, then looked at Robby. "Give him a few moments to adjust before ye proceed."

The room grew quiet except for the moaning of a few wounded escaped convicts.

"I need to call an ambulance," Barker said.

"No' yet," Angus replied. "We have to let Whelan handle this."

"We'd better erase their memories before they go back to prison," Connor said.

Barker kicked at a pile of dust. "Some of these dead vampires were escaped prisoners. Why didn't they teleport away like the Malcontents?"

"They were newly turned," Emma explained. "They hadn't learned how to teleport yet. I doubt they even realized they had the power."

Robby took a deep breath. Time to proceed with the next step. He removed the dagger from the sheath on his calf.

"What are you doing?" Olivia asked.

"I have to feed him." Robby's eyes misted with tears. "If he rejects my blood, he'll die. I will have killed him."

She touched Robby's arm. "Whatever happens, it won't be your fault. You've done your best."

He gave her a wry smile. "Still trying yer therapy on me?" He sliced his forearm and hissed in a long breath. Blood oozed from the wound. He pressed the blood against J.L.'s mouth.

Nothing happened. Drops of blood dribbled down J.L.'s cheek.

"Come on, lad." Robby grazed his wounded arm against J.L.'s nose to make sure he caught the scent.

J.L.'s nostrils flared.

"That's it." Robby held his arm above J.L.'s mouth. Drops of blood landed on the closed lips. "Drink, lad."

Olivia leaned close, with tears glistening on her cheeks. "J.L., please. If you can hear me, you have to drink."

More drops plopped onto J.L.'s mouth, staining his pale lips red. His mouth opened.

"That's it." Robby pressed the wound to J.L.'s mouth.

A shudder racked J.L.'s body. He suddenly grabbed hold of Robby's arm and sucked.

"It's working." Robby blinked back tears. He hadn't lost J.L.

Now if he could just hang on to Olivia.

Olivia perched on the edge of a bed where J.L. was resting. Robby had teleported her back to Romatech, while Angus had brought J.L. They'd placed him in one of the bedrooms in the basement.

She'd cleaned the blood off J.L.'s neck. To her amazement, the wounds were actually healing. Robby had explained that a Vamp's body could heal during death-sleep.

Robby and Angus had then teleported back to Kansas City to hunt for Casimir and make sure Whelan cleaned up the mess at the storage unit.

Alone with J.L., Olivia recalled how difficult the transformation process had been on Robby. He'd suffered both physical and emotional pain. His eyes had glistened with tears. Would he have to do the same process on her someday?

She slipped into Robby's room next door to take a shower. Then she rummaged through his chest of drawers for something that wouldn't fall off. She ended up with a pair of flannel pants with a drawstring she could cinch tighter. She topped it off with a T-shirt that reached her thighs.

She went back to J.L.'s room to keep him company. He was still in a coma, so he wasn't aware of her presence, but she needed to be there.

An hour later Robby strolled into the room. "I brought you some clothes from yer apartment." His mouth twitched when he saw she'd already changed.

"Sorry." She tugged at the baggy T-shirt. "I helped myself."

"They look better on you than me." He walked over to the small fridge and removed a bottle of blood. "Tomorrow night at sunset you'll need to be here with a glass of warm blood ready for J.L."

Robby set his bottle in the microwave. "In fact, ye'd better have several glasses ready. He'll awaken with a terrible hunger, and he may be tempted to jump you."

Olivia winced. Poor J.L. He was going to be in for a shock when he woke up.

"I'll be awakening next door." Robby removed the bottle from the microwave. "I'll come here right away."

She nodded. "Thank you for saving him."

Robby sighed. "He may not like being Undead."

"It's better than dead." She perched on the bed next to J.L.

Robby took a long drink. "There is a process for changing Vamps back into mortals, but 'tis verra dangerous."

"You—you could become mortal again?"

"Nay." He settled in the easy chair. "It requires a sample of yer blood and original DNA from when ye were human." He motioned toward J.L.'s bloodstained clothes. "We have that for J.L., but 'tis impossible for us old-timers."

"Oh." She tried to hide her disappointment.

He gave her a wistful look. "I'm afraid ye're stuck with me the way I am."

She took a deep breath. That was what it all boiled down to. Could she accept him as he was? Could she accept the consequences of her acceptance when it meant she might become a vampire, too, someday?

"How did it happen to you?" she asked.

Robby took another sip from his bottle. "I was a soldier back in 1746. Dougal and I went to fight for Bonnie Prince Charlie and the end of English tyranny. We lay dying on the field of Culloden as the sun set. I was drifting in and out. I thought I was imagining it when a voice asked me if I wanted to keep on living so I could fight evil."

"And you said yes."

"Aye." Robby drank some more. "'Twas Angus who asked the question. I dinna realize at the time what I was agreeing to. I just knew I dinna want to die."

"Of course you didn't," Olivia whispered.

"Angus changed me, and Connor changed Dougal." Robby finished his bottle of blood and set it on the table.

She frowned. Robby was being macho and completely glossing over the pain and fear he must have experienced. "I guess you had to bite people back then?"

"Aye, but I was careful never to hurt anyone. I tried to go back to my farm, but I could only farm at night. And my wife—"

"Your *what*?" Olivia stiffened.

His mouth thinned. "I had a wife and daughter. They were repulsed by my new condition. Mavis taught my little girl to run from me for fear I would bite her."

"I'm so sorry." Olivia didn't need empathic powers to know this had caused Robby a lot of pain.

"Then I learned that during the day while I was hiding in a cave in my death-sleep, Mavis declared me dead and took a new husband. A bloody English soldier."

Olivia winced. "This is why you value loyalty so much, isn't it?"

Robby arched a brow. "Are ye being my therapist again?"

"I'm just trying to understand you." Now she knew why he hated betrayal so much.

He glanced down at his bloodstained T-shirt. "I need to wash up. I'll be back soon." He strode from the room.

She thought back on his story. He hadn't asked to be a vampire. He'd only wanted to stay alive. And he was using his prolonged life to fight evil. There was no denying the fact that Robby MacKay was a good, honorable man.

And she loved him.

She couldn't bear to wound him with rejection. She couldn't let him feel betrayed all over again.

She rose slowly to her feet. She was going to accept him. And love him, no matter the cost.

She eased into his bedroom and locked the door. She could hear the shower running in the bathroom. She glanced up at the surveillance camera to make sure it was still turned off.

She padded into the bathroom. He was soaping up in the clear shower stall, his back turned to her. Rivulets of soapy water meandered down his strong back and tight buttocks.

She sighed.

He turned and his eyes widened. He cracked open the door. "Are ye here for the view, or did ye need something?"

With a smile, she pulled his baggy T-shirt over her head and dropped it onto the floor. "I do need something." She tugged at the drawstring holding up his flannel pants. "I need you."

He leaned back into the water spray and turned the water off. He looked at her, his eyes glinting with a reddish tint. "Olivia, I canna play at this. If I take you, I willna let you go."

"Good." She wiggled the flannel pants over her hips and let them drop. "Because I'm not letting you go."

He burst out of the shower and swooped her off her feet.

She laughed. "You're all wet."

"Ye will be, too." He tossed her on the bed and landed beside her.

"Do ye know how much I love you?" He kissed her brow, her cheeks.

"About as much as I love you." She ran her hands into his long, wet hair.

With a growl, he took her mouth. She opened and welcomed his tongue, stroking it with her own. She invaded his mouth and tested the sharpness of his fangs against her tongue.

He pulled back. "Careful with those."

She smiled. "I'm not going to live in fear of you. And you don't have to keep punching holes in my pillows."

His eyes widened. "Are ye saying ye're no' opposed to a wee nip here and there?"

She laughed. "That depends on where."

"Oh aye." He cupped a breast. "There are definitely places I would never want to puncture." He brushed his thumb over her nipple.

She shivered, and her nipples pebbled.

"Och, now would ye look at that? Is there no' a lovelier sight in the world?" He leaned over and sucked a nipple into his mouth.

The rasp of his tongue sent goose flesh shimmering down her arms and legs. Heat pooled between her thighs, and her core felt empty and aching with need.

"Robby." She dug her fingers into his back.

"Are ye rushing me, lass?" He trailed kisses down to her belly.

"Yes, yes, I am." She wrapped a leg around him.

He slid a hand between her legs. "Do ye know what happens when ye rush a Vamp?"

"I . . . no." She closed her eyes, enjoying the slow and gentle exploration of his fingers.

"Ye might end up with me moving at vampire speed." Suddenly, his fingers were rubbing her as fast as a vibrator.

She squealed. "Oh my gosh. That's . . . that's . . ."

She spiraled out of control and shattered with an orgasm.

"Oh my . . ." She pressed a hand to her chest as she struggled to breathe.

His mouth tilted up. "So maybe we should slow it down a wee bit?" His hand returned to its more leisurely pace.

"You rascal," she breathed. "You're good at every speed."

With a grin, he buried his head between her legs and continued his languid exploration with his tongue.

She moaned and writhed in motion with him. This time the climax hit her without warning. It was sudden, deep, and thorough, pulsating through her with throbs that stretched on and on.

She was so sensitized that when he plunged into her, she came again. And she wanted more. She couldn't get enough of Robby. She wrapped her legs around him and met each hard thrust. The pace escalated, becoming frantic and frenzied.

He licked her neck, and it ignited spasms of pleasure. With a shout, he climaxed with her. She felt a small pop on her neck as her core clenched rhythmically around Robby.

When her breathing and heart rate returned to normal, she realized what had happened. "You bit me?"

"Just a little." He licked the wound, and she shivered. "I couldna resist marking you. Ye're mine now."

She hugged him tight. "I'll always be yours."

Chapter Twenty-seven

The next day at dusk, Olivia paced nervously beside J.L.'s bed. Carlos waited at the foot of the bed, ready to pounce, in case he needed to restrain J.L. from biting her. She had three glasses of warm blood ready on the bedside table. Emma had recommended she have some straws on hand.

Olivia had spent half the night making love to Robby before finally succumbing to sleep. She'd wakened around noon. It no longer freaked her out that he was lying next to her not breathing. She'd showered and dressed in the clean clothes he'd brought from her apartment.

Carlos checked his watch. "Any minute now."

"Do you like working for MacKay S and I?" she asked.

"Yes." Carlos smiled. "Are you thinking about applying for a job?"

"Maybe."

"Angus is a good boss. He's been very helpful and supportive with my . . . particular problem."

"Fur balls?"

Carlos snorted. "I wish it were that simple. My kind is an endangered species. The village where I grew up was destroyed and most of the were-panthers were killed."

"I'm so sorry. That's terrible."

"I've made a few excursions to hunt for more of my kind. Angus not only gives me the time off to do it, but he finances my trips."

"Where—" she stopped when J.L.'s body jerked.

His chest expanded as he dragged in a big breath of air. His eyes opened.

She leaned over him. "J.L.?"

He snapped his head toward her. His brown eyes possessed a strange new amber glow. "What . . . where . . . *aargh*!" He curled up, grasping his stomach.

"That's a hunger pain," Carlos whispered.

Olivia wanted to explain the situation before shoving a glass of blood at him. "J.L., you were attacked by vampires. They nearly killed you. The only way to save you was—"

He shouted and covered his mouth. He moaned in pain.

She winced. "I'm so sorry. We had to change you, J.L. It was the only way to save you."

"Change me?" he whispered. He cried out as fangs ripped through his gums. He touched the fangs with his fingers, and his eyes widened. "I'm a . . . ?"

"You're a vampire, dude," Carlos said.

Olivia's eyes blurred with tears. Poor J.L. looked so shocked. In the past, she'd always known exactly how he was feeling, but now he was blank. It was like she'd lost a part of him forever in exchange for making sure he survived. "I'm sorry, J.L. You were dying, so close to dying. It seemed like the only way to save you."

He looked at his hand, which had touched his new fangs. The fingers were smeared with blood from his ripped gums. His nostrils flared. "I'm so hungry." His gaze shifted to Olivia and the amber glow in his eyes intensified.

"Here." She held a glass of warm blood up to his mouth. It clinked on his fangs, so she plopped a straw in it. "Drink."

He took a hesitant sip, then grabbed the glass and drank it all. "Still hungry."

She passed him the second glass, and he finished it. His fangs retracted and there was color once again in his cheeks.

"I have another glass if you need it." She motioned to the bedside table.

He glanced at it with a bemused look. "It's so weird. It actually tastes good to me." His gaze drifted about the room. "Everything's more sharp and clear. Where am I?"

"Romatech Industries," Carlos replied. "The manufacturer of synthetic blood, or in your case, the local food store."

J.L. looked confused. "Do I know you?"

"I'm Carlos Panterra, day guard for MacKay S and I. And I'm a were-panther."

"Wow." J.L. looked at Olivia. "This isn't some kind of weird dream? I'm really a vampire?"

"I'm afraid so." She squeezed his hand. "I begged Robby to do it. But if you're really miserable, I heard there's a way to reverse it and make you mortal again."

"I'll consider it, but I think I'm going to be all right with this."

She heaved a sigh of relief. "I was afraid you would hate me."

"No." J.L. shook his head, frowning. "It was my fault. I shouldn't have gone back."

"What happened?" She perched on the bed next to him. "Do you remember?"

"I was at the hospital when Yasmine called. She said she was trapped inside the storage unit, locked in with a bunch of vampires, and if I didn't save her, they would wake at sunset and kill her. So I rushed back to get her. I thought it would be safe, you know, 'cause it was still daylight, and all the vampires would be dead."

He dragged a hand through his thick black hair. "It was a trap. There were some escaped convicts locked in there with her. I guess the Malcontents kept them alive to be breakfast. They attacked me and knocked me out. I think they were hoping to save themselves by offering me up as the entrée."

"It must have been terrifying," Olivia said softly.

He nodded. "I thought I was a goner." He smiled suddenly. "But hey, it could be worse."

She smiled back. "You could be a zombie?"

"Exactly. So when do I get to kick some Malcontent ass?"

Carlos chuckled. "Easy, bro. You need some training first to learn how to use your new powers."

"Superpowers!" J.L. grinned. "Sweet."

Robby was in the security office at Romatech, discussing strategy, when he spotted Olivia on a monitor. She was approaching the office with Carlos and J.L. He had checked on the newly turned Vamp earlier and was relieved to find him and Olivia in good spirits.

Robby opened the door to let them in, then introduced J.L. to the others.

"If ye'd like a job at MacKay S and I, we'd be happy to have you join us," Angus said.

J.L. shook his hand. "That would be great. Thank you."

"Everything's fine," Olivia whispered to Robby. "He's happy with the change."

"Wow, I could hear that," J.L. said as he crossed the room. He studied the weapons in the caged armory. "You guys have some awesome swords."

"We've decided to teleport back to Kansas City," Robby announced. "We believe Casimir will still be in the vicinity, mainly because his new buddy, Otis, will be there, looking for Olivia."

Olivia frowned. "I suppose you need to use me as bait to draw him out."

"Nay," Robby said quickly. "I'd rather come up with another option." He took her hand. "But for now, we're moving to Barker's office at the FBI building."

"I'm coming with you," J.L. insisted. "I don't know how to teleport yet, but I do know how to fence."

They armed themselves. Robby made sure Olivia had a dagger in addition to her pistol.

He slipped on some gloves, so he could load her pistol with silver bullets. "These willna kill a vampire, ye ken, but it will hurt like hell and slow them down."

"Thank you." She snapped her gun into her holster.

He stuffed a silver chain into one of the pockets of his black cargo pants. He'd learned months ago that he could teleport with the chain as long as it didn't touch his bare skin or wasn't wrapped around him. "This could be the night. If I can get this chain around Casimir, he willna be able to escape."

"And you'll finally have the revenge you've wanted for so

long." Olivia touched his face. "Be careful, I couldn't bear to lose you."

He kissed her brow. "Lass, ye're going to be stuck with me for a long, long time."

She called her supervisor on the speakerphone. Robby teleported her to Barker's office, and Connor brought J.L. Angus and Emma arrived with Carlos.

Barker grinned when he saw J.L. and slapped him on the back. "You're looking good."

"Thanks." J.L. peered into the main office. "Everybody's gone home."

"Yep." Barker led them all into the larger outer office. "They think all the escaped prisoners are accounted for. Of course, Otis is still out there. Any ideas for finding him?"

"Maybe Yasmine used her debit card again." J.L. headed for his work area. "I'll check."

"I'll help." Olivia followed him.

"Do you know how many vampires we're up against?" Barker asked.

Robby sighed. They'd compared notes earlier about the battle in the storage unit. Three Malcontents had managed to teleport away in addition to Casimir and Otis. "We believe they have a total of five, but Casimir could have had more of his followers teleport in."

The Vamps had five vampires, including J.L., plus two shape-shifters and Olivia.

"We could call in reinforcements," Emma suggested. "Jack, Ian, Dougal, and Jean-Luc would be happy to help."

"Let's do that," Angus told her, and she pulled out her cell phone to make the calls.

Robby glanced at Olivia. She was at her work station, turning on her computer. "I willna allow Olivia to be used as bait. Otis may have learned how to teleport. If he gets his hands on her, there's no telling where he might take her. We would never find her."

Jack and the others appeared. Robby introduced them to Barker, and Angus brought them up to date.

"Robby!" Olivia called from her desk. "I just received an e-mail from Yasmine."

He dashed over to her, followed by the others.

"It was sent via a BlackBerry," Olivia explained. "She wrote, 'Help me, Olivia. They will kill me. I'm texting so they won't hear. Come to the old warehouse at Pier 6 by the river.' "

"'Tis a trap," Connor grumbled.

"Aye. Otis will be there waiting for you," Robby told Olivia. "We canna let you go."

She frowned. "I'm not helpless, you know."

"Ye're no match for a vampire," Robby argued. "They dinna let Yasmine call 'cause they dinna want us using her voice to teleport."

"I've located an office on Pier 6," J.L. said as he typed on his keypad. "We can call the number and teleport there."

Angus patted him on the back. "Lad, ye're going to fit right in at MacKay S and I."

J.L. smiled. "Just let me hitch a ride with one of you."

Olivia sighed. "And what am I supposed to do?"

"I'll stay here with you," Barker said.

"Verra well." Robby stepped back and drew his sword. "Call the number on speakerphone, J.L."

All the Vamps drew their swords and waited for the beacon to teleport. The phone rang.

"Be careful," Olivia told Robby.

He smiled. "Doona fash. I'm finally getting my revenge."

"Kansas City Exports," a female voice answered the phone. "How may I help you?"

Robby and his eight companions teleported, landing in a small office with a shrieking woman. Angus quickly erased her memory, and they all dashed from the office building. They headed toward the old warehouse.

Angus silently divided them into three groups of three, then they slipped inside. Angus took his group to the right, Jack veered to the left with his group, and Robby led Connor and J.L. down the wide path in the center.

Dim lights shone overhead with dust motes dancing in the weak, golden glow. The air was musty and stale. Robby passed rows of stacked wooden crates and boxes, then came to an open area in the center of the warehouse.

On the far side of the open area, close to a double stack of crates, Yasmine sat tied up in a chair. Definitely a trap. She couldn't have sent the text to Olivia with her hands tied behind her back.

A clash of swords sounded on the right, then another clash on the left. Angus's and Jack's groups were under attack.

Robby slowly advanced into the open area with Connor and J.L.

Yasmine spotted them. "Help! They're going to kill me!"

"That's what you said last time!" J.L. yelled back.

"I'm sorry," she wailed. "The prisoners said they would kill me if I didn't find someone else for the vampires to feed on."

"So you chose me?" J.L. glared at her.

"Please!" Yasmine cried. "I'm so scared. I didn't know Otis would become a vampire!"

"Doona approach her, lad," Connor said.

"Don't worry," J.L. grumbled. "I'll never trust her again."

Yasmine's desperate look vanished and she glared coldly at them. "Where's Olivia? I promised him Olivia."

"He will never have her," Robby said.

Yasmine lifted her chin. "Fine by me. She'll never love Otis like I do. I can make him happy—"

"You stupid bitch!" Otis zoomed from behind the crates and backhanded Yasmine across the face. "You failed me again."

"Otis," she cried. "I'll do anything for you."

J.L. charged toward Otis, but he teleported away just as J.L. lifted his sword. "Damn!"

Yasmine laughed. "You'll never catch him. He's too smart for you."

Connor ran behind the crates to see if another vampire was hiding there.

J.L. gave Yasmine an incredulous look. "What is your problem? How can you help a monster like that?"

"Otis needs me. He said I was different from the others. He said I was special. He hates other women, but he loves me."

J.L. scoffed. "He loves Olivia."

"No!" Yasmine struggled against her ropes. "He said I would be with him forever. All I had to do was help him drive Olivia crazy."

"You're the crazy one!" J.L. yelled.

"Enough." Robby held up a hand. The clashing of swords in the distance had stopped. He pivoted, searching the warehouse, then focused on Yasmine. "Is Casimir here?"

She glowered at him. "Why should I tell you anything? Otis hates you. I told him Olivia was dating you, and that's when he had me put the apples in her apartment to punish her. I'm the one who really loves him. When he realizes that, he'll change *me* into a vampire. Not Olivia. And then we'll be together forever."

"He's just using you, Yasmine," J.L. muttered.

Connor emerged from behind the crates. "It's clear."

"He loves me!" Yasmine shouted. "Otis loves me."

"Enough, woman!" Connor shot a vampire mind zap at her, and she slumped unconscious in her chair.

"Wow," J.L. whispered. "I need to learn how to do that."

Connor shrugged. "'Twill no' make you verra popular with the ladies."

The other Vamps ran into the open area.

"We killed two," Angus reported.

"We killed one," Jack said.

"Bravo," a voice said from above. Casimir stepped off a rafter far overhead and floated down to land on top of the crates. He held his sword in his right hand. His long coat didn't hide the fact that his left arm was bent in an unnatural way. His left hand was gloved and curled up against his chest. "It only took nine of you to kill three of my men. How very brave of you."

Robby reached a gloved hand into his pocket to grab hold of the silver chain. He teleported to the top of the crates and whipped the chain out.

Casimir pointed his sword at him. "Do you think you'll get revenge? The joke is on you, MacKay. I found a new way to torture you, and the wound will cut deep. You see, Otis stole the Asian's cell phone last night while I was feeding on him."

J.L. felt his pockets. "He's right. It's gone."

Casimir chuckled. "I wonder if the lovely Olivia will answer a phone call from her friend? If she has, Otis has already teleported there."

Robby's blood turned cold.

"What will you do, Robby?" Casimir sneered. "You can make a feeble attempt to kill me, or you can rush back to your woman and discover you were too late to save her."

Olivia was pacing in Barker's office, waffling between anger and anxiety. She was worried about Robby and J.L., but also angry that they hadn't allowed her to go with them.

"Relax," Barker said from behind his desk. "They'll be fine."

"J.L. isn't used to being a vampire yet. He shouldn't be fighting so soon." Her cell phone rang, and she checked the caller. "Oh my gosh, it's J.L."

She flipped the phone open. "Hello?" She shot Barker a worried look. "J.L.? Are you there?"

"I'm right here, darling."

She gasped and spun around. Otis was in the office, holding J.L.'s phone.

"Shame on you, darling." Otis affected an injured look. "You were supposed to come to the warehouse. But lucky for me, I had another way to find you."

She dropped her phone and drew her weapon.

Barker jumped to his feet, aiming his pistol.

Otis tossed the phone on the floor and stepped toward her. "Now, at last, we can be together."

Barker shot at him, but Otis vanished. Olivia spun around, looking for him.

She heard Barker gasp. His face contorted in pain, then he slumped to the floor. Otis was standing in his place with a bloodied knife in his hand.

"They left you poorly protected, didn't they?" He wedged the knife under his belt.

Rage exploded in Olivia. She fired her gun. And missed.

Otis had moved out of the way at vampire speed, his body zooming across the room in a blur. He knocked the gun from her hand. She jumped back and drew her dagger.

Otis smiled. "You like knives, too? I knew we were perfect for each other."

She lunged forward, stabbing at his chest, but again he vanished. He was suddenly behind her, yanking her up against his chest and ripping the dagger from her hand.

She elbowed him in the ribs and stomped on his foot. When his hold loosened, she broke free and ran for her dagger on the floor.

He tackled her from behind, slamming her onto the carpet. Before she could catch her breath, he flipped her over. She swung punches at his face, but he grabbed her wrists and pinned her arms down.

"At last." He breathed heavily. "I'll make you mine forever." He reared his head back and his fangs sprang out.

She kneed him in the balls. He hissed, and lifted her up just to slam her back onto the floor.

Pain shot through her skull. Her vision cleared in time to see him drawing closer to her neck. She struggled, but he was too damned strong.

He flinched and pulled back. "What?" He regarded her with horror. "You've been marked. You let someone else bite you?"

"I'll never be yours. Never," she hissed.

"You bitch!" He pulled his knife from his belt.

A silver chain was suddenly looped around Otis's neck and he cried out in pain. The knife tumbled from his hand.

Robby yanked the chain tighter, and Otis's skin sizzled. He hauled Otis off her. Otis flailed his arms, trying to reach Robby behind him.

"His knife," Robby growled. He yanked Otis to his feet, still squeezing him around the neck with the silver chain.

She spotted Otis's knife on the floor beside her, grabbed it and scrambled to her feet. "This is for all the women you tortured and killed!" She plunged it into his chest.

He turned to dust.

She dropped the knife to the floor. Robby dropped the chain and pulled her into his arms.

She held him tight. Even so, she started to shake.

"'Tis over, sweetheart." He hugged her. "He'll never threaten you again."

"Is it really over? Did you kill Casimir?"

"Nay. I left him to save you." Robby kissed the top of her head. "I couldna bear to lose you."

A moan sounded behind the desk.

"Oh my gosh, Barker!" Olivia skirted the desk and found him on the floor. Blood oozed from his wound.

He blinked up at her. "You're all right?"

"Yes." She fumbled for the phone on his desk. "I'll call an ambulance."

Robby stopped her. "Ye may no' need to. Barker, will ye heal if ye shift?"

"I think so. But I've lost a lot of blood." He winced. "I'm sorry, Olivia. I wasn't much help. I passed out."

She squeezed his arm. "Don't apologize."

More Vamps appeared in the room.

J.L. ran toward Olivia and Barker. "Are you guys okay?"

"Otis stabbed Barker in the back," Olivia told him.

Connor stepped forward. "I can teleport him to a Vamp doctor in Houston. We'll make sure he heals properly."

"Oh, thank you," Olivia said.

Connor gathered Barker up and vanished.

Olivia gave J.L. a hug. "I was worried about you. Did you find Yasmine?"

"Oh yeah." He made a face. "The woman's crazy. We called the police to come get her."

"What happened to Casimir?" Robby asked.

Angus sighed. "The bastard teleported away right after ye did." He motioned to the pile of dust on the floor. "I gather this was Otis?"

"Aye. Olivia killed him." Robby smiled at her.

"We did it together." She stepped into his arms.

He hugged her tight. "We make a fearsome couple."

Angus chuckled and nudged his wife. "I think we'll have some wee bairns in the family soon."

Emma grinned. "Oh, I hope so."

Robby scoffed. "Do ye mind if we get married first?"

Olivia touched his cheek. "Are you proposing?"

"No' here." He kissed her brow. "But I know the perfect place."

She smiled. "It's a date."

Epilogue

Patmos, one week later . . .

Olivia sat at the kitchen table in her grandmother's house, nervously awaiting her Yia Yia's re-action. Eleni Sotiris was staring into space with a stunned expression. It wasn't every day that you heard your grand-daughter was in love with a vampire.

Eleni had been thrilled when Olivia had suddenly arrived early in June. She'd been even more thrilled that Olivia was leaving the FBI. But this latest news shocked Eleni so much, Olivia felt her grandmother go blank for a few minutes.

"Are you sure?" Eleni asked. "Some people just have very pointy teeth."

"I'm sure. I know it comes as a shock, but it's true."

Eleni sighed. "I can sense you're telling the truth." Her emotions took a dark turn, with disbelief and suspicion swirling around her. "He's not hurting you, is he?"

"No, he's a sweet and gentle man."

"How can that be? Isn't he some kind of demon?"

"No. Robby was dying on a battlefield when his grandfather transformed him. He was a good, honorable man, and he still is. His death couldn't change who he is."

Eleni pursed her lips. "I thought vampires were evil."

"Some of them are. An evil person will turn into an evil vampire. Actually, I suspect they become even more evil. All that extra power goes to their head."

"He's not a devil worshipper, is he?"

Olivia snorted. "No. He was raised Roman Catholic. And he says he's willing to become Greek Orthodox."

"Oh." Eleni's aura of suspicion cleared away. "That's good news."

"And we can still have children."

"What?" A surge of joy emanated from Eleni. "Why didn't you say so from the beginning? Of course we'll welcome your young man into the family."

Olivia exhaled with relief. "Thank you. It'll mean a lot to Robby that you've accepted him."

Eleni waved a hand in dismissal. "I always knew he was the man for you."

"I thought you had your hopes up for Spiro."

Eleni shrugged. "Spiro ran off last month to get married." She winced. "To Dimitrios."

Olivia laughed. "I'm going to meet Robby on the beach after sunset. I can bring him back here if you like."

"Of course!" Eleni bustled over to the refrigerator. "What would he like to eat?"

"He doesn't eat, Yia Yia. He drinks synthetic blood out of a bottle every night."

"You mean you won't have to cook for him?" Eleni shut the fridge door, smiling. "That is perfect for you, child. I'm afraid you were never much of a cook."

Olivia hugged her grandmother. "Thank you so much for understanding. I knew I needed to tell you the truth about Robby."

"Of course." Eleni wagged a finger at her. "I will know if you ever lie to me."

"This is something we need to keep secret. I know you like to gossip with—"

"I do not gossip," Eleni huffed. "And I can keep a secret. Now go on, go see that young man of yours. And tell him I expect you two to get married here in my church."

"Yes, ma'am." Olivia left the kitchen and crossed the courtyard. Memories flashed through her mind. This was where she'd first talked with Robby, where she'd first started falling in love.

She hurried down the stairs, then headed down the beach toward Petra. The sun was low on the horizon, turning the sky pink and gold and setting the sea ablaze with golden sparkles.

The Draganesti villa came into view. Robby had left a message on her phone that he'd arrived shortly before dawn. She'd been waiting all day for him to wake from his death-sleep. She stayed on the beach to watch the sun disappear over the horizon. It was a beautiful end to a day, and a beautiful beginning for her new life.

"Are ye sure ye're no' a Greek goddess?" Robby called out to her.

She turned and grinned at him. He was standing on the bluff, looking gorgeous as usual. "I won't object to being worshipped."

He jumped off the bluff and landed neatly beside her. "I missed you." He brushed back a curl that the breeze had blown across her cheek.

"It's only been two days since I saw you last." She wrapped

her arms around his neck and kissed him. "I told my grand-mother about you."

He winced. "How did she take it?"

"As far as I can tell, you could be an alien from another galaxy, and it wouldn't matter as long as we can have children."

He chuckled. "I like yer grandmother." He stepped back. "Remember when ye asked me yer three questions?"

"Yes."

"Ask them again." He took her hands in his. "Ask them again, and I will answer."

She smiled. "What do you want more than anything in the world?"

He squeezed her hands. "I want you."

Her heart expanded with joy. "And what do you fear more than anything in the world?"

"Losing you."

"And if you get what you want more than anything, will it make you a better person?"

"Aye, it will." He knelt on one knee. "Will ye marry me, Olivia?"

"Yes!" She fell on her knees and wrapped her arms around him. "Yes."

He hugged her tight. "I love you, Olivia."

Tears filled her eyes. "I love you, too."

"I looked up yer last name in a dictionary, and it means salvation. That's what ye've done to me, lass. Ye saved me from a life filled with hatred and vengeance. I'm free now."

She rested her hands on his face and gazed into his glittering green eyes. "We're free together."

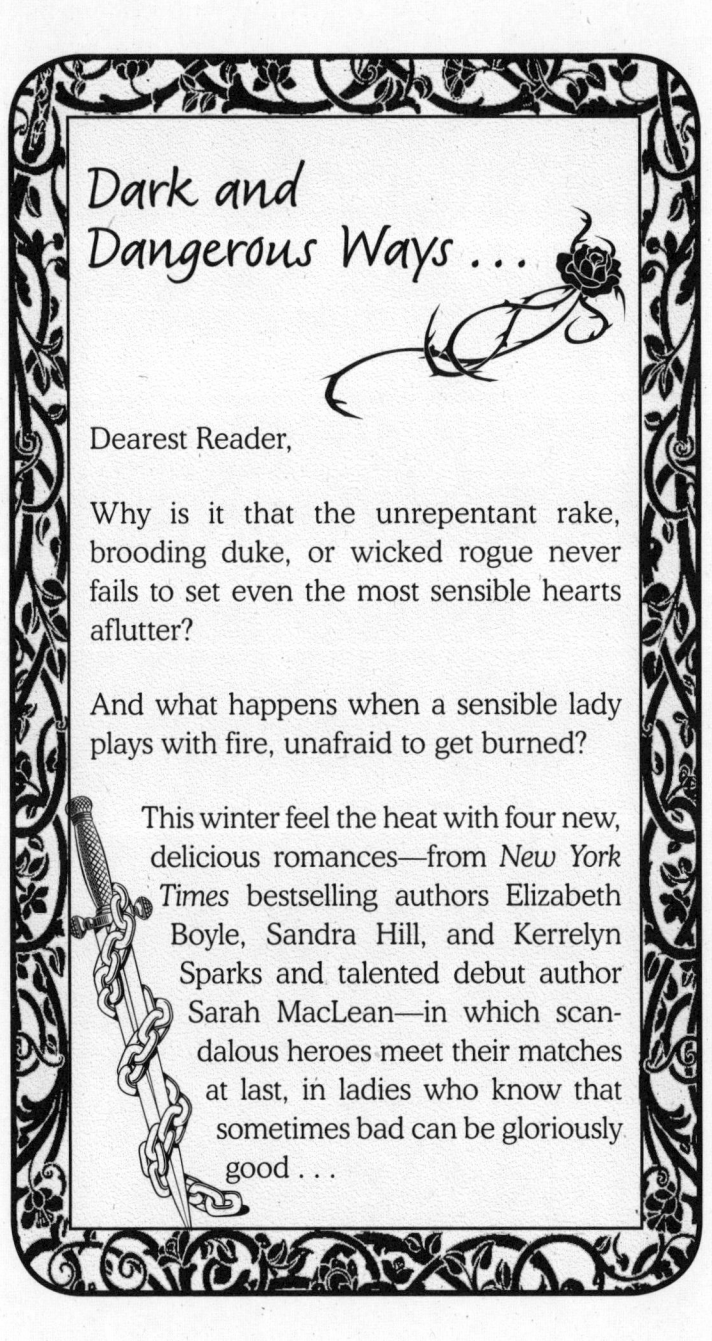

Dark and Dangerous Ways . . .

Dearest Reader,

Why is it that the unrepentant rake, brooding duke, or wicked rogue never fails to set even the most sensible hearts aflutter?

And what happens when a sensible lady plays with fire, unafraid to get burned?

This winter feel the heat with four new, delicious romances—from *New York Times* bestselling authors Elizabeth Boyle, Sandra Hill, and Kerrelyn Sparks and talented debut author Sarah MacLean—in which scandalous heroes meet their matches at last, in ladies who know that sometimes bad can be gloriously good . . .

How I Met My Countess

The first in a new series
from *New York Times* bestselling author

Elizabeth Boyle

When Lucy Ellyson, the improper daughter of an infamous spy, saves the Earl of Clifton's life, he decides to make her his countess. But then the irresistible chit vanishes and Clifton is certain he's lost her forever . . . until he discovers she's living in Mayfair, as scandalous as ever and in the sort of trouble only a hasty marriage can solve. But before Clifton can step in, secrets from the past emerge, threatening to ruin them both.

While the Earl of Clifton had been expecting a scullery maid or even a housekeeper to respond to Mr. Ellyson's shouted orders, the gel who arrived in the man's study left him taken aback.

Her glorious black hair sat piled atop her head, the pins barely holding it there, the strands shimmering with raven lights and rich, deep hues. They were the sort of strands that made one think of the most expensive courtesans, the most elegant and desirable ladies.

Yet this miss wore a plain muslin gown, over which she'd thrown an old patched green sweater. There were mitts on her hands, for the rest of the house was cold, and out from beneath the less than tidy hem of her gown, a pair of very serviceable boots stuck out.

This was all topped off with the large splotch of soot decorating her nose and chin.

She took barely a glance at Clifton or his brother before her hands fisted to her hips. "Whatever are you doing shouting like that? I'm not deaf, but I fear I will be if you insist on bellowing so."

Crossing the room, she swatted Ellyson's hand off the map he was in the process of unrolling. Plucking off her mitts and swiping her hand over her skirts—as if that would do the task and clean them—she caught up the map and reshelved it. "I doubt you need Paris as yet."

There was a presumptuous note of disdain in her voice, as if she, like Ellyson himself, had shelved their guests with the same disparagement that she had just given the errant map.

And in confirmation, when she cast a glance over her shoulder and took stock of them, it was with a gaze that was both calculating and dismissive all at once. "Why not begin with ensuring that they know how to get to the coast," she replied, no small measure of sarcasm dripping from her words.

Ellyson barked a short laugh, if one could call it a laugh. But her sharp words amused the man. "Easy girl, they've Pymm's blessing. We're to train them up."

"Harrumph," she muttered, putting one more stamp of disapproval on the notion.

Clifton straightened. It was one thing to be dismissed by a man of Ellyson's stature, but by a mere servant? Well, it wasn't to be borne. He opened his mouth to protest, but Malcolm nudged him.

Don't wade into this one, little brother, his dark eyes implored.

"I need to start with Lisbon," Ellyson said. "But demmed if I can find it."

"Here," she said, easily locating the map from the collection. "Anything else?" Her chapped hands were back on her hips and she shot another glance over her shoulder at Clifton, her bright green eyes revealing nothing but dismay, especially when her gaze fell to the puddles of water at his feet and the trail of mud from his boots.

Then she looked up at him with a gaze that said one thing: *You'd best not expect me to clean that up.*

Clifton could only gape at her. He'd never met such a woman.

Well, not outside of a public house.

Bossy termagant of a chit, still he couldn't stop watching her, for there was a spark to this Lucy that dared to settle inside his chest.

She was, with that hair and flashing eyes, a pretty sort of thing in an odd way. But she held herself so that a man would have to have a devilish bit of nerve to tell her so.

Then she shocked him, or at least, he thought it was the most shocking thing he'd ever heard.

"Papa, I haven't all day and I've a roast to see to, as well as the pudding to mix."

Papa? Clifton's mouth fell open. This bossy chit was Ellyson's daughter?

No, in the world of the Ellysons, Clifton quickly discovered, such a notion wasn't shocking in the least.

Not when weighed against what her father said in reply. "Yes, yes, of course. But before you see to dinner, I have it in mind for you to become Lord Clifton's new mistress. What say you, Goosie?" he asked his daughter as casually as one might inquire if the pudding was going to include extra plums. "How would you like to fall in love with an earl?"

Lucy glanced over her shoulder and looked at the man standing beside the door. Very quickly, she pressed her lips together to keep from bursting out with laughter at the sight of the complete and utter shock dressing the poor earl's features. He had to be the earl, for the other man hadn't the look of a man possessing a title and fortune.

Oh, heavens! He thinks Papa is serious. And in a panic over how to refuse him.

Not that a very feminine part of her felt a large stab of pique.

Well, you could do worse, she'd have told him, if the other man in the room, the one by the window, the earl's brother from the looks of him, hadn't said, "Good God, Gilby! Close your mouth. You look like a mackerel."

The fellow then doubled over with laughter. " 'Sides I doubt Ellyson is serious."

Lucy didn't reply, nor did her father, but that was to be expected, for Papa was already onto the next step of his plans for the earl and his natural brother, and therefore saw no polite need to reply.

"Sir, I can hardly . . . I mean as a gentleman . . ." the earl began.

Lucy turned toward him, one brow cocked and her hands back on her hips. It was the stance she took when the butcher tried to sell her less than fresh mutton.

The butcher was a devilish cheat, so it made ruffling this gentleman's fine and honorable notions akin to child's play.

Clifton swallowed and took a step back, which brought him right up against the wall.

Literally and figuratively.

"What I mean to say is that while Miss Ellyson is . . . is . . . that is to say I am . . ." He closed his eyes and shuddered.

Actually shuddered.

Well, a lady could only take so much.

Lucy sauntered past him, flicked a piece of lint off the shoulder of his otherwise meticulous jacket, and tossed a smile up at him. "Don't worry, *Gilby*," she purred, using the familiar name his brother had called him. "You don't have to bed me." She took another long glance at him— from his dark hair, the chiseled set of his aristocratic jaw, the breadth of his shoulders, the long lines of his legs, to his perfectly polished boots—everything that was wealthy, noble, and elegant, then continued toward her father's desk, tossing one more glance over her shoulder. "For truly, you aren't my type."

Which was quite true. Well, there was no arguing that the Earl of Clifon was one of the most handsome men who'd ever walked into her father's house seeking his training to take on secretive "work" for the King, but Lucy also found his lofty stance and rigid features troubling.

He'll not do, Papa, she wanted to say. For she considered herself an excellent judge of character. And this Clifton would have to set himself down a notch or two if he was going to stay alive, at the very least, let alone complete the tasks he would be sent to do.

No, he is too utterly English. Too proud. Too . . . too . . . noble.

And Lucy knew this all too well. For she'd spent a good part of her life watching the agents come and go from her father's house. She knew them all.

And she also knew the very real truth about their situation: They may never come back. As much as she found it amusing to give this stuffy earl a bit of a tease, there was a niggle of worry that ran down her spine.

What if he doesn't come back?

Well, I don't care, she told herself, crossing the room and putting her back to the earl. She opened a drawer and handed a folder to her father, who through this exchange had been muttering over the mess of papers and correspondence atop his desk. "I think you need these," she said softly.

Her father opened it up, squinted at the pages inside, and then nodded. "Ah, yes. Good gel, Goosie." He turned back to Clifton. "Whatever has you so pale? I don't expect you to deflower the gel, just carry her love letters."

"Letters?" Clifton managed.

"Yes, letters," Lucy explained. "I write coded letters to you as if I were your mistress and you carry them to Lisbon." She strolled over, reached up, and patted his chest. "You put them right next to your heart." She paused and gazed up at him. "You have one of those, don't you?"

Viking in Love

The first in a new series
from *New York Times* bestselling author

Sandra Hill

Breanne and her sisters are more than capable of taking care of themselves—just ask the last man who crossed them. But when a hasty escape lands them in the care of a Viking warrior, the ladies know they have at last met a worthy quarry. After nine long months in the king's service, all Caedmon wanted was . . . well, certainly not five Norse princesses running his keep. And after the fiery redhead bursts into his chamber on the very first morning . . . Caedmon settles on a wicked plan far more delightful than kicking her out.

*B*eware of women with barbed tongues . . .

Caedmon was splatted out on his stomach, half-awake, knowing he must rise soon. This was a new day and a new start for getting his estate and his family back in order. In his head he made a list.

First, gather the entire household and establish some authority. Someone had been lax in assigning duties and making sure they were completed. The overworked Gerard, no doubt. And the absent Alys.

Second, take stock of the larder. Huntsmen would go out for fresh meat, fishermen for fish, and he would send someone to Jarrow to purchases spices and various other foodstuffs.

Third, designate Geoff and Wulf to work with the housecarls on fighting skills and rotating guard schedules.

Fourth, replenish the supply of weaponry.

Fifth, persuade the cook to return. The roast boar yestereve had been tough as leather, made palatable only by the tubfuls of feast ale and strong mead they had consumed.

Sixth, the children . . . ah, what to do about the children? One of the cotters' wives . . . or John the Bowman's widow . . . could supervise their care, and a monk from the minster in Jorvik might be induced to come and tutor them, although his history with Father Luke did not bode well for his chances.

The door to his bedchamber swung open, interrupting his mental planning. The headboard of his bed was against the same wall as the door, so he merely turned his head to the left and squinted one eye open.

A red-haired woman—dressed in men's attire . . . highborn men's attire, at that—stood glaring at him, hands on hips. She was tall for a woman, and thin as a lance. As for breasts, if she had any, they must be as flat as rounds of manchet bread. "Master Caedmon, I presume?"

"Well, I do not know about the 'Master' part. What manner dress is that? Are you man or woman?" He smiled, trying for levity.

She did not return the smile.

No sense of humor.

"You are surely the most loathsome lout I have e'er encountered."

Whaaaat? He had not been expecting an attack. In fact, he needed a moment for his sleep-hazed brain to take in this apparition before him.

"Your keep is filthy, pigs broke through the sty fence and are all over the bailey, I saw dozens of mice scampering in your great hall, thatch needs replacing on the cotters' huts, you beget children like an acorn tree gone wild, your staff take their ease like high nobility, there are several blubbering servants arguing over who will bury the priest who is laid out in your chapel, and you . . . you slothful sluggard, you lie abed, sleeping off a *drukkin* night, no doubt."

Whoa! One thing was for certain. This would not be yet another woman trying to crawl into his bed furs. "Stop shrieking. You will make my ears bleed." Caedmon rolled over on his side, tugging the bed linen up to cover his lower half, then sat up.

"Bestir thyself!"

"Nay!"

"Have you no shame?"

"Not much."

"Are you lackbrained?"

"No more than you for barging into my bedchamber."

"Even if you have no coin, there is no excuse for the neglect."

"Not even the fact that I have been gone nine long months in service to a king undeserving of service?"

"Where is the lady of this estate?"

'Tis just like a woman to think a woman is the answer to everything! "There is no lady."

"Hmpfh! Why am I not surprised?"

Now he was getting annoyed. "Sarcasm ill suits you, m'lady. Have you ne'er been told that?"

"The blade goes both ways, knave."

His eyes went wide at her foolhardy insults. "Who in bloody hell are you?"

"Breanne of Stoneheim."

"Is that supposed to mean something to me?"

"She's a princess," someone called out from the corridor. He saw now that a crowd of people were standing just outside the open doorway, being entertained by this shrew's railing at him. Geoff and Wulf were in the forefront, of course, laughing their arses off.

"Well, Princess Breanne, what do you in my home and my bedchamber?"

She had the grace to blush. "My sisters and I came here, on our way ... as a stopping-off place ... for a ... uh, visit ... on our journey. Your castellan offered us hospitality."

He could tell by the deepening red on her cheeks that she was either lying or stretching the truth.

"Sisters?"

"She has four sisters," Geoff offered. "All princesses."

Five princesses? Here? Oh, Lord!

"And they are accompanied by two scowling Vikings who are about this tall," Wulf added, holding a hand high above his head. And Wulf was a big man by any standard.

"They were only scowling because your archers aimed their bows at them," the lady declared, doing her own good job of scowling.

" 'Tis a comfort, your explanation is. I feel so much better."

Caedmon could practically hear the grinding of her small, white teeth.

"And there is a wise man from the eastern lands who has opinions on every bloody thing in the world, most of it involving camels." As usual, Geoff was enjoying himself at his expense.

"Why me? I mean, why stop here at Larkspur?" he asked the bothersome woman. "Surely there are better places."

"My sister Tyra is your cousin."

He frowned. "I have no cousin named Tyra." Leastways, he did not think he did, but then he was still wooly-witted from sleep.

"Her husband, Adam of Hawkshire, is your cousin by marriage . . . um, slightly removed," the flame-haired witch explained.

He knew Adam, or rather he had heard of him. A famed healer. But their connection by blood was far removed.

"Did you know there is a child still in nappies walking about nigh naked? He could be trampled by dogs the size of small ponies roaming about indoors."

"Have a caution, wench. You have already passed the bounds of good sense. Any more, and you may taste the flavor of *my* wrath."

She started to respond, then stopped herself.

"I told Emma to take care of Piers," Caedmon said.

"Would that be the same Emma who spent the night spreading her thighs for the blond god?"

"She is referring to me," Geoff preened. "The blond god."

"And, by the by, why do all the females in this keep appear to have big bosoms?"

"Huh?"

Geoff and Wulf were laughing so hard they were bent over at their waists, holding their sides. When he was able to speak, Geoff said, " 'Twould seem that Gerard has a preference for big breasts when choosing maids for inside work." He gave particular emphasis to "inside work."

"Gerard? Bloody hell! He is old enough to . . . never mind."

"Not yet in his dotage, if he can still appreciate a buxom bosom," Wulf observed.

Breanne waved a hand airily. "You are not to worry. My sisters and I will set your keep aright whilst we are here."

Alarm rippled through Caedmon's body. "How long do you intend to stay?" he asked bluntly.

Another blush. "I am not certain. But you are not to worry."

"I was not reassured the first time you said that."

"You will hardly notice we are here."

"I doubt that heartily."

She went stiff as a pike, apparently not liking it when the sarcasm came from his direction, but she pressed her lips together. Very nice lips, he noticed, if he were attracted to tall, skinny, red-haired women with barbed tongues, which he was not. At least she was making an effort to be polite now.

Something very strange was going on, but he had more urgent matters to take care of. He'd drunk a tun of ale yestereve and now he needed to piss. Badly.

"Go down to the great hall and wait for me. We will discuss this later."

The shrew lifted her chin defiantly and said, "I am not leaving until you get your lazy self out of bed. If no one else cares about those children . . ." On and on she blathered in her shrill voice.

Really, this woman's tongue flaps like a loose shingle. I could rebuke her in a way she would not soon forget. Hell, I could kick her cheeky arse out the door, if I choose. But wait. I know another way. "You say me nay? Be careful, you may find I am more than you wagered for."

"Do you threaten me, troll?"

"So be it," he said, tossing the sheet aside and standing. *How do you like that trollsome part?*

Immediately her eyes fixed on a part of his naked body, which was displaying a powerful morning thickening, standing out like a flagpole. "You, you, you . . ." she sputtered, but could not seem to raise her eyes, which he noticed, irrelevantly, were a beautiful shade of green, like summer grass on the moors.

"Do not be offended, m'lady." He pointed at his nether part. "*This* is not for you. Your virtue is not forfeit . . . from this quarter. 'Tis just that I must needs visit the garderobe."

"What an insufferable, crude, arrogant, loathsome lout!" she exclaimed as she sailed through the doorway, where the crowd had magically parted like the Red Sea of Biblical lore.

"Damn, but it is good to be home, is it not, Caedmon?" Geoff inquired sweetly, then ducked just in time to miss the pillow he sent his way.

A short time later, Caedmon realized he had one more thing to add to his list of things to do today: Get rid of princesses.

The Vampire and the Virgin
from *New York Times* bestselling author
Kerrelyn Sparks's
Love at Stake series

After doing battle with evil vampires intent on world domina-
tion, Robby MacKay is in dire need of a vacation. And calm,
cool nights on a tropical island are exactly what the doctor
ordered . . . but there's nothing cool about Olivia Sotiris. Also
on vacation, the very sexy, very hot psychologist can make
Robby's eyebrows singe with just one look. Soon, those nights
aren't calm or cool . . .

Olivia rested her elbows on the patio wall and gazed at
the beach below. A breeze swept a tendril of hair across
her face, and she shoved it aside. Most of her long hair was
secured on the back of her head with a big claw clip, but
as usual, there were always a few unruly strands that managed to escape.

She took a deep breath, savoring her solitude. There
were times, like during the party that evening, when the
constant bombardment of everyone's emotions became
hard to bear. It would feel like she was drowning, her own
emotions submerged under the flood of those around her,
to the point that she feared losing herself entirely. She'd
learned over the years to handle it, but still, every now and
then, she had to escape the maddening crowd.

Being an empath had certainly helped her with her job.
Unfortunately, her unique abilities had also caused the

monster to become obsessed with her. *Don't think about him. You're safe here.*

A movement far to the left caught her eye. She focused on a grove of tamarisk trees but only saw them swaying with a breeze. Nothing strange there.

Then she saw him. A lone figure emerging from the dark shadow of the trees. He was jogging along the beach. At this time of night? He reached a clear, sandy expanse where the moon shone brightly, and Olivia forgot to breathe.

His body was beautiful and she suspected his face was, too, but it was hard to tell at this distance. Dressed in dark jogging shorts and a plain white T-shirt, he moved quickly and easily along the beach. His skin seemed pale, but that could be caused by the moonlight.

She sucked in a deep breath as he came closer. He was a big man. His T-shirt was stretched across wonderfully broad shoulders, the short sleeves tight around his biceps.

If only she could see his face better. Her gaze drifted over to the telescope. Why not? She rushed over, pointed the telescope in the man's direction, and peered through the eyepiece.

Oh, yeah, he did not disappoint. His eyes looked sharp and intelligent, pale, though she couldn't tell the color. Green, she hoped, since that was her favorite. He had a straight, strong nose, a wide mouth, and a strong jaw with a sexy hint of dark whiskers. There was a grim expression on his face, but it didn't make him unattractive. Quite the opposite. It added to his aura of masculine power.

He passed by the house, and she admired his sharp profile for a few seconds, then lowered the scope to his body. His chest expanded with each deep breath, and she found herself matching her breaths to his. Even lower, she noted his muscular thighs and calves. His white running shoes pounded on the sand, leaving a steady trail.

He continued down the beach toward the rock known as Petra, giving her a glorious view of his backside.

"Opa," she muttered as she continued to spy on him through the telescope. She'd seen plenty of fit men during her training days for the Bureau, but this guy put them to shame. While their muscles had seemed forced and clumpy, this guy looked completely natural, moving with an easy, graceful control.

She was still focused on his rump when she noticed the attached legs were no longer moving. Did he run out of steam? He hadn't seemed tired. His jogging shorts slowly turned, affording her a long look at his groin. She gulped.

She raised the scope to his chest. Oh dear. That huge expanse of chest was now facing her direction. Surely, he wasn't . . . she lifted the scope to his face and gasped.

He was looking straight at her!

She jumped back, pulling her blanket tight around her. How could he see her? The courtyard was dark and the walls reached to her waist. But then the walls were white-washed and she was cocooned in a white blanket, and the moon and stars were bright. Maybe he *could* see this far. Surely he hadn't been able to hear her? She'd barely spoken over a whisper.

He stepped toward her, gazing at her with intense eyes. Oh God, he'd caught her ogling him with a telescope! She pressed a hand against her mouth to keep from groaning out loud. Apparently, the smallest of sounds was carrying across the beach.

He took another step toward her, and the moon glinted off his hair. Red? She hadn't met any redheaded men at the party that night. Who was this man?

"Olivia," Eleni called through the open door. "Your tea is steeping."

She strode into the kitchen and waited impatiently for her mug of tea. "There's a man on the beach."

"Are you sure? It's almost two in the morning."

"Come and see. Maybe you know him." Olivia wandered back to the patio and peered over the wall.

He was gone.

"He—he was there." Olivia pointed south toward Petra. There was no sign of him anywhere.

Eleni gave her a sympathetic look. "You're exhausted and seeing shadows. Drink your tea, child, and go to bed."

"He was real," she whispered. And the most beautiful man she'd ever seen. *Dear God, please let him be real.*

Coming April 2010

Nine Rules to Break When Romancing a Rake

A delightful new romance from debut author

Sarah MacLean

Kiss someone passionately, fire a pistol, attend a duel . . .

Lady Calpurnia Hartwell has had enough. Sick and tired of following rules and never having any fun, the inveterate spinster decides it's time to throw caution to the wind . . . at least just this once. But when a little fun leads her into the arms of a devastating rake, good Lady Callie must decide if she'll retreat to the life she knows . . . or succumb to a most ruinous temptation.

Who are you?" The Marquess of Ralston's eyes narrowed in the darkness, taking in the soft angles of Callie's face. "Wait . . ." She imagined his eyes flashing with recognition. "You're Allendale's daughter. I noticed you earlier."

She could not contain her sarcastic response. "I'm sure you did, my lord. It would be rather hard to miss me." She covered her mouth immediately, shocked that she had spoken so boldly.

He chuckled. "Yes. Well, it isn't the most flattering of gowns."

She couldn't help her own laughter from slipping out. "How very diplomatic of you, my lord. You may admit it. I look rather too much like an apricot."

This time, he laughed aloud. "An apt comparison. But

I wonder, is there ever a point where one looks *enough* like an apricot?" He indicated that she should resume her place on the bench and, after a moment's hesitation, she did so.

"Likely not." She smiled broadly, amazed that she wasn't nearly as humiliated by his agreement as she would have expected. No, indeed, she found it rather freeing. "My mother . . . she's desperate for a daughter she can dress like a fashion plate. Sadly, I shall never be such a child. How I long for my sister to come out and distract the countess from my person."

He joined her on the bench. "How old is your sister?"

"Eight," she said mournfully.

"Ah. Not ideal."

"An understatement." She looked up at the star-filled sky. "No, I shall be long on the shelf by the time she makes her debut."

"What makes you so certain you're shelf-bound?"

She cast him a sidelong glance. "While I appreciate your chivalry, my lord, your feigned ignorance insults us both." When he failed to reply, she stared down at her hands and replied, "My choices are rather limited."

"How so?"

"I seem able to have my pick of the impoverished, the aged, and the deadly dull," she said, ticking the categories off on her fingers as she spoke.

He chuckled. "I find that difficult to believe."

"Oh, it's true. I'm not the type of young lady who brings gentlemen to heel. Anyone with eyes can see that."

"I have eyes. And I see no such thing." His voice lowered, soft and rich as velvet as he reached out to stroke her cheek. Her breath caught and she wondered at the intense wave of awareness coursing through her.

She leaned into his caress, unable to resist, as he moved

his hand to grasp her chin. "What is your name?" he asked softly.

She winced, knowing what was to come. "Calpurnia." She closed her eyes again, embarrassed by the extravagant name—a name with which no one but a hopelessly romantic mother with an unhealthy obsession with Shakespeare would have considered saddling a child.

"Calpurnia." He tested the name on his tongue. "As in, Caesar's wife?"

The blush flared higher as she nodded. "The very same."

He smiled. "I must make it a point to better acquaint myself with your parents. That is a bold name, to be sure."

"It's a horrible name."

"Nonsense. Calpurnia was Empress of Rome—strong and beautiful and smarter than the men who surrounded her. She saw the future. She stood strong in the face of her husband's assassination. She is a marvelous namesake." He shook her chin firmly as he spoke. "It is a name to be lived up to. And I think you are well able to do so, if only you would attempt it."

She was speechless in the wake of his frank lecture. Before she had a chance to reply, he continued. "Now, I must take my leave. And you, Lady Calpurnia, must return to the ballroom, head held high. Do you think you can do that?" He gave her chin a final tap and stood, leaving her cold in the wake of his departure.

She stood with him and nodded, starry-eyed. "Yes, my lord."

"Good girl." He leaned closer and whispered, his breath fanning the hair at her nape and sending a thrill through her, warming her in the cool April night. "Remember, you are an empress. Behave as one and they will have no choice but to see you as such. I already do . . ." He paused, and she held her breath, waiting for his words. "Your Highness."

And with that, he was off, disappearing deeper into the maze and leaving Callie with a silly grin on her face. She did not think twice before following him, so keen she was to be near him. At that moment, she would have followed him anywhere, this prince among men who had noticed *her*, not her dowry or her horrible dress, but *her!*

If I am an empress, he is the only man worthy enough to be my emperor.

She did not have to go far to catch him. Several yards in, the maze opened on a clearing that featured a large, gleaming fountain adorned with cherubs. There, bathed in a silvery glow was her prince, all broad shoulders and long legs. Callie held her breath at the sight of him—exquisite, as though he himself had been carved from marble.

And then she noticed the woman in his arms. Her mouth opened in a silent gasp, her hand flying to her lips as her eyes widened. In all her seventeen years she'd never witnessed something so . . . wonderfully scandalous.

The moonlight cast his paramour in an ethereal glow, her blonde hair turned white, her pale gown gossamer in the darkness. Callie stepped back into the shadows, peering around the corner of the hedge, half wishing she hadn't followed, entirely unable to turn away from their embrace. My, how they kissed.

And in the deep pit of her stomach, youthful surprise was replaced with a slow burn of jealousy, for she had never in all her life wanted to be someone else so very much. For a moment, she allowed herself to imagine it was she in his arms: her long, delicate fingers threading through his dark, gleaming hair; her lithe body that his strong hands stroked and molded; her lips he nibbled; her moans coursing through the night air at his caresses.

As she watched his lips trail down the long column of the woman's throat, Callie ran her fingers down the same path on her own neck, unable to resist pretending that the feather-light touch was his. She stared as his hand stroked up his lover's smooth, contoured bodice and he grasped the edge of the delicate gown, pulling it down, baring one high, small breast to the night. His teeth flashed wickedly as he looked down at the perfect mound and spoke a single word, "Gorgeous," before lowering his lips to its dark tip, pebbled by the cool air and his warm embrace. His paramour threw her head back in ecstasy, unable to control her pleasure in his arms, and Callie could not tear her eyes from the spectacle of them, brushing her hand across her own breast, feeling its tip harden beneath the silk of her gown, imagining it was his hand, his mouth, upon her.

"Ralston . . ."

The name, carried on a feminine moan, sliced through the clearing, shaking Callie from her reverie. In shock, she dropped her hand and whirled away from the scene upon which she had intruded. She rushed through the maze, desperate for escape, and stopped once more at the marble bench where her garden excursion had begun. Breathing heavily, she collected herself, shocked by her behavior. Ladies did not eavesdrop. And they *certainly* did not fantasize in such a manner.

Besides, fantasies would do her no good.

She pushed aside a devastating pang of sorrow as the truth coursed through her. She would never have the magnificent Marquess of Ralston, nor anyone like him. She felt an acute certainty that the things he had said to her earlier were not truth, but instead the lies of an inveterate seducer, carefully chosen to appease her and send her blithely off, easing his dark tryst with his ravishing beauty. He hadn't believed a word of it.

No, she was not Calpurnia, Empress of Rome. She was plain old Callie. And she always would be.